SAVING GRACE

SAVING GRACE

Alison Scott Skelton

GraftonBooks
A Division of HarperCollins*Publishers*
77–85 Fulham Palace Road
Hammersmith, London W6 8JB

Published by GraftonBooks 1991

A CIP catalogue record for this book is
available from the British Library

ISBN 0–246–13488–7

Phototypeset by Input Typesetting Ltd, London
Printed in Great Britain by
HarperCollinsManufacturing Glasgow

This fictional story is dedicated to the real family that was its very distant inspiration. Were they to recognize anything of themselves herein, I would ask that they forgive any intrusion upon their privacy, and accept it instead as the tribute to their courage and dignity that is intended.

I

When Anne got to the country house that evening, she lit the first fire of winter. She thought briefly of saving the ritual until the next night, when Bob would be there, but chose not. She was wary of allowing him too great an ingress into her private festivals.

The woodstack was in the back yard, propped between two maples, but she was pleased to find that the local boy she paid to cut grass and trim hedges and see that the gutters were cleared and the lawns raked had shown initiative and brought a weekend's worth of wood up on to the back porch. There was no kindling, however, and before she took off her coat, Anne got the axe out of the still open garage to make some. She exchanged her shoes for her gardening boots which waited on the porch, and took a log down to the chopping block. She felt incongruous in her business suit, her nylon clad feet sliding around the boots' rough interiors, and she made a mess of splitting the log; jamming the axehead against knots, missing her swing and burying the blade deep in the block. It took fifteen minutes to make a small stack of kindlers. She was rusty, not just because of the fireless summer, but because all last winter Bob had made kindling, stacked wood, lit fires, fixed the plumbing. Anne was annoyed with herself. It had taken so long to get good at those things, and now she had let just a year of a man around the place rob her of her skills. She got the second log, split and divided it so there would be enough for all weekend, and only stopped when the wooden kindling box on the porch was satisfyingly full. She returned with the axe, pulled down the garage door, and went into the house with an armful of firewood and her city shoes clutched beneath it in one hand.

And then, quite suddenly, she was tired. It hit her like that, in alien, startling moments, as if her body was briefly someone else's. Irritated, she put the wood in the basket, and sat down quickly and waited for it to pass.

It puzzled her. It seemed early for it to matter; what difference could it make already? She wondered if that was how everyone experienced it, or if it was because of her age, and wished there was someone to ask; someone, that is, other than Bob. With belated sympathy, she remembered the past pregnancies of friends and colleagues, the litany of miseries she had dismissed with bored disinterest. Rueful solidarity swept her, and with it, loneliness. It must be fun, she thought wistfully, if you were really young, and half your friends were pregnant as well. She shrugged, and stood up and took off her coat. *Forty-three*, she thought. God, Anne, you're an idiot.

The fire was hard to light. The cold chimney refused to draw and billowed smoke back into the room. She went out to the garage again for more newspaper and was startled to find a late twilight sky as green and clear as mid-winter. The air was crisp and cold, touched by the Canadian winds that had overnight swept Indian summer away.

Anne had not been to the country place for three weeks and had left it with farmstands piled orange with pumpkins and the Expressway clogged with cars of the last summer people. She liked finding it suddenly wintry and nostalgic, smelling of dead leaves and salt water and all the things that marked her early childhood. She gathered mildewed newspaper from the stack beside the leaf rakes, carried them into the house, and shut and now locked the door.

Flaming newspaper turned the draught, and a pale thread of smoke uncurled inquisitively into the chimney. Anne piled kindlers around the burning paper and made a teepee of split logs around them. She spread a sheet of paper across the open-ing, and waited for the critical moment when the roar behind signalled the fire had caught before whipping the smouldering sheet away. She crammed it into a ball with the fire tongs and stuffed it under the logs. The flames held, yellow and flickering, but cast no heat. Anne got up, drew the mesh spark screen, and went down the basement stairs and switched on the oil burner, listening for a moment to its comforting rumble. The radiators

2

creaked and clicked and the house began to warm. She went back into the living-room and looked again at her fire. The twilight flickered with its heat and the smell of woodsmoke pervaded the house. She nodded to herself and said, aloud, 'Fine.' Then she lit the corner lamps, started to pour herself a malt whisky from the bottle in the kitchen, thought of the baby and opened a Perrier instead, and toasted winter. Again and as suddenly, the tiredness came back and she wanted to sit down with her drink and enjoy her pretty room and feel it grow warm. Instead, she took her glass to her desk in the corner, moved the telephone slightly aside to set it down, and switched on the machine. It clicked, whirred and began to play. She listened with her diary lying open before her, automatically making notes of who to reply to, or make appointments with, or ignore. The first two messages were from the man who serviced the oil burner, then the Forsyths asking them over for drinks on Sunday, then the contractors about the as yet uncompleted patio. She listened to the slow, East Long Island voice finishing its story of fatally unavailable kerbing stones and then briefly switched off the machine, made a note to fire the contractor, and switched the machine on. The oil-burner man made another try, more plaintive this time. The next voice was Bob's. She shut the machine off after *Hello, Anne?* and left it off, thinking, and mentally rehearsing the new hesitant tone. She drank from her Perrier, got up and carefully added two new logs to the warming fire, and returned. She still waited a moment before beginning the playback again, and as she listened she sat up straight, tense and unhappy.

I rang the shop, but you'd gone. Look, Anne, I'm sorry about that disaster at lunch, Wednesday. I've been thinking a lot; maybe I didn't express myself too well, either. Anyhow, I'm sorry. I think maybe we need some professional help . . . Let's talk about it Saturday. There was a pause in which Anne quietly shook her head. Then Bob continued, *If I'm still welcome. And, oh, Marion Forsyth wants us for drinks Sunday. I said she better ask you. And if you get a chance, maybe ring your mother. Joseph's had a rocky week.* There was another pause, then, *I love you*, and then the tone. Anne shut the machine off. She pencilled a tentative note to ring Marion and cancel Sunday, grateful that the depth of friendship between them ensured no explanation would be needed. Then she leaned back in her desk chair, sipped her drink and relaxed, admitting to herself that it was good to hear Bob's voice sounding almost ordinary once more – gentle, soothing and reasonable. The last time she'd heard it they'd been screaming at each other in the middle of Fifty-Seventh Street. She'd been certain she would never see him again; certain she never wanted to. Had they been young, that might have been exactly what happened. But they weren't young and both had too much civilized middle-aged sense to end anything that way. Which did not mean, however, that in its own way it might not yet end.

Her mother's message immediately followed Bob's. It was as she expected. *Hello, darling. Sorry to bother you. Maybe you could call back tomorrow if you have time.* Then a pause, and then, *Things aren't too good just now.* As always she had not actually mentioned Joseph at all. Anne wrote down that she must call her mother in the morning, knowing as she did so that more than likely she would call her tonight. She ran the machine on. A cool, professional voice followed smoothly:

Ms Conti, this is June Dawes from the Bayside Clinic. We are a little concerned that you haven't yet made an appointment for your amniocentesis and wonder if you would consider coming in for counselling? Our experienced staff are at your disposal, should you require them. Please ring us at your convenience. The same cool voice recited a telephone number and then a breezy, *Have a nice day.* Sure, Anne thought. You bet. An absolutely terrific day. She made no note in her diary.

The next caller was Sandi from the Fifty-Seventh Street store, her voice an argumentative Brooklyn whine pitched somewhere between apology and irritation. She didn't say hello, but launched immediately into protest. *Look, I know you're in the country and it's the weekend and all that, but damn it all she's your sister and I don't know what the fuck I'm supposed to do about her. The point is, the order came in, at last, just after you left, and I open it up and what do I find? Sixteen dumb sweaters in some shit-beige colour; no batwings at all, and no invoices. Never mind my special order she was supposed to be doing. Now what the fuck do I do with sixteen beige sweaters all size ten or twelve? No eights, no fourteens. For* Christmas! *Oh screw. You deal with her. I've had it, Anne.* The phone clicked dead. Anne, doodling gently with her pen, sighed slightly. Oh Jenny, she thought. She shook her head, listening through the

4

next two messages, both from local workmen; the first, her plumber inquiring if she wanted the outside faucets and the pool-shower drained, the second her contractor now proclaiming a miraculous discovery of hitherto unavailable kerbing stones. She penned a large question mark beside her decision to fire him.

She was still thinking about Jenny as she listened to the end of the contractor's speech. Thinking about her seemed to have the eerie effect of summoning her up into the recording, because after the next pause came the distinctive crackling of the transatlantic line followed at once by, *Oh shit, it's the machine*, and then the click of disconnection, and silence. All of which were unmistakably Jenny. Anne left the machine running, smiling to herself, and got up to pour a second Perrier. From the kitchen, she heard Jenny's voice again. *Hello, uh, Anne. Uh. Uh, this is Jenny, calling from Scotland*. Where else? Anne thought. The voice continued in its robotic inexpression. *Anne, if you're listening, I need to talk . . .*

'I'm listening, kid,' Anne said aloud. Jenny seemed to think the machine relayed its messages at will and at random, according to some inner mechanical whim.

Oh Christ, I can't talk to this thing. The line went dead.

'Jenny!' Anne said, exasperated. She groaned, sloshed more Perrier into her glass and returned to the living room, in time for the beginning of the third message.

'*Anne, is that you?*' Jenny addressed the hapless machine.

'Oh Jenny, get into the twentieth century,' Anne snapped, suddenly really irritated, 'I haven't time for this shit.' *If that's you, could you maybe call me back? Soon. Thanks a lot*. The last was breathless with relief, and then the voice suddenly shouted into the phone. *Oh, this is Jenny*, and then she hung up. Anne listened warily, but the recording was finished. Jenny's message, such as it was, was evidently complete. Anne switched off the machine, wrote 'Call the kid', in firm large letters, and went to the freezer to find supper. As she did she looked at her watch, calculated time zones, and briefly considered calling Jenny now, while Sandi's ire was still fresh in her mind. Besides, she had something of her own to talk about and she almost wanted to have it all settled before she even saw Bob. But it was eight o'clock New York time, one in the morning in Scotland. Jenny was an early

5

riser, and often early to bed. Anne imagined the chaos of a one A.M. phone call in Jenny's house, as dogs, cats, and Jenny herself galloped around, disturbed in their silent rural night. She decided to wait until morning.

But in the morning there was no time. Anne telephoned her mother at eight. A little guiltily, she had chosen to wait last night, after all, allowing herself a brief private respite before shouldering the responsibilities of the country place that came as surely as its peace. Her mother, or rather Joseph, was the foremost, the most difficult, and certainly the reason that her weekend and summer retreat was here on the Island rather than in Connecticut, or Upstate where she might have chosen.

She knew at once from her mother's flat, exhausted voice that she had been awake all night and had only just come back from the Home. She pictured her sitting at her kitchen table with her coat still on, drinking tea, her face as grey and colourless as her dry, limp hair. 'Were you going to bed?' Anne asked quickly.

'Later, dear. Thank you.' There was a pause. 'You got my message.'

'You didn't say much.'

'Oh, there isn't much really, dear. Just another infection. There's something going around. Frankly I'm *not* happy about that place, the hygiene isn't wonderful. Bob says so too.'

'Bob also says it's the best around,' Anne said quietly.

'Well.' Again there was the long, exhausted pause, in which Anne thought distractedly about age: how old her mother was, how old Joseph was. She did quick figures in her head. If she was forty-three, then Jenny was forty-one on her last birthday. That made Joseph almost thirty-five. And their mother? Seventy. No. Seventy-one. No wonder she's tired.

'Mom?' Anne said.

'Well, if that's the best there is, there's something wrong with the world.'

'I'll have a word with them,' Anne said. Meaning: *I'll kick some ass.* She wouldn't *say* that of course to her mother, but oddly her mother both knew and approved exactly what she meant.

'Oh, will you, darling? Thank you. Thank you so much. You're so good at these . . . you're such a *fighter*.' She laughed lightly. 'You've always been a fighter. I'm afraid I'm only just beginning to appreciate it.'

6

'If there's a fighter around here, Mom, it's you,' Anne said, her voice warm with affection.

'Joseph,' her mother said. 'There's the *real* fighter.' Pride swelled in the words and the affection Anne had felt diminished beneath it and cooled.

'Yeah, Mom. Of course he is. Look. I'll go in this morning. I'll see him and have a talk with the staff. Maybe I'll have a word with Bob if he's there.'

'God bless you, darling.'

'You go to bed now,' Anne said.

'Goodnight, darling.'

'Yeah,' Anne said. She put the phone down in a familiar surge of anger and remorse, taxing herself in frustration: *Oh when will I learn to control it?* And then she answered herself. *On the day she speaks my name the way she speaks his.* But it wouldn't happen. She knew it for certain now, with the double-edged realism of middle-age. As she got the car out to drive to the Home she reflected that human love was one of the few things where a little was not better than none at all.

The Baytree Center looked pretty in the cold November sun, its lawns neatly cut and the leaves of its tall maples raked into piles. A gardener was setting bulbs into the dark earth of the flower beds. The patio, where in the summer the wheelchair patients were parked in rows, was empty and windswept, its tubs of flowers bare. The main building was an old Long Island house with white clapboarding, a steep pitched roof, and a long white painted porch. It looked like it might hold a pleasant seafood restaurant, but inside it was discreetly modernized into offices and reception rooms, and corridors which led with only a subtle hiatus into the modern wings of low red brick that held the wards and therapy rooms and workshops. It was, as Bob said, the best of such places around, the best indeed that Anne's money could buy. Which was exactly what all the gardening and trim paintwork was intended to imply. But Anne was no fool, and on the day they first came here, seeking a place for Joseph, she had stalked right through the polished reception rooms into the kitchens, and poked about in closets and outside, where the rubbish was stored, making her own assessment. She even peered through windows into closed rooms with incensed staff watching in amazement. She made sure they were watching.

That was her message and she didn't stop prying until she was quite sure they had taken it aboard. Then, only then, she talked standards, conditions and money.

On the whole, she had been satisfied, at least satisfied that it was endurable and that she would not, except in a better world, find its superior. Jenny's husband Fergus, of all people, had been with her, laughing genially at everyone's consternation. Afterwards, he had said, 'Joseph will live like the king of Ireland there. You've scared the bejesus out of them all.'

'He's my brother. If he's going in there he's going on my terms.' And so he had although, just as she expected, it required regular reinforcement to make her terms stick. In the near twenty years Joseph had been there, they had seen two changes of management and a succession of nursing staff, and had come, in some ways, to know the place better than the people who at present operated it. There had been crises, and near-decisions to go elsewhere, but all had eventually worked out. The last had ended with the arrival of Bob Sheffield, under whose sharp, compassionate eye the last five years had produced significantly raised standards. By now Joseph was the grand old man of the place, having by the transient nature of its occupants out-stayed all others. His long-livedness had made him a modest celebrity within its walls, an achievement which Anne credited to the ferocious tenacity of their mother. Joseph had already doubled any predicted lifespan allotted him in childhood; survival was his chief trick, his major talent, his *raison d'être*, for better or for worse; the one, only thing he seemed able to do. Pretty hard-hearted to begrudge him it, Anne thought, whatever one's better instincts held.

Joseph was in the physiotherapy room which, at ten in the morning, was where he should be, Anne noted, pleased that there had been no back-sliding to the days, under a different supervisor, when she would find him still gurgling aimlessly in his crib at noon. The room was long and light, cheerfully painted in pale warm colours. It spanned the breadth of the building and rows of windows on either side let in sunlight both morning and afternoon. It was warm, with the steamy, nursery heat of hospitals. The floor was polished industrial linoleum, but a large rectangle of robust carpet, on which were spread two padded gymnasium mats, covered one end. Nearer the door was a table

8

where two young women sat in wheelchairs working with wooden puzzles. One looked up as Anne entered. She had a broad, plain face, spotted with acne. She smiled happily, waved her hand and shook her head, making her hair which was cut short and blocky at chin length bounce up and down. A pink barrette shaped like a poodle clipped the front off her forehead.

'Hello, Lisa,' Anne said, and then, 'Hello Marilyn.' The other woman never looked up, but Lisa smiled again and reached her arms out and Anne stopped by her wheelchair and hugged her, pulling away after a brief moment as Lisa hugged tighter. 'All right, Lisa,' Anne said, but Lisa had begun to giggle and tease, tugging at Anne's jacket.

'*Lisa.*' A young therapist spoke with practised severity, and Lisa let Anne go, sucked her thumb petulantly, and returned to her blocks. 'You really have to be rough with her, Ms Conti,' the therapist said, 'or she just takes over.' Anne nodded. The young woman was kneeling on the second mat. She wore green trousers and a short-sleeved green collarless blouse. She looked about sixteen, Anne thought, with her pretty pale hair tied in a pony tail. She simply had to be older than that, of course, but she was still very young. She was leaning over Joseph with both her hands clasping both his, doing exercises, stretching his thin arms out and folding them in, stretching them out, and folding them in. He giggled each time but contributed nothing. The action, all of it, came from her.

'Guess who's here, sweetheart,' the pony-tailed girl said, quite loudly, up against the hearing-aid on Joseph's good ear. 'Anne's here. Anne's come to see you.' Anne stepped closer, kicked her shoes off and knelt down on the mat on the other side of Joseph. She leaned forward and said, 'Hi, Joe. How are you today?' He was too occupied with his therapist to notice, giggling in anticipation of her commencing his exercise again. He lay on his back, his knees partly curled up, like a small baby. He was dressed in tracksuit trousers and a pale green sweater with a maroon stripe at the neck and sleeves. The bulk of his diaper distorted the trousers. Anne sniffed but there was only the faintest residual smell of urine. Fine. She fingered the collar of the sweater, 'This is new,' she said.

'Your mother brought it for him yesterday. Doesn't he look nice?' Anne looked coolly at her brother. The therapist had

9

released his hands, and he had drawn them up to his chin, his elbows pointed awkwardly outwards, his long, white fingers bent habitually into slack fists. His face was the same creamy white from a lifetime in rooms, and his eyes, a murky version of her own dark brown, wandered their separate blind pathways. The marks of the heavy, thick-lensed glasses that therapy demanded he wear for part of every day to salve his negligible sight, were red on the bridge of his nose. The skin around his eyes was shadowed dark, unhealthy and bruised. As she studied him his fists crept up to press against his lids, and were intercepted gently by the hands of his attendant. She began separating them and clapping them together, singing, 'Patty cake, patty cake, baker's *man*.' On 'man' she bent her forehead until it touched Joseph's and he shrieked a sudden, loud gurgle of delight. Anne smiled. She reached one hand towards him and for a brief moment cupped it gently at the back of his head, her palm just brushing the bristly, close-shaven hair. With his face turned away, the roving eyes less apparent, and the almost ascetic curve of cheek and cleanly-shaved jawline in half profile, he looked more or less all right. He did not look nice. He had never once since babyhood looked nice, and that totally because though infancy left him, all of its attributes remained stubbornly behind. No, Anne thought grimly. He looks like hell. Like a thirty-five-year-old baby crossed with a praying mantis. But the girl was leaning her perfect, peaches-and-cream cheek against Joseph's and crooning with real affection. 'I could eat you up, you're so handsome in that,' she said, and Joseph snorted and giggled.

'You're a lucky guy, Joe,' Anne said. She stood up and slipped on her shoes. With someone else she might have been angry. She had always hated the false cheer piled upon the lolling heads of the disabled, but there was nothing false in the pony-tailed child now hugging her brother. She was a rare creature, with stores of natural caring in her that passed comprehension. Anne left them together and went out, dodging Lisa's outstretched arms. When she looked back the young woman was lying full length on the mat beside Joseph, rocking him in her arms. *Never*, thought Anne, *never in a million years could I be that*. She thought it calmly, with admiration, but with little remorse. She had long passed the years when she thought life demanded that of her because of the accident of sibling relationship. No, she could never do that, but she had her own talents. Her talent was making money to pay for someone who could. She shrugged, letting the split doors of the physio room close behind her.

She went down the corridor to Joseph's room. It was a double room, but it was empty at present because Matthew, Joseph's roommate, who was fourteen with a mental age of three months, was home for the weekend. It had been his birthday last week, and Anne's mother and Matthew's parents had sat together around the two big cribs and shared birthday cake and shovelled it messily into their respective sons. A paper-chain in pink, yellow and pale green still hung on the wall above Matthew's bed. The bed was stripped down to the mattress during his absence, which made Anne uneasy because it was also how beds appeared when their occupants had recently died. But the paper-chain and Matthew's stuffed pink rabbit perched on his locker promised his intended return.

Anne went to Joseph's bed, drew back the smooth cover and studied the soft flannel sheet. The room was dim, with drawn curtains, and she crossed to the window, opened it, and returned to the bed where, bending down, she studied the faint outlines of a stain. She leaned over and sniffed, then stood up and stalked out. Outside the door she steeled herself before walking purposefully down the corridor. In the administration block she found the supervisor and berated her bitterly and loudly, aware that her voice was carrying throughout the building.

'*And* it was damp.'

'I am sure it was not damp, Ms Conti. The sheets feel cold. They may seem damp but they are not, I assure you. We launder thoroughly, and although a stain may remain, the sheets are sterile when we make up the beds. How*ever* . . .'

'It stank of piss,' Anne said loudly, exaggerating for effect. The woman turned red but shut up. She excused herself, left the room and, after some muffled shouting, returned. She was still red but her voice was beautifully controlled.

'I am terribly sorry, Ms Conti, there may possibly have been some confusion with the laundry room this morning. The bed will be stripped and remade as a precaution. If anything *was* neglected, I assure you there will be no recurrences.'

'There damn well won't,' Anne said, ominously. She turned

11

and walked out without looking back. In the corridor her careful veneer dissolved abruptly in shaky legs and trembling fingers. She stood in front of the shiny glass of a framed print and nervously readjusted her smooth black hair in its faint reflection. She straightened the lie of her jacket, resetting the shoulders. She was less ruffled from her conflict with authority than from Lisa in the playroom, but the calming effect of those familiar female gestures was good. She was not really angry, but even the false anger raised for effect quickened the pulse and reddened the cheeks. She wanted to look calm as a nun when she went to see Bob. As she walked back down the corridor to the children's wing, she stopped briefly and glanced back into Joseph's room. A hurried figure darted about, with armfuls of sheets and blankets. Good, she thought. Fine. On their toes. She was secretly glad of the stain on the bedsheet, and the lingering smell of urine that may or may not have come from it. A principle was at stake, and whether it was a lazy bed change or a twice-used cutting board in the kitchen was irrelevant. The principle remained and that was simply that Joseph Conti, though he had been here twenty years, was not without resources to leave.

She knew exactly where she would find Bob, his schedule was regular and after years of his companionship, as familiar to her as her own. His morning round began with the geriatrics, progressed through the assessment centre and ended with the residential children. She stopped outside the door and looked in through one small circular window. Within was a room with bright-painted walls hung with finger-paintings, cheerful splodges of red, yellow or blue. There were small tables and instructive toys, blocks and puzzles, paints and crayons. It looked like an ordinary kindergarten, except for the disparate sizes of the several children, the presence of two institutional wheelchairs, and two young women dressed not as teachers but in the same green trousers and shirt as Joseph's therapist.

Bob was sitting on a little short kindergarten chair, his knees half up to his chin, his back to her. Before him a small, angular blond boy with perfect features and a belligerent vacuity in his eyes stood facing him. Bob's hands gently imprisoned his forearms and Anne could actually feel the intensity of his gaze as if reflected from the boy's face. The boy's name was Scott. He was eight and autistic and would do anything rather than meet anyone's eyes. She had seen Bob sit with him for fifteen minutes at a time, locked in gentle combat. He had done this once a day for over a year. He had never won. Once he said to Anne, 'God almighty. If we could harness it, we'd rule the world.'

While Anne watched, a chubby red-haired girl came between her and Bob, peered up at the window, waved and smiled the beatific grin of Down's Syndrome, and then turned and clambered up on the back of Bob's chair hugging him frantically. He continued his one-sided staring match, unperturbed. Something caught in Anne's throat. She turned away, cursed herself, felt stupid and wanted to cry.

'Shit,' she said aloud.

Someone laughed. She turned and saw a boy tangled up in his wheelchair like a shell-less crab, grinning all over his face. He laughed again. Anne glared. He croaked out a sentence in his hoarse, spasmed voice. 'I did not,' Anne lied.

'You said shit,' he said again. And Anne said, 'What if I did, Big Ears? Buzz off.' He laughed again and jabbed at the controls of the electric wheelchair, spinning in a circle.

'*You* buzz off.' Then he was flying away, still giggling, before Anne could make a menacing move in his direction.

Anne looked back through the window. Bob had not moved; nor had Scott. The red-haired girl, Monica, still clung to him. They looked like a family. The feeling came again, in her throat, and another feeling inspired by the simple familiarity of the line of Bob's shoulder and neck, the shaggy, sandy-grey hair, the thin patch at the crown that he pretended he didn't care about but she had yet caught him observing ruefully with a mirror over his shoulder. She felt love, and horniness, and was irrationally irritated. *Hormones*, she thought. *Damned hormones, all over the place*. The horniness had come with her pregnancy right from the start, embarrassingly inappropriate. It had sprung up astonishingly for the young gynaecology student examining her at the Dawes Clinic, vaulting happily the obstacles of medical detachment and antiseptic atmosphere, fixing itself stupidly on a gawky boy she wouldn't give a second glance to in the street. *This isn't supposed to happen*, she thought wildly, while her body accepted his examination with hot enjoyment. She was disgusted with herself, ashamed, imagining he could sense her response, imagining the disgust he would feel in return. *Horny old pre-*

13

menopausal cow. She could hear his laughter among his compatriots. She knew what med. students were like. Bob had told her. *No wonder she's knocked up at her age.* No wonder indeed. And the funniest thing was, when it all started, it was menopause she thought of and the real truth never crossed her mind.

The damned feeling wouldn't leave. She wanted to go in and climb all over him like Monica, smiling no doubt the same irrepressible smile. She wanted her hands on him.

'Oh fuck it,' she said aloud, but softly, glancing around for the boy in the wheelchair. But he was cruising the corridors, apparently, because he hadn't returned. She had just decided she would simply leave, being in no condition for a controlled encounter with a half-estranged lover, but then the therapist, Susan Hill, looked up, and saw her and gave a bright smile and a little wave. Anne could see her saying something to Bob, and sensed a stiffening in his posture, though he neither released Scott from his hold, nor turned. Now she couldn't go. It *would* be Susan who saw her. Susan was thirty, tall, good-looking, a little too aggressive for Bob's taste, but she had lusted after him for years, ever since he came to the Center. Anne suspected they might briefly have been lovers, in the year after his wife died, when sex was still a drowning of misery. They were not lovers now. But that limited neither Susan's desires nor her hopes, both of which made her perversely Anne's compatriot. At cocktail party, medical luncheon, coffee morning, Susan would seek her out, peer into her eyes, pry into her life with endless questions. Sometimes Anne felt like an invisible screen through which Susan Hill made love to Bob. It wearied her and bored her, and she wondered privately whether it would end at last if she were Bob's wife. Perhaps, she felt coldly, remembering Wednesday and the shouting on Fifty-Seventh Street, it would end differently and Susan Hill would be Bob's wife. Which would be a pity, because he did not love her.

Bob's hands lifted gently off Scott's arms and Scott instantly whirled around and bolted for the furthest corner of the room. He crouched down on his haunches by a low window and stared out, blank and mesmerized as brown leaves blew past. Bob watched for a long while, then gently detached Monica, set her down and turned to welcome Anne.

They had coffee together in an ante-room he used as an office.

14

The coffee made her slightly nauseous. She left it half finished. Bob talked about work and then Anne talked about Joseph. Then, those subjects exhausted, they fell into an awkward pause which they both broke at once, stumbling over each other's words.

'Have you been back to the Clinic?' he said, as she was saying, 'Jenny called. I'm going to call her back this afternoon.' She stopped, looked up at him and said, 'No.'

'Anne.'

'*No!*' Their eyes met. Bob's were blue-grey, gentle and intelligent. He used his reasonable, clinical voice.

'It won't go away.'

'I'm not the one who wants it to,' Anne said at once. Then she added, 'I'm going to Scotland for Christmas.' She recoiled faintly from her own gall. She hadn't even spoken to Jenny yet, much less asked. Still. That's what sisters were for, or so the world said.

'That's cutting it close,' Bob said. Anne said nothing, and then could think of nothing other to say, and so his words hung in the air, growing rather than diminishing in import. Finally Anne managed, 'I suppose you've your own plans, anyhow.' She heard her voice take a familiar and distinctive note of calm, become what she called her 'mistress voice', the voice of incomplete claims, saying clearly, 'I know where the boundaries are. I am not crossing any.' Christmas, birthdays, public and intimate festivals were subtle ground when a man had celebrated all with someone else. And when the children of that lost union remained to coalesce suddenly into the tight knot of family. Two Christmases had passed since she began seeing Bob. During the last they had been virtually living together. Both were spent apart.

The change of voice confused him. He lost impetus and said only, half to himself, 'Well yes. Of course.' He looked unhappy as he said it. 'I suppose Mandy and John will want me for Christmas dinner. Or at least they'll *say* they want me and then stick by it so firmly that I'll never know if they mean it or not.' He paused. 'You'd think they'd *want* to be alone. Especially this year, with Mandy . . . well they won't be alone again.' He looked embarrassed and Anne felt for him. He said slowly, 'I don't understand them. They seem to need me still. It's like they don't believe they are really adults yet. Last Christmas Mandy came

15

running into my room in the morning and climbed on my bed with my present like she's done since she was five.'

Anne laughed softly and said, 'What did John say?'

'Nothing. He just came and joined her. Like another big kid.' He grinned whimsically. 'I'm sure we grew up faster than that.'

Anne shrugged. 'It's nice,' she said. But then she pictured the same scene with her in the bed beside Bob and knew why it bothered him so. 'What about Robin?' she said. He stared into his coffee, still seeming preoccupied with Mandy and John. Then he said quickly, looking up, 'Oh, she wants me to come up to New Hampshire skiing, for Christmas and New Year. Like last winter. She says I promised.'

'I think you did.'

'Yeah,' he said, turning the cup around slowly. 'So I suppose I'll go.'

'You'll love it,' Anne said kindly. She was conscious of sounding too generous, as if it must be false, but it wasn't really. He stayed silent and then suddenly burst out, 'I'd love it a lot more if you were there too.'

Anne sighed. They'd been through the same argument last year. She said, 'I don't ski. I'm certainly not going to learn *this* year. And Robin would hate it.'

'Anne, where do you always get that idea? She doesn't *hate* you . . .'

'Of course she doesn't,' she replied brightly. 'But she loves you. And she'll hate sharing.'

'Give her a chance.'

'That's what I'm doing, Bob. I'm giving her a chance. If she's ever going to like me, it won't be for taking away her favourite vacation with her Dad.'

He looked at once both sorrowful and relieved. The relief hurt. Anne said, 'Anyhow, I'll be in Scotland, like I said.' Unwittingly, she brought him back to where they had started from.

He said, 'You must make an appointment at once. You must have it done before you go.' He was looking at the calendar on his desk, counting weeks, suddenly professional. 'Yes, *just* before you go. You're nineteen weeks on 12 December.'

'No,' Anne said, quietly. He looked up. He was completely controlled. She had become a patient.

'Anne, if you leave it until after you'll be running very close to the limit by the time the results are in. If something *does* turn up, God forbid, we'll really have to move fast.' He sat back and said solemnly, 'I don't like these things done late. I don't.'

'I'm not having it done before, Bob,' she said, and she cut off his argument with a quick wave of her hand, 'because I'm not having it done. I'm not having it done at all.' For a moment exasperation crossed his face, exasperation not with her, but with the patient she had suddenly become. It was replaced by sorrow. The sorrow was for her. For them.

'Anne,' he said softly. 'Anne.' Quite suddenly he dropped his forehead into his hands, the fingers splaying out through his coarse, shaggy hair. She wanted to touch, to kiss them. He lifted his head. 'Anne, it's irresponsible,' he said at last. 'It . . .' he paused. And then his face animated and he made a sweeping gesture around the small office that encompassed the invisible wards beyond. 'This is my life. It is my work, my choice, my . . .' he paused, with a sudden, technician's ill-ease with emotion, 'My love. I love them. Most of them. Some of them are such hopeless . . . even them, sometimes I love. But Anne, I swear it, if I could have kept any single one of them from being here, from *being* at all, I'd have done it. I swear it. Oh God, Anne, there's times here on a bad night when I've been ready to do it now. *Now!* Do you know what I'm saying? Do you know the amount of *suffering* . . .' He went quiet, looking away, and still looking away he said, 'Amniocentesis is a compassionate window into the future. When the future is *this* . . .' he waved his hand, tiredly now, as he had done before. 'And we can see it . . . we have a duty, Anne. Knowledge is a gift from God. We must use it.'

'As we see fit,' said Anne.

'As we see fit,' said Bob, and it meant something she had not meant at all.

Anne made the call as soon as she got home. She made it standing by her desk with her coat still on, knowing if she delayed in any slight way, her resolve might fail. It being Saturday, there was no one at the Bayside Clinic, but she left her name and number and her request for an appointment in the soulless charge of their answering machine. Then she put the phone down and felt herself engulfed by bleak depression. She wanted desperately to talk to someone, and thought of calling Bob, but then she imagined him repeating his same good advice; how it was only sensible at her age, how the risk to the baby was minimal; perhaps with a slight lift of relief in his voice. Abruptly she knew she would neither call him, nor even tell him, or anyone. It was her concern, hers to deal with alone. She slipped briskly from her coat and hung it in the spacious closet behind the sliding doors in the entry hall. Then she went to the kitchen and sought normality in preparing lunch, a meal that in the past she had usually skipped but in which she now indulged with superstitious care, as if by guarding her pregnant body scrupulously, she could keep all harm away.

In the afternoon, she called Jenny. She calculated time zones carefully and chose an hour when her sister would likely be in from tending to animals, in her workshop with any luck, but the phone rang on and on anyhow. Anne stood tapping her fingers by her desk, the phone in one hand, the receiver under her chin, listening to the distinctive British double tone. She knew more, by now, than to suggest Jenny invest in an answering machine, but she still wondered how many orders were lost while her sister chopped wood, mended gates, or milked goats. *They'll ring back*, Jenny would always say, infuriatingly confident that people liked her scatty rural charm. And no doubt some of them did. But more, Anne was certain, did not.

'Hello, hang on just a moment while I get the door before the kittens get out,' Jenny's voice suddenly shouted breathlessly across the Atlantic. There was a heavy clunk as the old-fashioned receiver was dropped on something, and distant scurrying sounds over which came the clear, pretty blur of Jenny's voice, the words muddled to indistinction. Then, after another scrape and scuffle, '*Hello*, Jenny O'Brien here, can I help you?'

'Ah, so, velly important order, two thousand sweaters for big store in Tokyo, cannot wait for kittens. Velly solly. Goodbye.'

'Anne, is that you? Hi, how are you?' Jenny's voice was bright and happy, as it had been so much of the time since Simon's arrival in her life. Anne hated to hit her right away with Sandi and her complaints.

'Fine, dear, look . . .'

'How's Mom?'

'Fine . . .'

'And Bob?' Anne sighed. Jenny had never learned the art of the transatlantic call, indeed of any telephone conversation, and so Anne was doomed to spend large amounts of money on these senseless ritual litanies, usually confused by crackling lines and capricious echoes. This line at least was good.

'Bob's fine. Look, dear, I'm . . .'

'How's Joseph?'

'Great. Training for the New York marathon. Jenny, this is three dollars a minute . . .'

'Oh, I'm sorry. And it's your call.'

Anne felt mean then. Jenny was as loquacious on her own, scant, money, and Anne, if anybody, could afford a few minutes family chit-chat if it made her sister happy. Only it didn't. The questions weren't real and the answers weren't listened to; it was just a habit that Jenny couldn't break, a tribal response to the unholy devices of the computer age, which the telephone, in Jenny's reckoning, was one. But having won the field of play, Anne held on to it.

'Look, Sandi rang yesterday. She's just got your order in.'

'Oh, great. I was afraid . . .'

'No. Not great.'

'What's wrong?' Jenny said, with such innocent surprise that once more Anne was thrown back on the old uncertainty, was Jenny actually as naïve as she certainly acted, or was she powered rather by a subtle and truly monumental stubbornness?

'Jenny,' Anne began quietly, 'I specified in June. Plum, raspberry and emerald. So you send Sandi sixteen quite magnificent sweaters in beige.'

'Natural,' Jenny corrected.

'Beige, natural,' Anne paused to retain her calm, 'Jenny, they weren't plum. Or raspberry. *Or* emerald.'

'But they were my Jacob's wool,' Jenny said with an indignation that stood in as its own explanation. 'I put a little label on, you know, with the four-horned sheep . . .'

'Sandi didn't notice.' Anne paused again. 'Look, how do I tell you this any clearer? This autumn's colours are plum, raspberry and emerald. The whole line is colour-co-ordinated. All *New York* is colour-co-ordinated. So when my ladies come in with their plum-coloured jeans from Macy's looking for something special in Anne Conti to dress them up, they don't give a damn how many horns the fucking sheep had. They want *plum*. And while we're at it, where were the batwings with the lurex thread?' There was a determined silence on the other end of the phone. Finally Jenny said in a small, dignified voice, 'I couldn't bring myself. It's so tacky.'

'It's fucking Christmas,' Anne shouted. 'We *want* tacky.'

There was another silence and then Jenny said, 'I didn't do them.'

Anne sighed, wearily, and Jenny bubbled up with protest, her dignity diluted slightly by self-pity. 'Surely there must be *some* discerning shoppers about.'

'Jenny, your discerning shoppers have long since gone to the Great Shopping Mall in the sky. What I have is customers. And they want *plum*.' Anne said it with vengeance, but she knew already she had lost. Jenny would neither agree nor disagree, and if the occasion arose again she would still steadfastly refuse to dye her Jacob's wool, or make any other concession to a taste that offended her own. Compromise in her craft did not exist, though in her life, with children, lovers, or God, she compromised at will. *This is the stubbornness of geniuses*, Anne thought. *This is why they starved in attics. What's it doing with my little sister?* 'What are you trying to be?' she asked, 'The Chatterton of the knitting machine?'

'Was there anything else you wanted?' Jenny said. Her voice was hurt, quiet and controlled.

'No,' Anne said, and then immediately, 'Yes, of course there is. Look kid, I'm sorry, and before we get into this again, I do respect what you do, I do think your work is beautiful and all that. And most of the time I even like your surprises, though I promise you Sandi never will. And by the way, you *must* include invoices. You just can't do business on this scale as if you were trading sheep.'

'Stop treating me like a peasant,' Jenny said, adding 'I'm as American as you.' Anne started to say, *Then stop acting like one*, but was brought up suddenly by Jenny's plaintive afterthought. *You're not*, she thought. *That's just the trouble. You're not. Somewhere along the way you lost it. To Fergus. Or the kids. Or that wet green place you live.* She said, 'I'm going to come to London next month. I thought I might fly up to Edinburgh and check out the new extension on the store. I'll stay with Gordy and Elizabeth.'

20

She paused, awaiting an invitation. It didn't come. She said, 'I could take a run up and see you all.' There was a silence, and Jenny's voice, hesitant, said, 'It's a long way, you know,' forgetting apparently that she wasn't talking to a stranger, some American buyer who'd never seen Scotland and thought she could trip around it in an afternoon.

'I've been there,' Anne said drily.

'I meant just for a day . . .' Jenny trailed off and Anne struggled with the thin wisp of a person that a disembodied voice provided. If she could only see her, see her open, blue eyes, watch her hands, tugging at her unstyled hair: then maybe she would know – was this anger, resentment, or that old wistful uncertainty that kept Jenny on the edge of her life, untrusting always of her motives? She thought, *I'll put my neck out. It doesn't hurt me as much as it hurts her*, though even in thinking it was uncertain if it was true. She said, 'I didn't mean just a day. I meant to come up for a few . . . for Christmas. I meant to spend Christmas with you.'

'Oh Anne!' Jenny burst out in delight, 'Would you really?' And then, instantly, the barriers fell; Jenny became gay, animated, humorous, and Anne realized that she had found the key, this time. But another time it might not work at all. Sometimes it was love, expressed openly, sometimes it was apology, sometimes it was anger; the key was never the same. Jenny kept changing the locks.

They talked happily now for fifteen minutes, Jenny forgetting, and Anne not caring, about the cost. They arranged dates, promised to check trains and flights, talked about delicacies to be brought from the New World to the Old, as always the silly, nostalgic things that exiles missed. 'If you could get some of those peppermint candy canes for my tree. And some candy corn. I remembered it at Hallowe'en and I've been craving it ever since. You'd think I was pregnant.' She laughed, and Anne felt her insides do a neat flip-flop at the word which in a handful of weeks had become the biggest word in her life. She said nothing to Jenny. And Jenny seemed to follow her own irrelevant train of thought because she said, suddenly, 'Anne, you know this thing that happened in October with the stock market?'

'The crash?' Anne said.

'Yeah, the crash.' Jenny's voice was distant. It turned faintly

21

sadly querulous. 'I thought that couldn't happen any more. I mean, Dad used to say that after the Depression they set up safeguards and it wouldn't happen like that . . .'

'Nobody's yet devised a safeguard against greed, kid,' Anne said smoothly.

'You mean it's really just the same?'

Anne thought briefly, wondering what on earth had evoked this totally atypical conversation. She said, 'Actually, I don't know. No one quite knows yet. They're certainly feeling it in Wall Street. I suppose we'll feel it eventually . . .'

'But what about the people who have, you know, shares and things?'

'They're hurting,' said Anne. 'Look kid, what's this about? I can't imagine you've started playing the market,' she said drily.

'Oh no,' Jenny laughed, comfortingly, 'Not me.' Anne wondered wildly who in Jenny's remote Highland world was even likely to have *heard* of the market. Then a miserable thought hit her.

'Oh kid, don't tell me Simon has been messing around with it?' She chose Simon because he was the only one of Jenny's acquaintances who had ever belonged to that world, but Jenny laughed with rich reassurance. 'Oh, not Simon,' she said. 'No chance.' And then, quite suddenly, she wouldn't say anything more. 'I was just wondering, that's all. It just sounded sort of scary. Maybe because we're so far away.' Her voice was smooth, adult, and final. *OK, kid*, Anne thought, rebuffed. *You're the one who asked.* But she didn't let it threaten the warmth of their communion of words, or the promise of the meeting to come.

'Right, kid, you get baking. I want Christmas cake, and plum pudding, and brandy butter. I want the works. A real English Christmas,' she said. Jenny laughed, and Anne realized at once the dumb, American thing she had said, but Jenny's laugh was sweet.

'We'll try and get the border shifted,' she said, 'Just for you.'

II

Jenny put the phone down and scooped up the two kittens who'd been tumbling over her stocking-feet. She held them up to her face, one in each hand, pressing their grey foreheads against her own. 'Auntie Anne's coming for Christmas!' she said with soft delight. She kissed them both and nibbled the edge of one furred ear, enjoying her own sensuality. There was no one about, no man about, to look huffy and object. 'Gorgeous babies,' she whispered and set them gently down. It was only when she'd gone through to her workroom again and sat down, humming cheerfully a snatch of one of Fergus's old songs, that she remembered. 'Oh Christ,' she said aloud, 'Simon.'

She sat staring at the machine in front of her for half a minute and then gave up, stood up, kicked the table leg and turned away. Her pleasure dissolved in guilt, and annoyance. Guilt that she had made arrangements for the holidays without consulting Simon, and annoyance that she felt the need. Of course she had not consulted Angus or Sarah either, but children were different. Children, even grown children, could be simply overridden if necessary; they were accustomed to it. An adult lover required formal notice.

'I have a right to see my sister,' she said aloud, and then wondered to whom in the silent house she was justifying herself. A pang of nostalgia came over her for the years before Simon. The best thing about being *truly* single was making plans without the endless barter with a partner. It was the thing that everyone outside assumed to be lonely, but actually it was a relief.

Jenny walked disconsolately around the workroom, tugging at the sleeves of a hanging rack of jumpers, prodding the piled up skeins of soft, many-coloured wool, removing a surreptitious kitten from the centre of a great mound of raw fleece beside her wheel. 'Hey, you, how'd you get in? This is off-limits.' She tucked it into the sagging pocket of her cardigan and surveyed the room moodily, remembering now Sandi's complaints as relayed by Anne.

She let the prickly argumentativeness, rising within herself towards Simon, spill over and transfer neatly on to Sandi's head. She had never met Sandi Lang. She probably never would meet her, and she didn't care. She knew she would not like her. The necessity of dealing with her, in her capacity of manager of the New York Anne Conti shop, irked Jenny. Initially she had attempted to circumvent it by addressing her correspondence and her shipments directly to Anne, but Anne perfunctorily eluded any attempts at personal involvement, passing Jenny's business, like everyone else's, back to her manager. For years Jenny had envisioned Sandi as a slick, hard, heavily made-up woman, like one of those masks of femininity on the cosmetics counters in Boots. It was a satisfying image, one to which she could comfortably assign everything that emanated from the place that she did not wish to assign to Anne. It had come as a shock to see a snapshot of Sandi sitting at the poolside at Anne's Hamptons house last summer: plain, slovenly, rather dumpy, devoid of make-up or style. On the telephone she had expressed her amazement to Anne who had replied, 'It was her day off. She looks good in the shop,' and then, after a pause, 'It's a *business*, Jenny. Not a spiritual undertaking.'

Jenny looked at the softly carded wool that lay like gentle clouds on the workroom floor. She envisioned its growth from the tight, spongy, Afro curls on the back of a lamb, to the heavy luxury of shearing time. It seemed filled with all the cool, wet beauty of the land. It was an honour to touch it, to work with it, to wear it on one's back. She thought of Sandi and her constant requests for glitter, for gaudy shades, crinkly lurex, seed pearl appliqués, synthetic mixes. 'I want something new, Jenny. Different. Something to catch the eye.' When Jenny explained painstakingly that her work was classic, timeless, would look as good next year as this, Sandi laughed.

'Next year? Next year they want something new.'

'Only because you tell them so,' said Jenny.

'And where the fuck would you be if I didn't?'

'The throw-away society?' Jenny said archly.

'You bet your sweet ass. And be glad of it.' Sandi's laugh was as rough as the laugh of a man.

Jenny had said to Anne, 'All life is a spiritual undertaking.'

Anne had said, 'Fine. Send your next shipment to the Pope.'

She smiled, remembering. Her anger had decided to fizzle out, rather than to settle and grow brooding. She thought of Simon with more fairness. Simon, after all, would not argue. Simon would be lovely about it, cheerful and understanding. That was his nature. He was not demanding and he liked, longed, to be involved more directly in her life. A family Christmas would please him. But she knew what would please him more: Christmas with just the two of them, a hotel somewhere, log fires, brimming glasses, bed. She could see it all clearly, an ad from the *Sunday Times*. It touched a small romantic chord, but immediately the thought of her house thus cold and treeless, empty of children and glitter and laughter, filled her with dismay. She felt herself sliding inexorably into the resentment that arose whenever she was certain that their motivations, hers and Simon's, were not the same. She felt them, silently tugging in opposite directions and knew that although she would win, her guilt would undo her enjoyment. 'He'll have to bloody well like it or lump it,' she said, walking out of the workroom and back into the kitchen. *Poor Simon*, she thought, *if he rings now, I'll snap his head off, and as always he'll never know why*.

In the kitchen she removed the kitten from her pocket and dumped it in the basket with the others. They slept in a grey and spotted amorphous heap. She lifted the cover from the hotplate of the Aga and slid the kettle on to the heat. As she crossed to the cupboard for the coffee jar, Honey, the big old labrador, wandered out of her bed and pressed her heavy head against Jenny's corduroy trousers.

At once the black and white collie, Dhileas, scuttled out from under the table and pushed his sharp nose in between. 'Jealous,' she said aloud. 'Dog in the manger. You didn't want patting until *she* came.' She talked to them like children because they acted like children. Not, as Simon imagined, because her own children had grown.

'When *they* grow up, I'll treat them like adults too,' she said.

25

But she found herself curbing some of her affection when Simon was around. She crouched down waiting for the kettle, her arms around the lab's loose-skinned, velvety neck. 'Who's a beautiful girl?' she whispered. 'Who's Mommy's darling?'

She didn't go back to work when she had made her coffee. It was getting late, and her mind was too restless from Anne's call. Instead she walked comfortably about the big old house, drawing curtains that had been forgotten, lifting newspapers on to tables, gently tidying, tucking the place up for the night. Eventually she remembered to lock the doors, but did so casually and, as often, so late at night that it was hardly worth bothering. She was not afraid of living alone, remote as the house was. That always surprised Anne, because Jenny had been a fearful child. 'Of course, you've got the dogs,' she had said, but Jenny only laughed. Honey, with her soft toothless mouth, Dhileas, scatter-brained enough to welcome in a troop of burglars.

'No,' she said. 'It's just that I know everyone. There's no one to be afraid of up here. Nobody comes up this hill at night, unless they live here.' And it was more or less true; true enough that Jenny recognized individually the motors of every car that passed.

When Fergus had died, everyone assumed she would leave the house they shared on a remote hill above Loch Ness, but that was the last thing she would have done. Now, with the children grown, the same suggestion was sometimes made. It's my home, Jenny replied. Not Fergus's. Not the children's. Mine. Why should I go? And where? But she knew what they meant: somewhere more suitable, more practical, without a dozen rooms to heat and a half-mile driveway and winter snows. Without all the things she liked best. She felt their objections like an attrition, and wavered between annoyance and guilt, as if there was something selfish in remaining. Sometimes she thought of marrying Simon to settle the thing that way. Not one of her friends' objections would stand if there were just one other person there, and that person a man. But it was Jenny who ploughed the driveway, Jenny whose workshop and animals made use of the space, Jenny who loved the solitude. And Simon, if anybody, who might choose to move away.

Just before she went to bed, she looked into the children's rooms. It was a nightly ritual, ingrained from their babyhood. It

26

seemed normal to continue, even though now they were rarely there. She flicked on the light in Angus's room, glimpsing briefly the neatly made bed, with an indentation from some departed sleeping animal, the wardrobe with one door slightly ajar because the latch had never worked from the day she bought it in the saleroom, the desk that had weathered finger-paints and play-dough, O-levels and Highers, and now the stacks of incomprehensible Economics texts. There were papers, desk-tidies, pens, books, rubbish. Even the note to himself listing what he must pack for the Michaelmas Term lay where he had left it in the dark morning before they set off for the train. She never touched anything on the desk. She had three reasons: respect for his privacy, sentimental superstition, and lazy rebellion against twenty years of picking up his things. The room was shabby, carpet and wallpaper inappropriate legacies of the previous occupant. There had never been the money nor the time nor the expertise to change them. And now it was too late. Bit by bit he would move more of his things out until none was left. She was suddenly afraid to change the room at all, as if doing so would hasten his departure. She switched the light off and crossed the corridor to Sarah's room as if for refuge.

Sarah had not yet begun to move out, instead she brought things back from her new outside world, filling her room with them, bringing change into the heart of the family rather than following it outwards. Jenny switched the overhead light on and went in and sat on the bed. Sarah's favourite cat, Smokey, slept patiently at its foot. Sarah made a great fuss of the cat each time she came home, but if Jenny mentioned it on the phone she sounded uninterested, even annoyed. She had thought it odd and told Simon, but he said, 'Don't you remember how different home and University were, and how you always wanted to keep them apart?' But Jenny didn't remember. It was longer in the past for her than for Simon; much longer. And too much had happened. She didn't think like a student any more. Sarah's walls were covered with large glossy religious posters, among which her own sketches and water-colours, once secure in pride of place, now struggled to be seen. The fashion magazines that still so mystified Jenny were stacked around her bed. Her make-up and hair gels spilled across her desk as they always had. That much was not new, the source of old arguments and confusions, but familiar, and like old friends. But the posters that now crowded the design sketches and fashion mannequins for space, were. Bright and brilliantly photographed – flowers, rainbows, animals, all somehow too vivid in colouring, too lacking in shading or subtlety to appeal – they repelled Jenny and made her more sceptical than she might have been of their messages. JESUS SAVES. FOLLOW HIM. HE CAME TO GIVE YOU FULLNESS OF LIFE. Jenny looked at them wryly as she looked at the stack of shiny blue, red, and yellow paperbacks lying invitingly on Sarah's desk. She knew the posters were a message to her, and the books and pamphlets remained by no accident. The room, cheerful and innocent, was a lure, a snare laid for her by Sarah, and she found its mix of old comfort and new challenge as upsetting as Angus's subtle withdrawal from her house. Over the bed, the wood and metal crucifix that Fergus had placed there still hung from the same old nail. It looked dusty and worn beside the bright posters, as if its Christ, and theirs, had never met. She picked up one of the thick, shiny paperbacks, studied its title and leafed through its pages. It was divided into sections: Sin. Redemption. Revelation. There were small cartoon type drawings of the questioning new Christian, his parents, girlfriend, football companions, none of whom understood him apparently. At the end was a drawing of Christ, bearded, solemn and Palestinian, looking out of place. Jenny took the book with her when she went out of the room.

She had fallen asleep reading it when the telephone rang. Because she had been thinking of Sarah, and reading Sarah's book, she expected her daughter's voice when she answered the phone.

She said, sleepily, as she was fumbling for the light switch, 'Yes dear?'

'It's me, Mom,' Angus said, and she wondered in confusion how he seemed to know, just from her voice, that she was expecting his sister.

'Hello darling,' she said, sitting up.

'Can you call me back?' he said, and rattled off a phone box number. Jenny nodded and put down the receiver, clasping the number in her foggy head. She dialled the Cambridge code with her finger, deliberately not engaging her brain. Another set of figures and all would dissolve in chaos. *A note pad* she thought while the phone rang. *A note pad by the bed.* She had been saying

28

the same at night for three years. She had not yet remembered in the morning. Angus answered on the second ring, 'Hi, Mom. Did I wake you?' He sounded slightly, but not seriously, guilty.

'No,' she said. She did nothing ever to discourage them calling whenever they chose.

Then Angus said, more cautiously, 'Are you, uhm . . . alone?' This was newer, within the last year.

'I'm alone,' said Jenny. Sometimes of course she was not, and once Simon had been making love to her. Not that Angus ever heard that. She had slipped from her lover's embrace and answered the phone on the first ring. She'd gone through the familiar routine of calling back and listened and chatted for twenty minutes while Simon for some dumb reason to do with embarrassment actually got out of the bed, dressed, and sat in a chair. After, when he returned to the bed and she had laughed at his self-consciousness, he had got angry and incautious.

'Couldn't he ring at some more convenient time?'

Jenny had looked at him in such a way that he didn't even dare start a fight, knowing that it would be the sort of fight that might end everything. 'No,' she said. 'He can't.' It was not mentioned again, and if the possibility of the phone ringing again inhibited Simon's lovemaking, he had not said, and she did not ask.

'How are you?' Angus asked.

'Fine? How are you?'

'Oh great.' His voice sounded restless.

'How's Amanda?'

'She's fine. Everybody's fine.' She was reminded suddenly of Anne, and she consciously reined in her list of social inquiries. But Angus did not say anything then, so she was then obliged to continue. She said:

'Auntie Anne rang this afternoon.'

'Yeah?' He sounded distant.

'She's coming for Christmas.'

'Oh yeah? That's nice.' The faraway quality was still there, but it often was when she discussed family affairs. Jenny said, 'You don't mind, do you?'

'No,' he said, and then as if forcing himself to pay attention, 'No, that's great. I'm looking forward to seeing her.' He paused again, but before Jenny could say anything more, he broke in quickly, 'Look Mom . . .' In the pause, she knew already what he would ask, 'Look, I'm afraid I need some money.' She was quiet and then she said uneasily, 'Already?'

'I'll pay you back.'

'You've just had your grant, Angus.'

'I *will* pay you back. Out of next term's grant. Or I'll get a job at Christmas . . .' He trailed off. There were no such jobs where they lived.

'But why do you need it? You've surely not gone through this term's money already?' She asked uneasily, a bit terrified that the answer was obviously yes.

'Not exactly. I mean . . . there are some extra expenses.' He paused again, and she had an awful feeling that if she pressed him further, he would lie. Angus, who never lied, not even in childhood. Unlike Sarah to whom lying had often been the first, quick avenue of escape. She said quickly, 'OK. I mean, how much?' She felt an empty feeling, like she got when the mail came full of brown, windowed envelopes.

'Would thirty pounds be all right?' She felt partly relieved. It wasn't *that* much. Enough, God knows, but not *devastating*. Relief bred rebellion.

'Look, love, I sent you thirty pounds a fortnight ago.'

'I *said* I'd pay you back.' He was frustrated at her backing off. She dodged back into compliance.

'OK love. Don't get angry. It isn't worth getting angry about. The honest truth is I'm not sure I have it. I'll try and get it together, OK?'

'Can't you promise?' He sounded desperate, like his little boy self, and it evoked a wave of sympathy.

She said, 'I can't promise if I don't have it, pet. I promise I'll try to find it.' There was a long, awkward pause. Jenny sat up higher in the bed, her mind darting around to where she would find an uncommitted thirty pounds without overdrawing even more and outraging her bank manager further, or borrowing from the sanctified money set aside for essential bills and the upcoming threat of Christmas. The fragile balance of her household economy allowed absolutely no margins, something neither friends nor family ever fully grasped. Then Angus said with delicate wariness:

'Could you maybe borrow it?'

'From who for God's sake?' she snapped.

'I don't know,' he said disingenuously. He paused again. 'Maybe from Simon?'

'*No.*'

'All right, all right. Don't get angry.'

'I *am* angry.' She tried to hold back but burst out, 'You know I can't do that. You *know.*'

'All right, all right. I know. I'm sorry.'

'Then why did you say it?'

'I said I was sorry.'

'But why did you *say* it then?'

'Oh, please, Mom. Don't get on to me. Please. I've got so much . . . so many people getting on to me for one thing or another . . .' She heard the high break in his voice, near tears. *Oh, Christ, why did she always manage to achieve that?*

'All right, pet. I won't. I promise. Look, I'll get your money. Don't worry about it. Just go to bed now and stop worrying. Or go back to your work. I'll sort it out.' She heard the smooth authority in her own voice, and so did he.

'Oh thanks, Mom, thanks so much. Look, I *will* pay it back.'

'Fine. When you can. But try not to go through it so fast.' There was the slightest hesitancy before he said, very softly, 'Yeah, well . . . thanks, Mom. Sorry if I woke you. Goodnight.'

'Goodnight, love.'

It was only after she put the phone down, had turned off the light, and made a petition to St Anthony to help find the money, that the meaning of that un-reassuring hesitancy raised a question in her mind and she wondered why Angus who was independent and clever with money, and scrupulously undemanding, should suddenly find himself repeatedly without it.

She lay in the darkness of her room, looking out, between the curtains that on her remote hill were never closed, on to the starry Highland night. The obvious thing – drugs, gambling, a girlfriend 'in trouble' – that in her era would have been first considered, were startlingly inappropriate. *I should be grateful*, she thought. But instead she was simply mystified.

In the morning, Jenny was up at five-thirty. It was Sunday, and there was the long drive to town for mass at eleven; but before that, as every day, beasts must be fed, eggs collected, goats milked. Jenny hadn't had a lie-in in so many years that she

31

couldn't recall what it was like not to be up and moving about with chores done long before most people were awake. In the summer when daylight came at three, it was pleasant to be out in the cold, clear air. In the winter, in the frost and dark, it was a teeth-gritting trial.

When the work was done she came in, trailing her flotilla of dogs and cats, made porridge for herself, and coffee, and got out her cheque book and accounts book and the little stashes of petty cash that she tucked around in jam jars and biscuit tins labelled 'egg money', and 'cash for coalman *do not touch*'. Once, when Anne was visiting, she had watched Jenny do her accounts at the end of the month with amazement, making small sounds of despair and murmuring occasionally, 'I don't believe this.'

'It works,' Jenny answered grimly. Because although it did work, in that she had managed in the twelve years of her widowhood to somehow stay out of debtor's prison, she was never quite sure why. Or, indeed, how long it would continue. Not much longer, she thought, if Angus didn't get his act together.

Eventually she found a bill for feed that could be put off for another month because she had not taken that liberty with the supplier recently. That left a temporary padding in her bank account against which she could write a cheque to her son without stretching her overdraft irrevocably. Then she remembered that one of her neighbours owed her at least a tenner for eggs, and she closed her accounts book and put away her treasure troves positively elated.

Then suddenly it was late, and she dashed upstairs to pull on a slightly less tattered jumper, braided her hair, found her missal and her rosary and ran back down the stairs, still in her jeans, with thick man's knee-length socks pulled over them. *Thank God she was Catholic and dressing up wasn't part of it. She hadn't* time *to be Church of Scotland, or Anglican, with their tweed skirts and proper hats.* In the sheet-tin back porch she stepped into her stiff, cold welly boots, grabbed her anorak and ran out the door. Honey followed her to the car, so she opened the tail-gate of the Subaru and stuffed her into the space behind the dog-grate. The Subaru was scruffy, with wisps of hay on the floor and an animal smell. Jenny pulled the anorak on and scuffed her feet across the slick spots on the frozen ground. 'Shit,' she said. 'Ice.' There would be no mad dash to town. She'd be late to mass and sit apologet-

32

ically on the floor at the back. So what. Angus wasn't here to be embarrassed. And Sarah, who wouldn't have been embarrassed, wouldn't be coming any longer, even if she were here. 'So, it's just me and You,' she said aloud. 'And You'd rather I'm late than skidding off this bloody road. You don't want me yet, I promise You.'

Jenny drove with caution down the long, winding, single-laned track. The nearer hills were dusted white, gracefully, like a sugared cake. The big far ones were thickly covered, shining pink in the early sun. Angus, who was a skier, would be glad. She would tell him in the letter that would accompany her cheque. She wished he were here, suddenly, long-legged and bony and masculine, filling up the passenger seat in his restless, argumen-tative posture, making the car, the house, the farm interesting and uneasy with his presence. They fought a lot whenever he was home, but it didn't make her miss him any less.

She stopped at her neighbour's, leaving the engine running, and collected her money, eleven pounds fifty, and ran back to the car. The clock in the car was five minutes fast, habitually, to give her five minutes extra time, but she'd used that up already. She came down the steep hill as quickly as she could, feeling her way around the icy corners, and allowed herself some extra speed on the salted main road. Even so, they were on to the second reading when she crept into the back of St Mary's.

Dutifully, she crossed herself with holy water and, as was her habit when she was late and the pews were crowded, settled surreptitiously cross-legged on the tiled floor. It was warm in the church, and cosy, smelling of wool and winter coats. She felt immensely at home, and leaned her back against the radiator at the wall, shut off from any view of the altar by the rows of seated people. She felt like a little child, too small to see, and her mind wandered comfortably.

After mass she went back up the aisle to the altar and knelt in front of the statue of Mary. She looked up at the pink and white china doll face, the painted, uplifted blue eyes, and mentally superimposed her own personal Virgin upon it: dark, semitic, and strong. She lit a candle for Angus and the problem about money. Then she lit one for Sarah, remembering the bold, uncompromising posters. She was about to light a habitual one for Joseph when she stopped herself. Enough. Two was enough.

She never knew when to stop. 'I haven't changed,' she thought. 'I never change.' Once, in confession after Fergus died the priest had asked her if she prayed, and she had answered 'All the time. *All* the time.' And it was true. Her prayer life was as intense as a contemplative nun's. But without order, without discipline, only a frantic outpouring of words, building nets of protection over her loved ones. The priest had said, 'It can be too much, you know.'

Jenny went back down the aisle, genuflected, turned to go, and then stopped before the poor box beneath the statue of St Anthony. She folded up the pound note that her neighbour had given her as part of the eleven fifty, and slid it into the box. And then, after a moment, she put the fifty pence piece in after it.

Her relationship with St Anthony was ongoing and permanent. He found everything she lost, protected her family, saved her finances, and presumably her soul. In return she contributed her widow's mite with unstinting regularity, even in the rare weeks when no particular petition was called for.

'I should do a banker's order,' she said once to Simon. He was not amused.

'No wonder you're always broke,' he said.

'It isn't *that* much money,' she replied, quickly, sorry she had said anything to him.

'I still think you need it more than they do.' The 'they' annoyed her. It conjured an image of indulged priests and gold-laden altars that she suspected was Simon's true vision of the church.

'It goes to the poor,' she said. Then they fought. He brought out all the old chestnuts about the church and money, back to the Spanish Inquisition. She became stubbornly silent.

'It's just superstition,' Simon declared gloomily. 'And you fall for it still.'

'It works,' Jenny said. And, like her book-keeping, it did.

It was still cold when she came out from the church, but the sky had filled with clouds, and across the river the first strings of Christmas lights, yet unlit, were swaying in a strong wind. Jenny looked at them with disapproval. Early November. They seemed to start earlier every year, and by mid-October the shops were full of red and green cards, tinsel and artificial trees, clashing wondrously with the black and orange of Hallowe'en witches' hats and goblin masks. Jenny's love for Christmas still resisted the commercial sprawl. They seemed to have no decency about it here. Even in America, famed as it was as a shrine of materialism, there were strict rules, and Thanksgiving stood a firm barrier to the Santa barrage.

Of course, they had no Thanksgiving here. For a while she had celebrated it, but it became more and more difficult to remember when it was, and find cranberries and turkey when no one else wanted them, and find other ex-pats to create a lonely festivity. The children lost interest, since pilgrims and turkeys had not featured in their school lessons, and eventually Jenny gave up.

As she returned to her car, watching the dead lights swinging in the November gale, she remembered going to New York as a little child, with her mother and father and Anne, to see the decorations and the skaters at Rockefeller Center. The memory was vivid; she could feel the frost at her nose, and smell the burning chestnuts of the street vendors, and recall her own wonder at the mounting cascades of lights in the darkening evening outside Macy's and Gimbels. They had ridden home on the train, too early for her, before the black dark that would have made the lights perfect. She could even feel the disappointment she had felt then, and laughed at herself, gently, wondering how old she could have been. Really small, three, four maybe. Certainly less than six, because it had to have been before Joseph was born. They never went anywhere after that.

And then, thinking of Joseph, and Christmas together, she remembered that once again she had forgotten to send presents in time. It was already far too late for the surface mail deadline, and she would have to pay extravagantly for her errors in airmail stamps. And if she wasn't really quick about it, her gifts would arrive in February, their bright wrappings jarring and tawdry in a pale spring sun. She shrugged, annoyed with herself, both for the added expense and the necessity of a rush trip to town the following day, which would cost in petrol and, more seriously, in time: another day in the workshop gone. From the start, her widowhood had been like that. Work and family had driven her in a ring of frustration, devouring bits of each other, like two snakes swallowing each other's tails.

In the afternoon, to make up for it, she broke a private rule and worked on Sunday. She sat in front of the fire with a sketch pad, designing, so that even a strict Sabbatarian might imagine her just amusing herself. She laughed as she did so, thinking of an elderly neighbour who, having often seen her sketches of jumpers or jackets, said complacently, 'Aren't you clever, and how ever do you find the time with the family and the farm?' Thus dismissing the thing that earned most of her living as the hobby it apparently appeared.

Before she drove back into town the next morning, she rang Simon. She waited until she had finished the chores and had had breakfast, so that she would not wake him. He rose neither as early nor as forcedly cheerfully as she did. When he stayed over, her morning bustle annoyed him. She did not restrict it, however, to appease him, and he would not believe that morning efficiency was no more natural to her than to him.

But she was perversely sympathetic, spurred by dim memory of her slovenly student days, and the halcyon years with Fergus, coming home from parties in the dawn and sleeping until dark, before parenthood and husbandry took their tolls. He answered sleepily anyhow, and she felt a rush of sexy affection. 'I'm going to town,' she said. 'Meet me for lunch?'

'Oh lovely.' He spoke throatily, as if she had said not 'lunch' but 'bed'.

'Fine,' she said, and she gave the time and the place with a masculine authority that came from so long running her own life. He acquiesced happily. He was used to her running things, driving her own car, paying her own way. He was used to her running their affair, and if not totally happy about it, content enough not to risk what he had by asking for more.

That, the control, was what she liked most in the way things were. She liked the meetings on neutral turf, the lunches together outside of his home or hers – the choice of going home alone or together being always with her. It was the loss of those light, free meetings she most regretted when tempted towards the comfort of marriage. Sometimes they joked about it, and promised to go out separately and meet by arrangement, even when they were wed. But everybody made promises like that in the midst of an affair, and no one ever kept them.

'*We* will,' Simon said. 'We won't change.' But he had not been married before, and Jenny had.

III

Jenny loved her trips to town. It was a nice town, having all the facilities of a city with neither the noise, dirt, or threats of a real one. She had lived provincially for so long that even Edinburgh seemed exhaustingly cosmopolitan on her rare trips south. But she liked action and faces and shops and cafés, though she liked them in neat, controlled doses, with a safe line of retreat to green places and silence.

Her sister Anne regarded her as a rural hermit she knew, but in truth that had never been her, though it had been Fergus. Fergus, born in Glasgow and raised in its grey and shoddy rim, distrusted every city, though his livelihood depended upon them. He flitted in and out of urban centres in the early days of their marriage, shaking their dust off his heels before a disappointed Jenny could manage even a glance around. And when he had earned enough selling his country songs to city people to make his longed-for retreat, it was to some Hebridean outpost he first determined to flee. Jenny held her breath; she was too young and submissive to him to argue. But a dilapidated Great Glen hill farm had intervened, and Fergus had settled, reluctantly, for a tamer version of his dream. And before he had time to grow restless, he was dead. Sometimes Jenny woke in the dark comfort of her house imagining herself marooned instead on an island in the midst of a cold northern sea. And yet she suspected she would have coped well enough, and grown content. Her capacity for easy contentment was huge, a comfort in times of adversity, and a permanent frustration to her family and friends.

While Fergus was yet alive and the children were really small,

Jenny almost never came down off her hill. Eventually she hadn't even any clothes you could reasonably wear in a town, and she had only one pair of shoes. But even then she was content, living like a pioneer wife with her man going out on rare forays for provisions and coming back with an evening's worth of stories of things and people he had seen. That had suited Fergus fine, too. The town was smaller then, and simpler, even though it wasn't really very long ago. There were few supermarkets, and Fergus avoided the ones there were, frequenting instead a dozen small, old-fashioned shops, butchers', fishmongers', green-grocers', buying one thing here, another there. It took all day. Everything came home in damp, thin, brown paper bags, or loose, piled into a wicker basket she had bought from a tinker woman at the door. Their needs were simpler then, too. They were yet in the purity of their dream of self-sufficiency on their Scottish hill.

Now, as well as several supermarkets, there was a big, modern, American-style mall, which Jenny regarded with a complexity of resentment and delight. In the early days of her widowhood, she had clung to Fergus's way of doing things, partly to stay close to him, but as much because she had no way of doing such things on her own. She had only recently even learned to drive, and handled the battered Cortina he had left her with a nervous-ness approaching panic. Then, in a fit of post-bereavement rebellion she sold it, and bought the Subaru which somehow she could drive with no difficulty, quite probably because it had never been his. And bit by bit she abandoned his cosy corner shops for the slick practicality of Fine Fare and Littlewoods. She hadn't the time any more to wait in queues and chat about the weather. Trips to town were frenetic dashes, wild asides in her daily routine, held within the firm parentheses of the school bus timetable. Even when the children were surely old enough to fend alone, she had still made determinedly sure to be home before them.

Now, of course, there was no hurry. No one was coming home. Nothing but evening feeding and milking drew her back to the farm. Now surely she could stroll about, and look in windows, and try on clothes she wouldn't buy, and sample perfumes in the chemist's and sit in cafés watching town life. But the habit would not die. She rushed everything anyhow, and the darkening winter evenings still brought their old nervous dread, as if haunted by a ghostly school bus yet. It drove Simon mad, the way she would jump up half way through a leisurely meal, protesting her need to run. Consciously she disciplined herself by starting early and ensuring her appointments and shopping were complete before she met him. That way the nagging need was less.

She did the food shopping first, in the big Fine Fare in the mall, because it was the bit she liked least. It demanded of her, at once, the two things she most resisted: making decisions and spending money. Morosely she pushed her trolley up and down the wide aisles under the deadening fluorescent light, piling it full. As always, she bought too much. She was unused to cooking just for herself, and she retained a siege mentality from the early days.

Half the trolley was filled with pet food: tinned rabbit and chicken and fish for the cats, sacks of meal for the dogs, sacks of litter for the kittens. She knew it was ridiculous, knew what Simon would say if he saw it, and she covered it up quickly with a veil of vegetables and fruit. She still felt guilty. It should be beans and pulses, whole-wheat flour, nuts and grains. Loose, in big hessian sacks. That's what Fergus would have had. That, or less. She remembered the dream-farm of their honeymoon again, with its greenhouses, and rows of vegetables in black earth, and grazing obedient goats who never got out and decimated neighbours' trees. Somehow, in the dream, the sun always shone.

Scottish weather and Scottish soil had proved a rude awakening. She had her own eggs, and her own lamb in the deep-freeze, and the few hearty vegetables that grew in the teeth of the wind. But Jenny wasn't bred to live on eggs and lamb and kale. She imagined Fergus beside her, in his dungarees and boots, glaring at everything under the sad white light. Fergus would have hated it. He would have uprooted them, and moved, like a true frontiersman, further into the wilderness where the smoke from his neighbour's microwave would never be seen. But Fergus was gone.

'Screw,' said Jenny under her breath. She piled her trolley greedily with packaged bread, and bright tropical fruits. She bought French cheese, because she was sick of her own. She bought pasteurized cow's milk in a clean white and blue carton, and knew that some of the goat's milk would go to the cats. She bought MacIntosh apples from America, shiny and smooth, because the apples from her orchard were wrinkly with age in their cartons in the shed. She bought mushrooms from Ireland, rice from Thailand, pasta from Italy, grapes from Israel. She rolled her trolley to the checkout, piled it all through, and wrote out a huge cheque. As she trundled it all away to the car she remembered the day that she and Fergus had carefully worked out that all they would eventually need to buy from the outside world was sugar and toilet rolls. *Christ*, she thought. *If that had been all, we could have drunk our tea without and wiped our bums on the grass.* She couldn't believe that they had ever been so stupid, or so young.

It was only just after eleven when she finished stacking paper cartons of groceries into the back of the Subaru, and she felt pleased with herself, with two hours left before she met Simon in which to find Christmas gifts.

She went out into the town to choose something for her mother first, before tackling the subtle task of shopping for Joseph. Her mother was simple enough in a sad way; as long as it was something plain and practical that had obviously not cost much, she would be pleased. Jenny felt the way she had when she was a tiny child with pennies to spend on her parents' gifts, being directed by Nonna away from the extravagant and delightful towards the useful and dull. All she had ever bought for her father had been cigarettes: single packs when she was little, cartons when he was older – buff-coloured cartons of Camel cigarettes. It was all he ever wanted. Her mother had seemed never to want anything. Though Jenny was sure that in the early days before she had Joseph she had accepted chocolates, and flowers and once, from their father, black, frilly underwear. Anne denied it though, attributing that memory, like so many, to Jenny's notorious imagination.

She bought her mother a blue sweater, plain, unadorned shetland wool. *Coals to Newcastle*, she thought, as she paid for it. Her workroom was stacked with knitwear that Anne sold for lavish prices in New York. But there was no point sending those. She knew that now. For years she had designed something truly special each Christmas for her mother, just as she did for Anne and, out of courtesy, for Sandi. It was Anne who told her gently, with no malice, that her mother never wore them. 'She says the sleeves get in her way. Or she's saving them for special. Or they're too warm. She *does* think they're beautiful, kid. She's very proud . . . she shows them to *everyone* when they arrive . . .' The next Christmas she had sent a beige lambswool cardigan from one of the chain stores. Her mother had loved it, Anne reported with a kind, rueful laugh.

It was raining and cold out in the town, and Jenny, lulled by the climate-controlled shopping of the mall, had left her coat in the car. She ran about the streets and narrow alleyways between the grey, wet old buildings, moving fast to keep warm. Seagulls circled over the slate roofs, mewing and riding the wind. She felt different out in the town, among the old places she remembered from her days with Fergus: the old hotels where they had coffee and lunches before the new bright cafés came; the old pubs, now dressed up and trendy, where they shared pints. Jenny never drank any more. She was always driving, always, until this year, in charge of children. It had never occurred to her in the past to apply the same restraints to Fergus. She paused outside the seedy back door of his favourite old dive, the one where the folk club had met back in the sixties when they had first come North. Someone was playing the accordion inside, and the melody drifted out: 'The Bonnie Lass of Fife'. In a jolting moment she was back there, young, free, in love. She stepped back, looking at the doorway, as if the ghost of her old self might come through it with the ghost of her husband. It made her neither sad, nor indeed happy, but gave her a sense of achievement, the satisfaction that came from survival.

In the end she found the blue sweater in the new, modern Marks and Spencer's, back in the mall. She had tried all the Scottish woollen shops, decked with tartanry and furry Highland cows, for something more original. But there her stubborn American accent had cast her as tourist, and the neat ladies in their tartan skirts and frilled white blouses had plied her with mohair plaids she did not want or with cashmeres she could not afford. 'Spoil yourself,' they coaxed. 'You're on holiday.' Jenny fled, empty-handed, into the arms of St Michael. She paid with the credit card they had given her in a moment of corporate madness, relieved that she'd not see the bill for a month.

41

Joseph next. She braced herself, clutching the shiny green St Michael's bag, soft, with the sweater inside, for comfort. She walked up the mall, her boots rubbery and clumsy on the polished floor. She looked in the windows of the fashion shops, as if she wasn't looking for anything in particular, and arrived at Mothercare as if by accident.

Inside the open entrance, the shop was filled with young, young mothers with babies in pushchairs, babies in papoose packs on their backs, babies in slings. The mothers looked like children. They looked like Sarah. Jenny felt again the sensation of suddenly tumbling into middle age. She caught a glimpse of herself in a mirrored pillar in her jeans, anorak, and boots, her hair loose the way she had always worn it, a grey-haired girl. Rebelliously she brushed the long hair behind her ears in a gesture unchanged from adolescence.

She circled the periphery of the shop, examining the age co-ordinated displays of educational toys, until she found '0–6 months', and stopped before the selection of squeezy animals, textured balls, boldly shaped rattles and teething rings in bright reds and blues, greens and yellows. She liked them; they were familiar and largely unchanged from the toys her own children had been given at christenings and first Christmases, fumbled with in babyhood, bashed about in toddler years, and somehow never relinquished so that years and years later they were still lurking stubbornly at the bottoms of toy boxes. She lifted down a package of rattling dumb-bells, blue and yellow, serene within their plastic bubble. Angus had had one. She was sure she had seen Dhileas chewing on something remarkably similar but the day before. She looked around at the hassled, harassed young girl-women struggling with their armfuls of infants. She wanted to shout, *Don't worry, it'll be over soon enough*. And then, more sadly, to whisper, *Hold on, hold on, they are leaving you already*.

She put the dumb-bells back and walked to another shelf. There, displayed between a white stuffed rabbit and a blue elephant, she found a large pink plastic ball with geometric indentations for fingers. She lifted it and explored the chunky protrusions thoughtfully with her thumb. Texture was everything; Joseph's fingers were his eyes. She shook it experimentally and it jingled cheerfully. She held it at arm's-length and shook it again. The jingle was sweet and faint. She shrugged. He probably wouldn't hear it. Maybe with his aid? Anyhow, baby toys never made *loud* noises. She imagined herself going to the sales-desk and asking for a toy that jingled like Big Ben. She tossed the ball in the air once, caught it, and carried it to the checkout.

A girl in a checked smock looked up quickly and smiled.

'0–6 months?' she asked, in case Jenny perhaps couldn't read. Jenny nodded. 'Do you have one in blue?' she asked.

The girl smiled again, a little stiffly.

'Just a moment, I'll check.' She went away somewhere and came back. 'There's none on the shelf,' she said.

'I know that,' Jenny answered.

'The pink is nice,' the girl said, encouragingly.

'He likes blue,' Jenny said. The girl looked annoyed.

'They can't tell the difference at that age,' she said, sharply. She was a young girl, as young as Sarah. She had no time for babies. Or their mothers. 'It's just the parents . . .'

'It's not for a baby,' Jenny said. The girl looked blank. 'It's for my brother. He's a boy . . . a man. He's retarded.' The girl stared. Adolescent embarrassment pinked her small, sharp-featured face.

'I'm sorry,' she mumbled desperately. Jenny ignored that.

'He's thirty-five, actually,' she said calmly. 'And he really likes blue.' She stopped and waited stubbornly. The girl said, 'I'll ask someone,' and scuttled off. Jenny stood quietly fingering the small pink ball. She thought, *Oh, lassie, if I told you he's blind as well you'd throw me out.* But there was no need to tell her that, or to explain the necessity of choosing Joseph's presents with infinite care, a care developed thirty and more years ago in the compassion of childhood and maintained rigidly ever afterwards. No one outside the family could ever understand the essential battle against the logical and nihilistic, *What difference?* What difference what colour? He can't see. What difference the elephant, the duck, the rabbit? All beyond his comprehension. From the start Jenny had chosen gifts not for the Joseph who was, but for the inner Joseph who would have been. And that Joseph liked blue.

'You wanted the blue hand-hold ball, that's correct?' Jenny looked up. An older, grey-haired woman with glasses and a managerial manner was standing in front of her, the blue ball, in a windowed box, held in her neat, efficient hands. 'We had one in the storeroom,' she added. The girl in the checked smock hovered behind her, staring at Jenny like a curious child.

'Thank you,' Jenny said. She took the ball, wondering what the woman was thinking behind her pleasant, co-operative mask. Probably that she was a crazy fussy American, making things difficult. Jenny placed the box with the ball in it on the checkout counter. She had worse things to worry about than that.

The young girl rang up her purchase, took her money, gave her her change and her receipt and slipped the box into a plastic Mothercare bag. Jenny took it in her free hand, looping its handle through that of the green one with the sweater. She turned to go.

'I hope your brother likes it,' the girl said. Jenny turned back. The girl looked thoughtful and hesitantly kind, like Sarah again, when she was feeling her way carefully into a new, more adult attitude. A wave of love and compassion for the sheer honesty of the young swept over Jenny.

'He'll love it,' she said with a smile.

Jenny met Simon in the wine bar on Castle Street. It was what she thought of as a new place, although actually it had now been there quite a long while. But what mattered to Jenny was that it had not been there when Fergus was alive. It belonged to her new life, not her old. The building in which it was set, of course, was old, and she remembered it in two previous incarnations, most recently as a delicatessen, and years and years earlier as an emporium of Indian kaftans, embroidered velvet robes, and fringed and flowing hand-print skirts. A Pakistani refugee from Uganda had opened it in the early seventies and it had been her favourite shop.

She found it pleasantly strange to sit, as she would now, with Simon at a small table, lunching and sipping coffee, where once she had bought garlic and cheeses and black pepper and, in an even remoter time, had tried on the tapestry kaftan that still hung at the back of her wardrobe. It gave her the same feeling of stability as the sensation of brushing by her own ghost-self in the streets of the town, as if for all her being an immigrant and a stranger, she had roots here in another world underlying the present.

Simon was there before her. She saw him through the window as she approached, standing at the bar with three of his friends.

44

At once she felt less happy about the meeting, less assured of herself, less in control. Simon's friends were young. One was a solicitor named Michael. Tall and jovial, he was leaning over and chatting to a pretty blonde woman in an expensive grey dress and dramatic black cardigan. Her name was Antonia, and she worked for the Tourist Board, but she was writing a novel as well. Beside her, talking to Simon, was her husband. He was bearded, and tall also, and he seemed to do very little; but with his good accent and attractive clothes he was welcomed into congenial company. He was pleasant and decorative and it seemed perfectly natural that he be supported by his wife. Like all Simon's friends, they combined success with sufficiently evident artistic leanings to be interesting. Jenny thought of it as a passing phase, the way homosexuality was for some pretty, sensitive boys. They were not in any way people she would seek out as friends, nor, under any other circumstances, would they likely seek her. They were all under thirty, and the girl Antonia was twenty-four.

They greeted her with enthusiasm. Simon's back was to her as she entered the door, but the bearded man must have said something because Simon jerked around, and his face lit with delight and he rushed towards her, clumsily, with his long shambly arms outstretched. With his glasses and flop of yellow hair and awkward stooped stance, he looked like an academic or a scientist and not at all either the lawyer he had briefly been, or the artist-craftsman he was now. He also looked older than he really was, which Jenny found a relief. He bent down to kiss her cheek, circumspectly, not because he was shy of her, or lacked passion, but because he understood her. Jenny took time. There was a conscious necessary adjustment she must make from one role to another; from Jenny the mother and Jenny the widow to Jenny the lover. It had taken Simon a while to learn this, and he had endured hurt and rebuffs in the learning, but now he knew exactly what was occurring, and knew too that the place he would always meet the most resistance, the place where the whole transformation took the longest and was the least complete, was in the old farmhouse on her hill. For that reason alone he secretly wished she would leave there and come to live with him, though he had more acumen than to suggest it.

'That's a nice jumper,' the blonde woman, Antonia, said. 'Is it one of yours?' Jenny looked down. Her body seemed encased in fur beside the sleek grey dress. The jumper was indeed her own, one of her 'failures' that she wore rather than waste the wool.

'I'm afraid so,' she said.

'You're terribly clever,' Antonia said. She was trying very hard to be nice the way Jenny used to try very hard with one or the other of her children's friends that for some reason she found hard to like.

'Thank you,' Jenny said crisply. She had decided not to apologize for the jumper any further. Perhaps she should have changed. But she had been in a hurry feeding animals and had run out of time. Simon didn't seem to care, anyhow. He looked at her with an intensity of pride and pleasure that startled her. She really couldn't imagine quite what he saw in her, but she was pleased and grateful all the same.

His friends were equally baffled, and less pleased. She felt she was playing a kind of peek-a-boo game with them, so that their encouraging smiles and helpful compliments were like little hands held in front of their faces. And if she turned quickly to look at them the hands would be down and the true scowls revealed. She knew, through other, truer, friends, that each of this crew had at one time or other had a heart-to-heart with Simon in an attempt to deflect him from her. She was glad when they all made jovial, affectionate goodbyes, and left them to lunch alone.

They had their usual argument over who would pay. It was a genuine argument, not a posturing. Each of them wanted to pay very badly; she to preserve her independence, he to assert his. The girl behind the counter waited patiently while they carefully and politely sorted it out, each in the end agreeing to pay their own. Jenny was always polite with Simon; she had had enough verbal brawling with Fergus to realize that even humorous battling eventually did harm. Simon was polite in return because Simon was polite with everyone. Initially she had thought him slightly weak, but in time she learned that his reasonableness was a kind of power, and it came from his training in law. He could argue for hours and never get angry, never get bored and, because he never repeated himself but instead found endless new persuasions, never became boring either. It made Jenny uneasy because she was accustomed to winning arguments with

46

the children, having the unfair advantage of age and the parental right and inclination to bully. She had tried bullying Simon and he had drawn her up short: 'It's not right just because you say it, Jenny. You need reasons.' Her immediate response was to apply the same parental authority to him, but she stopped quickly, shocked into acknowledging his adulthood to be as valid as her own, despite the dozen years between them.

Simon was quiet while they ate; Jenny talked. She wasn't really eating a meal, only nibbling at two small portions of salad. Hunger could be satisfied any time and cheaply at home. She talked quickly, nervously, about anything that came into her head; the farm, the dogs and cats, her shopping in the morning, her mother's gift. She told Simon about the girl in Mothercare and the blue ball for Jospeh. He nodded, stopping eating sometimes to lean his head sideways, adjust his glasses, push back the silky flop of hair. Then he would carefully cut another piece off his quiche and lay his knife and fork down to listen again. Eventually Jenny ran out of steam. 'I'm always talking,' she said, apologizing.

'Good. You need to talk.'

'No I don't,' she said, defensively. 'I just talk.'

'You're still nervous with me.'

'Stop it, Simon. You're psychoanalysing me again.'

'No. I'm just listening.' He paused, laying his hands down on the table on either side of his plate. They were big, strong, long-fingered hands, out of proportion to his lanky, slight body. 'You're like a fountain. You overflow. Partly you're trying to hide from me. Partly you're needing to communicate. It comes from living alone.' As she started to bridle he said, 'I know. I'm like that in the morning when I come in to the shop. Particularly on Mondays if we haven't been together.' The way he said 'together' made Jenny instantly think of bed, just the way she always thought of sex when he lifted his glasses off, because there was a way he did that, too, just before he made love. She wondered if he thought of sex half as much as she did. He didn't seem to, to hear him talk. But then she didn't talk about it either. She said, 'I've lived alone for a long long time, Simon. I'm pretty good at it.'

'No you haven't. You haven't, Jenny. This is the first year you've lived alone. Just now, since Sarah's gone to Edinburgh.'

'Children don't count.'

He laughed suddenly, 'Maybe not, but it's certainly different now that they aren't around.' He grinned, boyishly, and slightly triumphantly. She knew he was remembering making love to her on the sheepskin in front of the fire the weekend before. Afterwards he had confessed that he had longed and longed to do that all the time he knew her, but was terrified that Sarah might walk in. He expected her to revel with him in their solitude. Instead she was angry and hurt.

'She had a right to walk in,' Jenny had said. 'It's her *home*.' She gave him a bitter look that said, *It's not yours, anyway, don't forget*. He had drawn back, baffled.

'Of course she had,' he said, his voice innocent, and sweet, and Jenny had hated herself because never, never had he ever presumed upon her children's rights. And yet, watching him savouring the memory raised her anger again.

'Sarah might be coming home next weekend.' She said it as a challenge, and indeed it was only the faintest chance. He looked concerned. 'Nothing wrong, is there?'

Jenny shrugged. 'Oh, probably not. She's not really coming to see me. It's some church thing those friends of hers are into. Some ecumenical thing.'

Simon laughed. 'Only you can make ecumenical sound like a dirty word.' He laughed again, 'Are Catholics all like you?'

She wasn't amused. She said, 'No. And besides, you know other Catholics. It's not the ecumenical bit I mind. It's all this damned born again . . .'

'Uh, uh,' he said.

'What?'

'You can't say that, Jenny. You don't know anything about them. You can't just condemn them out of hand.'

'I know enough.'

'*Jenny*.' He lifted the glasses up. 'Come *on* now. You're not *that* kind of parent.' He smiled, coaxingly, 'Hey, where's all that sixties tolerance . . . ?'

'What would you know about that?'

He paused and the smile cut off in a little grimace.

'I was around in the sixties, Jenny.'

'Yeah, sure.'

'I *was*, Jenny.'

'You were ten years old.'

'Jenny, I'm not going to argue the age thing again. There just isn't any point.'

'Then don't lecture me on my generation's values, OK?' She felt sure he would get angry; she wanted him to get angry. Instead, he again laid down his knife and fork and said, 'Some of us still like those values. Even some of us in this generation. Even if we haven't got the credentials . . .'

Jenny laughed, suddenly, giggling behind her hand, her loose hair falling forward. Simon thought she looked very young, exactly as she must have looked when the sixties and their values were still vibrantly alive. She said, 'What in God's name *are* my generation's credentials?'

He laughed also, at himself. Eventually he said, sheepishly, 'I don't know. Hashish dust in your pockets. Lovebeads tucked away in a corner somewhere.' He pushed the hair back, knocking his glasses askew. 'Sorry, Jenny.'

'I only smoked hash three times. And I never had any love-beads. I've got a rosary at the bottom of my handbag if that might help.' He looked suddenly serious, older, like he might look when he was her age, or beyond.

'No,' he said, 'I don't think that's going to help at all.'

She said, 'If you're going to be in love with my past, Simon, you can't be selective. You'll have to take it all. Dancing naked at a love-in. *And* making my first communion in a white organza veil. It's all me.'

'Give us a child until he's seven . . .' Simon said. He looked grim.

Jenny said, 'I wish *that* one were as true as non-Catholics always want to believe.' She was thinking of Sarah again he could see.

He said, 'One gone over the wall?'

'She'll be back,' Jenny said, with a cool assurance that chilled him, until he realized how scared she was underneath.

Jenny let Simon pay for the coffee. She was serious, but not ridiculous, about her principles. The small concession pleased him inordinately and he came back from the counter with slices of cheesecake as well. She couldn't argue; she didn't want to argue. The room was full of men buying things for women. She thought briefly how nice it would be to be that kind of woman,

49

wife, or mistress, who carried nothing but a little clutch purse filled with inconsequentials and, as an afterthought, a sum of casual change. Jenny perpetually lugged about an ugly practical sack, stuffed with all the necessities – chequebooks, credit cards, bank books, cash – that life required of her. How nice to be without that and, too, to be without the worries that followed her about like unruly dogs, snarling at every cheque she wrote. She looked at Simon. He had finished eating and was watching her in his protective, contented way. She tried to imagine him coping with the bills that lay on her desk, the way once Fergus had done. But that of course was the irony; for Fergus had not coped. That thought of the floundering terror in which his sudden departure had left her welled up and banished even the playful imagining of Simon in his role. Whatever happened, she would never ever trust to anyone the hard-bought security of her home. Trusting Fergus had proved a disaster.

When they finished their coffee, Simon took a small box out of his pocket and, without preface, handed it across the table. Jenny held back from taking it, the way, as a child, she resisted accepting wrapped gifts from relatives in case they were somehow really intended for someone else. Simon extended the box further, and then laid it beside her cheesecake plate.

'What's this?' she asked.

'Present.' She looked doubtful. She liked giving things, disliked receiving them: the first held power, the second potential weakness. Besides, she was always afraid with Simon that it might one day be a ring, and somehow if she touched it she would, like a woman in a fairytale, be under some essential spell. But the box was long and flat, the wrong shape. Tentatively she picked it up and lifted the hinged lid. On the satinized interior was written in gilt script: Simon Hamilton, Silversmith. Below, on its white cushion, rested a small silver fish, its back and dorsal fin enamelled a brindled brown and blue. It was suspended, by a loop on the fin, from a thin silver chain, the bulk of which was tucked neatly behind the satin.

'It's supposed to be a salmon but I got the fins wrong. Somebody said it looked more like a pike. So I've gone back to the drawing board.'

'Oh, Simon,' she laughed gently. She liked that he gave her his rejects, the way she wore her own. It took the seriousness

50

out of the giving. 'It's lovely,' she said. Girlishly, she took it out of the box and put it on. He let her fuss with the fastening herself, without adding the intimacy of his hands. The fish nestled into the blues and greens of her jumper, as into a rough sea. He looked at it critically. 'If you like pike,' he said.

The gift had relaxed her. She had another coffee, paying for this one herself, and talked for a long while, forgetting even to worry about the time. In the end, she was relaxed enough to talk about Angus. Even so, when she did, she masked herself in abstractions. 'What exactly happens,' she said, 'when people get caught out by the stock market?'

'Caught out?' he said.

'You know. Like what happened last month. When it crashes.'

'They lose money.' Simon looked faintly mystified.

'Yeah,' Jenny said, 'but, I mean, is it really money that they have? I mean, they don't get into debt surely. It's just money that they *thought* they had . . . paper money.'

'It's real *money*, Jenny. It's just like owning anything. Like your car. If you smash it up, and it's not insured or anything, it isn't worth anything. Shares that lose their value aren't worth anything, or at least not as much. At least, not for a while.'

'Yes, of course.'

'Jenny, this is the second time we've had this conversation. I can't imagine you're that interested in the market. Or, for that matter, in the fate of yuppie London. As far as I can see a lot of greedy people took a well deserved hiding . . .'

'I think Angus was one of them,' she said.

'Oh, shit, Jenny,' Simon stared at her. 'You didn't tell me he was playing the market.'

'He *wasn't*,' she said, and then added, 'He couldn't have been . . . he didn't *have* any money, except his grant . . .'

'He didn't use his *grant*,' Simon said.

'Of course he didn't.'

'Oh the little twit.'

'Don't call him that.'

Simon leaned back in his chair. His expression was irritatingly wise. He said, 'My first year, one of my friends lost his entire grant in a poker game in the first week of term. He lived on Mars bars until Christmas.' Jenny glared at him.

'No he didn't,' she said astutely. 'He called his parents up and they sent him more money. Students all have these wonderful disaster stories, but it's never true. The truth is, their parents bail them out. Their *parents* have the real disaster.'

'Angus has been at you for money,' Simon said.

'No,' Jenny said, and then, 'Oh, what's the point. I shouldn't have said anything.'

'I don't see why you're mad at me, Jenny,' Simon said in his most reasonable voice. He was smiling gently, his greeny eyes softening behind his glasses.

She said, 'I hate having to admit these things.' Then, her pride swallowed, she said, 'He's asked me for money twice. He says it's something extra . . . I don't think he used all his grant. I mean I don't know *what* he did, but the day after the thing happened he called up very cool and collected, kind of evasive.' She stopped. 'I'm his mother. I could feel him panicking underneath.'

'How much do you think he's lost?'

'How should I know?'

'Jenny, if it's just a matter of this term . . .'

'It *can't* be anything more. It can't.'

'Unless he borrowed.'

'Oh shit, Simon, what am I going to do?'

'Let him sort it out himself,' Simon said, coolly. 'If that's what he's done, it will be the best lesson in economics he'll ever have.' Simon said 'economics' with distaste. The way Jenny said 'ecumenical'.

She said, 'Oh that's so easy to say when it's not your child.'

'He's nobody's *child*, Jenny. He's twenty-one.' He leaned across the table. 'What were you doing at twenty-one? Were you still living off your parents?'

'I was married to Fergus,' Jenny said. 'Living off him.'

Simon went quiet. She knew he had worked all through school, and through university summers and holidays, because his parents were divorced when he was twelve and there was never enough money after that. He said, 'Do you need money, Jenny?'

'If I did,' she said, 'you wouldn't know.'

Quite suddenly, he got angry. He pushed back his chair and almost stood up, but thought better. It was completely out of his nature to walk out on her, or anyone. But he was still angry. He said, 'Jenny, why do we have to play this game? What are you hiding from? I know everything about you. I know you're the least demanding of women. I know you're honest to the point of lunacy. And I know you've no money at all. I'll *loan* it to you, for God's sake, but you're going to have to get it somewhere, and I know perfectly well there *isn't* anywhere else.' He crumpled up his paper napkin and flung it on his plate. 'For the love of Christ.'

'I'll get it from my sister,' Jenny said then, stubbornly, and she didn't tell him that she would rather die first. 'She's coming over for Christmas,' she added. 'I'll get it then.'

Simon was quiet for a long, long while, and his anger slipped away. He said, at last, warily, 'You didn't tell me that.' He seemed afraid, as if some new element had entered her life that might edge him out.

'I only just found out. I was going to tell you today. I just forgot.'

'So you'll have a big family crowd for Christmas,' he said.

'I hope so.'

He looked sad. She watched him struggle with his disappointment, and his loneliness.

'That will be nice,' he said at last.

It was because of the disappointment that she asked him home with her. It wasn't a good idea. She should be working, and he would have to leave ridiculously early because he had an appointment with a buyer at the Craft Centre. The roads would be bad. They would fight in the morning, with him sleepy and grumpy and herself with her chores to do. It would set the week off wrong, and they would both muddle through it until the weekend when perhaps they could at leisure set it right. And then, of course, Sarah might come home. Simon knew all those things, but of course he said yes. He was young enough not to turn down the offer of sex anyhow, no matter how inconvenient. That annoyed Jenny and made her feel used, until she examined her heart and realized quite how angry she would be if he'd said no. He had never once said no to her, and she felt quite sure that, if he did, she would throw him out of her life. Saying no was her last female right in the world of equals she occupied.

Jenny had been home for hours when she heard Simon's car in the drive. She had returned immediately after lunch while he had to go back to work, and then to his small rented cottage to collect his things. He was funnily meticulous and always brought a toothbrush and pyjamas which he didn't wear. Jenny herself wore long brushed cotton nightdresses, prim and Victorian, but only because the house was freezing cold at night, and in the black hours when she rose. Sometimes she looked with envy at magazine pictures of women in floating négligés, drifting about their fitted kitchens at breakfast. It brought memories of her American childhood where central heating was so universal that it was never mentioned and indoor temperatures were balmy, year round.

It was a cold night, with a hard, early frost, and Jenny had done her evening chores with freezing hands and had forsaken her unheated workshop early for the coal and wood fire in her sitting-room. She was finishing an experimental cardigan by hand, and she sat still working on it as she heard the familiar sound of the car turning on to the rough drive and bumping its way up through the potholes to the house. Lights flashed through the open curtains at the window, but she still sat, savouring a peculiar security. She remembered sitting like that when Fergus came home from town, or, in the earliest days of the farm, from Glasgow or Edinburgh, when he was still doing gigs. Then as now she would not go to the door, but would wait for him to come to her, glad to see him, glad that he was safe and home, but still reluctant to relinquish her solitude.

Simon knocked on the door. He was so careful not to overstep. Once, in a moment of warm gratitude she had said, 'Oh please, just come in. You know me too well to knock.' But he had said, 'I couldn't do that,' and later, when her sense of aloneness had reasserted itself, she was glad.

She rose and put her work aside and went, without haste, to let him in.

They sat in the kitchen while she cooked supper for him. Jenny had eaten earlier, after she did the milking. Now she cooked bacon and eggs for Simon in a big frying pan on the Aga. She was not a good cook. Any talent she had had, in the less pressured days of early marriage, had atrophied in the years of coping with children and work. She had a few Scottish specialities learned from her Grannie which she was rather proud of, but her children, like all modern children it seemed, disdained the hearty native diet of broths and mutton and smoked fish. They

54

subsisted for years on pasta and scrambled eggs, store-bought biscuits and peanut butter. They preferred white sliced bread to the grainy varieties that Fergus had taught Jenny to bake. None of that bothered her; she cooked what they liked and in the end silenced argument with parental tyranny.

But cooking for Simon was a challenge. He was not fussy, but he had genuine likes and dislikes which, unlike the fancies of children, could not be simply dismissed. She felt an uncomfortable need to please him, to demonstrate her womanhood and to justify herself before him. She resented it fiercely. It made her short tempered and cross.

'You're tired,' Simon said gently, as he finished his supper. He put the plate aside. Scraps of bacon remained around the edges, and most of the egg yolk still lay congealing in the centre. She resisted the urge to tell him to mop it up with his bread, the way she always did with the children. Instead she rather stiffly took the plate and scraped the remains into a dish for Honey. Had he not been here, she would have put the plate down to be licked.

'No,' she said, 'I'm fine.' She opened her mouth to apologize for the supper, but closed it again, the words unsaid. She had apologized to Fergus for most of their marriage, for her cooking, her child-rearing, her performance in bed. It had made her deeply resentful of him, and yet, after he was dead, she was unable to recall a single incident in which the demand for an apology had actually come from him.

He can take me as he finds me, she thought. Aloud she said, 'I'm sorry about the house. It's awfully chilly in here,' because Simon was rubbing his hands together thoughtfully in the cold.

They went through by the fire. At once, Jenny regretted it, because although Simon seated himself properly on the sofa, she saw his glance cross to the fur rug and knew he was remembering making love to her there. She was not ready for that. Annoyance over the supper combined with her usual awkwardness. She had not allowed herself to feel sexual yet and therefore felt put upon, and self-conscious. It was always like that when he was first here. Often it lasted well into the evening, and secretly she acknowledged that their lovemaking was better away from here, better by far in his little cottage, even though they could hear sounds from the neighbours through a shared wall. They were his neighbours, not hers, and strangers anyhow. And Jenny was not shy, or prim. Jenny had made love to Fergus in a mountain bothy, with another couple in a bunk six feet away, shielded only by the October night. And once they had done the same at a folk festival in America, outside, under a summer tree with people moving and talking all around. But none of that mattered like the ghosts of her past that haunted this house; Fergus's ghost of course, but that, a true ghost of the dead, was an acceptable observer. Far worse were the ghosts of her living children; the memory ghosts of their infant and growing selves watching with uncertain curiosity as their mother entwined with a young man on the floor.

Jenny sat in a chair, stiffly, her feet together, holding a cup of coffee on her knee. After a while, Simon got up and came to sit on the floor at her feet. She began by stroking his hair, smoothing it out in long hanks over his ears and the stems of his glasses. She waited almost impatiently for desire, irritated by its apostasy. Desire was so often with her now; she moved about the house in a state of repressed randiness, thinking about his body, about hers. At times, at the centre of her cycle, she could not keep her mind off him, and yearned, as she worked, to hear his car turning on to the rough road. She who had for so many years lived in conventual seclusion was now, through Simon's presence in her life, transformed into another kind of woman, neither nun, nor mother, but her own young self, alert for sex, restless, sensual, so even the coats of her animals and their soft wet tongues aroused her. And yet, whenever he came to her, a tremendous barrier arose of restraint and nervousness and repression, and she must painstakingly take it down, brick by resentful brick.

They made love in her bed, not on the floor. Deliberately she let the fire burn down, so that the cold would make the room uninviting, and Simon, clumsy with fires like most men, unwittingly let her do it. She did not want a custom to develop, a habit, a ritual, that might change the way she lived in the house, and make it less hers. Sometimes she wanted to lie on the fur rug with her dog and her cats and not think of him at all.

Simon was very good in bed. She hadn't expected it. She had thought, because he was younger than her, she would have to tell him what to do, how to please her, and she had dreaded the intimacy that involved. But Simon knew how. He was not younger than her in bed at all, and he did not defer to her there, although he deferred practically everywhere else. At first she resented it, but eventually liked it very much. Once, mistakenly, she had begun to explain how her sexual feelings fluctuated around her menstrual cycle and he had cut her off smoothly. 'I know what women are like.' And she was suddenly, grievously shocked, as if Angus had come to her and said the same.

Jenny put her long nightdress on before she got into the bed where Simon was already lying naked. He looked large and masculine and alien beneath her familiar eiderdown. She said, 'I'm wearing this because I'm freezing.' He laughed, held the covers up for her, and when she slipped in beside him, ran his big cold hands up beneath the nightgown, on her body.

'You're wearing it,' he said, 'because you're shy.' He reached over her, turned off the light, and let the darkness rush in from off the hill.

They were both asleep when Sarah rang. Jenny reached a familiar hand for the phone, but Simon sat up straight in the flustered confusion of strange surroundings. He shouted something garbled, but Jenny just patted his shoulder and, as she spoke into the phone, switched on the lamp. Simon glared at her with myopic eyes narrowed against the light. She waved her fingers to indicate that there was no cause for concern and said, 'Hello, darling, how are you?' Simon hauled himself up and out of the bed, wrapping himself quickly in his dressing-gown as if Sarah herself, not just her disembodied voice, had entered the room. The two cats that had crept up between them in the night clung determinedly to the rumpled bedclothes, closing their eyes miming sleep. Honey got up from her place on the rug and padded quickly out as Simon stamped across to the chair where he'd piled his clothes. 'No, that's fine, darling, it's nice to hear from you.' She looked quickly at the clock. It was half past one. 'Yes, I *was* asleep. It doesn't matter.' Simon, across the room, made a small, deliberate sigh. He looked as discontented as the ruffled cats. Jenny gave him a little smile, but said nothing. Sarah, unlike her brother, never referred to the possibility of his presence in her mother's bedroom. Instinctively Jenny did not mention it either.

'I wouldn't have bothered you, but I only just got in, and there was something I wanted to tell you . . .' Sarah's voice was unusually high, nervous, and she paused again and said with portent, 'I wanted to tell you first.'

'Tell me what?' Jenny said, cautiously.

There was a long silence, and the voice came again, a little defiant. 'I have some very important news.'

She's pregnant, Jenny thought, wildly, her throat catching with sudden fear. She forced herself to be calm and said carefully, 'Oh, have you, darling? What's that?' and braced herself for the answer.

'I've become a Christian,' Sarah said. Jenny was silent. Relief, confusion, and annoyance flooded her in equal measure. She looked across hastily to Simon. He was sitting on the chair, his body tense, his face turned away. She saw he was wearing his jeans under the dressing-gown, and had taken his glasses from the bedside table and was polishing them on his dressing-gown sleeve. She shrugged her shoulders, trying to extend her bafflement towards him, and to draw him into the conversation, but he deliberately did not look at her. She said, finally, into the phone, 'That's nice, darling.' She heard the irony that crept, unintentioned, into her voice. Sarah did not answer at once. Jenny heard her draw a breath and expel it in exasperation.

'It's not just nice, Mom! It's the most important . . .'

'Sarah, you *are* a Christian. I mean, we all are.'

When Sarah, after some time, replied, her voice was haughty and distant. 'I thought you wouldn't understand,' she said coolly. And then, with resignation, 'It's all right. I've made my witness anyhow.'

Jenny was suddenly angry. 'What does *that* mean?' she said.

Sarah explained patiently. 'I have to *tell* someone you see. It's part of it. I . . .' she paused, and her voice wavered with disappointment, 'I just wanted it to be you. I had this crazy idea that maybe it would make us closer. But I really *knew* underneath that you wouldn't understand.' Her voice was the exact blend of self-pity and self-righteousness calculated to most raise Jenny's ire.

'What *is* this crap?' Jenny shouted.

'This *crap*,' Sarah shouted back, 'as you so crudely put it, this *crap* is that I have taken Jesus Christ for my personal *Saviour*. *That's* what it is.' Jenny heard the tears of young fury, but was too angry to respond.

58

'Fine,' she said, 'fine. But put Him back when you're done with Him. The rest of us might like a shot, too!'

There was a tremendous, empty silence on the other end of the phone. Jenny sat hunched in the bed, listening to the black airiness, and hating herself. Then, after a long while, a small, strained voice said with weary disdain, 'Oh, *Mom.*' And then very quietly Sarah hung up the phone.

Jenny put her head on her hands and began to cry. After some time she remembered Simon and looked up. He was standing at the foot of her bed. He was dressed completely, and holding his rucksack with his overnight things in one hand and his shoes, a little ridiculously in the other. 'Goodnight, Jenny,' he said, and he stepped quietly to the door.

IV

Anne thought about the baby all the way to the airport. She was accustomed to travelling and good at it, but as Bob drove her to catch her plane she began imagining doing this same thing, one of her thrice yearly European trips, next year, at just this time, with infant and bassinet, diapers and feeding bottles, and all the paraphernalia she remembered Jenny carting around when her children were small. The memory of Jenny was vaguely comforting because Jenny, in the first year or so, had taken Angus everywhere. She even went on a last tour with Fergus before he retired. And it had worked. But then, Jenny *had* had Fergus, big, capable and doting in his fatherhood, and there was no guarantee that Anne would have Bob.

I'll have a nanny, for God's sake, she thought, stubbornly. *I can afford that.* When she had said that to Bob he had said, 'What's the point of having it then?' Anne had never heard him quite so cold, or so conventional. But then his wife had never worked, but stayed home for him and raised his daughters and was still raising them when she died. They had another tense and unpleasant fight, at the root of which was not child-rearing at all, but the child itself.

It had started over Joseph. Two weeks before, while Anne was in the thick of the Christmas chaos, coping with Sandi, and with the nervous young manager of the Hamptons store, hounding suppliers, haunting the competition to see what seasonal tricks she might be missing, overseeing the Christmas advertising campaign and simultaneously preparing the way for the post-Christmas sales, Joseph, with his immaculate timing, went critical. It was an occurrence none the less devastating for its thirty-five-year familiarity. Joseph's second talent, closely allied to his first of impossible survival, was near-misses. Throughout his life he had managed to brush death with excruciating regularity and with the high drama of an operatic heroine. As usual, it began with deceptive triviality. Late on a horrendous Thursday afternoon, Bob rang just to let her know that Joseph had a slight cold which appeared to be responding to treatment. There probably wasn't anything to worry about, but if she was coming out for the weekend . . . She wasn't, but she did, and by Sunday Joseph was in the hospital with bronchial pneumonia. There followed a week of sleepless nights, and vigils by bedsides and telephones, that in Anne's exhausted state had the tired, worn quality of an old black-and-white movie, rich in *déjà vu*. The hospital ward; the nursing staff with their unquestioning determination; Bob, his eyes haunted by the moral confusion that such crises in his hopelessly damaged patients always caused. And her mother, the same as she remembered her since the first, archetypal original of this event, fierce, intent, tireless, incandescent with love, crouched over the bed of her wounded child, willing every breath into him, encouraging, begging, praying, and cursing God. And, as always before, Joseph survived. His recovery was, in its usual way, as dramatic as his decline, his mercurial physique bouncing back like that of a young child. In a day or two he was giggling and chortling to his mother's voice. Within the week he was home. Or rather, back at the Center which all but their mother regarded as his home. And, as countless times before, when it was over and she slept a full night at last, Anne marvelled at two things: the first, how the sheer drama of Joseph's epic survival aroused all around to excitement and cheer, and banished in everyone's minds the compassionate cynicism that might question the true nature of the victory, and the second, how, even at seventy, her mother could rally such incomprehensible strength of will and body as she did to carry them all through.

'I could never do that,' she marvelled, aloud, to Bob. 'Never, never, never.' He looked at her with understanding and then, with cautious determination he said, 'Anne, have that test. Have it *now*.'

'What are you saying?' Anne heard her voice turn icy.

'Anne, look . . .' He had reached to touch her and she had jerked away.

61

'I can't believe you're saying this.'

'I'm not *saying* anything. I'm just saying you should take this test.'

'Because of Joseph.'

'*Not* because of Joseph . . .'

'Nothing's changed. Nothing's changed since I was a kid at school.'

'Anne, for God's sake.'

'My brother's a congenital wreck so that makes me a freak too. Now my baby's got to be a freak as well . . .'

'Shut up.' She stopped short. He was in a trembling rage, his hands working into fists. He looked taller, older, a bitter stranger. 'How dare you insult me like that? How dare you insult my profession? Have you no respect for me?' When he saw he had her attention he calmed down a little, lowered his hands, turned away. 'I'm not some bigoted old woman.' He turned back to her. 'I don't deal in superstition. I deal in science. I know what happened to Joseph has nothing whatsoever to do with you. Or your baby. But neither you, nor I, can look at him, can experience what his life has meant, to your mother, to you and your sister, and to himself, without thinking very carefully about what it means to bring a damaged child into the world.'

He stopped. Anne had turned her back to him. She said, 'There's nothing wrong with my baby.' Her voice sounded odd to her, high and unfamiliar.

He said, 'How do you know?'

She didn't answer. She longed for a rush of instinct that would well out of some primitive centre and assure her, but none came, and when she said again, rigidly, 'There's nothing wrong with my baby,' she realized she was hearing her mother's voice.

He reached to put an arm around her shoulders. She didn't fight him. He said, 'I'm sure you're right,' in his soothing, medical voice, but she was too tired to resent the hypocrisy of it. She wanted to be soothed and stroked and reassured. Bob said, 'But you know, at thirty we would call you an elderly mother. And you're forty-two.'

'Forty-three,' she corrected inanely.

'All right, forty-three.' She realized he had mistaken her age deliberately, to make *her* say it. He was clever, and she admired his clever psychological skill and hated him for using it on her.

'You're well into the extremes of childbearing . . . at the point where we must reasonably expect potential difficulties . . .'

I'll show you, she thought viciously, *I'll drop this baby in a field by myself, and it'll be perfect.* But a sardonic inner voice replied at once, *Listen to the hippie queen; who do you think you are, Jenny?* Aloud she said, 'My family are good at having babies. Look at my sister. She didn't even have a doctor for the second one. Fergus delivered it.'

'She was lucky,' Bob said smoothly. 'And she was in her twenties.' He paused, 'And it's not just you. It's the baby. There's a one in twenty chance of Down's Syndrome after forty, Anne, for a start.' He squeezed her shoulders. 'We have to be realistic.' And then, because she had run out of arguments and she knew he was right, she said it.

'You don't want this baby anyhow. It doesn't really matter to you.' She felt his arm stiffen across her shoulders, but he did not take it away. If he withdrew from her, it was within. Outwardly, he was calm. He had masterly resources of reason, and he drew on them now, the way he would, she knew, in a medical crisis.

'I want a healthy child. I don't pretend there won't be problems even then and, if you're realistic, you'll agree. But that is what I can accept and cope with, that and no more. There is nothing heroic about embarking on a grand adventure that you know will turn into a disaster. I know. I pick up the pieces of people's heroic dreams of self-sacrifice.'

'If you mean my mother, I despise you.'

'I don't mean your mother.' He stopped, took his arm from her shoulders and stood away from her. 'Your mother is a saint. I'm not. And neither, I think, are you.' He had looked at her grimly, and turned and walked away.

They would both have liked to end it then. But they did not end it. Wearily they made up, wearily they apologized, and wearily, to seal a less than satisfactory truce, they made love that night. Already Anne was too concerned about her pregnancy to enjoy it.

For the next week they were meticulously polite and kind to each other because Anne was going away and they did not wish to leave behind them a legacy of misery for the holidays. She helped him buy gifts for his daughters and plan his skiing vacation. When Joseph's illness shook Anne into nearly abandoning her plans, it was Bob who convinced her to go anyhow, shielding her with a wall of his confident strength. Her gratitude evoked a flash of realism in which her half-formed plans of running off to live alone with her baby appeared childishly naïve. Even if she managed just superbly, there would still be her mother, still be Joseph, and the thought of coping with that without Bob's comfort was devastating. And yet, for years she had. Like the chopping of kindling, that powerful independence seemed a lost talent, sacrificed to their union.

At the airport he gave her her Christmas present. It was a tiny box in silver and gilt paper. He had placed it inside a miniature shopping bag of the same silver and gilt, and slipped a perfect red rose bud in beside it. He said she was to open it on the plane, an hour out of New York, and girlishly she agreed. She kissed him goodbye in the departure lounge and went through the gate, carrying her soft leather hand case and the little shopping bag dangling from its satin ribbon. She looked back. He was standing watching, his face solemn, his hands clasped in front of him, his good grey wool coat hanging loosely open. He looked like someone's father, she thought, and with a jolt realized that that was exactly what he was.

Anne tucked the silver shopping bag into the netting on the back of the seat in front of her which held the airline magazines, the discreet paper sickbag, and the shiny card suggesting what to do if the plane chose to land in the Atlantic rather than London. She had taken the little rose out, and held it in her hand during the take-off. The feel of it and the sight of the little bag behind the netting comforted her the way a favourite toy had worked her through traumas in childhood. Bob knew exactly how frightened she was of flying, although she did it all the time, and had planned all of this for her solace. She was an idiot not to be married to him.

Dutifully she refused the stewardess's offer of alcohol, though her nerves yearned for the warm companionship of whisky, and accepted instead an orange juice. And then, when an hour's flying time had seen them into the clouds over Nova Scotia, she carefully retrieved the parcel from the netting and opened her present. She was aware of the man next to her half watching while he pretended to read, but ignored him, making herself an imaginary wall of privacy behind which to delight in her gift. It was a little jewel case, as she had known at once it would be. Inside was a tiny, perfect diamond on a lacy gold chain, simple and exquisite and exactly right. She undid the chain and slipped it under the short, cropped hairs at the back of her neck, and fastened it there, knowing that the jewel would fit into the hollow of her throat between the revers of her silk blouse and look as if she had never worn anything else. Bob was the only man she had ever known who knew exactly what to give her. He understood the way she dressed, the way she moved, the things that pleased her eye. It was a small but welcome talent, and one that no other man friend had managed. Throughout her adult life men had courted her, some had made love to her, some had tried hard to marry her, and all had given gifts which spoke in a dozen subtle ways of how inappropriate the giver was as a partner. One revealed meanness by shopping only in sales and bragging about his bargains. Another showed arrogance in his lavish extravagance, as if convinced that money could buy her. Another gave her trinkets and saved all his money for his children, invoking at once disappointment and guilt. Each had passed out of her life. She touched the tiny diamond, imagining him choosing it, leaning over the jeweller's display with the same care he had shown choosing a ski-jacket for Mandy, a personal stereo for Robin, oblivious of price or status, thinking only of a colour, a preference, a personal quirk. A poor gift, she thought, speaks loudly of the giver, the perfect gift speaks of the one who receives. She phoned him from Heathrow to thank him, and let him know the plane had landed in London and not the sea.

It was late when she got to her hotel, and she went straight to bed, slept out her jet lag, and rose midmorning ready for a tight cluster of appointments. First, over breakfast in her room, she rang Jenny. She settled back into bed between the crisp hotel sheets, setting her cup of coffee – definitely British but not too awful – on the bedside table. She smoothed out the satiny green bedspread over her knees and set the telephone upon them, and pushed a button to request an outside line. She was wearing a favourite champagne silk nightgown, the matching négligé cast over her shoulders, and she could see in the gilded mirror across the room that she looked good; suntanned from her autumn holiday in St Thomas, her hair well-cut and smoothly shining, black as nature intended with a little discreet help. The diamond

65

on its thin chain reflected morning light. She felt pleased, indeed buoyant, and wondered if that were due to pregnancy, too. She got her line, and pressed in Jenny's code and number with pleasant anticipation, ready to talk like sisters, without for once, the hefty transatlantic charge.

The phone rang so long that Anne was about to give up, and then suddenly it broke off and she waited for Jenny's chaotic, breathless hello. Instead, she heard the rough sound of a hand briefly muffling the receiver and through it her sister's voice, distinct and harsh, shouting to the distance, 'Don't you walk out on me, girl. You stay right there.' There was another pause and then, '*Sarah.*'

The anger communicated readily through to Anne. She recoiled slightly. She was always uneasy with Jenny as a parent when the parenting wasn't going well. To hear her little sister as disciplinarian, and a strict one at that, upset some deep conviction of her own. Suddenly she wanted to hang up.

'Yes?' Jenny said, her voice still sharp.

'It's just me, kid,' said Anne. There was a long silence.

'Oh. Hi. Are you here? I mean, in London?'

'I got in yesterday.' There was another pause. Then Jenny said, 'God, I forgot.'

Anne felt surprise and then, perhaps foolishly, hurt. She had imagined Jenny looking forward to her visit like a little kid. She said, 'I guess you've been busy.' It sounded lame.

She heard a quick rustling as the phone was moved from hand to hand, and then Jenny said in a curt breath, 'Just a minute. I've got to do something.' The phone rattled down on to something hard. Anne heard running footsteps, raised voices, and then clearly, 'You walk out of this house and you can bloody stay out.' There was a silence; the footsteps, hard and ringing, returned. 'You still there?'

'Look, kid, I think you're busy. I'll ring you again.'

'No, that's all right. What did you want?'

'Nothing. It's all right, Jenny. I'll maybe talk to you tonight. I'm taking the shuttle up to Glasgow tomorrow afternoon. Then Edinburgh the next morning and, look, maybe I'll ring you from Gordy and Elizabeth's Thursday evening, OK?'

After a little while Jenny said, 'Yeah. Fine. Look, I'm really looking forward to seeing you. I mean, we all are.'

'Great,' Anne said, with forced enthusiasm. 'Talk to you later. Bye, sweetheart.' Jenny's phone clicked down almost at once. Anne set her own down and said, aloud, 'Sarah, I suspect you'd better watch your ass.' She laughed softly to herself and then sank quickly into a depression of disappointment. She felt tired suddenly, as if the jet-lag had sneaked back, and she dreaded getting up now, and facing the day full of buyers and managers and over-awed counter staff; the jolly lunch and evening drinks, the obligatory dinner with Michael and Laura who headed the London operation. She felt small and vulnerable and no longer up to playing the executive, jet-setting around her little empire of Anne Conti shops. She looked at her reflection gloomily in the gilded mirror and it gave her less pleasure. 'Damn her,' she said aloud, furious with Jenny. 'Why does she matter so much?' Then she felt sorry and selfish. Jenny had problems of her own. But rational thought did not undo the emotion and the mystification at the power family, *any* of her family, still wielded over her. Nor could it undo the hurt that always remained when Jenny's children took precedence over herself.

Being out in London buoyed her spirits up. She liked the city; not as much as when she first knew it, when it was filled with foreign excitement and also cleaner, tidier, and safer than it was today; but still enough to find a day in its unique old streets a pleasure.

She went to the Carnaby Street shop first. It was small, really just a branch of the main shop on Regent Street, carrying a narrow, selected line. But it was the oldest, the original London shop, and she had a sentimental attachment to it reaching back into the sixties, when she, a long-legged girl in a mini-skirt and patterned tights, had wangled its lease from the lovelorn Italian who owned it. She'd been shameless, she was so desperate for that site; she'd done everything but sleep with him, and she would have done that as well, but fortunately he capitulated first. Standing before the narrow frontage, now gleaming with paint in her distinctive dark red and cream colours, she could summon that bold young self up in a moment, kohl-shadowed eyes and Mary Quant hair, triumphant, with a foothold in Carnaby Street and London at her feet.

Forewarned she was coming, the manager and her two young assistants were lined up respectfully waiting for her when she entered. The manager was an older woman, well-dressed and assured. She showed Anne around the newly decorated interior, confidently pointing out changes in layout, lifting one or another garment from a rack or shelf for Anne's benefit. The two assistants watched, awed, only tugging themselves away occasionally to assist a customer. They both wore black skirts and white blouses. Only their hair, dyed with bright streaks of blue and red and very modestly spiked, revealed their true selves, and how they would choose to be seen. They would not buy their clothes here, even if they could afford to, Anne knew. They would go to the little shops where the music was loud, the décor and the staff raucous, and find the cheap, shoddy and gloriously outrageous things they sought. Anne knew, because once, in another generation, they had been her clientele. But her sixties rebels had grown older and richer and more discreet, and the Anne Conti look had grown with them. It made sense; she went where the money was. But sometimes, looking at those kids with their purple lips and black drapery, their deathly black or bright orange hair, she thought it would be fun to be back there again, in grimy shops crammed with over-stuffed racks, and bald, communal changing rooms full of careless, perfect young bodies. One of her designers had said, not long ago, with the same wistful yearning, 'In those days, I decorated bodies. Now I disguise them.' Anne looked around the new look Carnaby Street interior, with its beige carpets, open spaces, and discreet shelves lining the walls upon which were folded a restrained number of perfectly colour-co-ordinated garments.

'Restful, isn't it?' the manager said proudly.

'Like the grave,' Anne said. 'Get some colour in here before we all die of good taste, hey?'

Regent Street was better. The shop, her British flagship, was bigger, brighter, busier. In the larger, lighter space, the minimalist décor that Michael and Laura assured her was *de rigueur* this year in London was more successful. Across a blank space of a pale cream wall, someone had imaginatively hung three brilliantly coloured knitted cardigans, stretched out on pine poles. They looked like kimonos, and in their distinctive reds and blues Anne recognized Jenny's work. 'Selling well?' she asked casually of the young woman showing her around.

'Those!' she exclaimed. 'They're marvellous. I can't get enough of them . . .' Anne nodded, pleased. 'If only that woman would answer my calls.'

'What woman?' Anne said, alert.

'That Mrs O'Brien who does those. I've been trying to order more all week. I can never get her in.'

Her voice trailed off and Anne said, 'Yes, well. These craft people *can* be erratic.' She looked up at the wool kimonos and sighed. Oh Jenny. But her annoyance was tempered with pride. They were still the best thing in the shop. No wonder everyone wanted them. The best there was, and her little sister made them. Her little sister who taught herself to shear, to spin, to dye, and weave and knit. Her little sister who gathered lichens and mosses and hunted out old lost dyeing methods and had entered the Royal Highland Show with hanks of wool thumb-tacked to a sheet of cardboard. And won.

Her pride swelled hugely, in Jenny, in herself, in the whole great success of the two of them, remembering the waifs they were when they first arrived, two decades before, on these shores. Wistfully, she wished her Dad was still alive, or Nonna, because she wanted to show it all to someone, and bask in deserved approval. And then of course she thought of her mother, and the whole warm glow of achievement cooled, and shrank, and tightened up into a small hard pit of disappointment.

Michael and Laura took her to dinner. She wore a black dress, belted, with a full ankle-length skirt, and Bob's diamond. They both made a fuss of how she looked. They had chosen a Soho restaurant that was sophisticatedly scruffy, and they talked a lot about the food. Michael and Laura were transplanted North- erners, a decade younger than herself, very proud of their knowl- edge of London. They pretended great unconcern about every- thing, but Anne knew they were excited by the chance to entertain her, had probably argued about the choice of restaurant, and would probably argue again when they got home, accusing each other of saying foolish things, or giving the wrong impression. Anne liked them, and wished they could simply like her without regarding her so clearly as a lynchpin of their careers in the fashion world. They drank a lot of wine over dinner, and towards the evening's end, grew casual.

'When are we going to meet this Bob?' Laura said, leaning

chummily across the table to admire, for the third time, the diamond pendant. Michael glared at her.

'Maybe next year,' Anne said, gently. *If there is a next year*, she thought. She was feeling tired and depressed, and too sober in the company of her drinking friends. The meal had been good, but too rich, and nausea kept flickering around the back of her consciousness.

'You should stay here tomorrow,' Laura said, the wine developing a whole strain of sisterly affection. 'We could take you out somewhere. The theatre maybe.'

'Laura,' Michael whispered.

'I have to go to Scotland,' Anne said.

'Whatever do you want to do *that* for?' Laura said. Anne smiled. She was perennially fascinated by the insularity of the British, the walls they erected across their small island, and their astounding lack of interest in anything occurring beyond their immediate bounds.

'My sister lives there,' she said.

'Oh, of course,' Laura muttered, still staring boozily at the diamond pendant. 'Poor you.'

The Glasgow shuttle flight was quick, an arc up into the sky and then down again, while drinks were hastily served, swigged, and cleared away. In between, briefcases were opened and little computers came out to sit on knees. Everyone worked at something. It was a serious flight, full of people intent on making money. The man next to Anne, a Highland hotelier back from a promotions tour to Florida, was wearing a gaudy red and green kilt. 'The Americans love it,' he said, and then apologized when he realized she was American as well. When she forgave him, he suggested dinner. She declined, but rode into Glasgow on a comfortable wave of flattery. As always, the reminder that she could attract men without even trying boosted her confidence in every other aspect of life. She completed her business in Glasgow, dined with the raucous red-haired woman who managed the Sauchiehall Street shop, comparing reminiscences of their Glaswegian grannies, retired early to her hotel, and the next morning took the train to Edinburgh. As always, rolling past the stony shadow of the castle and pulling into Waverley, she felt she was coming home.

It had been twenty years since she lived in this city, but, unlike Glasgow, which had been stripped down and rebuilt in that time, it was largely unchanged. Familiar sights and timeless landmarks blended the present comfortably into the past. A black cab dropped her at the door of Gordy and Elizabeth's New Town house, in a circle of Georgian splendour perfectly preserved from the day she first saw it. The only difference being that in those years neither she nor Jenny nor Elizabeth could possibly afford to live there. Time had improved things for all of them, Anne considered. Except of course Jenny, but that was another matter.

A girl with white-blonde hair, jeans, and a sweatshirt with a picture of a skier on the front, answered Elizabeth's door. For a moment Anne thought she was one of Elizabeth's daughters, but she said, 'Hello. I am Ingrid. I am au pair. If you please come, Mrs Fraser is up the stairs.' She looked to be concentrating very hard.

Anne said, 'Thank you,' and followed the girl inside, leaving her case at the door. The interior hallway had been redecorated in Laura Ashley stripes. Huge gilt mirrors reflected the curving stone staircase, the white painted railings and polished banister. Anne had remembered the house with bicycles and clutter beneath the stairs, but it had grown pristine, magazine-perfect. A child's antique rocking horse sat on the first landing, its buffed leather saddle too exquisite for any infant bum.

Elizabeth was in her first-floor drawing-room, once the children's playroom, now carefully restored. There was a white marble fireplace and an oak writing desk, at which the mistress of the house was seated. She wore a mauve tweed skirt and a white ruffled blouse, a dark blue cashmere thrown over her shoulders. The blonde hair that had once cascaded to her hips was clipped to chin length and tied back with a black velvet bow, leaving a little whisk of hairs above her collar. In the moment before the au pair spoke, Anne saw Elizabeth had become the image of her own mother, the daunting Perthshire lady she and Jenny had met on a weekend visit her first year in Edinburgh. It was the occasion on which they discovered that the Elizabeth of bare feet and kaftans, whole foods and Laura Ashley pioneer frocks, was wealthy, pampered and public school educated. Of course all of their friends had known it all along from Elizabeth's accent and manner, but they, as foreigners, had missed all the

71

clues. They had crept about the country mansion awestruck all weekend, avoiding Elizabeth's mother, a nice enough lady divided from them by a cultural chasm, and dodging Elizabeth's hard-drinking, lecherous father who bore an inexplicable conviction that American girls slept riotously with everyone.

Now Elizabeth had slipped gracefully across the cultural chasm herself, but it no longer awed Anne and she did not mind. In their youth, she had not comprehended why Elizabeth's family had been content for her, a bright, intelligent girl, to spend her time cooking in a restaurant rather than at college. It was a while before they understood that when the British talked about 'school', they meant high school, or its elevated fee-paying equivalent, rather than university, and when they spoke of a good education, their references were social, not intellectual. They had known just what they were doing with Elizabeth. In her brief spell as a cordon-bleu Cinderella she had met the young solicitor Gordon Fraser and, in due time, abandoned work for the sort of marriage that featured in *Scottish Field*. It was exactly what her parents had had in mind.

'Darling,' Elizabeth cried, seeing her in the doorway. 'How marvellous. You look *wonderful*.' She rose and embraced Anne, kissing her cheek. 'However do you *do* it?' Anne nodded, never quite sure if Elizabeth's praise was genuine. 'It must be *wonderful* to be so stylish. I do envy you so.' She gave her another kiss and then turned to the au pair, 'Don't just *stand* there, darling. Go make coffee. Remember? *Cof-fee*.' The girl look blank, but Elizabeth gave her a beaming smile and her face lit up happily and she barged out of the door. She walked like a man, and Anne heard her steps clumping down the stairs. Elizabeth made a face. 'She's useless,' she said. 'They *all* are. I don't know why I bother.' She grimaced again but added, 'But she is such a gem when the children are home. And they do love her.' Anne was looking at the photographs on the mantel and on Elizabeth's desk; the old familiar ones, of Elizabeth's wedding, with herself as maid of honour, the artfully innocent snapshots of the children looking, as Elizabeth's daughters always did, like storybook children, and the newer ones of each of them in their school blazers and ties. The older girl, Annabel, had the same masses of golden-brown hair that Elizabeth had once worn.

Anne said, 'She looks just like you. That's the way you were when I met you.'

Elizabeth looked at the photograph, critically. She said, 'She doesn't look at all like that now. She's gone punk.' She sniffed and turned the picture slightly aside.

Elizabeth took her to Henderson's for lunch, because it was old and they both remembered it from their early days. They were wallowing in nostalgia, summoning up names and trying to put faces to them and guess where they were now. Elizabeth complained a lot about how hard life was being married to Gordon who was married to his work, and how difficult raising the children was. She said, more than once, that Anne was wise not marrying anyone at all. Then she said, 'Or Jenny even. I really envy Jenny up there with no distractions. No social duties . . .' She sounded wistful.

'No money,' said Anne.

'I could live without money,' Elizabeth said. 'Somewhere else. But here! You can't imagine how demanding Edinburgh is.'

It was only after lunch, while they were finishing their coffee, that Elizabeth remembered that Bob had called.

'Oh, I'm such a pea-brain,' she said cheerfully. 'I quite forgot. That delicious man rang for you yesterday.'

'Who?' Anne asked, alert.

'You know. Your doctor. I told him he was a day out.'

'What was it?' Anne asked, the familiar unease creeping over her. 'What did he want?' Elizabeth looked unperturbed. She wrinkled her clear-skinned brow prettily.

'I don't think he said. I imagine he was just missing you hideously.'

'Did he want me to call?' Again Elizabeth looked vague. 'Did he mention anyone?'

'No,' Elizabeth chewed thoughtfully on the perfect pink nail of her smallest finger.'Oh, I *am* sorry, but I was in the middle of the most frightful row with Ingrid over the hoovering, which she never even *dreams* of doing until I have guests and then she's thundering about all over the place like a berserk rhino, and you know these old New Town houses, how they echo.'

'Did he mention Joseph?' Anne broke in.

'Who?'

'My brother Joseph.'

Elizabeth blinked. 'You don't have a brother . . .' She stopped, and her cheeks reddened under her make-up. 'Oh, the retarded boy,' she whispered. 'I'd forgotten. Surely he's . . .'

'He lives in a home. But we see him all the time. Bob works there. I thought there might have been something wrong. Joseph has been sick a lot.' Elizabeth was absolutely silent. Her mouth opened and closed again and then she dropped her glance and said, mumbling to her empty plate, 'I'm sorry.'

Anne said gently, 'It's my fault. I don't talk about him enough.'

Elizabeth said, 'I'm a shit, Anne. I thought he'd died years ago. I haven't thought about him for years.' She looked up. Her eyes were wet. 'Some friend I am.'

Anne shook her head. She said, 'I hardly go around advertising him. It's not your fault. Really it isn't. But you're sure Bob didn't say anything?'

'Honestly, I don't think so. If it were important, surely he would have wanted you to ring back . . .'

'Yes,' Anne said. 'Of course.' She finished her coffee and set the cup aside. 'I'm neurotic. I never go away without thinking he's going to pop off while I'm gone. I've *always* been like that. And why should I think it when he's gone on the way he has? He'll probably outlive me.'

'Oh, surely not,' Elizabeth said. She looked away and asked, 'How does your mother cope?'

'Ask God,' said Anne.

Elizabeth was apologetic for the rest of the day. Not verbally; she finished that at lunch. But in every gesture, every deference, every careful courtesy as they went about the city together. Anne had expected a fun day, tramping around the narrow medieval streets of the Old Town, revisiting girlhood haunts, indulging themselves with pastries in tea shops and moaning about their diets. Now everything was serious, reverential. She had experienced the same so many times throughout her life that she had a name for it; she called it the St Joseph Effect. There were other patterns, of course. There was the Black Hole of Calcutta; wherein every reference to her disabled sibling dropped into a dark silence, never to be referred to again. There was the Under the Carpet approach, characterized by a wave of sympathy and then a determination not to mention the subject again 'lest it upset you'. Elizabeth, being kind, made up her careless error by an outpouring of niceness, as if a steady flow of Edinburgh good manners might prove an antidote to all.

The Edinburgh Anne Conti shop, where two decades before she had begun her enterprise with borrowed money and a few bales of cut-price Indian cloth, was still in its original Grassmarket site. It had expanded, swallowing up a fishmonger's on the left and a second-hand book shop on the right, and it was much dressed up; now, like all her shops, it carried her cream and red international logo. But inside it had retained something of its original flavour, the only one of her shops to do so. It seemed almost antique now with its bare pine floorboards and high old-fashioned ceilings. Anne vividly remembered teetering on a ladder up beside the broad plaster mouldings, painting the walls. Jenny had been with her, moaning she was afraid of heights, and a couple of boys from the University, and Elizabeth as well. As they stood in the door waiting for the manager to come out from the poky office at the back, Anne said, 'Do you remember painting this the night before we opened?'

Elizabeth looked around, 'Christ,' she said. 'Was that really us?'

Anne had a customary chat; a by now familiar pep talk. She praised the deep green velvet bows and gleaming red baubles of the Christmas decorations, remembering as she did how for her first Christmas she had criminally removed a small fir tree from a Forestry plantation near Elizabeth's home, carried it home on the train from Perth and decorated it with baubles from Woolworth's. It sat in a pot of sand, shedding needles all over the floor. She had thought it wonderful. Now, the décor of each shop was decided carefully at head office in New York, and identical velvet bows and red globes filled windows in Manhattan, Southampton and London. Elizabeth walked around the shop while Anne was talking to the staff; when Anne rejoined her, she had bought a blouse and was carrying it in a dark red plastic bag that said 'Anne Conti' in curling letters on the side. Anne wanted to give her a discount, but the shops were too big, too formal and remote for that; it was no longer in her hands.

'Good God,' she said, looking at the tag, 'at least you should have waited for the sales. That will be half price on the twenty-eighth.'

75

'I want it for Christmas,' Elizabeth said.

Anne knew she really wanted it as an expression of the St Joseph Effect. She smiled, sadly, and said, 'Do you know what gives me the biggest thrill?' Elizabeth shook her head. 'It's not the shop fronts, or the kowtowing from staff, or the dinners with designers and buyers. It's that.' She pointed to Elizabeth's purchase, swinging from her delicate, manicured hand as they walked up the cobbled centre of the Grassmarket. 'It's seeing my name on those goddamned plastic bags.'

Anne rang Jenny that night, a little nervously, afraid of what she might find. The voice that answered the phone was a woman's, cool and sophisticated, and not Jenny's. 'Is that the O'Brien residence?' Anne asked, uncertainly.

'Auntie Anne?'

'Sarah?'

'Mom's milking the goats. Shall I get her?'

'No, no darling. Just tell her I'm catching the morning plane to Dalcross. Is that really you? You sound,' she paused, having been about to say grown-up, and remembering that Sarah had regarded herself as that from fifteen. 'You sound *older*,' she said finally.

Sarah's answer was a surprise. She said, 'I've been through a lot,' in a serious voice, and added, 'I've changed.'

She has a lover, Anne thought. Aloud she said, 'Well, going away to college does that, doesn't it?'

'Oh, it wasn't college,' Sarah said smoothly. Then she added, 'College *helped*,' as an afterthought.

'How *is* college?' Anne asked.

'All right.'

'All right?' Anne asked. It seemed very moderate for a girl who had been yearning to study art from the first years of high school, a girl who had worshipped the fashion industry, and begged Anne's advice regarding a fashion career. 'Don't you like it?'

'Oh, I like it,' Sarah said. She was quiet and then added, 'It just doesn't seem very important now.' She sounded solemn, and Anne thought, *Oh God, not just a lover, she's in love as well*. 'I'll explain when I see you,' Sarah finished.

Anne said, 'Great, kid. Look, I've brought the original drawings for the spring coat line. I thought you'd maybe like them for your wall.'

Sarah thanked her with polite disinterest. Then suddenly she remembered. 'Oh, Auntie Anne. There's a message for you. Someone called Bob rang from America. Wait a moment, I wrote it down.' Anne felt a sick lurch of the nausea that seemed never far away. She waited, her fingers trembling on the receiver while Sarah went for the message. She looked around the bedroom where Elizabeth had sent her to make her call, as if all calls were excruciatingly private. It was Elizabeth and Gordy's own room, with a huge bed and dramatic draperies, fitted, hand-painted wardrobes and glass-fronted cupboards. There was a Chinese carpet on the polished pitch pine floor. A memory of sandalled, long-haired Elizabeth again wafted through, like a breath of summer wind. The phone rustled, then Sarah said, 'Hi, Auntie Anne?' She sounded more normal, the arch dreaminess gone from her voice. 'Here it is . . .'

Anne said, 'Go on, read it,' and braced herself.

'The builders have *finished* the patio. Alleluia. Merry Christmas to everybody. And love to you.'

'Oh God,' Anne laughed. 'Is that all?'

'Why did he say Alleluia for that?' Sarah asked. She sounded quarrelsome. Anne said, 'Because it's a damned miracle.'

Sarah was quiet. Anne asked, 'Are you still there?'

'You shouldn't swear so much, Auntie Anne,' she said. 'It offends the Lord.' Anne was briefly stunned, and then suddenly outraged at the impertinence, but fairness asserted itself. No doubt adults had said that to Sarah for eighteen years, so why shouldn't she say it back? She paused until she was sure of her calm and then said reasonably, 'I'm sorry if I offended you, Sarah. I'm not very religious. Your Mom will tell you . . .'

'You didn't offend me,' Sarah said coolly. 'You offended God.'

'Oh?' Anne said, 'Did I?' She paused again, 'When did He tell you?'

' "You shall not take the name of the Lord your God in vain;" ' said Sarah, ' "for the Lord will not hold him guiltless who takes His name in vain." '

Anne let out her breath with a long sigh. 'There's no answer to that,' she said. She waited in an awkward silence and said at last, 'I'm sorry, Sarah, I really didn't know you took the Church so seriously.'

Sarah said, her voice firm, 'Oh, Auntie Anne. It's got nothing to do with what *you* call the Church. I'm *so* glad you'll be with us,' she said, and then she said goodbye. Anne put the phone down, mystified.

In the morning Anne had her first bout of morning sickness, arriving ignominiously at Elizabeth and Gordon's Georgian breakfast table. The boiled egg set before her by the boisterous hand of Ingrid had forewarned her; just the sight of it brought an unfamiliar unease. Foolishly, she chopped the top with her knife, caught a whiff of the hot, sulphury scent and instantly was up and running for the nearest bathroom with her hand over her mouth. While she vomited wretchedly down the bowl, Elizabeth made little cooing noises of sympathy outside the door and she heard Gordy say in his loud, public school accents, 'That frightful girl can't boil water, much less cook a decent boiled egg,' as if Anne's condition was the au pair's fault entirely. Anne retched again and thought wildly of Sarah. *This is my punishment,* she thought. *He's heard me at last. I'll never swear again, Lord. For that matter,* she thought as she struggled upright and mopped at her face with a wet cloth, *I'll never get pregnant again either.*

Elizabeth drove her to the airport. Anne was subdued, white-faced and queasy, and not looking forward to the flight. She clutched at Bob's diamond, for luck, as they arrived at Turnhouse. At the departure gate, Elizabeth kissed her, smiled sweetly, and said cheerfully, 'You're preggers, darling, aren't you?'

Anne gasped and struggled for words. 'What a ridiculous idea. Of course I'm not.'

'Thought so,' said Elizabeth. She patted Anne's cheek, 'My, my. *That's* certainly getting in under the wire, isn't it?'

78

V

Jenny was in the barn milking the goats when the Saints came that morning for Sarah. She had heard an alien clatter on the driveway and, when she had emerged from the barn, their big red van, dust-caked and dented, was again parked just outside the gate. The van was the sort that hippy families once travelled in, or rock bands on the road. Across the side, where her eye expected psychedelic flowers, doves, and peace signs, was written JESUS in large white letters. There were stickers across the front bumper, reading, 'Christians aren't better, Just Forgiven', 'He Is Risen' and, 'We've Found Him'. The door of the van swung back and a young man got down into the frozen ruts of the drive. Again her eye expected long hair, bright clothing, an apostolic beard, but the young man was very ordinary, wearing jeans and a neat pullover, a padded ski jacket flapping open in the wind. He fumbled for a long while with the gate latch until Jenny took pity and went to help.

'It's just a bit of old wire,' she shouted as she approached. 'You have to undo it. I've meant to fix it for years.' She used her apologetic voice, but the apology was only half-hearted. She had meant to fix everything for years – gates, fences, roofs, guttering – but as she settled into the land, the great Highland lethargy absorbed her in its slow, unhurried time. *Mañana*-land, Simon called it having not stayed long enough yet to get absorbed himself. 'Yes, it's terrible,' Jenny always answered, but smugly, because she liked it. It took her only a moment to unhook the bent wire that held the gate. The young man smiled and extended his hand, like an American executive.

79

'Hi,' he said, 'I'm Mark. You must be Sarah's Mum.' She shook his fingers. Her own hand was grubby and smelt of goat.

'Sorry,' she said, 'I've been milking.'

'This is really beautiful,' he said, looking around. He smiled again and the smile was too familiar. It was Sarah's smile, the one she'd come home with; the Christian smile, broad and bright, aggressively happy, certain. She stared at him, as if to see if the smile were a mask, hooked over his ears. But it wasn't. It flashed on with every word he spoke, and, she had found already with Sarah, it was impossible to break that smile down. 'Sarah told you we were coming?' he said.

'No.' The smile continued.

'That's all right,' he said, as if Sarah's neglect was Jenny's fault. 'She's in the house?' He made to move towards the house and Jenny suddenly, and quite instinctively, stepped into his way. But the other van door had rattled open and two young women climbed down. They both said 'Hi', and smiled the Christian smile. Like the boy, they were dressed neatly and nondescriptly, exuding safety and good sense, and Jenny wished wildly that they were outrageous, with safety pins in their noses and rainbow coloured hair.

Before Sarah went to Art College Jenny had imagined her returning with student friends, painted faces, black gothic dresses, a whiff of marijuana for spice; and herself comfortable among them, like an older sister, sharing memories of her own wild times. *This* she could not have imagined in a million years. She said, still standing in front of the smiling, pleasant young man, 'It's early. Sarah's still in bed. And anyhow . . .'

'She's expecting us,' one of the girls said. She was big with soft, honey-coloured hair and a heavy jaw. She kept looking towards the house as if willing Sarah out of it, and then seemed to succeed, because a window rattled open upstairs and Sarah leaned out into the winter air and shouted. 'I'm just coming. Wait for me,' as if afraid they would leave her behind. The big girl smiled and waved.

Jenny said, bluntly, 'My sister's coming from America this morning. We're going to meet her.'

The young man, Mark, said, 'Of course, we all have families.' Then he added, 'But the family of the Lord comes first.'

Sarah came running from the house, leaving the front door

standing open. She wore jeans and a brilliant sweater that Jenny had made for her and was pulling on a long black coat that flapped about her ankles. Her face looked freshly scrubbed and her hair tousled, and Jenny knew she had leapt from her bed when she heard the van arrive. She wore no make-up, but she had abandoned that since she had taken up with the Saints, and now Jenny, who had been appalled at the swathes of artificial colour that Sarah painted upon her face, wished it back, as she wished everything back that recalled the daughter she had sent away to college. But that daughter – bright, quarrelsome, moody, fiercely aggressive – had vanished, and what had come home was the Christian smile. Sarah brushed by her to greet her friends. They all exchanged a kiss on the cheek which struck Jenny as terribly County and upper-crust, but Sarah said it was a kiss of peace and quoted St Paul. When Sarah was done kissing, she said, 'I'll be back tonight,' and climbed up into the van beside the big girl with the stern jaw.

'What about your aunt?' Jenny said.

'Tell her I love her,' Sarah said happily. She was bright-faced and excited. With her fingers she combed her smooth black hair back into its geometric point at the front. The spiked bits at the top were growing out, flopping into softness.

'That's not good enough,' Jenny said. Sarah raised her chin. She looked down at Jenny through the open van door, and for a moment a spark of her old temper flared. She visibly repressed it. 'The work of the Lord comes first,' she said, and Jenny found herself looking into four pairs of equally confident eyes, four certain, confident smiles.

The van engine started and she knew they were really going, and her mother instinct grew huge as it always did at moments of departure. 'You haven't had any breakfast,' she called sadly.

'Man does not live by bread alone,' Sarah said with no self-consciousness, and all her friends laughed happily and chanted, 'But on every word that comes from the mouth of God.' The van pulled away, turning awkwardly on the rough field grass beside the drive. Across the doors at the rear was a crude picture of Christ, holding up one hand, like a Russian icon. She watched its brown, mournful eyes all the way to the road.

Back in the house, a trail of biscuit crumbs down the hallway led back to the kitchen and an open tin proclaiming that Sarah was surviving on chocolate digestives as well as the word of God. The discovery warmed Jenny with humour, easing the desolation of her daughter's departure. In the week Sarah had been home from Edinburgh, Jenny had scarcely seen her. The red van of the Saints arrived every day. Different young people came each time. Jenny had no idea how many Saints there were, only that they appeared uncountable and identical and apparently all lived in perfect unity and chastity in a rambling house in a remote glen when they weren't like Sarah, studying at college or university, or evangelizing around the country.

At first she had comforted herself that they were but an eighties incarnation of a sixties phenomenon; a modern day ashram, Christian rather than Eastern in bent. But now she knew that the only resemblance was the superficial common ground of youth. In every other way they were different; rigidly chaste, severely disciplined, naïvely unquestioning, and somehow, and mysteriously, financially independent. There was money somewhere; money that paid for Bible colleges, for printing leaflets and posters, for feeding evangelists, for cars and rail fares, for renting halls. When she asked Sarah where the money came from, Sarah had answered with perfect assurance that it came from God.

Angus and Simon came in together from the back porch. They were carrying wood and coal for the Aga, being determinedly masculine and helpful. She wished they wouldn't bother. She had her own system of wood-stacking that no one other than herself understood. The wood in Simon's arms was green, from the wrong end of the stack. She thanked him anyhow and put the kettle on the hotplate while they struggled jointly stoking the stove.

She kept falling over Angus every step she made, bumping into him whichever way she turned. He had grown even larger in this latest term; he was at least as big now as Fergus had been. Cats hid on shelves and dogs scuttled under tables when he was around. He had big feet, like a puppy, and although he was skilled and agile on playing fields, indoors he was inordinately clumsy. Fergus had not been clumsy. He had moved with a light-footed theatrical grace and no one ever noticed how big he was; with Angus it was the first thing one saw. Perhaps, Jenny hoped, it was youth, and he would grow into himself in time; but secretly she doubted it, secretly she acknowledged he had gained his clumsiness from herself. She had always been a fumble-fingered, bumbling child, and was yet a clumsy person – except when she was working, and then her blunt fingers grew wisdoms of their own. Nobody ever noticed her clumsiness because she was so small; adults even called her dainty when she was a child. But grace, like beauty, had gone to her sister Anne. She might have complained to God about the unfairness had she not had a perfect example, in Joseph, of what God could manage when really in the mood to mess things up.

Aside from his size, Angus was her child in every physical way. He had her blue eyes, her lank, shining hair, falling forward now as he peered into the firebox of the Aga. He had her somewhat gawky but not unattractive face. But the resemblance ended with the physical. In all other ways, he was Fergus's son: self-confident, extroverted, cheerful, optimistic. He inherited traits that should not be hereditary, a taste for exotic food and good wine, for instance, as well as Fergus's fine musical ear. But music, in which he was gifted, had not drawn him. Perhaps it had intruded too much on his early childhood, when Fergus was still with them and the house was filled with guitars and lutes, bagpipes and dulcimers, and myriad people playing them. Jenny remembered a small Angus stamping about amongst them demanding silence.

In their musical household, both their children sought silence. Sarah painted and drew, and Angus, alone in his room, wrestled with numbers and computers and Rubik's Cubes. He was a puzzler, an intricate worker of details, and he used the same puzzle-working traits now, mentally tinkering with the economic systems of the world, making sense out of something Jenny regarded as pure mythology. He was ten years old when he first outstripped her in mathematics. It was a moment she did not forget; her first child first stepping beyond her. Now he was so far beyond her that they lived in different worlds. Sometimes, when she heard him arguing with Simon, she would recall the few short years since she gave birth to him and marvel at the capacity for human growth.

Argument filled her house when Angus was home. Jenny, dimly socialist, Simon, fervently Green, and Angus, a bold young Thatcherite, the cuckoo in her counter-culture nest. 'Where did this *come* from?' Jenny wailed and Angus grinned good-naturedly and sliced her arguments to ribbons. Justice and compassion were on her side, but Angus was a master of facts. They had argued until two in the morning the night before. And then Sarah had come in, breezily high on gospel music and good deeds, blessed them all archly and wafted off to her bed. After that, they had argued until three about Sarah.

When Simon and Angus learned she'd gone off with the Saints, they both jumped on Jenny again.

'Really, love,' Simon started, 'I don't like to interfere . . .'

'But you're going to,' Jenny said mildly, stirring the porridge with a wooden spurtle.

'Well, if *you're* not going to do anything, Mom . . .'

Jenny put the spurtle down. She turned, her back to the Aga, and leaned against the towel rail, wiping her fingers on her jeans. 'Any suggestions?' she said.

'Well, not sug*gest*ions as such, Jenny,' said Simon.

'Several,' Angus said. He glowered across the kitchen table at her, big and burly in his corduroys and loose pullover. 'You could have called me when they came, for a start.'

'Oh, that would have done a lot of good,' said Jenny. She turned back to the porridge.

'A lot more good than doing nothing.'

'There isn't anything to do.'

'I'll throw them out,' Angus said, his voice rising. 'I'll just throw the sods out.'

'Come on,' Simon said. 'Stay reasonable. That wouldn't really get us very far.'

'It'd be bloody satisfying,' Angus said.

'And they'll charge you with assault,' Simon answered. 'They're not stupid, these people. They're very clever and they'll know all the ins and outs of the law. And they'll use them.'

'She's going with them by choice,' Jenny said quietly. She set bowls of porridge before each of her men. 'That's what both of you insist on forgetting. She's a free agent. Nobody's kidnapped her. She comes home every night.'

'And every day she goes back,' Angus said. He sat down heavily and pulled his napkin from its ring and shook it out impetuously. 'And for all your talk about rights and the law, I don't credit them with half so much intelligence. They're a bunch of inadequate, unthinking automatons; they get away with this stuff because people like you are too liberal-minded to stop them. If I do a couple of them over, they're not going to stand around turning the other bloody cheek; they'll be off.'

'And Sarah with them,' said Jenny.

'Jenny,' Simon said gently, 'we need professional help.'

'A good lawyer,' Angus said quickly. 'Or one of those de-programmers who get kids out of these cults . . .'

'She believes in this, Angus. You're not going to deprogramme faith.'

'She's brainwashed.'

'A psychiatrist,' said Simon.

Jenny gave him a hard look across her refectory table. 'My daughter is religious,' she said, 'not crazy.'

'What's the difference?' Angus said.

Jenny looked around to her son. Her eyes narrowed. 'How can you say that?' she asked. He shrugged and she pursued, 'You go to mass. You're religious.'

'Sure,' he shrugged again. 'But I'm not some bloody Jesus freak, am I?'

'Fine,' said Jenny. 'That's fine. As long as it's conventional it's all right.'

'Mom, for Christ's sake, I'm on *your side*.' He flung up his hands, shoved his porridge aside and left the table. Across her mind flashed an image of his two-year-old self doing the same. Only then the porridge would be thrown at her, or turned upside down on his head. Or Fergus, unhappy about sex, complaining that she failed to provide his favourite foods. Or Simon, picking fastidiously around his burnt bacon and eggs. All her life she had extended food to men out of some ritual duty and had it tossed back at her as punishment for her failings.

'Eat your fucking breakfast,' she shrieked. They both went silent, looking at her in amazement.

'Sorry, Mom,' Angus muttered. He came, sat down, and began to eat.

Simon said, 'Sit down, Jenny, you're tired.'

'And I'm not fucking tired, Simon. It's eight in the morning. I've just fucking got up.'

The air in the kitchen went thick and silent. They sat there, munching away, eyes down, terrified. Jenny burst out laughing. They glanced at her, and at each other, as if she were mad. Very quietly she said, 'I'm always reminded of this sketch I saw on the telly once. There are these parents, middle-aged, the wife with her handbag on her knees, and they're telling this counsellor or something all about their son. He's been lured away by this religious group. They make him dress in funny robes and chant in a foreign language and get up at weird hours and read things in the middle of the night.'

'Sounds like Sarah,' Angus said.

'He's in a seminary,' Jenny said. 'He's going to be a Catholic priest.'

Simon laughed, a quick burst of nervously happy laughter. Angus said, 'So?'

'Well, that's the point. That would have been all right. Wouldn't it?'

'I don't see that it would,' Simon said.

'You mean if Sarah wanted to be a priest?' Angus said, intentionally obtuse.

'If she wanted to join the Poor Clares?' Jenny met his eyes. 'What then?' And since there was no answer available for her son, she said, 'I wanted to be a nun until I was twenty. I even wanted it sometimes after. Even after I was married.'

'Are you saying that this thing of Sarah's is the same?' Angus said ponderously. He had his 'I'm listening before I cut you down' face on.

Jenny leaned over the table to him.

'No,' she said, 'Because I know it's not. But I can't justify *why* not.'

Simon said, 'When I hear religious people talk, I'm really glad . . .'

'Yeah, yeah. You're glad you're an atheist. Look, Simon,' Jenny said, 'do me a favour. Don't be a pompous prick.'

She turned away from the table and left the kitchen. Outside the door, she calmed down and thought, *Oh great. Anne's coming in an hour and Simon and I are at each other's throats; Angus is furious with me, and Sarah's bolted with the Holy Rollers. Some family Christmas.* She felt devastated. Family was one thing, the only thing, she had to offer Anne. Everything else Anne and her sleek circle of friends could do better; work, play, entertainment. They lived in beautiful houses untouched by Highland lethargy; houses where the carpets didn't wear down to shiny mats of nylon, where wallpaper wasn't stained at the corners, snagged with kitten claws, peeling from damp walls. They had interesting jobs, secretaries, cool elegant offices. They dined out every day in restaurants she couldn't afford once a year. They met famous people at parties and were unimpressed. They had everything, and with them Anne had everything, except the one thing she envied Jenny for, children and harmony under her roof. Jenny couldn't bear to think of her seeing it in disarray.

She stiffened her back and returned to the kitchen. 'Look, you two . . .' she began, but they fell over each other apologizing, and she was ashamed. They were so *nice*, both of them, so reasonable, backing off from conflict, regretting hard words, rushing to iron out differences. She felt a tyrant, a termagant, aware how effortlessly and unintentionally she cowed them both.

They each offered to accompany her to the airport. But she didn't want either of them. She wanted to see her sister alone, to be just the two of them for a little while. She had looked forward to this meeting for weeks, had planned what she would wear, how she would arrive early and enjoy a coffee in the café, alone, savouring the arrival of the plane. How she would see Anne coming across the tarmac, since it was a little airport and the planes arrived singly, at long intervals, and parked in front of the terminal building like over-sized cars. And how Anne would see her in her lovely Jacob's wool tabard, her hair neatly braided, her figure neat and slim from working on the farm, and be proud of her, for all their differences.

As it was, none of that happened. She was late leaving the house because Simon had lost an essential order book, and was in a panic until it was found. Then the labrador, Honey, got out, and everyone had to chase around and find her because she was stupid enough to get in among a neighbour's sheep and be shot. And then, just as Jenny was bolting for the car, the telephone rang. She answered it as she flew by it, doubting it was for her. Angus had a huge network of friends and his visits home were preceded by telephone calls which kept up throughout his stay and only gradually receded behind his departing back. As she expected, the voice was male, well-bred, and young. It also sounded irritated. Jenny ran to find her son at its slightly imperious request.

She searched for ten minutes until she remembered that Angus

87

had gone with Simon on to the hill to mend a line of fencing, part of their dual attempt at masculine usefulness. She returned to the phone and explained. The voice on the other end sounded pained and dissatisfied.

'All right,' he said, as if deciding, after thought, to believe her, 'I suppose I'll have to try again. I don't imagine you have any idea when he *will* be available?' Jenny had enough of the tone.

'No idea,' she said. 'None whatsoever.'

'Great,' said the voice, and then in a belligerent hurry, 'Look you can tell him from me, this is just not good enough. My father's after me for the money and I'm sick of making excuses.' He paused, possibly regretful, because when he spoke again his voice was quieter. 'Well, look, sorry to bother you and all. Just say Matthew called, all right? He'll know what it's about.'

When Jenny got to the airport the plane was in. She was still in her milking clothes, and Anne was waiting beside the ticket desk. Jenny left the Subaru with the engine running outside the entrance and ran in, red in the face, her loose hair in a tangle, her welly boots scuffing on the polished floor. Anne had not seen her. She was standing beside her one soft leather case, holding an armful of flowers she had just purchased, looking vaguely around. She wore tan wool trousers and a long soft wool coat, belted at the waist, and high cuffed leather boots. Her black hair, which Jenny had envied all her life, was cut in its shining sculptured cap and topped with a tan beret. She stood there with her flowers and every man or woman who crossed the small waiting room turned briefly to look.

Jenny shouted, 'Anne, Anne, I'm here.' She waved, her anorak sleeve flapping, 'It's me.' Anne looked up. She looked a little pale, as if the flight had been rough, but she smiled a small smile that slowly spread wider, sardonic at the corners.

'Who else?' she said, looking Jenny over carefully, and then still smiling she opened her arms, the flowers held theatrically outwards, and gathered her little sister into her embrace.

Jenny chatted in her faintly hysterical way half the distance home. It wasn't just with men that she was like that. Simon was partly right; living alone had something to do with it. Those long stretches of isolation filled her head with ideas, and there was no outlet for them but dogs, cats, and goats. Some thoughts rattled around for weeks until she found the *right* person to release them to, and sometimes she never found anyone at all. Anne understood. Anne understood most things, because Anne had known her longer than anyone and knew her better, better even than her husband had known her, or her children knew her, or her lover. And yet, between them at times the bleakest, most insurmountable silences fell.

And even now, Jenny had said nothing of true consequence; nothing of the myriad things that worried her, nothing of Angus and his money problems, or of Sarah and the Saints. They were on the hill road, not far from home, when her string of trivialities finally ended.

Anne said, 'You done?'

'Yeah,' Jenny said, laughing at herself. 'So how *is* everything, really?'

'I've been telling you. Business is great and driving me crazy. Bob is great and driving me crazy. New York . . .'

'Would drive anyone crazy,' Jenny finished for her. 'How's Joseph?' she said then, in a clear, even voice. Next to her in the car, Anne turned away, looking across the low hills by the roadside to the more distant and larger ones, beyond the great hidden chasm of the Loch. She turned back.

'He's dying,' she said.

'*What?*' Jenny whispered. Her hands tightened on the wheel and the old car bumped and swerved.

Anne said quickly, lightly, 'He's been dying for thirty-five years, kid.' She touched Jenny's forearm. 'No need to get *too* concerned.'

'What are you saying?' Jenny said. She kept her eyes on the hummocky, twisting road. 'Is something different? Has something happened, or what?'

'No, no. Just the usual. I don't know, kid.' Anne reached up and pulled her beret off. It had begun to feel hot and sticky within the car. The bumpy journey was reviving her nausea. 'Hey, you couldn't slow down a little, could you? I'm still getting over the plane.' At once, Jenny slowed the Subaru and stopped throwing it around bends. 'It's just,' Anne continued, 'a feeling I have, that things have sort of speeded up.'

'What does Bob say?' Jenny asked.

'Bob's a doctor. He says everything's functioning.'

'To you?' Jenny shouted, outraged, 'He talks that mumbo-jumbo to you?'

'He can't help it,' Anne said softly. 'They don't teach them the word "death". The "D" section is missing in the textbooks . . . Oh, don't blame Bob, please, he's so good really, he's so good . . . Oh Christ, Jenny, stop this car please.' Jenny glanced across, saw Anne's white face and swung the Subaru off the road, into a lay-by. Anne flung her door open and stumbled to the wire fence beside a green, thistle-ridden field and leaned over it, vomiting, while a large, somnolent ewe watched with glittering yellow eyes. Jenny was beside her, fussing with Kleenex.

Between gasps Anne said, 'Oh piss off, please. Don't mother me.' But she appreciated the care all the same; and when she was done, she took the Kleenex, mopped up carefully and allowed Jenny to lead her to a hummock of rocky heather where she could sit down in the fresh, cool air.

'Didn't you take a dramamine?' Jenny said, still mothering.

Anne smiled to herself. She said 'Somehow, in the circumstances, I didn't think it would work.' She stood up. 'Is there anyone at the house?' she asked suddenly.

'Angus,' Jenny said. 'And Simon.' There was a slight catch in her voice when she mentioned Simon. On the occasion of Anne's last trip to Scotland, Simon had been a pleasant young man whose evident infatuation with Jenny was a source of amusement. Neither of them had quite expected what was to follow. 'Sarah's away with some friends,' Jenny added, elusively. 'She'll be back later, though.'

Anne nodded. 'Could we go for a walk?' she said.

'Now?' Jenny asked. She looked at Anne's costume. 'Like that?'

'Toss me that old jacket from the back of the car,' Anne urged. She slipped out of the long beige coat.

'It's Honey's bed. It stinks of dog.'

'I don't care.' Anne grabbed it from her and pulled it on over her white silk blouse. 'Great,' she said. Jenny was staring at her cuffed black leather boots.

'I can walk in them,' she said.

'You'll ruin them.'

Anne looked at her, almost pityingly. She said, 'Please don't take offence. I know they're expensive and I know you can't afford them. But I don't give a fuck if I ruin them. I can buy new ones when I get back, and besides, I get them half price. I get *everything* half price. All my friends are in the rag trade, too.' She looked hard at Jenny, watching her struggling to overcome her indignation at the waste. 'I know it isn't very fair,' she said, 'but that's the way the cake breaks. *I want a walk.*'

She flung one long leg over the wire fence and stepped into the field, swinging the other over to follow. She was halfway up the first grassy hummock when Jenny, who needed to scramble over the thing since her own short legs wouldn't make the stretch, caught up. Anne kept striding on, over the wet, rain-soaked grass, stepping neatly around sheep pellets and mole hills, impatiently tugging her soft trousers free of the spiny thistle leaves. They were out of sight of the road when she began to speak.

'When was the first time,' she asked, turning quickly to Jenny, 'that you wanted Joseph dead?'

Jenny stopped walking. She stared, silently, her blue eyes round. Her loose hair was blowing all over her face, and she clutched at a handful of it and ground a mess of grey-brown against her cheek. She looked devastated and Anne chose to soften the blow. 'I don't mean like all kids wish people dead sometimes. Like you must have wished me dead, or Marion. That's normal. That's everybody. But the first *real* time when you wanted him *really* dead. Gone. Out of the way.'

'When I was nine,' Jenny said, calmly. 'And we moved house. The night before we went. I wished he'd die so we could stay.'

Anne nodded. She said gently, 'That was fair enough.' She started walking again, and as Jenny followed she said, over her shoulder, 'I held out a bit longer, but it was just because he was never so much in my way, at first. I didn't *care* about moving house like you did. I made friends anyhow. And I always had Marion. She was always my best friend even when I treated her like shit. And I'd known her forever so she was Joseph-proof. It didn't get me until later.' She paused, and scrambled up on to a smooth back of rock and stood looking over fields and heathery hills, up towards the big mountain that hung over the moor. 'Even then, I got out of it by keeping away from the place. Never bringing anyone home. But eventually of course people found out. Remember my junior prom?'

Jenny climbed up beside her sister. She looked at the mountain while she said, 'What an asshole he was.'

'It wasn't his fault,' Anne said. 'He didn't know how to handle it.'

'Leaving you waiting for hours in your prom dress wasn't exactly a great solution.'

'What else? Call up and say, sorry, I'm standing you up because your brother's a freak and my parents think it might be catching? Jesus. Anyhow, he didn't have to tell me. I knew why. Marion told me.'

'Did you blame Joseph?'

'I'd have spit-roasted him if I could that night. Poor old Joe.' She turned and looked at Jenny. 'But the worst thing was trying to hide it from Mom.'

'I wonder,' Jenny said coolly, 'why we bothered?' Anne heard anger beneath the calm voice and gentled her own again when she answered.

'Jenny, when you were pregnant, did you ever think . . . did you ever think about her? How she must have felt? Did you ever think, maybe, it might happen to you?'

'Constantly. For nine whole months, with Angus. With Sarah,' she added lightly, 'I was more confident. I only thought of it maybe ninety per cent of the time with Sarah.'

Anne was quiet. Jenny had never told her that before. Of course, she had never asked. She said, 'It must have been a terrific relief when they were born.'

'I kissed God's feet.' She looked away again to the mountain, dark brown against grey winter clouds. It was starting to rain and high up the rain was snow, falling in sheets and curtains against the sky. 'Which was silly,' she said, 'because *she* must have felt fine when Joseph was *born*. It didn't show apparently. Nobody seemed to know . . .'

'She knew,' Anne said. 'She knew something was wrong, even if nobody was saying. That's why she was so weird about him, not letting anyone near him. Remember the christening?' Jenny nodded. She caught her lower lip in her teeth, chewing at it. The memory still hurt. 'She was like a mother dog or something, protecting the runt of the litter.'

'Dogs don't do that,' Jenny said quickly. 'If the bitch finds something wrong with a pup, she's more likely to kill it.' Jenny's face was expressionless. Animal behaviour was familiar, unemotional ground to her. She added, 'You don't get these problems in nature.'

'No,' Anne said slowly. 'I guess not.' She thrust her hands into the pockets of the borrowed jacket. It felt grimy. She wrapped it up closer to her throat against the rain. The smell of the bitch, Honey, was rank. She said, 'Jenny, if, when you were having Angus, or Sarah, if it *had* happened to you, knowing what we know, what would you have done?'

'You mean after they were born?'

'Before. If you'd known before.'

'She *didn't* know, Anne. That was the whole point . . . anyhow, there weren't any options then.'

'But just *if*, I said, if it were you, and you did know?'

'I'd have had an abortion.'

Anne stepped back shocked. 'You *would*,' she whispered. 'Just like that?'

'*Absolutely.*'

Anne paused again, uncomfortable, and said awkwardly, 'What about the Church?'

'I'd have come to terms with that. Somehow. But I'd have done it anyhow.'

'You're very certain,' Anne said softly.

'Savagely certain. Now that you ask.' Jenny raised her face and looked straight at her sister. Anne looked away. Finally she said, wrapping the scruffy jacket tighter, 'Poor old Joe.'

'What he never knew he wouldn't have missed,' Jenny said coolly. 'And, while we're at it, who says he would have missed what he did know?' Anne shrugged. 'Anyhow,' Jenny added, 'it wasn't just him. It isn't just *that* child affected. I'd have done it for the others.' She paused. 'If I'd been her, I'd have done it for us.'

'Is that what you wanted?' Anne said. But Jenny dropped her eyes and looked away. Anne watched her for a while, picturing all the other ages of Jenny she remembered; tiny wispy-haired Jenny in Indian headdresses at five. Jenny at thirteen, stubby and pudgy in her brief spell of puppy-fat; Jenny blossoming and startlingly lovely in her kaftans and lovebeads; Jenny high-strung and tearful in pregnancy; Jenny with her babies, heavy-breasted and placid as a Jersey cow. And now this Jenny, her body irrevocably marked by childbearing, her face by experience. At last she said, 'You wouldn't, you know. Not you. You least of all.' And before Jenny could argue, she added the old soothing oil, 'Anyhow, you said it yourself. There weren't any options then.'

'There were,' Jenny said. 'After.'

'After?' Anne whispered. Her mind filled suddenly with all the unthinkable late night thoughts; a heavy hand on the pillow, a moment of calculated carelessness in the bath, the turning over and drifting to peaceful sleep when the coughing began in the night . . . 'Never,' she said fiercely. 'Never. It would never have occurred to her.' *But it would have been so easy.*

'What wouldn't?' Jenny asked. Anne shook her head.

Jenny watched her a moment longer and then said, 'I meant, she could have put him in a home, then, before he had time to mess up our lives.' Anne raised her hand and brushed the rain water from her hair. She lowered it and held it before her and studied the clean fresh water dripping from her sun-brown fingers, beading on her polished nails.

'Oh that,' she said relaxing. 'Of course.' And then she added drily, 'Remember what happened the one time they tried?'

'I was a child. I didn't understand what it was going to mean. We were both children. They shouldn't have listened to us.' Jenny slid down the sloping rock easily on her heels. She started walking back, towards the road. It was too wet to stand talking in the middle of the heather. Anne followed, slowly. She said to her, over her shoulder, 'Anyhow, it didn't matter what I thought. Or you thought. Or anyone. She'd never have given him up. She loved him . . . adored him. She loved him more than any-thing, more than any of us.' She stopped and turned around to face her sister. 'She had to. She gave up everything for him. She had to love him more than everything.' She resumed walking and felt Anne catch up and stride, long-legged, at her side, through the soggy ground. She glanced down. The black kid boots were crusted with mud. She said, thoughtfully, 'She loved what he *wasn't* more than what the rest of us were. He filled all the space the theatre should have had . . .'

'The theatre was a toy,' Anne said sharply. 'Joseph came and they both grew up. Dad was a voice teacher, and Mom was a housewife. And mother *extraordinaire*. Can't you ever love them for what they were, not what you wanted them to be?'

94

Jenny said, with her back to Anne so that the words were barely audible, 'At least I didn't want them to be rich.' She turned and faced Anne angrily. They had reached the fence beside the car. They were both soaking. She said, 'What I wanted was what every child wants and has a right to want, a fair share of love.'

'You had it.'

'I had it after Joseph took his whack. You've never wanted to face it, Anne, but it was true. If the ship sank, the last to go overboard after you and me and even Dad would be good old Joe.'

Anne stopped at the fence. She placed both hands on the thin wet wire between two posts and leaned forward. Solemnly she intoned, 'In the beginning, there was Anne and there was Jenny, and then the Lord made Joseph and botched it all up. Forever and Ever. Amen.' Jenny leaned against a fence post and giggled, her weatherbeaten face hidden in her hands. When she finished laughing, Anne said, 'I'm pregnant, Jenny. I'm having Bob's child.'

VI

Jenny in a yellow sundress, bare arms sunburned, bare legs red with jellyfish stings, stands amidst rotting seaweed at the edge of the bay. She is holding the seining net; at her feet is the metal bucket from the Uncles' boathouse, filled with tepid saltwater in which a few battered minnows swim. They have been bait-fishing; as always Anne has a scheme to earn money and get rich, and Jenny and Marion, Anne's best friend, have been pressed into service. Now it is all forgotten. Anne and Marion are wrestling in the sand, punching and snarling at each other like boys.

'You bitch. You lying bitch. It's not true.'

And Marion, stubborn and pedantic as ever, 'There's no point in fighting about it. It's going to *happen* anyway.'

Then they're rolling over and over in the sand, but Jenny is standing gripped in the shock of what she'd heard, what Marion the know-it-all said in her smug, superior way: *Your Mom's having a baby. She's pregnant.*

'Take it back!' Anne is howling. She has her best friend down in the sand, arm in a hammer-lock, face open-mouthed and shrieking in the fly-ridden seaweed. But Jenny says nothing. She thinks, *It's over. The family. Nothing will ever be the same again.*

Her mother *is* pregnant. Jenny knows it, and so does Anne because Marion, for all Anne is shouting 'Liar!' at the top of her lungs, never lies, and is rarely wrong.

Marion and Anne have been best friends forever, since before they were born; their mothers were best friends before them. They've been thrown together so long they cannot help but love each other, like sisters. But it is a ferocious friendship, because they are not a natural combination. Circumstance, not attraction,

96

joined them, and now, like sisters, they are stuck with each other. Anne is a tyrant; Jenny knows, Jenny bows, buckles, submits, and worships. What else? She is tiny, and two and a half years younger. Marion is bigger than Anne, tough and strong. But good nature undoes her, and she too submits. Still, she has her limits, and knows what to do when they are passed.

Marion is an only child. She came late in her parents' lives, unexpected, much delighted in, but faintly inconvenient. Her tardy solitary arrival lacked impact; they have never seen the need to arrange their lives around her, as young parents and parents of large broods do by instinct. Instead, she is wedged in neatly. She plays properly in appointed rooms; others, off bounds, retain their adult sanctity. Adulthood, not childhood, is the accepted norm in her home. She rises to join them; they do not stoop to her. They have never been careful in front of her; they speak freely, tolerantly, and expect her to absorb adult information. She has no cute names for body parts. She knows where babies come from. She knows who's having them too. She's no blabber-mouth, though. Marion is too clever for that. She guards her secrets well, and uses them. And this time Anne pushed her too far with her tyrannies and her shouting and bossing, because the net was tangling, and there were few fish, and stinging jellies were driving them mad. So Marion waited until Anne stopped shouting to catch her breath, and came out with it. *I know a secret.* Now she was paying for it, with a mouthful of salty weed and a pummelled back. And being as honest as her proud parents always claimed, she hadn't even the luxury of recanting.

And so it's out: a secret no longer. And Joseph has blundered into their lives.

By the time he actually arrived, the original annoyance had faded; they couldn't hold Marion's big mouth (or Marion's *parents'* big mouths) against their Mom and Dad forever. Anne rather quickly came around to enjoying the idea; she had a younger sister already, an addition to the family was no loss to her, and quite likely an advantage. If nothing else, it gave her one more superiority over Marion, who had only a dog. She began to talk a lot about the New Sister, which appalled Jenny. Her picture of the family, her Mom and Dad, Anne and herself, was rudely shaken. She saw the new sister as an exact replica of

97

herself; she would be duplicated, replaced. She played obsessive baby games with dolls and carriages, trying desperately to at least be seen to be liking the idea. Instinct told her that under such a threat the best course was angelic co-operation. And then, quite suddenly, she had a joyful revelation.

'What if it's a boy?' she said to Anne.

'It's not a boy.' Anne was furious. 'Who wants a boy. I *hate* boys.'

'*I* want a boy,' Jenny said boldly. 'I *like* boys.'

Anne was disgusted. Jenny was soft on boys. She was always following them around the playground at school, getting them to chase her, letting them steal her snack, or her scarf. Anne and Marion regarded her as a turncoat. Anne said, ominously, 'You'd better *hope* it's a girl, that's all I can say.'

'Why?' Jenny asked, nervously. Anne had her wicked look. 'Tell me, tell me,' Jenny shrieked.

'Right, you little pig,' Anne hissed through her teeth. 'Here goes.' She cocked her head sideways. 'What do you think Dad wants anyhow?'

Jenny hesitated. 'A girl?' she said cautiously.

'A *boy*, you dummy,' Anne said. 'Fathers *always* want boys. Always.'

'*Dad* doesn't. He likes daughters. He likes *us*!'

'He *likes* daughters because he's *got* us. You wait until he has a boy.' She leaned back, one hand on her hip, smirking. Her black shiny hair swung, glistening over her shoulder. Her perfect creamy brown cheek glowed with warm pink light. She said, '*I'm* all right. I'm the oldest. And Nonna likes me best, anyway.' Nonna was their paternal grandmother, and no one doubted she favoured Anne, who looked like her, and worked hard to be like her, drying dishes in the kitchen of the restaurant that Nonna ran with their Grandpa and sometimes even waiting on table to show off. Anne said, with treacherous candour, 'You're *Dad's* favourite, of course.' She looked very adult when she said it, and Jenny glowed with pride. 'At least you *were*,' Anne finished. She grinned, her little white teeth gleaming. 'Boy, if I were you I'd be *praying* like mad for a girl.'

Jenny did pray for a girl. She felt guilty, knowing her Dad was probably praying for a boy, but she mumbled the prayer anyhow, tagging it on to her long list of prayers that always got longer and longer. She lay in her bed with her eyes squeezed shut, saying them all; first the Our Father and the Hail Mary that Sister Magdalena was teaching her so that she could make her first communion; and then all her bidding prayers, for all the family, even her Grannie in Scotland, for all her friends and her teachers and everyone's pets. She even prayed for the chickens that Nonna kept for the restaurant, and the minnows Anne caught to sell for bait. The list got longer and longer. Sometimes she fell asleep in the middle and had to finish it in the morning, if she remembered, while she dressed for school. But sometimes she would have enough, get angry with God and refuse to say any of them, and for a while her nights would be blissful and free. But then, one by one, in guilty succession, new prayers would clamber in to take the place of the old. Jenny was compulsively religious; she could be no other way. She prayed non-stop on the day her Mom was in the hospital having the new sister. So whatever happened, it wasn't Jenny's fault. Which is what she told Anne when their Dad came home and told them that Joseph had been born. He told Anne first. Then Anne stamped upstairs and found Jenny.

'She's had it,' she said grumpily and when Jenny started jumping up and down she said, 'For your information, we've got a brother. I hope *you're* satisfied.'

'A brother!' Jenny shouted. She couldn't hide her glee. She bounced up and down some more. 'A brother, a brother!' she shouted.

'You were *supposed* to be praying for a girl.'

'I did. I did. I prayed real hard.' Jenny couldn't stop her mouth grinning. 'Annette's got a brother,' she said, thinking of all the children at school. 'And Harry. And Stevie McLaughlin has a brother, only he's older. And now *we've* got a brother, too.'

'I hate him,' said Anne.

A cold day in February, bright with strong winter sunshine; there is snow lying on the ground. Jenny begs Anne to come out and make a snowman, but Anne won't leave her mother and the new baby. It is Joseph's christening day and the whole big family has gathered in Anne and Jenny's house. It is a Sunday, and because it is winter anyhow, Nonna and Grandpa have closed the restaurant and Nonna is in the kitchen of the house making food for the party when they come back from the church. There is a huge white cake, and Anne and Jenny have been casting it hungry glances all morning. Their other grandmother, Grannie Reilly, is in the kitchen too. She has come all the way from Glasgow in Scotland to see Joseph. The two grandmothers are too different, Nonna tall and black-haired, wearing high heels and silky dresses; Grannie tiny and wrinkled in flat shoes and old-lady clothes; they look surprised whenever they see each other and talk only about the baby. The baby, Joseph, is tiny. He is so small that the doctors at the hospital kept him extra days before letting him come home. He cries all the time.

'Such girning, that wean,' Grannie Reilly says. Nonna holds Joseph and rocks him back and forth. He howls.

'All babies cry,' their mother says. She is curt and short-tempered with everyone since she brought Joseph home. She takes everything as a criticism.

'Let *me* hold him,' Anne asks, reaching her arms out as if there were strings attached to them and attached to Joseph. Something aches inside her when she thinks what it will feel like to have him in her arms. She has found that she doesn't hate him at all. From the moment she first saw him, tiny, eyes squeezed into little lines, wet puckered mouth, damp, spider-web hair, she has felt that ache. Nonna looks up at her mother.

'He needs a feed,' her mother says, and snatches him away. Her father is watching. He looks hurt, puzzled.

'Anne's a big girl, Louise,' he says. 'She can hold a baby.' But her mother has taken Joseph away.

Joseph cried all through his christening. He cried so much that his whole tiny body, lost in cascades of lace and blankets, went stiff, his arms out like two little poles. His shrieks echoed through the church all through mass and twice before the baptism their mother took him out, carried him about in the foyer of the church, his cries distant through the glass doors.

'An opera singer, that one,' their Uncle Eddie whispered to Grandpa. The men all smiled. They sat in a row, Uncle Eddie, Uncle Ricky, Grandpa, their Dad. Jenny sat beside her Dad, looking down the row, feeling proud to be with them. Her Grandpa was small, white-haired, wiry, and his two brothers, Eddie and Ricky, were both tall and lean. They were dark from the sun because they worked on the farm, growing things for the restaurant. They were always outside and always together. Often they talked Italian, not American, as if they had never left Italy at all. Jenny loved Eddie who was kind to her and made a fuss, and was frightened of Ricky who didn't like children. Neither of the Uncles ever married and they lived together in a house by the bay and worked together, and occasionally they fought and did not speak to each other, even in Italian, for weeks. Now they were all on good behaviour because of Joseph's christening. Ricky only came to church for christenings; Jenny's had been his last visit; but Eddie came every week, and Grandpa got up every morning at six and came every day. Jenny's parents came when they felt like it, and sometimes just sent Anne and Jenny with Nonna.

Jenny liked it best when everyone was there, like now, even their Aunt Rosemary from New Jersey; she liked the whole family together with herself and Anne, and now Joseph, at the core. Afterwards, when the house filled up with people, she went up to her room and lay on her bed soaking in the delicious sounds and smells of festivity, like a second Christmas. Through it all she could hear Joseph wailing yet.

When she went downstairs, the adults were all in the big living-room with a fire in the fireplace, and through in the dining-room the table was covered with a cloth, and there were plates of food, and the big white cake, and rows of glasses with golden wine. Uncle Eddie sneaked Jenny a glass of wine with water mixed in it. Jenny walked around between the adults seeing nothing but skirts and trousers. Anne was by Joseph's bassinet, like she always was. Jenny joined her. Joseph was asleep at last.

'Hey, Joseph,' Jenny said, 'you're christened now.' His hands opened and shut and his face wrinkled and he began to make the chirping sound that preceded crying. Nonna picked him up, waltzed him around the room and then, quite unexpectedly, handed him to Anne.

She stood transfixed, the ache satisfied at least. He was unbelievably light and warm. 'Oh,' Anne whispered. 'Oh.' She began to cry and the Uncles pointed and laughed. But Anne rocked him gently, happily, and even when he opened his eyes he did not cry. At last, when the feeling of holding him became too special to stand, Anne handed him back. But it was Grannie who

101

took him, not Nonna, and Grannie carried him across the room to where Jenny was sitting by herself. Jenny was Grannie's favourite, exactly because Anne was Nonna's, and Grannie was fiercely fair. 'Here's your wee brother,' she said, offering him to Jenny.

'I'm too little,' Jenny cried, terrified.

'I'd a wean on my hip all the day at your age,' Grannie said. And she handed Joseph over as casually as if he were a doll. Jenny gasped, and clutched at him, and Joseph fretted and wailed, and then suddenly their mother appeared in the doorway.

'What are you doing?' she shouted, and she ran across the room and grabbed Joseph roughly out of Jenny's arms and held him to her. Everyone turned, alarmed, and Jenny, in the middle of their stares, sobbed softly.

'I didn't hurt him,' she said. Grannie patted her shoulder and said, 'Dinna greet. Your Mam's thinking she's got the first baba in the world.' She said it sourly, but their mother ignored her and took Joseph to his bassinet. After a while Grannie stood up and went across and looked down at the baby for a long time. He was sleeping at last. She watched quietly, her eyes narrowing. Then she spoke, aloud, for everyone to hear. 'That bairn's no' right,' she said.

It is spring. Joseph is lying in his bassinet making small sounds. Their Dad is leaning over him waving his fingers and playing peek-a-boo. He is in his dungarees and a plaid shirt because he has been working in the big barn that in the summer is a theatre, getting it ready for the season. Jenny likes spring because she likes the theatre. In the winter, everything is ordinary, and they are an ordinary family. Their Dad teaches piano and singing. One room of the big rambling house is shut off to them and music comes out of it all day. Their Mom is just a housewife in the winter. In the summer, she is an actress. The big barn which is dark and empty all winter is full of people watching the plays and applauding her Mom and Dad and the other actors and actresses. Jenny is allowed to watch the plays on Saturday afternoons and when they rehearse. She has to be quiet and in fact she is utterly silent for fear of losing the privilege. Anne doesn't bother to watch; she is bored with the theatre because it takes all her parents' time and she doesn't see the point of the plays; people talking in silly voices and pretending to be something they're not. But Jenny loves them. She wants to be an actress, like her Mom. In the summer a girl called Margaret looks after Jenny and her sister while her parents run the theatre. They have two lives: a winter life and a summer life. Jenny prefers summer, and Anne winter. Jenny wonders which Joseph will prefer. While her Dad plays finger games for Joseph and Joseph lies there, not crying, but not doing anything else either, Jenny pushes her face in close and watches for a long while. Then she says, 'He's not watching.' Her father waves his fingers more and puts them in front of his face. 'He's still not watching,' Jenny says. She waves her own fingers, but he pushes them impatiently away. He waves his fingers again, then his whole hand, moving it back and forth across the light. Then he gets a bright red toy, a little hammer that Anne has bought for Joseph with some of the money she earns, and waves that back and forth.

'He doesn't like his hammer,' Jenny says. 'Joseph doesn't like toys. He's too little.' She explains it all carefully to her Dad, but he keeps waving the hammer and waving it and waving it.

Anne crouches behind the door to the kitchen at the foot of the back stairs. Joseph has been away to a hospital, for a day and a night, and she has bitterly missed him, the sweet-sour smell of him, the tiny and yet imposing presence of him. She has even missed his endless crying. Now he is back. In the kitchen her parents are fighting.

'What do they know, these doctors?' her mother shouts. Her father is talking so quietly Anne cannot hear him. She hears sobs. 'There's nothing wrong with my baby,' her mother cries, and then the door bursts open and her mother, sobbing, rushes past and Anne runs to be with her father, but he pushes her away, because he is crying too. And so they learn that Joseph is blind.

That was when the tests began. They went on for almost a year and took in an ever-widening circle of doctors and clinics and hospitals, until the names of physicians and assessment centres took over all family conversations, and Joseph's progress or lack of it became the focus of all attention. It cost a great deal of money, and even more of time, and by the year's end, in subtle switches and stages, the family had changed until it ceased forever to centre on ordinary things; work and play, report cards from school, squabbles between Jenny and Anne, triumphs and failures in the summer theatre; and came instead to centre entirely upon Joseph. Throughout it all they learned a great deal about blind children, and about deaf children (since in time an indeterminate degree of deafness was added to Joseph's original disability) but strangely little about Joseph himself. There was still disagreement about quite how much he could see, and more disagreement about what he could or could not hear. The most dissension remained regarding the degree of further damage. And about one thing there were no answers at all: the inevitable and bitter, why? Why Mike and Louise's son, why Jenny and Anne's brother? Why this baby among so many? There were murmurings about infections, genetic flaws, a difficult birth, but there were never any answers. Except what Anne and Jenny's grandmother said in a letter from Scotland: 'It's the will of God and you accept it. That's all.'

Jenny stands in her parents' darkened bedroom, leaning over Joseph's crib. He is awake, jerking his arms and legs, clenching and unclenching his fists. His eyes are murky blue and they seem to look at her, but she knows they can't. She watches for a while, and then experimentally puts the straight fingers of each of her hands over her own eyes. It is dark, but not really dark. She can see pink edges around her fingers. Her eyelashes feel bristly and uncomfortable. She tries closing her eyes as well, but abandons that. Joseph could close his eyes too. It is always black with anyone's eyes closed. She tries to imagine it black with them open. She takes her hands away. Anne has been telling her lots of cheering-up things about Joseph: how he'll learn to read Braille and have a Seeing-Eye dog and be able to go to school just like them. She pictures Joseph older; running around, playing in the snow, riding a bike. She pictures the three of them, Anne, herself and Joseph, riding in a line. Joseph is at the back with trainer wheels and blocks and his bike is fastened to hers and Anne's with a rope. In her imagination Joseph looks like a boy she knows at school. She and Anne look just the same as they do now. 'I've got a great idea, kid,' she says. 'I'm going to practise for you.'

In her bedroom she finds a blue scarf. She spreads it flat and folds it carefully into a long strip and holds it over her eyes. When she turns to the window she sees dark blue and nothing else. She takes the scarf outside and gets her bike from the garage and wheels it across the lawn to the big empty parking lot of the theatre. She climbs on to the bike, standing with one leg on either side of the sloping bar, her skirt piled up in the middle. She ties the cloth around her eyes. She can't see anything, not even the handlebars right in front of her. 'Right,' she says. 'Pretend this is Joseph, riding his bike.'

She starts off, wobbling. Her balance is wrong; she feels dizzy with the bike moving under her in blue darkness. She wonders what she'll hit first, and goes more slowly. She thinks of Joseph and how she'll be able to teach him, and makes herself pedal harder. She tilts the bike, turning in a dark circle. She sees herself circling, like a bareback rider, blindfolded and brave. She goes faster and begins to sing a tuneless chant. In the dark distance she hears the front door slam. Her mother's voice, irritable, shouts, 'Jenny? What are you doing, Jenny?' There are footsteps and then the voice again, low, 'Oh for Christ's sake. Jenny, stop that. Get off that bike and get that thing off.'

Jenny back-pedals on to her brakes. The bike stops. She jumps down, straddling it. 'What?' She puts her hand up to the blindfold. 'I can't see you,' she explains.'I'm blind.'

'Get it *off*. Now. Get it off.' Then her mother's hand is on the scarf, jerking it from her head, careless of pulled hairs caught in the knot. Jenny's eyes sting and she sees her mother with her face screwed up and white, just before the hand comes down across her face in a slap that cracks across the yard.

'You bloody child. You little bitch.'

'*Mom,*' Jenny wails. She reaches for her mother, but she whirls around, her back to Jenny, clutching herself.

'Get away. Just get away.' Jenny wails again. Her mother turns on her, 'If you ever, *ever* mock your brother again . . .'

Jenny crumples the scarf up into a ball in her hand and flings it at her mother. 'Keep it,' she shouts. 'I was going to help him. I was going to help. Now I never will, thanks to you.'

She runs, out into the woods beyond the house, to her secret place. She crouches there, leaning against her favourite tree on the wet, snowy ground, and plans to run away. She'll go to Scotland and live with her Grannie. While she plans she waits for her mother to come and get her, but no one comes, neither her mother nor her Dad. In the end she goes back to the house alone, and she vows she will never do anything for Joseph, never teach him, nor speak to him nor even touch him, ever again.

Jenny didn't keep her vow. She knew well enough that it wasn't Joseph she was angry with, but her mother. After a day or two of ignoring Joseph she went back to her familiar, sporadic devotion to him. She was too young to hold for him the fierce protective love that had sprung upon Anne. But she did love him. He grew on her, quietly, so that she found the house empty and hollow on the occasions of his absences, when he was undergoing one of the many tests, or when, more frighteningly, he was whisked away to the hospital with another of his recurrent chest infections.

The first time that happened Jenny was terrified. She and Anne had come home from school on the last day before the Easter vacation with their report cards. Jenny was ebullient, school was her *forte*; she got gold stars on everything and her report cards were always a perfect row of 'A's'. Anne was sullen. She hated school and she didn't care who knew about it. Except at times like this when the reckoning came. They had come in together, Jenny grinning all over her face, Anne glaring at her, wanting to kill her, and suddenly everything was turned upside down. Their parents were gone. Joseph was gone. Nonna was in the house instead of her restaurant, nervously waiting for them. She gave them milk and cake, and after they had eaten it she told them that Joseph had gotten sick and he had gone to the hospital.

'Why didn't they just call the doctor?' Jenny asked. She looked up for a moment, and then down at her plate.

'He was too sick for that,' Nonna said.

Inside her stomach Anne felt a lurch, like she was going to be sick herself. It was funny, because nothing like this had ever happened before, but somehow she felt she knew all about it, and had been waiting for it to happen since Joseph was born. 'Joseph's going to die,' she said.

'What?' shrieked Jenny, her eyes going round. Nonna's hand fluttered into the air and rested like a bird on the gold crucifix at her neck.

'Of course he's not,' she said.

Jenny prayed all night, and Joseph got better and came home. But from then on, both of them knew there was another dimension, and that his stay with them was fragile and unassured.

Anne and Jenny's report cards were a week old before anyone looked at them at all. They had lain in their brown envelopes on a counter in the kitchen, getting covered over by newspapers and stained by coffee cups. Jenny kept uncovering them and hoping her Dad would notice hers each time he came home. But he never seemed to see them. Only when Joseph was back to normal, in his crib, lying there and doing nothing, and their Dad was standing at the counter looking at all his unopened mail, did he find them at last. He lifted Anne's and slid the card out, looked at it, and laid it down. Anne watched from the far end of the kitchen, her mouth open. Then he opened Jenny's and while Jenny waited, her face glowing happily, he just nodded and laid it down as well. And that was all that ever happened. He just went out of the back door and they saw him walk across to the theatre where he was rehearsing a play.

'Maybe he's waiting till he tells Mom,' Jenny said. Her lip kept trembling. She turned away, not wanting Anne to see. Anne shook her head. But she felt sorry for Jenny.

'He liked yours,' she said unconvincingly. 'I could see by his face.' Jenny sobbed, undone by the kindness in Anne's voice.

'No he didn't,' she wailed honestly. Anne stood next to her and patted her shoulder. She wasn't very good at it. Touching people made her feel awkward. But she felt really sorry for Jenny, and angry at her Dad. The funny thing was she should have been so relieved. Joseph had rescued her from an awful yelling session, and all the threats about being kept in, and no television, and no friends, that always followed report cards. But she didn't feel relieved or happy at all.

It is late spring, a Saturday. Anne is shopping with her mother and Joseph. They have driven into town and parked the car and now her mother is carrying Joseph in her arms. He is five months old, but he doesn't look it. Anne knows, because she knows another baby who is Joseph's age. His name is Gary and he's the cousin of a boy in Jenny's class. He holds himself up in his carriage and looks at you. He rolls around on the floor and he giggles and laughs. When you try to hold him he is as strong as a puppy, struggling in your arms. When you hold Joseph he just sags. His head is floppy and warm against your shoulder. He makes little noises but he neither smiles nor laughs. His eyes wander; his mouth is flaccid, without shape. He was pretty at first, but he doesn't look pretty any longer. Anne knows. Jenny knows, Marion knows. But their mother doesn't seem to know at all. Once, Anne tried to talk about Gary, and how he's different in ways that have nothing to do with hearing and seeing, but her mother said only that Gary was older than Joseph, and that explained it all. When Anne patiently pointed out that Gary was definitely younger (she even knew his birthday) it all blew up into a fight; her mother shouting and her Dad coming in and giving her hell for upsetting her Mom. So Anne didn't say anything again. Now she watches, fearfully, for the signs of Joseph's difference that no one's allowed to see.

In Woolworth's they meet a woman they know, one of Anne's father's piano students. 'There's Mrs Corliss,' Anne says. Her mother looks up. Mrs Corliss looks up. Their eyes meet and the woman turns red, looks aside, and quickly turns away. She pounces upon some dish towels and begins talking about them in a loud voice to the sales-girl, her back to Anne and her mother and Joseph. They brush by her; she never turns. Anne's mother's pretty face is white, her mouth in a tight line, but she says nothing. They do their shopping, but she forgets half the things they came for and halfway through suddenly gives up. They hurry back to where they have parked the car and Anne's mother dives into it and sits on the broad front seat holding Joseph and sobbing, her tears wetting his soft white shirt. Anne throws her arms around her mother. She shouts, 'What do we care? She's a stupid fat old bitch. We don't even like her. What do we care?'

The first play in the theatre that year Joseph was born was *Our Town*. It opened at the beginning of the summer vacation, and in the hot days of June Jenny and Anne watched the rehearsals sitting beside Joseph's carriage. Their mother played the heroine, with her hair in a ribbon and her Scottish voice loosened into an American drawl. Anne didn't like the play at all. She didn't like her mother acting the young wife and dying having a baby. It made her think of Joseph all the time. She left Jenny to watch the rehearsals alone.

Anne had a job that spring, helping her Uncle Eddie pick strawberries. She worked at it after school and all weekends and she made a lot of money. The first thing she did was buy a big blue stuffed dog for Joseph, and after that she just kept the money and each Monday her mother put it into the bank for her. Anne had a bank book with all the money she had earned written down in rows of ink numbers. She showed it to everyone. Her Dad said, 'That's a lot of strawberries,' patting her head with a quizzical look on his face. Her Mom just said, 'It'd be fine if she did her homework as well.' Nothing had changed. Jenny still got all the 'A's' and gold stars and 'Very Goods'. Anne's next report card was as bad as the last. She didn't see the point of school; they didn't teach her anything she wanted to learn.

When Anne showed Jenny her bank book, Jenny wanted one, and she pleaded with her Dad until he gave her a dollar so she could have a bank account too. Anne was furious. She went and demanded a dollar so argumentatively that her father refused to give it to her.

'You've got lots of money,' he said. 'Don't begrudge your sister.'

'I earned it. I worked for it,' Anne shouted. There was a fight. Their parents were busy with the play and Joseph had a cold again, and no one had time to be patient with Anne. She got sent to her room without supper. Later, Jenny sneaked up to see her, and found her sister glowering at her bank book on top of her school books on her desk.

'Get out,' she said, but Jenny came in and stood by the desk too.

'You can have my dollar,' she said.

'I don't want *your* dollar,' Anne said. But she looked interested.

'I don't want it,' Jenny said. 'I just wanted a book like yours. You can have my dollar now.' She watched as Anne glowered yet, suspiciously. 'I know it wasn't fair,' she said.

Anne said, 'Keep your dollar, kid. The book has to have a dollar in it or it doesn't work.' Gently she tugged at the end of Jenny's straggly hair.

The real trouble, for Jenny, with Anne having a job, was never having anyone to play with. Marion went along with Anne to the strawberry field and helped her pick, or at least stood around and talked while Anne worked. So there was no one for Jenny, except Joseph. Jenny pushed him around the house in his carriage, or tickled him in his play-pen – which he seemed to like, though it was hard to tell with Joseph – but he wasn't much use for filling up a day.

When her parents were in the theatre rehearsing *Our Town*, Joseph was in his play-pen just outside, under the green and white striped awnings that sheltered the play-goers in the evening. Jenny sat on the steps of the back porch of the house, watching. She could see Joseph, and twice while she sat there her mother came out in a hurry, peered at him, and ran back in a hurry. She let Margaret look after Jenny and Anne, but she kept Joseph to herself. Jenny watched and thought about the end of her second year in school and how different everything was from last year. She tried to picture what everything would be like if Joseph had never come. But she couldn't imagine it. When she tried she got nothing but a kind of blank emptiness, like the bare, blank stage-set of *Our Town*. *He's meant to be here*, she thought. Like her bank book that wouldn't work any more without its dollar, their family wouldn't work any more without Joseph lying in his play-pen doing nothing at all.

Jenny got up and walked across to the theatre and stood in the cool shade of the awning, looking at Joseph. She leaned over the wooden railing and stretched down to tickle his tummy. He was lying in his floppy way; his eyes, which were brown now but murky, without focus, wandered unaware across her face. As often, she tried to imagine what it was like to be inside Joseph, in the dark and the silence. She no longer acted it out; that had got her into a trouble that she still didn't understand. And besides, it frightened her. *It's not scary for him*, she reassured herself. *He doesn't know any better*. It was something she told herself all the time but still, occasionally, the fear solidified: supposing he was as frightened inside as she would be if darkness and stillness engulfed her? 'You all right, Joseph?' she said, awkwardly. She put her hand on his round stomach and rocked him back and forth. He jiggled, jelly-like.

He seemed to like Jenny rocking him back and forth. He made little sounds and his mouth quirked. She speeded up the rocking, and the sounds got louder and quite suddenly they exploded in a giggle and his mouth stretched up at the corners tentatively, and then more surely, into a smile. Jenny opened her own mouth and stared in surprise. She wriggled him back and forth and he giggled again and smiled and made a sudden squawk of delight. 'Joseph,' she shouted. 'You're doing it! You're doing it!' He squawked again and then suddenly took fright at his own mirth, curled his lip into its familiar scowl and began to wail. 'It's all right, Joseph, it's all right,' Jenny soothed. But of course, in moments, her mother was there.

'Oh for God's sake, Jenny, did you have to wake him now?'

'He smiled at me,' Jenny said, swept with her own excitement. 'He smiled.'

Her mother stared at her, stopped midway through her impatience. 'Really smiled, Jenny? Not just you pretending?'

'*Really* smiled. I swear it. I was rocking his tummy . . .' She reached to do it again but her mother had swept Joseph up and was cradling him joyously against herself, stroking his smooth blond hair.

'Oh clever pet, clever pet,' she whispered. 'We'll show them, you and I.'

'*I* made him smile, not you,' said Jenny, but her mother, lost in intimacy with her brother, didn't hear.

A dark night in July; under the thick shadows of the maple trees the lightning-bugs flicker like green stars. Anne is running, barefoot, in her pyjamas across the gravel to the warm yellow circle of light at the back of the theatre. Moths flutter at the doorway; she brushes them off. Her tough calloused feet pad silently down the narrow corridors, stuffed with costumes. She is breathing hard, panting, as she searches the maze of dressing-rooms and cupboards. There is no one, but she can hear voices echoing through the timbers of the old barn, a man's voice and her mother's voice, sweet and wistful as a girl's. Anne's heart thumps. She is breaking every rule; she should never be here. But Joseph is sick. He has coughed all night, and now there is vomit in his crib and Margaret who is meant to look after them is dancing to records with her boyfriend in the living-room and shouting, 'In a minute' whenever Anne goes downstairs and pleads with her to come. Jenny is asleep, her eyes tight shut, her hands still clasped from saying her prayers. Anne is alone. There is no one else to go to, nothing else she can do.

She creeps through the theatre to a gap in the curtains at the side of the stage, and crouches low on the floor. There are two tall step-ladders on the stage, just within her view. On one is a young actor with shiny blond hair. On the other her mother, in a blue dress with a bow at the back, her hair tied up in a ribbon in the same soft blue. She looks wonderfully pretty. Hot bright lights shine down and Anne is close enough to see the sweat shining on the actor's face. Across the stage, in semi-darkness, she can see the others waiting in the wings. Her father is with them. Desperation to reach him envelops her. She stands and begins to creep from the place where she has waited, in the dark shadows that rim the stage, feeling her way, bare-footed, around the tangle of ropes, the cables of the lighting, a stack of waiting chairs. Her toes scrape on a splintered board and she winces and flings out an arm to catch her balance and tips the top chair and the whole pile collapses with a tremendous clattering crash.

Anne stands mortified in the midst of them, her eyes staring wildly across the stage to her father. A murmur of surprise sweeps the darkened audience like a breeze through summer leaves. On the stage her mother and the blond actor never move. Their faces keep their same wistful calm and their voices the same smooth tenor as they finish their lines. Then the curtain comes softly down and the lights brighten backstage and her mother leaps off her ladder, strides across the bare wood floor and grabs Anne's arm with fingers that pinion flesh and bone.

'What in the name of God are you doing here?' Anne looks up and sees her father crossing the stage to join them. He looks very young and handsome in the bright lights of the stage.

'You little idiot!' he whispers, and yet he seems only half angry, and half amused.

Anne says, 'Joseph's sick and Margaret won't come.' Her mother's grip goes slack. She seems to shrink behind her make-up so that the young girl painted on her face becomes a mask disguising an old woman.

'My baby,' she whispers, and starts to walk away from them, away from the stage, towards the corridor and the door. Anne's father runs after, calling her name, but she starts to run. Anne squeezes past her father and runs after her mother, who flees in the jewelled night as fleet as a long-legged child, her long costume dress fluttering about her ankles as she runs.

* * *

112

In the autumn, the theatre closed forever. No one said that that was what was happening, but everyone knew. It stumbled on through the summer, with understudies in Louise Conti's roles, but it was not the same. It was for her wit, her charm, her bright, blond beauty that people had come; she was the star. But to return to it meant leaving Joseph again, and she no longer trusted him to anyone. Besides, she had lost interest; her tiny sickly son drew it all away and she never left the house throughout the rest of that hot dispirited summer. And, without her, Mike Conti lost heart. By mid-winter he had sold the barn to a man who filled it with old furniture instead of actors, and hung a sign out that said, 'Antiques'. Anne didn't really care; it had never meant much to her. But Jenny mourned the old dusty stage, the deep red velvet curtain, the wardrobe trunks filled with costumes in which she was sometimes allowed to play. Her mother and father seemed plain and ordinary without the theatre; she felt their lives grow dull. Her classmates no longer envied her. Glamour had deserted her. She had become a piano teacher's daughter.

Throughout the summer, Joseph was often ill. The family doctor, a young man called Tom Walsh, who was also a family friend, became a regular visitor. Sometimes, on Sundays, he came to lunch, when the whole family – Nonna, Grandpa, Uncle Eddie – gathered after mass. He was sad when the theatre closed; he said, quite harshly, 'Louise, don't let this happen to yourself.'

'Nothing's *happening*,' she said. 'I want to look after my baby. Just until he's a little older. What's so bloody unreasonable about that?' She was smiling, but her voice was angry and her hands, fiddling with a dish towel, were trembling suddenly.

There was a long silence and then the doctor looked straight at her and said, 'Louise, this kind of child doesn't get older. Not in the way you mean. You must realize that.' He shook his head, facing her, his expression open and innocent and baffled, as if he carried knowledge like a burden. 'What can I say to you? We've had *all* the tests.' He paused and looked at the ceiling and said,'I keep running out of words.' He looked around the room for help. The whole family was watching but no one said anything. He burst out, 'I've been telling you for months. Look at him yourself, Louise. He's eight months old. He can't turn over, or sit up, or communicate in any way. He responds to nothing . . .'

'What can he respond to if he can't hear or see?'

'Louise, stop fighting me. Even allowing for that, he still – oh, for Christ's sake . . . Mike, *you* can see it, surely?'

'I know he's slow.' Their father whispered it, like he didn't want any of them to hear.

'Slow,' the doctor said wearily. 'You know he's slow. Mike, he's so far retarded, so *profoundly* damaged . . .'

'My baby's not retarded,' their mother said. Her voice was steady again and matter of fact. 'He's slow because he has no way of learning. Of course he's slow. But I'll get around that. As he gets older . . . there are schools, you said so, special schools . . .' her voice grew brighter, her face animated.

'This child's never going to school,' the doctor said. 'He'll never go to school because he will never speak, never walk, probably never even crawl. He will never know you beyond a source of immediate comfort. He will never *be* a child in the sense you are imagining. He will be nothing more than a vast, uncomprehending baby for as long as he lives, which thankfully in the case of such children, is not usually very long.' He stopped, closed his eyes and breathed deeply, his fists clenched. He opened his eyes again and fixed their gentle blue stare on their mother's face, 'Oh, God forgive me, but they leave it to us to say these things. I know I'm not good at this, but you have to see it and know it and face it. You'll never raise this child, Louise.'

She stood very quietly looking at him, as if carefully considering and absorbing all he had said. She shrugged slightly, a small, hurt gesture. Then her eyes hardened and she looked straight into his. 'Get out of my house,' she said.

He nodded, twice, sadly, as if he agreed that was what he deserved, and he backed away towards the door. But then Grandpa said, 'Oh come on, come on. What's happening here?' He lifted his shoulders and dropped them, the palms of his hands held out in front of him. 'Is everyone crazy?'

Their father stepped between their mother and the doctor. 'We can't throw Tom out,' he said, and she shook her head wearily, overwhelmed by reason. She stepped forward to him and the young doctor and the three of them met and embraced awkwardly.

114

'We'll take care of your baby,' the doctor said. 'Whatever comes.'

Jenny and Anne were sent to set the table for Sunday lunch. Jenny carried the box with the silverware and Anne set the places carefully, remembering where everything went. Jenny said in a whisper, 'What did he mean?'

'What did he mean about what?'

'About Joseph not getting older?'

Anne shrugged, 'I don't know,' she said.

Jenny persisted. 'Will he just stay a baby? Forever?'

'How should I know?' Anne concentrated on lining up the big forks beside the little forks, the big knives beside the little knives.

'Isn't he going to get any bigger?'

'Who knows?' Anne said, keeping her head down.

'He has to get bigger, doesn't he?' Anne turned around and grabbed a bundle of spoons out of the box.

'What are you asking me for? Go ask Mom. Or ask the doctor. He's the one who's supposed to know everything.'

Jenny shied away from that. She shrugged slightly and at last she said, 'I don't care if he doesn't get any bigger. I like him like he is.'

Anne took the box away from her and laid it on the low table in the dining-room window, beside her mother's pots of houseplants. She said, 'Joseph's retarded. That's what they're talking about.' Jenny looked puzzled and Anne said, 'You know what it means, do you?'

'Danny Vignato says that Stevie McLaughlin's retarded,' she said.

Anne shook her head, patiently. 'No. Stevie's just stupid. That's what Danny meant. He was just calling names.' She paused. 'Joseph's *really* retarded. It means really, really stupid.' She sighed slightly. It made it easier saying it. She'd heard it whispered so many times behind her back, by kids at school, and people in stores, and even by Marion's Mom when she thought Anne couldn't hear. It was a relief saying it out loud.

Jenny said, '*That* doesn't matter.' She looked confidently self-satisfied. 'I'm really bright, so if Joseph is stupid I can teach him.'

'Sure, kid,' said Anne. 'You can teach him.' She smiled and flicked Jenny's straggly pigtails. 'I bet you'll teach him a lot.'

115

VII

Jenny stands in front of the big mirror in her mother's bedroom while Grannie lowers the white dress over her head. She holds her arms up straight and shivers as the clouds of organza envelop her. Then she stands very still while Grannie sets the veil on top of her head, tucking hairgrips through the ringlet of silk flowers, securing them to her hair. It is Jenny's First Communion day and she is wearing the most beautiful dress in the world. Nonna made the dress, three years before, when Anne made her First Communion. This time she just re-sewed the dress so that it would fit Jenny. Jenny is smaller than Anne was at seven. She looks funny in the dress, pale and skinny and awkward, but she loves wearing it anyhow. There is a picture in Nonna's house of Anne in the dress to remind Jenny how it is meant to look. Jenny doesn't mind. She knows Anne is the pretty one; it makes up for her being lousy at school.

Jenny has been preparing for her First Communion for months and months. She has learned all her prayers and goes every Wednesday to Sister Magdalena's catechism class. She goes to mass every Sunday and goes back sometimes in the evenings for benediction. On Friday evenings she goes to mass, too, and confession on Wednesday nights. Her mother goes with her, always. Jenny loves it. She loves sitting up close by her mother or kneeling beside the soft folds of her skirt, looking up to see her closed eyes and moving lips and the beautiful crystal beads of her rosary clutched in her folded hands. Often it's just the two of them, because her Dad stays home in bed and Anne goes with Nonna later, or not at all. Jenny feels holy all the time. She says a huge list of prayers at night, and she lights candles in church. Her mother lights them too. The candles are all for Joseph. Anne is sick of all the holiness. She tells Jenny, 'It's nothing special. They just give you this piece of bread like a piece of cardboard and it's supposed to be Jesus. But it doesn't *taste* like him or anything.' Once, late at night, she tells Jenny a horrible story of a time when the wine really turned to real blood and the priest was drinking it, like Dracula. Anne is good at horrible stories.

Jenny doesn't care. She feels wonderful, the centre of everyone's attention. The whole family is coming. Grannie has come all the way from Scotland just for her. Aunt Theresa is coming from New Jersey. Everyone will be in church, even Joseph.

Jenny watches herself in the mirror while Grannie ties her hair back under the veil. It takes two rubber bands and two barrettes to make all the wispy bits stay. Granny fusses, but Jenny smiles happily at the mirror and her face smiles back, with a dark gap where her two front teeth are waiting to come in. *Anne's the pretty one*, she reasons carefully. *I'm the smart one*. And Joseph? She thinks a long time. *Joseph's the Joseph one*, she decides at last.

Jenny had meant to make a special prayer for Joseph when she made her communion, but when she lined up at the altar rail with all the other children there was so much to think about – remembering to say 'Amen' at the right time and hold her mouth open and her tongue out, and not to drop the wafer, and to walk back to her seat with her hands clasped and her eyes reverently downcast – that she forgot. She only remembered Joseph when she was sitting down next to him and Grannie and then she felt sad. She was sure that if she had made her special prayer right then, at such a powerful time, something good might have happened to Joseph.

She had begun to think a lot about praying for Joseph; Sister Magdalena was always reminding her to pray for him. Sister Magdalena had been on a pilgrimage to Lourdes and brought them all Lourdes medals and little books about Bernadette. Once, Jenny had asked her if Lourdes would make Joseph able to see, but instead of answering she talked about the real purpose of Lourdes being to make people love Our Lord and Our Lady. It didn't stop Jenny thinking about it, though. She told Anne,

'When I'm bigger, I'm going to take Joseph to Lourdes.' Anne made a whole lot of arguments.

'How are you going to get there? Who's going to pay? How will you carry Joseph when he's bigger too?' until Jenny shrugged and ran away. She gave up her plan for Lourdes. Instead she thought up a really wonderful daydream in which she found a spring in her special place in the woods, and she took Joseph there and came back with him walking along behind her, on fat little legs like Stevie's cousin Gary. He was looking at things and pointing and making loud shouts like Gary did. She wasn't a saint or anything like Bernadette, in the daydream, but everyone thought she was pretty smart anyhow, even Anne.

'You looked really dumb,' Anne said, outside the church, while Grandpa was getting his camera ready to take Jenny's picture. Anne was feeling sour because Grannie scolded her for yawning in church, but mostly because Jenny had looked so privately happy. She made a face and walked with her hands together and her eyes rolling up to heaven. But Jenny was determined to preserve her new, sin-free holiness, and she just smiled benignly at everything Anne did.

Grandpa took pictures of Jenny in her white dress on the green lawn of the church, first by herself, then with her mother and father and Anne and Joseph and Aunt Theresa and the Uncles; then with each of her grandmothers; then with Father Gerard and Sister Magdalena. When he ran out of film, they went off to Nonna's restaurant and had a special family lunch with even Grandpa and Nonna sitting down with them. Jenny had lasagna which was her favourite food and Uncle Eddie gave her wine from his glass. Everyone kept mentioning her name and talking about her and Jenny wished the day would go on forever.

But when they all went home after the lunch, the adults all suddenly left them and went into the living-room and Anne and Jenny were sent off to play. Jenny was hurt by their sudden desertion, and more hurt when Marion arrived – like it was any ordinary day – and Anne wanted to play with her.

'Come with us,' Marion said.

'I can't. I'm all dressed up.'

'Go change. Get out of that dress and put your dungarees on,' Anne said, with some satisfaction. She wasn't pleased with Jenny having all the attention all day.

'I don't want to,' Jenny said. She knew that once she took the dress off she would never be able to put it on again. It was like a bride's dress, for one day only. 'I want to wear it still.'

Anne shrugged. 'Then stay,' she said unconcerned. They went off and Jenny was left alone, on her First Communion day. She felt desolate, like on the morning after Christmas. The day was empty and cold. Sulkily she went upstairs and into her parents' room. Joseph was asleep, but she wanted something for company so she jiggled him until he woke up. He started to cry, but she tickled him some more and he giggled instead.

'Hi, Joseph, old pal,' she said, the way Marion said 'Hi' to Blackie, her dog. 'Old pal, old pal.' Joseph cackled. 'Did you like my First Communion?' Jenny asked. She jiggled him again and he cackled some more. 'Sure you did.' She waited a while and then she said, 'I'm just going downstairs for a while, I'll see you later,' and she went out.

Jenny crept down the back stairs and sneaked on tiptoe up to the living-room door. She leaned on it, listening petulantly to the conversation from which she had been excluded. She heard her Aunt Theresa's voice. She heard Dr Walsh and wondered when he had come. They were talking about adult things. She sat down on the carpet and leaned her back against the door, and spread the skirt of her dress around her folded knees in a pool of white organza. She was still wearing her headband of flowers and her white veil, under which her hair now straggled loose from the barrettes and rubber bands. As she listened she played with the ends of the veil, stretching them out taut over her hands. She was almost asleep when she heard Dr Walsh say, 'They're always happier with their own kind. Believe me, I know.'

Jenny sat up straight and alert. She heard her mother say something, but it was too soft to understand; but everyone else in the room started to say things, agreeing with the doctor.

'It's a wonderful place, Mike,' Aunt Theresa said. 'Molly Levy's little girl was there until she died. And she was happy, poor thing, as much as you could tell . . .'

'You've got the other children to think about,' said Nonna. 'You must think of Anne and Jenny.'

Jenny heard her father say, 'Jenny's all right.'

'And Anne?' said Dr Walsh.

After a long while her father said, 'Anne's having a hard time at school.'

'Children tease,' said Aunt Theresa.

'If they tease now,' said the doctor, 'wait until they're older.'

Her father said, 'We shouldn't give in to that. It's like running away.'

'You can't fight Joseph's battles through Anne and Jenny's lives,' Dr Walsh said. 'Is she falling behind?'

'They wanted to leave her back. She gets "D's" in everything.'

'It won't get better.'

'So how d'ye make it Joseph's fault, that Anne cannae thole schooling?' Jenny heard her Grannie say. 'She just cannae be bothered and you're all making it easy for her. She needs the strap, like we had, to make her learn.'

The doctor said gently, 'Children show stress in different ways, Mrs Reilly.'

'Away with you,' said Grannie. 'Stress.' Jenny could imagine her face with her sharp little eyes and her thin mouth set firm, like it was when Anne or Jenny were telling fibs. She grinned, thinking of the doctor and Grannie. But then the doctor said, 'Then we *are* agreed?' and Jenny froze. She waited to hear her mother protest or her father argue. But nobody said anything and the doctor said then, 'I know you'll be glad in the end; it's the best for everyone. I'll let you know as soon as they have a place.'

Again there was a silence, and then Jenny heard people getting up and walking as if someone was leaving through the front door, and just then Grannie said clearly, 'Och fine. Sweep him under the carpet wi' the rest o' the dirt. The poor wee soul.' And then steps came to the door where Jenny was sitting and she scrambled up in her fluffy dress and ran into the kitchen and was hiding there when Grannie came in, with her cheeks bright red, and her old hands clenched in two small fists.

'Grannie?' Jenny whispered.

'Who? Och, child.'

'What are they doing to Joseph?' Jenny felt tears coming.

Her grandmother looked at her for a long time and then she said, 'You poor thing, and you on your special day.' Then she sat down on one of the kitchen chairs and held her arms out to

120

Jenny, and Jenny climbed up on to her lap, feeling her small bony knees through her woolly skirt. 'You shouldnae have heard.'

'But what?' Jenny cried.

'It's for your Mam to tell ye,' Grannie said. She cuddled Jenny sadly, smoothing her crumpled white veil. Jenny knew then that the doctor was taking him away. But she didn't say anything, but sat there pretending that she didn't know, until she had stopped herself crying and could slide off Grannie's knees and say, as if nothing were wrong, 'I think I'll go take my dress off, upstairs.'

She stopped in her own room only long enough to stuff a blanket and the candy Anne had given her as a First Communion present into her blue overnight case. The blanket was for Joseph; the candy for her. She closed the case with its two stiff latches and lugged it down the hall. She was glad Joseph had gone back to sleep because she was able to root around in his crib for the two toys she had arbitrarily decided were his favourites, and stuff them into the case. She wished she had one of his baby bottles with milk in it, but the bottles were all in the kitchen with Grannie. She was pretty sure he'd eat candy if he was really hungry. She lowered the side of the crib, stretching to reach the safety latches. When she lifted him out and held him up against her shoulder, his bland soft face pressed up against the ruffles of her dress. She wished he could hang on, the way Gary hung on to you, but Joseph wasn't much good at that. Jenny leaned over, and managed to lift the case with her hands around Joseph, holding it by the handle with two spare fingers. 'OK kid,' she said carefully. 'Whatever you do, don't make any noise.' Clutching him tightly, she crept out of the room and down the stairs.

She tiptoed, with her nose pressed up against Joseph's silky hair and the blue case banging at her knees, through the now empty living-room, listening to distant voices in the kitchen. She levered her way backwards out of the front door and went down the broad steps to the gravel path.

By the time she reached her special place in the woods, which was only a small part of the way she must go, she knew the case must be abandoned. Carefully she lowered Joseph down on to the grass. His mouth puckered at the feel of it, but he didn't cry. She opened the case, took out the blanket and spread it out and piled the candy and the toys on top of it. Then she untied the white ribbon that Grannie had used to cover the rubber bands in her hair, pulled it free, and carefully tied the blanket up by its corners to make a little sack. She lifted Joseph, clutched the sack behind his back and plodded on through the woods.

She had only found the place once before, and then it seemed a long remote way. Now, carrying Joseph, it seemed forever. It was across the Uncles' hay meadow with its hummocky lumps of fallen grass, and beyond, into the viney wood that ran into the saltmarsh beside the bay. She picked her way carefully, expertly eluding the shiny-leaved fortresses of poison ivy. Twice she had to stop and lay Joseph down and rest her arms. He kicked and stretched and giggled when she lifted him. As she walked he made little contented noises. Knowing how much he liked her made Jenny more determined as she struggled against the fear that she would never find the place again. And then, quite suddenly, she was in it; a soft perfect clearing, with viney trees high above and moss and soft grass in a patch of sunlight on the ground.

She laid Joseph down, untied the blanket and spread it out on the springy moss. When she put him on it he wiggled and chortled with delight. 'Right, kid,' she said. 'You play there and I'll make camp.' He waved his hands and kicked his legs, but that was all. As she went off to the edge of the wood to gather the reeds that grew up to the clearing, she was glad, for once, that Joseph could not run away the way Gary would. She broke the reeds off at the base, one by one, wishing she had her penknife to help. As she stacked them she began to picture herself and Joseph in the Indian shelter she was building, living the Indian life they would live. 'I'll fish,' she said. 'With a sharpened reed. And I'll make a snare and catch rabbits. You'll probably like rabbit,' she added, confidently. 'I might catch a little one to keep as a pet. Just one though. We'll have to eat the rest.'

It was Anne who found her. 'Lucky for you,' as Anne said. Lucky for her it wasn't Mom or Dad, or the Uncles or Aunt Theresa, or Marion's parents, because all of them were looking for her, all with that wild frantic adult fear that would turn, in the instant of relief, into fury. Anne was furious too. 'Jeez, you've really done it. Mom's crying, Dad's shouting at everybody. Marion's Dad was going to call the police until they found your stupid overnight case in the woods, and they *knew* it was just you being dumb. Come on,' she said, picking Joseph up and giving the blanket a prod with her foot. 'Get that stuff and get going. They might *still* call the police if you don't get back quick.'

'I didn't do anything,' Jenny wailed.

'You didn't *do* anything! You'll be lucky if they don't arrest you. For kidnapping,' Anne said ominously. 'Boy are you in trouble.' Jenny sat down in her half-built Indian shelter and pulled the blanket over her head.

'I want to die,' she cried. Anne looked at her with disgust.

'You big baby,' she said. She kicked the reed shelter and it collapsed on top of Jenny in a slithering heap. Jenny shrieked and sat up and then scrambled to her feet.

'It's your fault anyhow,' she cried. 'It's your fault they're taking him away.'

'What?' Anne whispered.

'They're taking him away. They're taking Joseph away. Dr Walsh is going to come and get him. And it's all because you're so bad at school.'

'You're lying,' Anne whispered, and she kicked viciously at Jenny because her hands were occupied holding Joseph. 'You bitch.'

'It's true. They're taking him. They're taking him. I heard them . . .'

'Bitch,' Anne shrieked, kicking again; and Jenny cowered away from her but still shouted, 'And Dad said it was because of you.'

Anne turned and clutched Joseph up tight and, forgetting Jenny, ran through the woods and out of the viney shadows into the rough grass of the hayfield, where Jenny, struggling with the blanket and the toys and candy, caught up with her. But Anne kept running, with Joseph joggling against her and beginning to cry and Jenny sniffling after.

Their Mom saw them a long way off, and came running across the field, crying, her arms outstretched, and in the moment of meeting them was so joyous with relief that she swept up not only Joseph, but Anne and Jenny too, and held them all against her as she sobbed. For a wonderful moment Jenny thought it was all going to end just like that, with no retribution, but then their father arrived and the Uncles, and Marion's parents and Nonna; and Jenny, standing in the midst of them in her torn and muddy First Communion dress, knew horribly that it had only just begun.

It went on for days, the scoldings, the threats, the punishments; later the explanations, the arguments and debates, and Jenny conscious always of hideous embarrassment, that she had done what to her was a serious adult thing and was being treated as a foolish baby. Long after the initial furore was over, the serious family talks went on, and she was trapped, by constant reminders, in the misery of her transgression. Eventually she thought that if they'd just take Joseph and it was over, that would be best.

But now no one was certain what to do. In stiff, awful family conferences they sat and talked about what would happen if Joseph stayed with them; what would happen if he went away. Their father and Nonna talked a long time about all the things they wouldn't be able to do, or have, if Joseph stayed. But Anne and Jenny sat as stubborn as Grannie watching it all with her sharp blue eyes, and all they would say was, 'We love Joseph.'

Jenny lay in her bed at nights, imagining Joseph alone in some faraway place, in a lonelier, further dark. She had a nightmare that the doctors made a mistake and came and took her away instead, even though she was screaming, 'I can see, I can talk,' and no one, not her parents, or Nonna, or even Anne, seemed to realize that they were taking the wrong child. She woke up howling, and after that the worst and scariest thing happened, because a new doctor came who wanted to see not Joseph, but herself and Anne, as if her dream were coming true.

The doctor was a tall woman who took each of them away into a room and talked about all sorts of things, like school and friends and whether they wet the bed. Jenny was just terrified, but Anne was disgusted. She was ten; she hadn't wet a bed since she was three. Anne refused to see the doctor on her second visit, but her father forced her because it was Anne they were worried about most of all. Of course when the woman doctor started asking about school, Anne knew what it was all for.

'It's not *Joseph*,' she said plainly, 'it's me. I don't like school. It's boring and stupid.' The doctor kept asking about her friends, and what people called her brother and what she did if they teased her. 'I hit them,' Anne said. Still, she knew what was required of her now.

The next day she brought all her school books home instead of leaving them at the foot of her locker. She straightened out the bent pages, and laid them all on the kitchen table where everyone could see. She got lined paper and pencils and laboriously began doing sums, writing English stories, and making long lists of true and false answers and multiple choice letters for history and science. 'What's this?' her father said, warily. She worked on without answering, her shiny cap of black hair hiding her forehead. When she had finished all that week's homework, and that of the week before, she stopped, stacked her papers and handed it to him.

'The answers are at the back of the book. You can check them,' she said. She stared at him with hard, dark eyes.

'What's made this happen?' he asked lamely.

'I'll get straight "A's" on my next report card,' Anne said coolly. 'If,' she added, 'Joseph stays.'

A cold spring day, wind making ripples across silvery puddles in the sandy playground. Anne and Marion are twelve, in their last year at elementary school. Already they are too grown-up for the place, embarrassed by it, and uncomfortable. The playground, full of baby swings and climbing frames, has become a frustration. They no longer climb, or swing or slide, but stand around talking endlessly, marooned in the landscape of their own childhood. They are both changing, but Anne is changing faster than Marion, and so they argue all the time. They are in their habitual meeting place, beside the grey teeter-totter, glaring sullenly at each other. Anne has spent the lunch hour trying to get the attention of a boy called Lee. Marion is outraged. Two little first graders, riding up and down on the teeter-totter, laugh and giggle, oblivious of their adult troubles. Anne says, 'Well, are you going to sulk about it forever?'

'I'm not sulking,' Marion says in a small cold voice.

'You could have fooled me.' Anne shrugs her shoulders. There is something new in Marion's expression, a look of vengefulness.

'I'm not sulking,' Marion says carefully, 'I'm just thinking.' She lets it hang in the air.

Anne rises to the bait, 'About what?'

'I'm just thinking about something I know. Something I know about your family that I'm not supposed to tell.'

125

'Oh sure,' Anne says. 'How convenient. You're just making something stupid up.' But she is nervous.

'I've known it for a month. And I've never told.'

'So what,' Anne says. 'It'll be some dumb thing about Joseph that I know already. That he's getting a hearing aid, right? Well forget your big surprise, because I know about it and it's not going to happen anyhow, because we tried and it didn't work. So big deal.'

'My Dad's going to buy your house,' says Marion. For a moment Anne doesn't say anything. It is so different from all the things she'd expected Marion to say, and it makes no sense.

Marion looks uncertain, watching her, and Anne whispers, 'That's a lie.'

'It's not.' Marion's bald honesty outshines every other expression on her face. She says matter-of-factly, 'He's going to buy it. They were going to tell you next week anyhow.' Already she is sorry she has spoken. To placate, she says, 'It's too big for you anyhow. Your Mom can't manage with Joseph. Besides, you need the money.'

Anne screws up her mouth. She hisses, 'Bitch. Shitty-assed bitch. You're lying. You're always lying.' Marion just stares at her, bewildered, unsure how to undo what she has done. Anne cries, 'We'll never sell our house. It's ours. We'll never sell it.'

Marion shrugs. 'You can say what you like; it's going to happen anyway.' She smiles, shakily, and says, to encourage; 'It doesn't matter *that* much. You're not moving far *away* or anything.'

'We're not moving anywhere,' Anne shrieks. 'We're not moving.' She is crying, unable to help herself, and that just makes her madder. She balls her hands into fists. 'You're not living in my house. Not ever. I'll kill you. I'll kill everybody. I'll burn the house down. You'll never . . .'

'Jeez,' says Marion. 'Stop getting so excited. *We're* not moving into your stupid house. Why would *we* want it?' She looks scornful. 'I'd never have said anything if I'd known you'd get so excited.'

'Oh yeah, then what's he going to buy it for, if you're all too snooty to live in it?'

'I don't know,' Marion says. She adopts a grown-up, father-mimicking voice. 'I guess we'll hang on to it for a while, watch the market, maybe rent it, or sell it for a good profit.' She pauses.

'You should be grateful, you know; we're helping you out. It's a bit of a dump actually.' Anne knows Marion is just echoing her parents. She can hear them, talking among themselves in their smooth, reasonable voices; Marion's parents talking about her parents as if they were real poor people from the development across the highway. Anne crouches down in the playground and clutches for a heap of stones from around the feet of the teeter-totter. 'What are you doing?' says Marion.

'I hate you,' Anne cries. She stands up and flings the stones at Marion's face. Marion never moves, but just stares at her through the hail of gravel and Anne actually sees the one that cracks into her mouth, and sees the bit of her front tooth spinning bloodily away. Blood from Marion's cut lip spatters on to her neat white buttoned shirt. Marion puts her hand up. She feels her mouth, feels the jagged stump. She doesn't cry.

'You've broken my tooth,' she says. She keeps feeling it, and blood runs down her fingers from her lip, and the two first graders on the teeter-totter stare and one starts to shriek. Marion says, 'Your parents will have to pay to have it fixed. We'll have to sue you.' She says it very practically, as if she is a little sorry about it, but still acknowledges the devastating necessity.

Chill terror grips Anne. She thinks of her father sitting every night at his desk with his bills. She wants to scream, to cry, to beg Marion not to tell them, to make an alibi and protect her. Instead she whispers, 'You can sue all you want. I'll pay for it with my own money. I'll quit school and work all day. It's worth it,' she says dramatically. She starts to walk away, but stops. 'And remember this,' she says ominously. 'If you tell Jenny what you told me, I'll break every tooth you've got left.'

Marion never did tell. She never told Jenny about the house and she never told anyone about the tooth. Anne waited in terror for three days for the announcement of lawsuits and family devastation and then her mother casually mentioned that Marion had been to the dentist to get her tooth capped because she'd fallen off a slide. Anne was so grateful for that loyal subterfuge that she was on the verge of making up when the true blow fell. Her parents called her and Jenny into the living-room the following night and told them everything exactly as Marion had said. They had decided to sell the house because it was too big for them, and had too many stairs to carry Joseph up and down and it was hard to keep warm. Marion's Dad was going to buy it, and maybe rent it to someone, but he didn't mind how long they stayed in it while they waited to find a new house of their own. Their Mom and Dad sounded gentle and grateful whenever they mentioned his name, and Anne hated him the more for it. Jenny sat white-faced, not even crying, her big eyes bigger with shock. Their Dad said, 'You'll like the new house. I promise you.'

It was a stupid promise. There was no way they could possibly like the house. When, later that year, they moved to it, they both simply hated it. It was a tiny house, and it had only three bedrooms, and one was taken up with Joseph and his special chair and special bed, even though he still slept most nights in their parents' bed. Still, he had a whole room, and therefore Jenny and Anne, for the first time ever, had to share just one room between them. Jenny didn't mind that as much as Anne; in fact that was the one thing about the new house that she liked, having Anne's company in her room. Everything else she hated so much that she wanted to die.

The worst part was where the house was. It wasn't at all near their old house, or near Nonna's or Marion's, or on any of the tree-lined streets near the bay. It was far away, across the highway in a barren development. The house had a tiny yard in front with two square patches of worn grass. In the back it was just mud with a rusty old swing left by the people who had sold it. Beyond the fence was the backyard of another house. There wasn't even a single tree and there was nowhere secret, or even private, in which to hide. Jenny's Dad took her to see the house on the night before they moved to it, and she cried in the car all the way home.

Jenny lies in her bed in her own room for the last time in her life. She lies awake until everybody is asleep and the house is utterly still. She makes up escapes in her head; all the old escapes, running away to Grannie in Scotland, living like an Indian in the woods, riding a boxcar to the Rocky mountains and becoming an explorer. But they don't work any more. She is getting too old for little kids' dreams. She says her prayers, but she is getting too old for some kinds of prayers too. She can't believe any more that God could *really* change things that are as settled and completed as the sale of the house. She gets tangled up in all the complications of where God would find the money and how he'd get it to her Dad, and also, how he'd make the stairs not matter for Joseph. There is only one thing that God could change, right away, one thing that would make a real difference. Late, late at night, Jenny prays, 'God, since he'd really be happier in heaven, please let Joseph die tonight.' She puts her hands over her face in horror, and falls asleep.

In the morning, Joseph hasn't died. Everything is normal, except that the house is almost bare, with the furniture moved out. Their parents are putting the last things they are taking – Anne and Jenny's toys, suitcases of clothes – on to Uncle Eddie's pick-up truck. Joseph is lying on his blanket in the middle of the empty living-room. Jenny comes in and looks at him. She thinks of what God knows, about what she asked. She leans over and kisses Joseph's face. It is damp and dribbly, and he makes a small squawking noise. Then she goes out and sits in her special place on the steps in the cold February sunshine for the last time. As long as she sits there, she knows it hasn't really happened yet, and she still lives in this big wonderful house, and has the woods and the fields and the saltmarsh for her own. While people clamber around her carrying boxes and saying, 'Come on, Jenny, move!' she plans how she will still sneak back into the woods and play, no matter who lives here. But then her father comes and tells her to get in the car, and she stands up slowly, and leaves her special place behind.

Jenny drew a line across her life, marking the day they moved house. She was nine years old and, nine years later, when she went away to college, she drew another line, ending the division in her life the first had begun. For all those nine years she never accepted the new house as home. When she was thirteen, and fourteen, and everybody at school had forgotten she had ever lived anywhere else, when someone said, 'You come from Berry Hill, don't you?' she would still deny it.

Berry Hill was the name of the development she lived in now. Coming from there was nothing to brag about, so the other kids thought she was just lying to make herself look big. But Jenny *really* never came from Berry Hill; her inner private self remained wedded to the meadows and woods of her first home, even when those same lovely places had fallen to the bulldozers and cement mixers of developers. They lived forever in Jenny's mind, transferred now rationally to other, further places, with mountains and farms and rivers where she knew she would live when she was grown.

Jenny had sworn she would make no friends, speak to no one, help with nothing in the new house at all. At every chance she would run away, back to her own *real* yard, and play in her secret place in the woods. She had it all planned out, but none of it worked out in the end. She did try, but only once, to run away back home. She got as far as the highway, which lay like a river between the old town where she belonged and the new town she had come to. She was old enough to cross it alone now, but somehow she did not dare. To act out the rebellion that lay in her heart ran too raggedly across the grain of her natural obedience. Anne would have done it with hardly a thought. Jenny could not. She returned instead to the new house with a sort of resentful relief, and she never tried again.

It was a lonely time for Jenny. Her parents were always busy. For a while, when the piano and voice lessons weren't going well, her Dad had a part-time job driving a school bus. He got up very early, and was already out of the house on the frosty mornings of February and March when Jenny got up. Though she and Anne shared a room, it did not make them closer but seemed rather to drive them apart. Anne had changed. She was in junior high now. She grew fussy about her clothes, and shouted at Jenny if Jenny was in her way by the dressing-table, or if Jenny crumpled her skirt by leaving her books or toys on it. Mornings always began with fights and with their Dad out and their mother busy with Joseph, there was no one to mediate. Anne made all the rules, and some were tyrannical and unfair. She divided the room and kept all the best parts – the window, the dressing-table, the bookshelf – for herself. Jenny was wedged into a dull corner by her bed, with just her bedside table for keeping things on. Sometimes, when Anne was in a good mood, she would relent and let Jenny's toys and games sprawl into her domain, but when she was grumpy – and she was grumpy a lot of days and almost all mornings – she shouted and kicked Jenny's treasures out of her way. Then she stormed off, with her school books, to eat her breakfast and go out to school before Jenny could follow her.

At the breakfast table, Jenny ate her oatmeal with small unobtrusive bites while her mother struggled with Joseph. Joseph wasn't easy to feed. When he was little, you could just shovel food in, like into the gaped maw of a baby bird, and he would swallow everything. But he wasn't little any longer, and he had a surprising strength when he stiffened his body and flung his arms out in recalcitrance. Once even Jenny could feed him; now only their parents managed. Jenny's Mom sat in a solid chair at the end of the big table, which had been in the dining-room of the old house and was now crammed unhappily into the open-plan dinette of the new. Joseph sat on her knee, his arms pinioned by her free hand, his legs sticking out at their bent, awkward angle. He crooned the low sound he made when he was happy. His eyes wandered around the room, and sometimes rolled up a little, showing the whites. Jenny didn't like when that happened, and when she was alone with him she would say, 'Stop it, Joseph. You make me sick.' But she never said it when her mother was around.

Her mother never talked, except to Joseph, during breakfasts. Mostly she just repeated a string of cajolements while she battled oatmeal into him. Half the oatmeal came out again and dribbled down his face. Whenever Jenny looked up, she would see her mother, with her hair pulled back tight and pinned with hair-rips, her face lined with concentration. Her mother was still in her robe; she didn't have time to get dressed until after Joseph was fed. Jenny always dressed herself and made her bed. When she finished her breakfast she got her jacket and her paper-bag lunch, and went out of the door. Behind her, her mother called, 'Goodbye, honey,' in a thin, distracted voice.

Anne wasn't lonely. She saw less of Marion because of living further away, but she plunged into the new street full of children like it was a high adventure. She knew everyone's names, and where everyone lived, and whose brothers and sisters belonged to whom. She was in and out of everyone's houses and rode or walked home with different girls every day, and sometimes even with boys. On the first day they were in the new house she had gone boldly off with two older girls to drink cokes outside the Carvel stand, and when they came back there was a big boy called Greg with them and Anne was teasing and joking and punching him like she had known him all her life. Jenny was terrified of him; he was as tall as a man and had pimples on his chin. Now Anne spent half her time with Greg and the rest of it at the restaurant, working for Grandpa and Nonna. Jenny hardly ever saw her any more.

Once when, on a Saturday morning, Jenny begged Anne to play with her, Anne said, 'I'm too old for you. Go find your own friends.' She was sitting in front of the dressing-table mirror, where she sat most of the time, putting lipstick on her mouth. She wasn't allowed lipstick, but an older girl called Jo-Jo had given it to her. She sometimes wore it around the house when their Dad wasn't home, but she always wiped it off before she went to see Nonna.

'I haven't got any friends,' Jenny said. Anne swivelled around and looked at her as if she had never seen her before.

'No wonder,' she said.

On Saturdays, the boys race up and down the street on their bicycles so fast that Jenny dares not ride hers. At one end they play baseball, hurling the hard leather ball with ferocious force into the catcher's mitt. They swing at it with the bat and send a pop fly arcing into a yard, bringing someone's Dad out to shout at them. Jenny is afraid of the shouting Dads, the whizzing baseballs, the sharp angry crack of the bat. The girls cower inside the yards or play hopscotch on the sidewalks. Jenny watches them chalk squares and snail shapes on the concrete. She does not understand the games. No one asks her to play.

Bored with baseball, the boys attack the girls. They ride bicycles through the hopscotch games, shout taunts into the play-houses in the yards, snatch scarves, scatter chalks, wreak havoc until the street is theirs. The little girls run away crying. The bigger ones shout indignantly, but with a new excitement, as if this was what they've been waiting for all day. Jenny cowers in the middle, entrapped by circling bike wheels and sweaty shoving bodies, while the boys tie up a girl with her jump rope. Then they see her.

'Who's she?' A skinny boy in a Yankees jacket peers at her. He has narrow dark brown eyes and his hair is crew-cut, so it looks grey. He is the leader; everyone wants to please him.

'Aw, she's nobody.'

'She's the new girl. The little pipsqueak.'

'The one with the cuckoo brother.'

The boy in the baseball jacket looks interested. 'You mean the moron?'

They agree happily, and the boy signals to Jenny with a crooked finger. 'Hey you. Come here.' Jenny does not move. 'Look, you, I called you.' He adopts an exaggerated attitude of tried patience. Still Jenny does not move.

'Aw, she's just a moron too.'

'Let's get her,' another shouts.

'Yeah, get the pipsqueak.' And then they are all around with their grinning faces and their rough boy smell. One grabs her hands and ties the jump rope around them, another wraps his scarf around her and around her. They chant, 'Moron, moron,' as they lead her down the street. 'She's our prisoner. We're taking her prisoner.' The girls all shriek and shout but they don't do anything. 'Take her to the fort,' the leader says. 'We'll hold her for ransom.'

Terror fills Jenny. She is all alone. No one will help her. Her Dad isn't in the yard fixing the car like other Dads, but shut away with a music student. Her mother is in the house with Joseph. Anne is at Nonna's, working. The boys can take her away and keep her in their fort forever, until she starves to death tied to a tree. They tug at her arms.

'Stop crying, you little baby. We don't like prisoners that cry.' He grabs Jenny's woollen hat and waves it in front of her face. Then he crams it on his own head, until another boy grabs it off and then the hat goes whirling away from one head to another as if it is more interesting than herself. She watches its red and white bobble disappearing down the street.

'Give it back,' she cries. 'My Grannie knitted it.' The big boy holding her laughs and suddenly she hates him. She jerks hard and the bonds of the scarf and jump rope loosen. Another jerk and they unwind.

'She's getting away,' another boy shouts. Jenny takes the end of the jump rope and swings it hard and the wooden handle cracks into the boy's chin. He howls and begins, amazingly, to cry. Jenny explodes into a punching frenzy, kicking with her hard leather shoes, slapping, biting. The boys shrink away and space appears around her.

'Gee, leave her alone,' one of the boys says, awed.

'She's crazy.'

'Like her brother. Crazy, crazy.' The others take it up, a new chant. 'Crazy moron, crazy moron.'

Jenny runs, pounding up the street in her leather shoes, skidding around the corner of the driveway, across the patchy lawn, stumbling over the concrete front steps and in, safe, the door shut behind her in the darkness of the house, quite still but for the distant notes of a piano, and Joseph's plaintive, petulant cry.

VIII

The summer of Anne's seventeenth year; late June, sticky with heat, the maples heavy with leaves under a white sky, the sun too hazy to cast proper shadows. Anne, Jenny and Greg walk home together from mass. Everyone is fractious with the heat; Anne and Jenny frazzled with exhaustion as well. Joseph cannot breathe well in the humid air, and the night has been restless with the noise of their parents moving him about to make him comfortable, worrying, arguing. Now he is sleeping; their mother sitting vigilantly beside him, their father sleeping awkwardly on the couch in the living-room.

The usual argument about mass has been forsaken; Anne has the good sense, if not the good grace, to keep quiet and go, however unwillingly, without complaint. Only she and Jenny attend mass regularly any more. Their father is too tired. Sometimes he goes in the evenings if he isn't working at the odd jobs he does to fill in for the school bus in the summer. Their mother never goes at all. Anne sees religion as a disease in their family, a sporadic affliction, jumping generations; a recessive trait, like Jenny's blue eyes. Grannie in Scotland has it. Grandpa has it. But it has flitted by her father and Nonna and Anne, to land on Jenny who has it, at present, worst of everyone. Their mother is different though; Anne cannot explain her simply or comfortably at all. Alternately she rejects God in anger and flings herself in desperation upon Him for Joseph's sake until, worn out with the struggle, she loses her grip and, like a drowning woman, slips away.

Still she sends Anne and Jenny, and brooks no arguments. From Jenny she gets none, of course. Jenny is thirteen and wildly religious. She wants to go to parochial school instead of the ordinary junior high, and she sits in front of her mirror draping towels over her head to envision what she'll look like when she becomes a nun. But Anne fights all the way, with a string of crass adolescent arguments, until her father steps in and shouts her down. And so she goes, sits at the back and refuses to take communion. Greg sits with her. He doesn't take communion either because he isn't Catholic. Greg's family are Episcopalian and he should go to their beautiful ivy-wrapped stone church by the lake. Instead he follows Anne to mass because he follows Anne everywhere.

After mass Jenny feels cool, peaceful and holy. She walks quietly behind Anne and Greg, holding the feeling like a soft cloak around her, shielding her from the hot, intrusive day. Anne feels like a released convict, giddy with freedom. She messes about with Greg, stealing his wallet from his jeans pocket, looking in it for pictures of other girls, pretending to find one. But there aren't any of course. There's just her picture, framed in clear plastic beside his driving licence. And a love note she sent him across the table of a diner, written on a napkin. Greg is sentimental; he loves her too much, she is in danger of despising him for it.

Anne is tall and beautiful. Adolescence blesses her. She has no acne, no puppy-fat, requires neither glasses nor braces. Her legs are long, her waist slender, her breasts firm. The sun tans her golden-brown and the salt water streaks her black hair with red and gold lights. 'You've got *everything*,' her best friend Marion says, and Anne just shrugs. She has always been attractive; she accepts it without thought.

Anne wears a long cream cardigan, much-washed, with Greg's varsity letter sewn on the pocket. Around her neck on a heavy gold chain hangs Greg's senior ring. She accepts those too, without thought. She is going steady with Greg because girls like her go steady; it doesn't stop her flirting with the Italian boys who work in the restaurant with her, stealing kisses behind Grandpa's back. She walks slowly in the heat, carrying her missal and her rosary and the square of black lace for her head. She looks straight ahead. Greg walks beside her, his eyes on her always. The missal, the rosary, the square of lace are holy objects, emblems of love, part of the mystery of Anne.

Behind them Jenny trails awkwardly. She knows they'd like her to go away, but there's only one way to walk to St Lawrence's; one way home. She does her best by keeping several feet back, her eyes on the ground. She too clutches a missal, and the rosary that Grannie sent from Scotland for her confirmation. She still wears her black lace mantilla so that people can see she has been to mass and is going to be a nun. Jenny teeters on the edge of adolescence, but does not look likely to be blessed by it.

The warm Mediterranean colouring of her father's family has passed her by. She is white-skinned, blue-eyed, mousy-haired. She freckles rather than tans, and burns before she freckles. Her shoulders and forearms are bright pink from yesterday's swimming, and across her nose white curls of peeling skin reveal pinker patches beneath. 'Jenny doesn't suit the sun,' her Scottish Grannie says, as if sun were something one could simply do without. Sunburn is an old penance, which has wrapped Jenny in T-shirts, towels, sun-hats, all her life. There are new penances now: Jenny is menstruating. Until a month ago, exactly, she envied Anne her grown-up miseries, her cramps and moods and boxes of smuggled Tampax. Now she wonders why. Womanhood has brought smells and stains, humiliation and pimples. She waddles like a duck, a sanitary towel between her legs. She is certain that Greg knows and the embarrassment is mortifying. Jenny detests her body, her face. She pictures herself with greedy disgust, sensually categorizing her many faults. She is no longer contented being the smart one, though no one doubts she's that. Anne, kissed by the sun and Italian boys, seems to have made a far better deal and Jenny's dream of holy orders is strictly qualified: she wants to be a *beautiful* nun.

Ahead of her, on the hot street, Jenny hears Greg laughing to Anne and reddens under her sunburn, sure they are laughing at her. But actually Greg is telling jokes. He stops in the middle of the road and stands with arms outstretched, head to one side. Jenny can't help catching up and she hears him say, 'Look, Anne. "What a way to spend Easter, hey?" ' Anne shrieks. Jenny is disgusted. Greg twists his feet around each other, arms yet outspread. ' "Cross your legs, will you, I've only got one nail." ' Again Anne guffaws. Jenny says sharply, 'You shouldn't laugh. That's a sin. That's blasphemy.'

'Oh shut up,' Anne says wearily. 'You little saint.'

'I'll tell Nonna. It's a sin.'

'Look you.' Anne grabs her by the collar of her sundress, scraping the fabric across her sunburn. Jenny winces and Anne hisses, 'You do, and you'll get it. And stop butting in on our talk.' Anne doesn't want Nonna hearing she'd laughed about the crucifixion. Nonna isn't religious like Grandpa, but she's religious enough to be shocked by that.

'I don't care,' Jenny says boldly. 'You shouldn't blaspheme.'

Anne pushes her away. 'St Jenny the Martyr,' she says. She walks away, furious, and Greg follows. After a while he says, 'Here's a good one. "Hey Mrs Smith, can Johnny come out to play baseball?" "Shut up kid. You know he hasn't any arms or legs." "That's OK, we just want him for second base." '

Greg turns red, spluttering at his own joke. Anne shrieks with delighted disgust, but Jenny jumps in and shouts, 'That's awful. That's really sick. That's like laughing at Joseph. That's what you're *doing*, you know. Laughing at Joseph.'

Anne is silent. She turns around and her eyes are shiny and black. She raises her hand, as if she will hit Jenny, but lowers it again. 'Get out of my sight,' she whispers, 'you little cunt.' And Jenny, cowed, turns and runs away.

She runs ahead of them, down the street to home, but when she loses her breath and has to walk, she can still see them walking behind her. They are walking side by side, not looking at each other, and no one is laughing any more.

Anne left Greg at the corner of the street. They kissed conspicuously, a long, open-mouthed kiss while Jenny looked away. Then Anne walked away from him and he stood watching after. She never asked him to her house. Neither Jenny nor Anne brought friends home often. It wasn't easy to explain to them about Joseph. If they told too much people got scared and made excuses and didn't come at all. Too little, and there was the inevitable shock when they first saw him. There were all the awkward things; the smell of Joseph's room, the big diapers drying on the line, the daunting prospect of meal times, and just the strangeness of him; his sudden squeals that they all knew meant he had lost his grip on his old blanket, or his shriek of delight when he rolled into a bar of sunlight and it fell full on his murky eyes. Really old friends were all right: Marion was as good as another

138

sister. She had grown up with Joseph too. She was used to the way he looked and smelt, the way he ate, the noises he made. She knew how to play Joseph-games; the tickling game, and patty-cake, and whispering in Joseph's ears which for some reason he liked a lot. She even invented a new game called Joseph-under-the-blanket, which was just that: covering Joseph with a blanket and then pulling it off which, again in Joseph's mysterious world, became an immense favourite. Marion knew too that it was important to go to his room, to greet him, to ask his mother about him, rather than to dash through the house as so many, even adults, did, as if it were a kind of deadly maze, and he the minotaur at its depths.

But it wasn't just Joseph that made Anne leave Greg at the end of the street. The one time he had come to the house he'd actually been pretty good. He swallowed hard at the sight of the eight-year-old baby rocking himself and drooling on the living room floor, but after that he'd come closer, and even got down beside him and patted him with rough, boyish pats. And when Joseph laughed once for him he grinned all over. The problem wasn't really Joseph, it was her father. The moment he saw Greg, Anne could see he knew everything; everything they did down at the beach under the big beach blanket; or in the back of his Oldsmobile at the drive-in, or in bedrooms at house-parties before the parents came home. He said only one thing afterwards: 'No, Anne. That's not your kind of boy.' But she knew just what he meant; knew he wished it were so and knew it was not. And the real joke was that when Greg's parents saw her, they said exactly the same thing. Only it was their son they were worried about, not her.

So Anne and Greg met at school, and outside the movies, or on street corners, and everyone knew about it and there was nothing anyone could do. As Anne walked through the front door into the cramped, stuffy house, she automatically slipped the chain that held Greg's ring over her head and stuffed it into her pocket unseen.

Because there was no shade in the development, the houses baked in the sun, soaking up the heat. Anne and Jenny's father had planted two wispy thin mimosa trees because they grew fast, but they hadn't yet grown enough to cast more than a lacy shadow over the front yard. In the back yard there was an awning

139

over an area of flagstones where Joseph's chair could be moved out into the fresh air.

The backyard contained too their one great luxury, a circular, above-ground swimming-pool, twelve feet across and four feet deep. It was the envy of all Jenny's friends, but Jenny explained primly, 'It's not *ours* really. It's for Joseph.' And it was; the result of consultations with the physiotherapist at the hospital which Joseph attended twice a month, and the fruit of scrimping and saving on everyone's part. Joseph's swimming-pool had cost Anne and Jenny dearly in missed treats, frugal birthdays, re-cycled clothing, but neither of them resented it at all. Anne had even put fifty dollars of her own money towards it with proud generosity. It was the delight of Joseph's life; water was his element. In it he became joyful, alert, even graceful. He could not swim, but he could kick and splash powerfully when securely held, and was fearless and, most of all, happy. Free of chairs, beds, restraints; free of gravity and his prison of floors, he floated and splashed, extending arms and legs into his new domain, exploring, luxuriating in a maze of simultaneous sensations: light-ness, coolness, wetness, turbulence. The laughter tumbled from him so vigorously as to almost become words. The family rose with him into his new dimension, splashing each other, playing, rejoicing, briefly healed in their circle of beneficent water. And that was the third reason Greg was not invited home; the har-mony of that family afternoon around the pool was something Anne would share with no one but Marion who alone had shared everything since Joseph was born.

Inside the house, Anne went to the room she shared with Jenny, wrinkling her nose against the urine smell from Joseph's bedroom that hung persistently in the humid air. She pushed her window up higher, but no air moved through the sun-hot screen. She shoved Jenny's plastic horses out of her way with her foot, ignoring Jenny's squeal. 'They're on my side,' she said as she hid Greg's ring in her underwear drawer. 'They're over the line.' The ring wasn't well hidden, but it didn't matter. Jenny was loyal and would not tell, and Anne's mother hadn't time to poke around in drawers anyhow. Jenny gathered her horses, setting them up carefully on her side of the imaginary line that divided the room.

Jenny had begged her mother and father for a room of her

140

own, which was like asking for the moon, since there just weren't any other rooms. 'I'll stay with Joseph,' she said. 'He's nicer than Anne.' Briefly she pictured herself hemming Joseph in with satisfying authority the way Anne did to her. He didn't need a whole room anyhow. He just sat in his chair or rolled around on his play mat. But her parents said it was impossible, and so she stayed with Anne and whenever she, rarely, brought a friend back from school, Anne would come in and announce, 'That little turd had better not have touched any of my things,' and invariably she would find something; a muddy footprint on her side of the rug, a broken lipstick, lines in the dust where one of her ceramic ornaments had been moved. Jenny dreamed of living in a huge house, like the old one, all by herself, and moving peacefully from room to room in utter silence.

Jenny was a great dreamer. It was a joke in the family, how she would be found, glassy-eyed and unresponsive, sitting in a chair pretending to read, or lying on her bed, or on the front patch of crab grass under the mimosa tree, dreaming to herself. Sometimes it even frightened her, her need for dreaming, which grew stronger that sticky summer when her periods started and she felt lousy all the time. Even at school, where she was usually so attentive, she would find herself drifting into rich, satisfying stories in her head, while history and math and English trundled past her unseeing eyes. A teacher had caught her out and made her stammer in embarrassment in front of the whole class about the lesson he had been giving which she simply had not heard. She had cried all through the lunch hour; she was unaccustomed to reprimands at school. But the dreaming continued anyway.

Her dreams were heroic; she was always saving someone: her parents, school-friends, teachers, and particularly those boys she had crushes on. A lot of her dreams were about Joseph. In one she started a secret programme of lessons and taught Joseph to talk. In another she learned of a famous doctor, and brought him home to work a miraculous cure. Sometimes she dreamed that instead of being a nun she would live in a wonderful house in the country when she grew up and look after Joseph so well that he would start walking and seeing all by himself. Once she made the mistake of sharing part of the dream with Anne.

'When I'm grown up, I'm going to have a farm and Joseph will live with me.'

'I thought you were going to college.'

'After I've gone to college. I'll have horses, and a little pony for Joseph to ride.'

'How are you going to buy a farm? Where will you get the money?' Anne's face was pinched and angry as it always was when Jenny was so disgustingly certain about something.

'I won't need money. I'll find the farm. I'll reclaim it from the wilderness. The house will be deserted and I'll fix it up.'

'You're such a dope, Jenny. There aren't any places like that. Everything belongs to *somebody*. There aren't any wildernesses any more.'

'Yes there are,' Jenny shouted. 'Yes there are. There are.'

The late afternoon sun streaks dull gold over the asphalt tiles of the roof, lighting the water in the pool. The water sparkles bright blue, reflecting the plastic walls and bottom of the pool. Anne and Jenny's Dad is standing with the water above his waist, holding Joseph carefully beneath his armpits. Joseph's head is back in ecstasy, his feet kick a white circle of froth. Jenny stands outside the pool in her bathing suit, stretching up on tiptoes, her elbows on its rim. She is conscious of the sanitary towel making a bulge in her crotch and doesn't want anyone to look at her, particularly not her Dad. Her mother says, 'Don't be silly. Your father knows about little girls' bodies.' It makes her feel worse. Still, she is happy being there, out of his sight and watching Joseph. Her father's shoulders are sun-tanned from playing in the pool with Joseph. He is dark, like Nonna, Grandpa, and Anne. But his hair, which Jenny remembers as shiny and black under the lights of the old theatre, is grey now, and thin. There is a bald sun-tanned patch on top of his head. Anne is in the pool with Marion. Marion wears a one-piece green bathing suit with a skirt across the hips because she is self-conscious about her weight. She has grown into a big young woman, placid, her long thick hair piled up on top of her head to keep it out of the water. She grins a lot. Nothing ever makes her mad. Jenny feels close to her because she is thoughtful in a way that Anne is not. She understands how Jenny feels about her pimples and her sunburns and her stubby figure. Jenny is chubby this summer; she has no breasts yet and no waist. Her bottom seems huge. Marion says, 'It's puppy-fat. It'll go away.' Anne only says,

'You're a pig. You eat too much.' Jenny watches Marion in the pool, her brown, soft shoulders, her big adult bosom. Even the soft double chin is nice. She grins again and makes a boat prow with her hands and swims towards Joseph, bumping him gently. 'Collision,' she shouts. Anne dives under the water, her long legs coming up like a seal's tail. Jenny can see the black bars of her bikini against the blue plastic as she swims underwater. Then Joseph convulses in giggles. Anne surfaces beside him, tickling. 'Submarine attack,' she shouts. Joyful, in silence and darkness, Joseph splashes on. Anne dives in close and kisses his wet face. Her black hair is smooth and glistening, making wet tendrils over her forehead, down her neck. The screen door bangs and her mother comes out, carrying a tray with cups and glasses. Marion climbs out of the pool at once to help.

Their Dad lifts Joseph and carries him up the ladder, out of the pool, and dries him off on a towel on the grass. Then he puts his T-shirt on and puts him into his chair and wheels the chair to the wooden picnic table where they all gather. Jenny wraps a towel around her waist to hide herself and joins them. Their mother pours Pepsi with ice in it for Jenny, Anne and Marion, and some into a special cup for Joseph. She pours tea for herself and their Dad. She is wearing a bathing suit too, but she hasn't been in the pool today because her back is hurting. She has a nice figure, slim and long-legged, and although her skin is pale like Jenny's she unfairly tans golden and does not burn. She is still probably pretty, though she seems too old now for Jenny or Anne to think of her that way. Her hair, which was blonde and curly, has been cut short to keep Joseph from pulling it when she feeds him, and her arms are strong and muscular from lifting him every day. She is gay and cheerful in the sunshine because they are all together; Joseph with them. She hands the tea to their father and he suddenly strikes a pose, one arm outflung and begins to sing, 'Tea for Two, and Two for Tea.' Their mother joins him, arms outstretched, holding the tea-cup at length, legs planted wide, hips slung sideways. She is vibrant, graceful. They sing together, and begin to dance together across the lawn, comically dramatic. Jenny laughs, and Marion applauds and even Anne smiles. Joseph is silent, absorbed in rubbing his fists against his eyes. But Marion applauds louder, cheering. Later she prods Anne to help clean up. Marion is staying overnight because her parents are sailing with friends from the yacht club. She has been invited but would rather be here. In the kitchen, before Anne goes out to the restaurant to work, Marion leans against the draining-board, looking out on the empty pool and the green crab grass where Anne's parents danced the tango. She puts her chin on her hands, dreamily. 'I wish I were in your family,' she says.

Grandpa and Nonna's restaurant, where Anne worked in the evenings, was beside the creek that bordered the land of the house that had once been theirs. It had been a boathouse when their old house and the Uncles' farm and Grandpa and Nonna's own house had all been part of one big old estate. Grandpa had bought it all in 1925, a few years after he had come from Italy. For years it was a big family compound, but bit by bit they sold it until now very little was left. The Uncles' farm had once supplied the restaurant, and the crabs and clams and fish were caught and dredged by the Uncles and Grandpa himself. Now it was all more modern. Nonna no longer kept hens, and the Uncles were getting old and grew smaller fields of corn, tomatoes and peppers. Most of the food came in vans from wholesalers and the fish came in from Montauk and the Hamptons. But the reputation of the restaurant remained and old customers still came and sat at the same tables with red-checked cloths that they had sat at for years.

To get to work, Anne rode her bicycle right past her old house, but she hardly glanced at it. It meant little to her and it looked entirely different now, anyhow. The new owners had painted the grey shingles brown, and the porches and shutters were now gleaming white. They had added stained glass to the funny windows on the third floor, and planted bushes and flowers shielding the house from the lawns that had once run to the barn-theatre. The Antiques were still there; an old horse-drawn buggy and a sleigh stood in front of the barn with signs painted on them. Beyond the barn and house some of the Uncles' fields had been sold and new houses had been built. Strange children rode bikes on new roads where she and Marion had played cowboys and Indians and camped out at night. When Jenny had seen the foundations for the new houses first dug, and the cement blocks and fresh earth scarring her old play places, she had cried. Anne had only been curious, poking about the outlines of the houses, finding where the rooms and doors and plumbing were going to go. Now she had friends who lived in those places, which Jenny regarded as a kind of treachery. She rode her bike by the new houses, waving to people she knew, and then up the long driveway to the restaurant, gliding to a smooth stop behind the kitchen doors, leaning her bike against the trash cans before she went in.

The front of the restaurant was very pretty, with decking built over the dark waters of the creek so people could sit out on the warm summer evenings. The back was plain, a tacked-on extension with asbestos shingles and functional metal-framed windows that housed the kitchens. That was the part that Anne knew; hot and steamy, smelling of food and dishwater, where everyone worked hard and fast, falling over each other in the cramped space, to create the lovely cool peace of the restaurant and bar beyond. She went straight in, took her apron from its peg, tied it on, and began at the sink, scrubbing the pots that Nonna had piled there. Her grandparents nodded to her, too busy to speak. They were a good team, the three of them, each out-doing the other in willingness to work. They were the core of the restaurant: all the rest – Uncle Eddie who helped out with the cooking, the girls who tended the bar, the two boys, Marco and Giovanni, who waited on table – drifted along, waiting to be told what to do, taking time out for cigarettes in the staff room, talking among themselves. It didn't mean anything to them. It meant everything to Anne; when she was grown-up it would be hers. Grandpa had promised her. And when it was hers, it was going to make her rich.

It wasn't making anyone rich the way it was now. Anne had realized that years ago when she was still a child. There were too many people working in it, too many wages paid out for too little done. There were other things wrong, too. There weren't enough tables, so people were often turned away at the busy times. And those who came sat all night, drinking coffee and waiting for Grandpa to come out from the kitchen and sit and talk with them, too. They were all old friends, cronies. Some just ate a bowl of spaghetti and still sat all night. Anne bitched about it in the kitchen.

'The cheapskates. Three dollars all night. And no tip.'

'So, Anne, what money has he got, that Tony?' Grandpa said, patiently.

'Enough to spend on beer,' Anne said. Grandpa smiled, wrinkling his tanned leathery face. He pinched her cheek. 'A business woman,' he said, laughing at her. 'What do I do? Tell him he can't eat spaghetti?'

'You could tell him to get moving,' Anne said.

Grandpa's smile faded. 'This is my friend you are talking about,' he said.

Anne knew when to stop. But she couldn't help adding as she returned to her dishes. 'You could make more money if you had a decent turnover.'

'We make enough money,' Grandpa said. Behind him, Nonna made a long, eloquent shrug. Nonna understood. It was too late for Nonna, though. She would work hard for the rest of her days and have nothing at the end. But Anne could tell by the way she dressed herself and did her hair and made up her face that Nonna would have liked a life with money. And it wasn't too late for Anne. Her sharp mind filled up with plans she would implement when the restaurant was hers, and in that way she contained her frustration.

When she took her break for coffee, Marco and Giovanni, the waiters, came and hung around her so long that their orders piled up on the serving counter and Nonna had to shout at them. They shrugged, ripply continental shrugs, and loped out with their platters. They were another of Grandpa's indulgences, grandsons of an old friend in Sicily. Grandpa had given them jobs and arranged their permits and found them places to stay. They said they wanted to come to America to become restaurateurs. So far, Anne knew, they had got no further than waiting on table and spending their days on the Fire Island beach. But she enjoyed them. They were different from American boys. They flattered and wheedled and made her feel they would die if she didn't go to the beach with them. She knew they were lying, but she liked the game. She liked their accents and their wild gestures and their dark, hairy bodies. They tanned wonderfully brown and wore bathing suits so small that she could see almost everything. They wore gold rings on their smooth hands and holy medals on silver chains and they flirted outrageously.

When she went out with them, she left her own chain, with Greg's ring, at home.

Grandpa reprimanded her for flirting with the Italian boys, and once he threatened to tell her father. When he saw them going off to the Ferry on Saturday mornings with towels and blankets and six-packs, he drew her aside.

'You, you're a nice girl. Why you throwing yourself at those boys?'

'They're my friends,' she would say sullenly, and her bold fearless look reminded him that she was an American, not a Sicilian girl.

'So behave yourself,' was all he could say. Anne didn't care. Grandpa couldn't see her under the boardwalk with the Italian boys and her Dad and Mom hadn't time to keep watch over her. She worked hard all week; Marco and Giovanni were her reward.

Jenny tries to say her prayers. She lies in bed in the dark with her eyes tight shut, trying to build a wall of silence around her side of the room. But Anne hums to herself, sings, flicks on her flashlight and reads from one of her secret books under the covers. When Jenny's eyes open, she sees a tent of soft blue light; Anne under her bedspread with *Lady Chatterley's Lover*. 'Jeez, you should hear this bit,' she says, provocatively.

'I'm saying my prayers.' Jenny's voice is small and prim. Anne doesn't really want to read to her; it's just a way of getting her attention. Jenny ignores her, reverting her concentration to God and His saints. Her litany is more complicated now. She invokes St Anthony, St Bernadette, the Blessed Virgin, with separate petitions for special needs. She includes as always all her friends, Anne's friends, her family. There is the usual prayer for money for her father, since the lack of it seems his chief misery. There is a prayer for her mother, amorphous and uncertain, requesting only that she 'be happy'. Jenny has no clear idea of what would make her mother happy – other, of course, than a miracle for Joseph. That, her final prayer, has become the essential core of all the others.

'Oh God,' she says silently, 'Please make Joseph able to see and hear and walk and talk and be normal.' It doesn't sound like a real prayer to Jenny, so she dresses it up with trimmings and explanations that go on for a long time. They too become essential and she clings superstitiously to the need to repeat all of them, each time, and to finish it all with an Our Father, three Hail Marys and a Gloria. It takes a very long time and it's almost impossible some nights for Jenny to win silence enough to say it. If Anne interrupts, she goes back to the beginning and starts again. It is part of the ritual and Jenny remains convinced that the prayer will not be efficacious if not said in one complete whole. Sometimes Anne drives her to spasms of frustration with her sudden bursts of chatter, but of course Jenny can't get angry without also spoiling the prayer and she bears all with silent fortitude. Halfway through the third Hail Mary, she hears Anne's intake of breath and braces herself. 'Gosh, you wouldn't believe anybody would write any of this *down*.'

'Anne,' Jenny says, 'I don't want to hear about it just now.' Anne is bursting with the need to talk. 'Want to hear a ghost story?' She's good at ghost stories. She tells 'The Monkey's Paw', and 'The Green Mist', and changes them to make them sound as if they were real and had happened last year to people who lived not far away at all. Sometimes she makes up her own stories about people and places they know. The most terrifying are the stories she makes up about Joseph.

'I don't want to hear anything,' Jenny said. But Anne is full of devilish high spirits. She has spent the evening at Nonna's, being fitted for the strapless evening dress Nonna is helping her make for her Junior Prom. Anne has chosen the pattern, altered it cleverly, and done almost all the sewing herself. 'You should be a dressmaker,' her grandmother says. But Anne only shrugs. It sounds boring, an old lady's job. Greg is taking her to the Prom and she is a candidate for Prom Queen. The Italian boys are fiercely jealous and the excitement of it has keyed Anne up to a rare pitch.

'How about "Joseph and the Swamp Monster"? ' Anne says.

'I *hate* that story. Be quiet, Anne, I'm saying my prayers.'

'Listen, it starts like this. One day, Mom goes out early and she has to leave Joseph alone. But she thinks it's all right because Dad will be back soon. Only, just as she starts out the door she hears this strange noise, and she sees this sort of mist coming in from down at the bay. So she locks the door really carefully, and she goes . . .'

'Stop it, Anne. It's going to be that one about the thing in the mist. I can't stand it.'

'No, this is different. Listen. So Joseph is lying there and the room sort of fills up with the strange fog, but he can't see it so he's not scared . . .'

'Anne, *stop* it.'

'And then he feels this strange thing. It doesn't *hurt* or anything, but suddenly he feels *stronger*, and he begins to sit up, and he finds he can stand up and then he grabs the bars of his bed and they just *crumble* into metal dust. That's how strong he is. And the mist starts drifting out of the house and Joseph knows he has to follow it. And he starts to walk, really awkward at first, like Frankenstein, but he gets better, and he gets to the front door that's locked and he just shoves it and it *splinters* and he walks out into the street, still in the middle of the cloud of mist so no one sees him. But now he's looking for someone. There's someone he has to find and he reaches out his hands and tightens them up like he's squishing something and he begins to say something.'

'Shut *up*, Anne, it's really rotten.'

'What do you think he's saying?'

'*I'll tell Mom.*'

'It's a name. Real muddled at first, but it gets clearer. That's it. I can hear it now. He's whispering it. "Jen-nee," he says. "Jenny." And there's this echoing voice in the mist that says, "Get Jenny." ' Anne giggles and Jenny whispers, 'You shut up, Joseph wouldn't be like that.' She paused, her prayers abandoned. 'Joseph loves me,' she says sadly.

Anne giggles again. Jenny hears a rustling from across the room and Anne says, 'Jenny, look at this.' Anne is out of bed, on the floor, in the circle of light of her flashlight. She shines it under her chin so it distorts her features horribly and she twists her shoulders and bends her arms around. Suddenly she is Joseph. She worms her way across the floor waving the light.

Jenny gasps and hides her head in her pillow. She hears Anne beside her bed, whispering wickedly, 'What was that?'

'What?'

'From Joseph's room. That noise.'

'No, there isn't.'

'He's coming, Jenny. He's coming. He's coming.'

* * *

149

On the day before the junior prom, Marion came to see Anne. She was serious and very grown-up, and she asked to see Anne alone.

'What's all this about?' Anne asked sarcastically, as they sat side by side on Anne's bed in the bedroom from which Jenny had been evicted.

Marion looked at the floor where Jenny's book lay, splayed open, as she'd left it. She said at last, 'It's about Greg.'

'*What* about Greg,' Anne said.

'Something I know about him,' Marion said.

'Oh sure,' Anne said. 'Here we go.'

'Greg's not taking you to the prom,' said Marion.

'*What?*'

'He's not taking you.'

Anne was silent, her mouth half open. Marion looked miserably unhappy. 'I thought it would be better if I told you now than if you found out the hard way.'

Anne suddenly exploded into words, 'The hard way? What are you talking about? That's a load of shit. Of course he's taking me. He's been taking me for months. I *saw* him just yesterday. He wanted to know what colour corsage to get me . . .'

'But he's not, Anne,' Marion said firmly. 'So you'd better just forget about it, the corsage and everything. You're not going.'

Anne stared again, her eyes widening. 'I don't believe this,' she said.

'It's true,' Marion insisted.

Anne said, 'I mean I don't believe you. I don't believe you're that jealous of me that you'd do a thing like this.'

'I'm not jealous, Anne.'

'Shitting right you're jealous. I know what you're up to, you slimey cow. Right, now I call Greg up and we have a huge fight and he breaks off with me and then you take his side like you always do and, guess what, he takes *you* to the prom. Jeez, if I was so hard up for a date I'd shoot myself.'

'Anne, what are you talking about? Greg's not taking *me* to the prom.' She shrugged, with honest naïvety. 'Who'd take me?'

Anne knew then she wasn't lying, but she wouldn't face it. 'Yes he is,' she shouted. 'You've set it all up. You're supposed to be my friend.'

Marion shrugged again and made a small, adult smile. She

said, 'Yeah, I'm supposed to be your friend. Sometimes I wonder why. Look, Anne, I came here to do you a favour.'

'I don't want your favours, you jealous bitch.'

'Yeah, well, you're getting it anyhow. Greg's not taking you because his parents cracked down hard. They don't want him to see you any more.'

'That's a lie.'

'His Mom was going on about it at the Yacht Club. My Mom overheard it.' Marion paused. She said reasonably, 'It's partly your fault. The way you mess around with those Italian boys. It's not doing your reputation any good. But it's *mostly* because of Joseph.'

'*Joseph?*'

'They don't want Greg involved.'

'With *Joseph?*'

'You're his sister. You're related. They're afraid Greg might be getting *real* serious about you. I guess they're worried there might be something in the family,' she added sensibly. When she saw the look on Anne's face she said, 'Look, they're a real bunch of snobs. My parents can't stand them.' She shrugged again, apologetically.

Anne looked murderous. She said, 'Sure, I bet. Your parents can't stand them. The *truth* is your parents are crawling up their assholes like everyone else because they're filthy rich. Talking of *snobs* . . .'

'That's not fair.'

'I don't need your favours or your *parents'* favours. You're as much of a snob as the rest of them. I bet you've loved this, getting all your Yacht Club shit and dumping it all over me . . .'

'I'm trying to help.'

'Oh yeah. The fuck you are. You're just lording it over me like the rest of them because we're poor and because of fucking Joseph. Well you can shove it, all of you, because whatever you say Greg loves me. And whatever his parents do, he'll be here tomorrow, even if he has to leave home.'

'Anne, he's already taking someone else. His parents have arranged it . . .'

Anne stood up slowly and looked down at Marion. 'Get out, you bitch!' she whispered. 'Get out of my house. I'm sick of you. I hate you. I've always hated you, you fat cow. I've been doing

151

you a favour for years, being friends. Now get the fuck out and don't come back.'

Marion went stiff and quiet. She stood up and walked silently to the door. Her eyes were wet and shining but she didn't actually cry. She said, 'You're a funny kid. I don't know why any of us put up with you. Maybe because you used to be such fun.' She looked very sad. 'Well you can yell at me all you like. It's not going to change anything. It's going to happen anyhow.'

It is ten o'clock. The night is warm and velvety black, filled with the sound of crickets. The high school gym is lit up bright and strung with streamers of crêpe paper, and on the stage at one end is a crêpe paper-draped throne. Girls and boys stiffly dance the Twist in strapless dresses and tuxedos. Neither Marion nor Anne is there. Marion is at home, where she expected to be, reading Cyrano de Bergerac. Anne is also at home, dressed in cream satin, sitting rigidly upright on the edge of the sofa in the living-room. On the floor her mother is sitting with Joseph sprawled on her knees. He is half asleep, exhausted, struggling for breath in the sticky air. Her mother is totally occupied with him. Only her father, standing miserably by the window still, seems aware of Anne's anguish. And Jenny, lurking at the door-way, afraid to enter the sanctum of unhappiness but unwilling to leave.

Every time a car's headlights come up the street, their father straightens up and peers into the night, but none of the cars stops. Anne has ceased even to look up.

Their father says, 'That car of his, it's so old. He's broken down somewhere.' But Anne knows he could borrow his father's car. Later, her Dad says, 'When I was that age, I never had the nerve to meet a date. Half the time, maybe, I just wouldn't show up. Chickened out. Your father was some chicken.'

Joseph, on their mother's knees, wakes and wails softly before she rocks him gently back into his sleep. Their mother says, 'He was two hours late for his first date with me.' She laughs softly, and he laughs too, but Anne has no laughter in her. She stands up and lifts the rhinestone tiara off her smooth black hair. She holds it, studying it for a long while, and then quite deliberately takes it also in her other hand, and then without expression she crushes it between the two. Her mother gasps and her father

152

opens his mouth, then closes it, and swallows hard. Anne twists the tiara into a glittery snake and then drops it on the floor. It falls with a loud clatter on to bare wood, and Joseph wakes and wails again.

Anne looks at him with hatred. 'Go on, cry, you little shit. It's all your fucking fault anyhow. I hope you choke.'

'Anne!' Her father, whose arms had been outstretched to comfort her, draws back, stunned. She turns to him, defiant.

'I mean it,' she says.

His sorrow turns quickly to anger. 'What's this? You blame your brother because that no good boy stands you up?'

'Yes, I blame him,' Anne says. 'I blame him for everything. Everything that goes wrong in my life is his fault. He's why I never have enough money to go out with my friends, and why I can't bring anyone home because they get sick looking at him. And why,' her voice breaks, her control loosening, 'and why Greg didn't come. Not because of me. Greg loves me. Because of Joseph. Because his parents won't let him because of Joseph. I know. Marion told me. Marion's my friend. My real friend. The only one I'll ever have because of *him*.' She kicks out with her cream silk shoe, the satiny tip just brushing Joseph's arm.

'Anne!' her mother cries, and instantly her father is upon her. He catches her bare shoulders in his hands, the big fingers closing roughly, and shakes her back and forth.

'Never,' he shouts. 'Never. Never.' Her mother is crying for him to stop, her face contorted. Joseph is wailing. Jenny freezes in the doorway, watching as Anne breaks free, batters her father with her fists and then runs past her, the satin of her cream dress brushing Jenny's arm, soft as a moth's wing. Anne runs out into the front yard and shrieks aloud, a great cry of frustration. She spins about and dashes back into the house and into her tiny hot room and flings herself in the darkness on to her bed. In the living-room she can hear her parents shouting at each other, and Joseph crying, and Jenny's baffled, miserable sobs.

After a long while Jenny comes into the room and puts on her bedside light. Through wet lashes, Anne sees her standing by her bed, the wreckage of the rhinestone tiara clutched in her hands. Tears of sympathy run down her acne-marked cheeks.

'I'm so sorry, Anne,' she sobs. 'I'm so sorry.' Helplessly, she holds out the ruined tiara. Anne raises her head from the bed.

153

She is done crying. She reaches her hand out to Jenny, takes the tiara and lays it on the pillow, and then takes Jenny's hand.

'It's not your fault, kid,' she says gently. She turns over, her back to Jenny, and is quiet.

Silently Jenny undresses, climbs into her bed, and turns out the light. She lies in the darkness, about to begin her prayers. Anger overwhelms her. *Damn you, God, I'm not praying to you. Not when you let that happen to Anne.* She shuts her eyes in fierce apostasy, and after a long, long while, she sleeps.

Jenny dreams of a farm; a backwoods American farm, from a Disneyland programme about the frontier. But the barn is different from the wooden barns she saw on television. It is built of stone, and is very dark inside. In the dream, Jenny is looking into the barn. Then she hears Joseph talking. She knows it is Joseph, though she has never heard him talk before. Joseph says, 'Here's a light, Jenny,' and when Jenny looks she sees Anne's flashlight lying on the floor of the barn. It makes a circle of blue light. Jenny knows if she picks up the flashlight she will be able to see Joseph, standing up and talking to her like she has always wanted. But in the dream she cannot move.

IX

Marco drops Anne in front of the house. He waits, a dark shape inside the dark outline of the car, until she finds her key and lets the door open a crack. When he sees the bar of light he revs the engine, and the red Mustang roars away. Anne slips through the door and closes it silently behind her. She checks her clothing in the mirror in the tiny vestibule hall, making sure her blouse is buttoned correctly, the waistband of her skirt properly fastened. Getting dressed again in the back seat of the Mustang is a comic nightmare. She sees her face in the dimly lit reflection, pale, tired, her eyes glowing softly from sex. It is three in the morning; she has been up since six, and will be up again tomorrow at eight. She thinks of her bed with sensual longing and hopes her father is asleep.

The living-room is dark, silent, and she seems to sense his sleeping presence, though she cannot distinguish his outline from the lumpy shape of the sofa where, as on most nights, he is probably sleeping. She walks softly by the door but is struck then by a shaft of light from the kitchen and his voice, old and tired, from within.

'Is that you, Anne?'

'Yeah, Dad,' she says wearily. 'It's me.' She steps into the kitchen. The bright fluorescent ring glares, and she squints her eyes shut against it, seeing the room and her father through a wicket of crumbling mascara. 'You weren't waiting up, were you?'

'No, honey. Just getting some cocoa.' But he is sitting at the big table with an already empty cup and the *Daily News*.

'You shouldn't wait up for me.'

155

'I don't,' he says. Then he shrugs. 'Sometimes I don't sleep so well.' She nods resignedly, finds the coffee pot, half full of cold coffee. She removes the basket and sets the pot on the electric ring.

Her father says, 'That coffee, that keeps you awake.'

'Nothing keeps me awake,' Anne says. She pours the coffee and flops into a chair, stretching her legs. Her calves ache from standing all day on the hard lino floor. Her clothes and hair reek of cooking oil, garlic, fish. But she is more conscious of other smells, Marco's sweat, and her own, the wetness yet between her legs, and the salty tang of sex. Her father looks dry and clean, scrubbed, a husk of an old man. She is ashamed in his presence. She says, 'You should be in bed.'

'He isn't sleeping well. He has a cough.' Her father nods towards the bedrooms of the house. 'He sleeps better with your mother.'

'So do you,' Anne says. And then he does something strange. He looks across the table to her, his eyes, brown, like hers, the whites yellowed with tiredness, suddenly alive and knowing.

'Once,' he says. 'Once, I slept so well, nothing kept me awake, either.'

Anne knows that he is not fooled. He knows about Marco, what she does in the back seat of the Mustang each night after work. Embarrassed, she looks away.

Her father says, 'Do you know what day it is?'

'November something,' she says, uninterested. 'Why?'

'November twelfth,' he says, proudly, and she remembers.

'Oh Dad, I forgot.'

'Our anniversary.'

'I know, Dad. Oh gosh, I'm sorry.'

But he pats her hand. 'Why should you remember? You weren't even there.' He smiles gently. He looks like Grandpa now, his black hair all grey and thin, his face no longer handsome but craggy, like an Italian peasant. 'Twenty-four years,' he says. 'Next year, our Silver Wedding. This year, twenty-four years.' He pauses. 'It must be something too. There's something for every year, a precious stone, or something. The first ones are nothing much, paper, or wood. But twenty-four must be something good.'

156

'Oh Dad, why didn't you say? You could have gone out. I'd have looked after him.'

'She didn't remember either,' he says.

Anne looks anguished, but he only smiles. 'She never remembered anything,' he says. His eyes are dreamy, far away. 'Such a giddy girl. I had to remind her twice what day we were getting married. First she told the priest the wrong day. Then her sisters who were bridesmaids – Eileen, and Marie, the one who was killed by the buzz-bomb in London – she told them both a different wrong day. If her mother hadn't reminded her to post the banns we'd never have gotten married at all. I didn't know about posting the banns, you see. That was new to me. And then she almost forgot to ask for leave. A giddy girl,' he whispers. 'A giddy Glasgow girl.'

'I have to go to bed, Dad,' Anne says quietly. 'I've got to get up at eight.'

'Sure, sweetheart. Sure.' He stands up quickly to let her go and, exhausted, she slips by him, leaving him alone in the bright light of the kitchen. Again, she knows, she has failed him. She should stay, encourage him, let him talk and reminisce, and tell all the old stories about the War and the theatre and how her parents met. But she knows it could go on for an hour. He would go to the basement and get the box of photographs and show her their wedding pictures, her mother in her dress of parachute silk, all the old, dead friends in war uniforms. And last always, the browned photograph of herself at eighteen months, old-fashioned and European in hand-knitted baby clothes, held in her mother's arms on the deck of a ship leaving Scotland. But she cannot bear it. She is too tired, too stretched between too many people to give anyone anything more. She wishes Jenny were here. Jenny loves the pictures, the stories, the grey Scottish past. She loves family and history. But Jenny is gone and Anne goes to their bedroom alone.

She was careful now of all Jenny's things. The invisible line remained in the room, but now it was Anne who respected it rigidly, ensuring nothing of hers drifted over to Jenny's unused side. She undressed and laid her clothes neatly across her own bedside chair. Before Jenny went away to college Anne had cleared a space for her on the dressing-table, and kept her lipsticks, mascara and nail varnishes all on her own half. Though even when Jenny was home there was nothing on her side but her brush and comb and a metal clip for her long hair. Anne wished they were there now; she missed Jenny fiercely and the thought of the metal clip evoked a wave of love.

Jenny was in her sophomore year at Harpur College, upstate, and although she came home for the long vacations, she hardly seemed to live here any more. Last summer she had travelled with friends in Europe with money their grandparents gave her for making the Dean's List. They went to France and Italy and on the way back Jenny stayed in Glasgow with Grannie and toured the Highlands. She fell in love with Scotland. She brought books home, full of Scottish stories, and folk songs and pictures of mountains and lochs. She brought everyone bright tartan scarves and hats. She brought Joseph a sheepskin rug. It all made Anne uneasy. She felt remote from Jenny and could not accustom herself to her new, travelled, educated sister who had worlds that were not her own.

Anne's world was narrow: home, the family, the restaurant, Marco. She had fallen into Marco's company in her seventeenth year, after Greg stood her up on her prom night. That was the year, also, that Giovanni gave up his American dream and returned to Italy to marry a fisherman's daughter, leaving Marco his half of their scruffy trailer behind the restaurant, his share in the red Mustang and, inevitably, his half interest in Anne. At once her friendship with Marco shifted from a game into a romance and then an affair. She was nineteen when they first became lovers in a hollow in the dunes on the Beach. Now they had been together so long that they were utterly bored with each other in everything but sex. It was rough, coarse sex, soured by the mutual knowledge that they did not love each other, but it was enough to keep them together. Anne needed it; she needed the release from the tension of work, and she needed something to think about when the tedium got too much for her or Grandpa was in one of his difficult moods.

Running the restaurant was gruelling work. Her childhood dream, consummated, brought disillusionment. Now that she was an adult and had lost her privileged position of doted-upon grandchild, she saw her grandparents through a harsher light. Her grandmother was a well-bred woman who had married beneath her for love. Her grandfather and the Uncles were not the brotherly union she had once imagined, but a knot of old resentments over family and money. Uncle Ricky was miserly, Uncle Eddie, kind but unimaginative, was ordered about by both his brothers. Grandpa, deeply religious, was also intolerant and unforgiving, holding grudges that went back fifty years. All three were subtly contemptuous of women. When Anne revealed deficiencies in the business they shrugged; when she suggested improvements, they ignored them; when she made criticisms, they bridled. Her youthful conviction that she would resurrect the failing restaurant and make a fortune from it broke on the rocks of their stubborn resistance and dissipated like froth.

Nonna saw it. Nonna understood. Sometimes she would stop, in cutting vegetables or preparing fish, and look up at Anne, the expressive lines still beautiful around her dark eyes. The eyes would meet Anne's and she would shrug, a sensual, soulful shrug that welcomed Anne into the unfairness of womanhood. At such times Anne felt a curious struggle within herself, between wild, desperate resistance, the certainty that she must escape now or never, and a kind of peaceful surrender, a communion with her grandmother and generations of her female kin.

But it was hard to break away. Her grandparents had been her mentors, her solace in a disrupted childhood, her source of wisdom and comfort. Without them she would be terribly alone. Already she was isolated. Her friends from school had all gone their ways, most to college, some to jobs in other towns or in the city. Greg, who had tried and failed to win her forgiveness for his desertion, was at Brown, studying law. Marion was at Bryn Mawr. Like Jenny, they came home, trailing an aura of growth and adventure. In the first year after she left school and Grandpa began paying her an adult wage, her access to money, to nice clothes, to Marco and his car, gave her a boost in maturity. But now they were overtaking her. Even Jenny, she sensed, was overtaking her. Dimly she saw herself drifting into marriage with Marco, and not even for love, like Nonna, but merely from habit. She lay in her bed in her darkened room, listening to her father shuffling about the house at four in the morning and trying to fathom up strength to plan, to change, to break out. But instead the trivia of life – tomorrow's menus, bills to pay, a new supplier

159

to be found, a new waitress to be interviewed – rushed in, filling every cranny of her mind.

Through the thin walls of the house, she heard Joseph's coughing begin.

Marco's trailer – old, dilapidated, rusted at the lower corners – sits behind the restaurant, tall weeds growing up through the rust-encrusted towing bar. The wheels are sunk deep in the sandy ground, the tyres flat, cracking with age. It will never move again, but disintegrate quietly here where it sits. *Like all of us*, Anne thinks. Occasionally Anne goes inside to get something – Marco's cigarettes, a clean apron – but aside from that she does not enter it. It is not a love-nest. It is too close to the restaurant, and under the watchful windows of Grandpa and Nonna's own house. And so they are reduced to the red Mustang, its dark, cramped back seat, its swaying springs, and the anonymity among other cars parked for the same reason beside the night waters of the Bay.

In November the car is stuffy with closed windows, the heater motor, their own shortened breaths. Marco moans his back is sore. Anne performs acrobatics. Half-satisfied, they drive to her house without looking at each other. One night, when the work is finished and they have locked the doors of the restaurant and the bar, Marco leads her to the trailer instead. Anne argues, embarrassed and worried, but he coaxes and pleads. Then they are in his bed, gloriously comfortable, grandly naked, enjoying the luxury as much as each other. They make love again and again. And then, just as Anne is rousing herself to dress and wake him to drive her home, she falls asleep. She sleeps wonderfully, and wakes with light outside and the warm curve of his back against hers.

Panicked, she peers at her watch and in the grey light reads six-thirty. She slips from the bed. Marco mutters something and curls up tighter, the blankets gathered around his dark head. She regards him almost tenderly, recalling the pleasure he gave her. Then she dresses in the clothes she wore the night before, opens the metal trailer door, and climbs down the crumbling steps into the weeds.

The dawn light brings an ancient memory of herself and Jenny camping out in the meadows behind the Uncles' house. Although

160

it is July, the night is clear and cold and they sleep restlessly, and wake so early that their own house is still silent and locked. But Uncle Eddie takes them in and gives them cups of milky coffee, thick with sugar, which Anne drinks with sickening relish. The taste of it lies treacherously in her mouth even in memory, and she creeps through the damp cold weeds now, assaulted by recollected nausea. At the corner of the trailer she meets Grandpa in his dark suit and hat, returning from mass. He stares at her, takes everything in.

'So,' he says. 'You will marry this boy now?'

And so Anne left home. It was a brave act, because she was leaving everything and going to nothing. The inheritance, tattered though it was, that she had worked for from childhood, was abandoned. Grandpa offered it to her now as Marco's wife. He would not offer it again on any terms. Marco was happy to marry her, having always assumed he would do so one day anyhow. With the promise of the restaurant as dowry, since Grandpa's offer was, in old Italian fashion, to him as husband, not to her as wife, the prospect looked golden. When Anne refused him, the twin loss of assured prospects and masculine pride turned him vengefully bitter. He allied himself with her grandfather and his brothers and they formed a united front. Only Nonna, boldly defiant of her husband, was on her side; and her father, who understood exactly what she had needed from Marco. Neither had much influence. Her mother understood nothing at all.

'But you must love him,' she said. 'If you did *that*. He's a nice boy. Who are you waiting for?'

'No one,' Anne said. 'I don't want to marry anyone at all.'

Her mother looked grieved. She said, 'This is my fault.'

Anne said fiercely, 'It's *not* your fault. You're a wonderful mother. You're wonderful to Joseph, and to Jenny. And to me. Jenny's brilliant and Joseph is getting on really well.'

'And you?'

'I make my own trouble,' Anne said.

She left her mother, standing at the washing machine, loading in Joseph's diapers and daily bed linen, and went through to the room she shared with Jenny. She took off her black skirt and white blouse that had been her uniform at the restaurant for five years and dropped them on the floor. She rooted in her closet and took out a pair of jeans and a college sweatshirt that Jenny had given her, and took them and fresh underwear to the bathroom.

She stood a long time under the shower, scrubbing herself carefully, washing her hair, watching the rivulets of shampoo run down her body. She was thinner than in her school days; cooking in the restaurant ruined her appetite, and her body had changed shape in some subtle way since she had become Marco's lover. She studied it, remembering his hands upon it, and then consciously she took it back from him and claimed it for herself.

She got out of the shower, dried, and dressed herself in the jeans and Jenny's sweatshirt. In the bathroom mirror her steamed up reflection looked young and innocent, free of make-up, her hair in wet spikes. Excitement filled her, and a childish sense of adventure. *Look out, world, here comes Anne Conti*, she thought.

She went into the living-room but found only Joseph there. He was lying quietly in a bar of afternoon sunshine, staring upwards into its full light, transfixed. She came closer, knelt and gently turned his face towards hers. He whimpered and turned back, seeking whatever dim light his eyes discerned. 'Come on, sweetheart,' she whispered. 'That's not good for you.'

She turned his face towards her again, and lowered herself to the floor so she lay beside him. *Joseph-Land*, she thought suddenly. It was what she and Jenny, as children, had called the floor. She turned on her back, briefly, and looked up at the ceiling, the dull, papered walls. She squinted her eyes shut so that only the barest light entered. *Joseph-Land*, she thought. She rolled towards him, slipping her arms about his bony shoulders, drawing him closer. His long, bent arms came up against her chest, the hands like thin white claws. She rested her chin against his crew-cut hair. His skin felt damp and cool, and smooth, like that of a baby. 'Sweetheart,' she whispered. He made a low sound of contentment, safe in the shelter of her arms. 'Sweetheart,' she whispered again, 'I'm going away.'

April 1966; spring has come overnight to the campus of the college. It is a new campus, bulldozed out of the rolling wooded hills, a discreet distance from the dull industrial city of Binghamton. The dormitories and classroom buildings are red brick,

162

trimmed with cool white marble, modern and simple. The land-scaping is basic, long sweeps of roughly tended lawn, now scattered with dandelions, concrete pathways, clumps of newly planted silver birch. Its students customarily dismiss it with rueful contempt, but Jenny loves it. After almost two years she is still childishly delighted to be here thanks to a Regents Scholar-ship, a special bursary for skills in English, and her father's gritty determination.

Her whole first year, Jenny worked frenetically, rarely leaving the library or study lounges, her only social life a series of secretly harboured crushes on unattainable boys. This year, she has loos-ened up. She has friends, shares long lunches in the snack-bar, spends evenings with her guitar in the music lounge, singing Scottish ballads. Since autumn she has had a lover.

He is a tall farm boy from upstate New York. Like Jenny he is Catholic. They met in a philosophy class, arguing about God. The argument has gone on all year, across snack-bar tables, on long snowy walks, on the ice-skating pond. It accompanied each step of their hesitant dance towards bed and, even now, months after their mutual surrender of virginity, it shadows and occasion-ally threatens to curtail their love-making. The boy, Tim, has traded off his Church for love, and is in misery about it, moping about on Sunday mornings, forbidding himself mass. But Jenny compromises gloriously, frequents the confessional, makes extravagant promises, extravagantly abandoned. She attends church, takes communion, shrugs off inconsistencies. Two years into the liberation of education, Jenny is Catholic to the core, an odd fish, swimming the wrong way in a world divesting itself of God.

She has had her flirtation with apostasy. Judaism entranced her throughout her first semester. A crush on an apostle of Alan Watt led her briefly into Buddhism. Dutifully she followed enlightened friends through a Unitarian service and all last spring she dabbled in playful amusement with a community of Mor-mons. Never, throughout two years of curiosity, has she failed to attend mass.

Tim has moved off campus into an apartment in the town, where they can make love. After, he lies in the rumpled bed, smokes cigarettes and mourns his soul. 'I'm going to hell for you,' he says dramatically. He is miffed that Jenny seems disinclined to accompany him. They both regard themselves as seriously in love, but they do not discuss marriage, except as an inevitable consequence of the dreaded accident of pregnancy. Today, Jenny's period is late and a cold shadow underlies the warm spring day.

She is late too for her nine o'clock class. They have spent the night off-campus. Her room-mate, and all the girls on her floor, lie dutifully, protecting her. She does the same on other nights for them. After a childhood of obedience she finds the rule-breaking as invigorating as the love affair. In the car, after an earthy and strenuous night, they argue philosophy all the way to the campus and part with a frustrated kiss. Jenny runs to the English department, boot-heels thudding on the concrete walk, long tail of clipped-back hair bouncing on the shoulders of her man's flannel shirt.

Her costume – tall leather boots, blue jeans, black turtleneck, red and black checked shirt – is an unvarying uniform. She has other clothes, but rarely wears them, preferring to wash these to faded death instead. She hasn't worn a skirt in a year.

Jenny is carefully careless about her appearance. She wears no make-up but washes fanatically, showering morning and night. She shampoos her long hair every day. It is dry and brittle, the ends splitting at their colourless tips. The mousy brown is paler than it was, and Jenny is pale too from the long winter and late nights. 'Pale and interesting' her honey-skinned Jewish room-mate calls her, enviously. The envy is mutual. The physical obsesses Jenny; she thinks of sex with Tim all the time and she no longer contemplates being even a beautiful nun. Nor does she dream of a home in the wilderness with Joseph. He has drifted from her mind. She has drawn away from him, from all the family. Sometimes she does not even think of them for days. Except, of course, for Anne.

Anne arrived just after Thanksgiving, her plans made in haste in the family turmoil of the holiday weekend. At first Jenny was piqued; her private free world intruded upon, her new friend-ships threatened by old family rivalry. She kept Anne at a dis-tance from her friends. But Anne lived her own life, even there, and moved in a different world. She had no interest in arguing about the universe, singing Scottish ballads, protesting the war.

She had no courses to complain of, no professors to ridicule. She was only there because Jenny was there, she needed a place to stay, and one upstate city was as good as another. She got a job tossing pancakes in an Aunt Jemima's restaurant near the campus, and begged a bed in the tiny back room of Tim's apartment. On the nights Jenny and Tim spent there, she slept in Jenny's bed on campus instead. She used all of the campus – snack-bar, dormitories, library, gym – as if she were as much of a student as Jenny. She did it with such confidence that no one thought to challenge her. Sometimes, for fun, she sat in on Jenny's philosophy class and threw irksome questions at the pompous young professor, leaving him floundering in a sophist tangle.

They met after Jenny's Chaucer class to drink coffee in the Student Center. Anne was wearing jeans and a sweatshirt and a green duffel coat; her student disguise. In a green book-bag she had stuffed her Aunt Jemima uniform. She said, 'I made your bed. Marcia wants your Shelley notes. And your roommate borrowed your brown turtleneck. Did you have a nice night?'

Jenny shrugged. 'Yeah, fine.'

'What's wrong?'

Jenny's freckled forehead wrinkled. She rubbed the side of her nose. She looked like she always did when in trouble, as a child. 'What is it?' Anne asked suspiciously.

'How late is late?' Jenny said.

'What do you mean?'

'How late is a late period?'

'Jesus *Christ*!'

'Be quiet,' Jenny whispered painfully. She ducked her head down low by her pile of books. 'You don't have to tell the whole world.'

'How late *are* you?' Anne whispered back.

'A day.'

'You're joking.'

'I'm not. I'm a day . . .'

'You can *tell* you're a *day* late?' Anne looked incredulous as well as relieved.

'I'm really regular.'

'You must be like clockwork. Look, kid,' she said with a wry grin. 'Come back in a week and tell me your troubles. In the meantime, go run around the gym or something.'

Jenny grinned. 'I'm really nervous about it,' she laughed.

Anne nodded and then looked suspicious again. 'Jenny,' she said carefully. 'You are *using* something.'

Jenny's face was calmly unexpressive. 'No.'

Anne's coffee cup halted in mid-air. She stared and said quickly, 'Well then, *he* is.'

'No,' Jenny said. 'He isn't either.' The cup hit the saucer, splashing coffee across the formica.

'*What?*'

'Anne, it isn't allowed. *You* know that.'

'You mean you're not using *anything*? Neither of you? Oh for Christ's sake, Jenny!' Anne was shouting again. Someone lowered a book and glowered. A party of bridge players looked interested. Anne got up, crossed the wide linoleum floor to the jukebox and stuffed a handful of coins in. The Byrds. Marianne Faithful. Baez. She waited for the first rowdy chords and went and sat down by her sister. 'Right,' she said, shielded by the jangly chorus of 'Mr Tambourine Man'. 'You and I are having a talk.'

'There's nothing to talk about, Anne. It's a sin.'

'Oh Holy Mother,' said Anne, burying her face in her hands. She looked up slowly, 'And I suppose screwing him every weekend isn't?'

Jenny looked away. She knew it was, but it was a pure, clean sin; romantic; almost holy itself. She said, 'It's different.'

'*Sure.*'

'Anne, leave me alone. It's my business.'

Anne leaned forward and caught her baggy sleeve. 'Look kid, my little sister getting pregnant is *my* business too.' She looked away, to the tall windows and the green and gold lawns. 'Mom and Dad don't need *another* disaster,' she said.

Jenny stiffened her back, pulled her sleeve away. She reached up and unclipped, realigned, and reclipped her long brown hair. She said, 'It wouldn't be that much of a disaster. I'd just get married, that's all.' Her voice was dull and practical.

'Jenny,' Anne whispered, 'don't be like that. Don't throw your life away. You've got so much, you've done so much.' She paused. 'It would be different if it were me, but *you*.' Jenny

166

looked up, amazed. 'You've got so many plans. And you're so brilliant at school. And what about Edinburgh? You're going to Edinburgh next year. How are you going to do that married and with a brat?'

Jenny dropped her head forward and studied the table, solemnly spreading out a coffee spill into a line with her finger. 'I'm not sure I'm going,' she said. 'Tim doesn't want me to go. And anyhow,' she added quickly, 'I haven't even been accepted yet.' Anne waved that away as the triviality she knew it was. No one was turning Jenny down.

'You're giving up Edinburgh, you're giving up Celtic Studies which you've been dying to do since last summer, you're giving up your *degree*, for God's sake, for this jerk?'

'He's not a jerk.' Jenny looked up, her eyes glittering. 'And I'm not giving up my degree. I can get my degree here.'

'You can't get Celtic Studies here. And if he asks you to give it up, he's a jerk.'

'I *love* him,' Jenny protested. 'Don't you understand?'

'You love getting laid. Don't we all,' Anne added, having not been laid for longer than she liked to think. 'But it isn't everything.'

'You're really crude, Anne,' Jenny said.

'Realistic. Come on. We're going to town to find a doctor to put you on the pill. That one Marcia uses. Unless Romeo would like to start using a sheath?'

Jenny glared. Finally she said, 'He thinks they're disgusting. He says he wouldn't touch them.'

'Oh great. Not just a jerk but an asshole. Come on then, kid, looks like it's up to us.' She pulled Jenny to her feet. 'Marcia's in her room; we'll get the address.'

Jenny followed, resentfully obedient. At the door of the snack-bar she stopped. 'What about the Church?' she said.

Anne stopped too, her pretty mouth twisted wryly at one corner. 'Jenny, there's plenty of time to be a good Catholic when you're old.'

Anne and Jenny stand crushed together in the crowded corner of the Student Center by the telephones. Jenny presses the receiver hard against her ear, covering the other ear with her hair and her hand. Around her people are shouting, shoving, laughing. She struggles to hear her mother's answering voice. Anne grins at her, waving the roughly opened envelope in triumph, making a thumbs-up sign.

'Mom?' Jenny shouts.

'Hi, Jenny. Wait a moment. I have to check him before I can talk.'

Jenny puts another coin in, nods vigorously to Anne, 'She's checking Joseph.' She waits, and hears her mother return.

'He'll be OK for a minute. What is it, darling?' The voice is strained, edgy.

'I've made it, Mom!' Jenny shouts.

'What, dear?'

'I've made it into Edinburgh. They're accepting me.'

There is a distracted pause. 'Oh. Oh, have you, dear?'

'I'm going abroad, Mom,' Jenny says. 'I'm going abroad for my whole junior year.' Saying it redoubles her excitement. Anne pounds her on the back in mock congratulation and she nearly chokes. 'Mom?'

'Wait a minute, darling. I can hear him . . .' Her mother is gone a long time. Jenny's excitement fades. The money runs out and she signals madly to Anne for more coins. Friends rally around, dimes and quarters are thrust in her hand. Eventually, her mother returns.

'I'm sorry, dear. What were you saying?' The voice is thin, cracking with exhaustion.

'I'm going to Edinburgh next year.'

'Oh that's very good, dear. That's very good. We'll have a good talk later, honey. I'm sorry. I have to go, darling.'

'Yeah, sure,' Jenny says. She hears the phone click off and slowly takes it from her ear, hangs it up. Her ear burns from the pressure. Her eyes sting. Anne is watching, the letter still clutched in her hands. Jenny grins, shrugs, wipes her eyes with the sleeve of the flannel shirt.

'Is she glad?' Anne asks.

Jenny grins again, lop-sidedly, 'Yeah,' she says brightly. 'She's really thrilled.'

Anne drove Jenny to the Pier to board the student liner that would take her to England. The logistics of a family send-off with the massive complication of Joseph were too daunting, and so

Jenny said her goodbyes in the dim light of a September dawn on the doorstep of the ugly little house that had been her home for eleven years. Instinct, utterly without rational foundation, told her this departure was large and final. She cried, hugging her father, still in his pyjamas and robe. He was very practical, reminding her of her travellers cheques, her bank draft, her passport, her tickets.

'For Christ's sake, Dad,' Anne said. 'She's been once already. She's a big girl.' She was half laughing and half annoyed. Emotion unnerved her, and Jenny's sentimentality irked as well; she would give anything just then to be in Jenny's shoes, going somewhere exciting, with no worries. All Anne had to look forward to was a return to Binghamton, the tiny apartment she had found to replace Tim's back room, and days divided between her job at Aunt Jemima's and her own new fledgling business.

She had begun the business in the middle of Jenny's final term at college. In the beginning it was very simple. Her customers were all Jenny's friends, and she had only one commodity: earrings. Not just any earrings, but the long, exotic, silver or base-metal dangling earrings that were *de rigueur* amongst Jenny's set on the campus. The neat pearl studs that their mothers wore, and which comprised the total stock of the old-fashioned Binghamton department stores, never appeared on a student ear. Earrings were bought in the city during vacations, coveted, borrowed, treasured; the more extraordinary, the more beaded, the larger and more fantastic the better. Anne saw a gap in the market and plunged in. A quick trip to the city and a day spending her carefully hoarded wages around the jewellery shops of Eighth Street, and she was in business. She created a series of display cards, expertly sewing black velvet on to stiff card, enclosed them in a large, beautifully decorated folder, and began hawking her wares around the dormitories at night.

Her presentation was professional and her pursuit of a market both vigorous and instinctive. She quickly developed a side-line in ear-piercing, with an ice-cube and a sterile needle, for fifty cents extra. She supplied gold sleepers for the initiate, dabbed iodine on ear lobes, and provided astute fashion advice, suiting the appropriate hoops, bangles, or cascades of Indian silver to face and hairstyle.

Rapidly, she expanded. She brought back a few silver rings in unusual shapes and, when they sold also, bought more. She added bracelets and strings of African and Indian beads. Skirts were getting shorter and shorter that winter, and extravagantly patterned tights filled the gap between high boots and hem-lines; Anne found the best and most interesting, bought up a selection and brought them North.

It was all getting too bulky to haul around the dormitories, and so she made an appointment with a local bank, dressed herself immaculately and brazened her way past a smitten Binghamton bank manager to secure a loan. Then she bought a battered Volkswagen and filled the back of it with her 'shop'. Parked in one of the big college lots, she did business in the open air, like a gypsy, moving from lot to lot lest the authorities take notice of her and object.

It was working well: with her salary from Aunt Jemima's as well she had enough to pay the rent on her own apartment in one of the shabby wooden Victorian houses in the poorer quarter of town, and she was now looking for a shopfront. But the price of success was high. She spent nothing on herself. She had no social life, no free time. Sleeping late on a Sunday morning was her only treat; she couldn't even afford a Sunday paper. She missed Marco. She had had no lover since him, and no companion either. Occasionally she still saw him, on trips home, and visits to her grandparents, and she could almost have been tempted back to him by sheer loneliness, had he not already found another girl. Grandpa had made him a partner in the restaurant; he was becoming the heir. Anne did not really mind. In truth she wanted neither him nor the restaurant. Her life was spartan now, but what she worked for and what she had were all her own. But she was sorry that Jenny was leaving; the prospect of the dull old town was drearier without her companionship, and the campus without Jenny would seem alien and cold.

'It's only a year,' Jenny told her. They looked at each other sadly in the dim light, the same finality which Jenny felt enveloping Anne.

'It'll be all over before we know it,' Anne said. They hugged each other.

Anne said, 'You'd better go in and say goodbye to Mom and Joe. We've got to hit the road.'

The house seemed distorted by her departure, her suitcases

and backpack crowding the narrow hall, the fluorescent lighting in the kitchen unseemly in the early hour. Her mother had been up since four, getting Joseph ready to see her off. He was fractious and unsettled as any young child whose routine has been broken. His father had lifted him into his chair; at fourteen, although thin and small for his age, he was still too heavy for anyone but their father to lift from his bed, or his bath, or into or out of his chair, and thus both his parents were required in almost permanent attendance. When Jenny went into the living-room, her mother was brushing Joseph's hair, gently smoothing it into place. He struggled and fought. *Like any boy*, Jenny thought, and wondered at it, that apparent touch of normal adolescent behaviour springing from the total abnormality of Joseph's life. As she watched, a vision flitted across her mind of the other Joseph, the fourteen-year-old, tall, bony, pimply, bumbling and graceless like any teenager; that Joseph who would have been had the thing that had happened not happened at all. She could, at times, see him so clearly it was as if a ghost walked through the room. He looked more like her mother than her father, more like Jenny than Anne. She *knew* him, knew his expressions, his voice, even the things he would say. *Piss off, Sis. It's going to be real peaceful without you.* She smiled to herself, and came and knelt down by his chair.

'Hey Joe,' she said.

'He's a right terror this morning,' her mother said. She leaned over fondly and said, 'Aren't you, hey? Are you a terror?' She stroked the side of his face. He jerked away.

Jenny reached to take one of his hands. She felt his manner change at her touch. She caught both hands in her own and patted them gently together. 'Patty-cake, patty-cake, baker's *man*,' she whispered. He giggled softly, flopping his head back, wriggling in the chair. Jenny looked up and met her mother's eyes. They were soft and wet.

'He's going to miss you,' her mother said. Jenny wanted to say, *And you? Will you miss me?* but her mother was looking down again at Joseph, fondling his hair.

'I'll miss you too, kid,' she said, hugging her brother, burying her face against his neck, drinking in the smell of fresh soap, baby powder, urine, the smell that was inextricable from her consciousness of home. 'Back soon, sweetheart, back soon.' He

171

giggled, enjoying her embrace, waiting for a new game to start. As always, she was his favourite. As she held him, an awful thought settled upon her, that a year was too long, far longer than she'd ever been away before, too long by far. He would not remember her. He would have forgotten her when she came home. It hurt desperately, and worse hurt came when she wondered, Would he miss her before he forgot? Would he long for her, in his secret silence, wonder about her, mourn for her, and abandon hope? She sobbed, holding him close, rocking him up against her, and then she let him go.

She stood up. Her mother was watching, her thin, lined face grey in the dull light, shabby, like the carpets and wallpapers of the worn shabby house. 'Will you be all right?' Jenny said uncertainly, realizing she had chosen a hopelessly late hour to ask.

Her mother shrugged. She made the smallest wry smile. Then she leaned over her son. 'Oh, we're all right. We're always all right, Joe and I.' When she looked up, her eyes were bright and defiant.

Jenny stepped back. 'I'm going now, Mom.'

'I'll say goodbye here, dear.'

She leaned over Joseph's chair and kissed her mother on the cheek. She wanted to hold her and be held, but with the chair between them it was impossible. And then she went out with her sister, and left her mother behind with her last, loyal child.

172

X

Jenny's first term at Edinburgh was lonely. She loved her courses in Scottish history, Celtic poetry and Gaelic, and she loved the grey, wet city, but she missed Anne and her family. She missed Tim. She even missed her roommate although they had done little together but quarrel. She stayed in a university bedsit in Bruntsfield that she had foolishly chosen for its size and grandeur; it was the first-floor drawing-room of a Victorian villa with a marble fireplace and rococo cornicing around the ceiling. But the fireplace was boarded up, a tiny metered gas fire sitting instead on the splendid hearth, into which she fed a constant stream of shillings in return for meagre heat. She sat at her typewriter in front of a vast wooden table in the huge, monastically furnished room, shivering as she worked.

Every other weekend, she packed her books and a spare pair of jeans and took the train from Waverley to Glasgow to stay with her grandmother. It was a journey of less than two hours, and Jenny regarded it as commuting distance, although her new British friends thought of it as a major expedition. The weekends refreshed Jenny. She needed the touch of family. The closeness she had always felt for her mother's mother ripened into a new, adult companionship.

She saw her grandmother now as a Glasgow type, one of an army of work-worn, bird-thin women, pinched in growth by poor nutrition, wiry and tough from a lifetime of unquestioned physical labour. She had raised eight children, lost two to the war in early adulthood, and lost four more, Jenny's mother included, to emigration. Two of Jenny's uncles had gone respectively to New Zealand and Australia. An aunt was in Canada.

They were all strangers to Jenny, but she loved to hear about them, and their rough and adventurous tenement childhood. She found it wonderfully romantic, and her own suburban upbringing dull and colourless by comparison. Talking to Grannie unearthed hidden memories, her mother's tales of street games and gang rivalries, her own young dreams of running away to live such a childhood under Grannie's care.

But the old tenement with its common stair and shared lavatories was gone, reduced to rubble by urban renewal, and Jenny had never seen it. Her grandmother had been moved to a new council estate sprawling on the amorphous edge of the city, a spiritless grey place of bleak, brown, two-storey houses running in long terraces before patches of battered grass. Jenny rode a succession of slow, crowded buses from Buchanan Street to get there. Inside, the house was plain and, to Jenny's American eye, primitive. The rooms were square and soulless, with bland overhead lighting. The wallpapers, patterned and ugly, clashed with gaudy carpets and curtains of cheap synthetics. Grannie loved it. It had central heating and no fireplace to spread dust, and its own lavatory and bath. She scrubbed and polished everything and hung photographs of Loch Lomond and Ben Nevis and Skye. But she was lonely there, because her friends were either dead, or scattered about other such estates, and she clung to Jenny as much as Jenny to her.

Each Glasgow Sunday they went to mass together with lace squares on their heads, carrying missals and rosaries. They knelt side by side to take communion, and lit candles together for her parents and sister and Joseph. Grannie had never thought to ask if Jenny still went to church, but assumed it without doubt. Jenny wondered if she knew that she was the last of the family keeping the faith.

On the Glasgow weekends, Jenny and her grandmother talked so much, made so many cups of strong tea, pored over so many albums of photographs, that she rarely had time for work, and ended in belated study on the train back to Edinburgh and her classes. History absorbed her life: a twin history of Scotland. At the university she learned of Scottish heroes and Scottish battles, kings and queens, ballads and poetry; and from her grandmother she learned of shipyards and football and tenement closes, of wartime deprivation, German bombs, evacuation. Grannie

174

brought out ration books and recipes and cut off a minute piece of cheese to illustrate a week's allotment. She sifted through boxes of newspaper clippings of Jenny's mother as singer and actress in the early days of the war. She found a snapshot of Jenny's father in uniform, and a brown studio photograph of Jenny's mother on stage in the ENSA production in which she was playing on the day they met.

'She was so pretty,' Jenny said sadly.

Her grandmother brushed dust off the picture. 'She was my beauty. The lads hung round like flies around honey.' She smiled, showing her too-straight National Health false teeth. 'But you're the image of her, right enough.'

Jenny stared at the picture. 'Am I?' Then she said quickly, 'But Anne's the pretty one.'

Grannie sniffed. 'Pretty? That wee tinker? Brown as a darky, and eyes like pissholes in the snow.' Grannie had never liked Anne. Jenny giggled, guilty and pleased at once.

Sometimes, when they talked, each of them was so wrapped up in their own thoughts that they didn't really listen to each other at all. Grannie would go on and on about old friends Jenny had never met, and Jenny would talk about her parents and Joseph, and the words would meet somewhere in the middle, mingle and dissipate, unresolved.

'Poor soul,' was all Grannie ever said of Joseph. 'God bless the poor creature.' When Jenny worried that he was getting too heavy and awkward for her parents to manage, Grannie answered calmly, 'God gives strength to those who need it.' Then she told a story about a boy like Joseph she had known when she was a young girl in a mining village outside the city, and how his father had built a cart for him out of the wheels of a pram and a tea chest and the children had taken him every-where. 'His brothers were sick to the death of him, but there was no gettin' out without the daftie, that's what they called him, though he wasn't daft, really, just simple, so the daftie came everywhere. He'd sit in his cart while they played at the football, and every now and then they'd kick the ball his way to make him feel part of it. He seemed happy enough. Though you couldna really tell.'

'Joseph would have died if anyone treated him like that,' Jenny said, appalled.

Grannie shrugged. 'The daftie didna die. He was tough as old boots.'

Later in the year, Jenny made more friends and she stopped going so often to Glasgow. She felt guilty, and told her grandmother it was because of the papers she had to write. She joined the Country Dance club and on Wednesday nights learned Strathspeys and Reels and was hurled about the floor by tall, ruddy-faced Lewismen, homesick for the islands, and dark foreign students who gripped her hands ferociously in desperate courtship. At the weekends she went to the King's Theatre or the Traverse and afterwards sat in student flats talking solemnly of theatre and politics.

She was often lost; British politics were a mystery to her. But her friends were equally ignorant of America, drawing wild assumptions based on glossy magazines and Hollywood films. They would not believe that Jenny was not rich and held her personally responsible for the crassness of fellow countrymen and the sins of her Government. Usually everyone was good-natured, but sometimes they all attacked her at once for being a materialist and an imperialist and napalming babies in south-east Asia. Each day when she went for lunch at the Student Refectory she passed under a white daubed sign on the lintel: US OUT OF VIETNAM. She grew to resent it – not the sentiments, with which she agreed – but the ritualized crossed lines that turned the 'S' into a dollar sign. Later, when experience had taught her to read the British class system by accent as deftly as her friends, she recalled those public school voices railing against her supposed wealth, and resented it more.

A rainy November night: Jenny's new friend Elizabeth pounced upon her in the history library. 'I'm working,' Jenny said.

'Not tonight. You're coming to the Folk club. They've got Fergus O'Brien. He's marvellous.'

'I've got this essay.'

'Oh don't be a *bore*, Jenny.' Elizabeth didn't understand about essays. She had had one year of university, and dropped out to study cookery. Now she worked in the Laigh Coffee House, serving salads and wholemeal bread all week, spent her evenings in the Refectory with the students, and at weekends went home to her parents in Perthshire. Elizabeth was very beautiful. She had blonde hair that was long enough to sit on. She wore sandals and peasant skirts except when she was home in Perthshire, where she wore twinsets and pearls. Jenny thought she had the best of both worlds: all the fun of university with none of the work. Elizabeth's mother said Elizabeth was 'being tiresome'. Elizabeth said her parents were frightful capitalists and a complete bore. Being a bore was Elizabeth's worst condemnation.

'OK,' Jenny said, worriedly. She stacked her papers, returned her books to the desk. Her mind was full of the travails of Scotland.

'He's *gorgeous* as well,' Elizabeth said, and Jenny knew Elizabeth fancied this Fergus O'Brien and was taking her along for moral support.

The Folk club met in a dismal room, lit by a bare bulb, in a half-abandoned university building. It was so old that the curving stone stairs were shored up with struts of wood, and the upper floor was unused because of a leaking roof. The room was cold and damp, but bodies crowded together and made their own warmth. They were mostly students, but there were some older people too. Jenny brought her guitar and allowed herself, sometimes, to be persuaded to sing. She sang Joan Baez songs, faithfully replicated from the recordings. Other people did the same. But there were some real folk artists too, old men with fiddles, penny-whistles, bagpipes. And this time there was Fergus O'Brien.

He was the first person she saw as she entered the room, a tall man with red hair and a luxuriant red beard. He was too old to be a student, but younger than the grey-haired ballad singers – former shepherds and fishermen – whom the club engaged for authenticity. Jenny thought he looked like a Viking. He was sitting amid a crowd of students, mostly women, enjoying their attention. Jenny assessed him quickly and passed a scornful judgement. She was not interested in men that other women lionized. Then he got up, stepped on to the low stage, bowed professionally, and played a reel on his fiddle. Later he sang, 'The Bonny Earl of Moray'. His voice was a clear, emotion-wrenching tenor. The song made Jenny cry.

Other performers took the stage, and then there was a break and people shuffled around the dusty room, talking and tuning instruments, and Elizabeth grabbed Jenny's arm and they pushed their way through the crowd to Fergus O'Brien. Jenny knew she was being used as a foil, and that if Elizabeth succeeded in making an impression it would be her duty to fade out of sight and go home alone. But Jenny also saw the tall, dark-haired woman in black tights and a black leather mini-skirt, who hovered behind Fergus, kept proprietorial guard over his fiddle and guitar, and lit his cigarettes, and she knew things were not going to be as easy as Elizabeth imagined.

Fergus was signing autographs. Jenny was startled. So he was famous, at least in this city, perhaps in this country. She felt remote. She had never heard of him. When Elizabeth dragged her into his presence she felt silly, an autograph hound, a fan, and looked aside, annoyed. Elizabeth was praising his perform- ance in her cool, clipped voice. She was talking about things like 'interpretation' and the 'true folk idiom'. The man chatted easily with Elizabeth. He was flattered, responsive. Jenny turned to leave, glancing as she did at the woman in the black mini-skirt. She looked faintly bored.

'And who are you then?' She turned back. He was looking straight at her. His eyes were dark blue where she had assumed brown, and faintly offended.

She stammered, 'Nobody. I'm just Jenny.' She looked at Eliza- beth and shrugged, awkwardly. Elizabeth laughed loudly and Jenny turned away again and pushed back through the crowd. From a safe distance she glanced back. Elizabeth was leaning on Fergus O'Brien's arm, giggling, her blonde head close to his. The woman in the mini-skirt was watching Jenny with narrowed eyes.

Four days later, there was a call for Jenny at her bedsit in Bruntsfield. Her landlady summoned her to the telephone with the irritation she always showed when Jenny's presence intruded on her life. 'I don't know *who* it is,' she said briskly. And added suspiciously, 'It's a *man*.'

'Hello?' Jenny said, trying to sound safely uninvolved.

'I'm looking for nobody,' said Fergus O'Brien.

On their first date, Fergus told her that the woman in the black mini-skirt was his mistress, that he was no longer in love with her, yet did not know how to part from her and so had not tried. Jenny thought it was a pretty sodden excuse, but was honest

178

enough to confess to herself that she was both relieved and glad. Her sympathy for the mistress dissolved in a new current of self-interest. She was intrigued, and hugely flattered, and a portion of her was already in love.

She went out with him all winter. Almost immediately her life changed: he was older, only by eight years, but that seemed quite significant to Jenny at twenty. What was really significant was that he was not a student. With him she moved out of the student world, into the real world in which people were married, held jobs, had children. The history of Scotland seemed airy and rarefied suddenly, the Celtic Studies of the university fossilized and academic after earthy evenings of bothy ballads among Fergus's friends. Jenny's work suffered; the history library saw less of her. Everyone saw less of her; her friends, her bedsit landlady, her tutors. Weeks passed between visits to Glasgow. She forgot to write home. Fergus filled her life.

He was big, boisterous and exciting to be with. In his company, Jenny bloomed. Suddenly she was at the centre of the world, not at its periphery. At parties she was with the one man everyone wanted to talk to; at concerts she was back stage, at the hub of the excitement, comfortable with the performers, attuned to their humour, their nerves, their triumphs and failures. Fergus's friends, after a brief flurry of loyalty towards the now departed mistress, welcomed her, at first hesitantly, then warmly. For the first time in her life she had no doubt that she was attractive to men.

Almost at once she knew she would sleep with him and, after their second meeting, she went surreptitiously back on the pill so as to be ready. As it was, since he travelled continuously, only touching down for occasional days at his Newington flat, it did not happen for over two months. When it did, they fell comfortably into bed like husband and wife, with neither physical nor moral trauma. Jenny had grown accustomed to making accommodations with God. Her apologies were brief. Fergus, who, like Jenny, had been born Catholic and had managed to cling to the Church through what was, in his case, an otherwise totally chaotic childhood, made no apologies at all. He attended mass faithfully, kept holy days and said his rosary nightly, but it had never occurred to him that God might be serious about the seventh

179

commandment. Still, he asked her to marry him the first time they made love.

Between January and March he asked her seven more times. Initially Jenny laughed, particularly on the first occasion which appeared nothing more than a sudden back-sliding into Catholic guilt. Later, she smiled indulgently, because he chose such romantic situations: beneath the battlements of the Castle in the gardens of Princes Street; on top of Arthur's Seat, overlooking the city; out in the Pentland Hills where they had gone walking. Beauty then, if not guilt, inspired him. But when he asked in the morning, before she'd brushed her teeth, and when they hadn't even made love because she had her period and had lain instead with a hot-water bottle on her stomach, she knew she had to believe him.

'Don't be an idiot,' Elizabeth said. 'The moment he's sure of you he'll start playing around. He's that kind of bloke.' Elizabeth was touchy about Fergus. She had not quite got over the tacit insult in being passed over in favour of Jenny. She was thoroughly miffed for a fortnight, and then patched up any bruised pride by declaring Fergus a bit of a clown and making fun of his working-class accent. But she had the good grace to stop when she realized Jenny was seriously involved, and became sportingly helpful, lending Jenny clothes, suggesting venues for meetings, and making herself a comfortable part of their affair. She cared far less about losing Fergus than she did about potentially losing Jenny, however, and marriage seemed an awkward interloper in a happy and casual threesome.

'He wants a family,' Jenny said.

'A family! Children! How perfectly grotty!' Elizabeth raised delicately plucked eyebrows. 'Oh Jenny, you're not preggers for Christ's sake . . . ?'

'Not yet,' Jenny said placidly.

In April, she accepted. It was during the university Easter holiday, and Fergus had a week off between engagements. He took her north, and west, to the Isle of Skye, in the dusty green Bedford van in which he toured. It was the longest time they had spent together, and they approached it nervously, convinced by custom and the dire warnings of their friends that constant companionship would prove the undoing of romance. Instead they fell headlong into a new kind of love, subsisting so desperately upon each other that separations of even an hour seemed unbearable. They slept in the back of the van, out in the wet moorland in Fergus's tent or, strictly as Mr and Mrs O'Brien, between the nylon sheets of bed-and-breakfast landladies. They made love everywhere, rapaciously, without restraint.

It was on Skye that Jenny realized that the journey was a pilgrimage, and that Fergus had taken her all that way to sit on a bare green hillside above a ruined crofthouse and propose to her in a setting that suited his sense of destiny and romance. 'This was my home,' he said. Below them, a roofless rectangle of grey stone let in the sea wind through paneless windows. A tin-roofed byre housed wandering sheep. Lambs hopped, stiff-legged, on the mossy mounds of fallen walls. Rusty wire fences leaned in sagging tangles around the fading borders of abandoned fields. It was an archetype of the Highlands as Jenny had seen them: ruin and abandonment.

'Here?' she said.

'This was where I was a boy.'

It was true, but only in the deepest and barest sense of personal myth. In the lost croft below them Fergus had spent three years in a foster home. It was an oasis of pastoral peace in a childhood of urban strife and deprivation, a house full of children, and fiddle music, and flawless Gaelic voices. He had gone there at eight and left at eleven; the years before and all the years after comprising a wandering existence with his alcoholic mother between the cities of Glasgow, Liverpool and Dublin, in all of which segments of her wide-flung Irish family gave them temporary shelter. The brief spell of fostering when, for a while, the rickety framework of support broke down completely, was the healthiest, most stable, and happiest of his life.

But his mother returned, in the company of the newest of the many 'uncles' who had plagued his childhood, gathering her various and scattered children together to make a last stab at family unity. It lasted five years. When it was over, his mother was in an institution and his stepfather in jail. But Fergus was an adult then, sixteen, and he moved out and took his first job, as a builder's labourer in Glasgow. When he was eighteen he went back to Skye, seeking the woman who had fostered him, but she had moved away from the croft and he was too shy and too ignorant to pursue her further. Instead, he sat in the cold shelter of the empty house and swore to himself that one day it would be his home. What he would do there with his urban skills, and his rarefied love of old music, he did not force himself to imagine.

'The roof came off in a gale in 1960,' he told Jenny. 'I meant to come up and repair it, but I was playing with a group in Dublin and I never got back. After a winter like that, there wasn't anything much left to save.'

'Anyhow,' Jenny said, 'it wasn't yours. It must have belonged to somebody. It must belong to somebody now.'

Fergus looked boldly over the barren fields. 'The land belongs to those who work it,' he said.

Jenny thought it sounded grand, socialist, and unlikely.

Fergus leaned over her, bent her down on to the dried grass and kissed her. 'Come and live here with me,' he said, and Jenny said yes. On the hillside, in the open air, and in full sight of anyone passing on the road, they made love yet again.

On the way home, in the van, she told him about Joseph. It was awkward, because she had talked a lot about Anne, and suddenly it made no sense that she had never mentioned her brother at all. She started cautiously. 'There's something about my family you ought to know,' she said.

Fergus glanced across quickly and looked back at the road. When he spoke, his voice was quiet, betraying unease. She had learned already that the loud, boisterous side of him was a mask hiding infinite insecurities. He said, 'They won't let you marry me because I'm a bastard.'

Jenny laughed, 'Who the hell cares about that?' she said.

He relaxed a little, laughed as well and said, 'Almost everybody, when you scratch them. I know.'

'Not my family,' Jenny said at once. 'Look, it isn't about you, it's about us. About me. About me and my brother,' she said at last. Before he could express surprise, she told him everything about Joseph; how he was born, how he grew up, how he was now. She found herself shaking as she said it, the words tumbling out in disorder. When she was done, she added awkwardly, 'We don't know . . . nobody ever told us what caused it. Except, it's supposed to be just him. I mean, it's not supposed to be heredi- tary.' She steeled herself. 'But of course, it could be, you know.'

Fergus leaned, hunched like a truck driver over the wheel of the van. She could see only his outline in the dim, late twilight. It looked comforting, rounded and softened with hair and beard. He said, 'Poor little bugger.' His voice was gentle. He turned towards her and said, 'Hey Jenny, have you got a picture of him? You showed me pictures of everyone else.'

They stopped the van and switched on the interior light, and in an empty lay-by on a deserted West Highland road, Jenny carefully withdrew the one photograph of Joseph that she always carried, quietly hidden in the centre of her wallet, tucked into a piece of cloth on which were printed the words of St Anthony's Brief. Fergus peered at the picture in the dim light. They were all together, one summer day, beside Joseph's pool. Her Mom, her Dad, Anne, and Joseph, held in her father's arms. Marion had taken the picture and Jenny had kept it always because it was the only one of Joseph in which everyone genuinely looked happy.

Fergus said, 'He's like you, isn't he?' And Jenny, nodding, began quietly to cry.

Fergus hugged her and, over her shoulder, before he put the picture safely away, he read, aloud, ' "Behold the cross of the Lord. Flee, ye hostile Powers. The Lion of the tribe of Judah, the root of David, has conquered." '

It was after midnight when they reached Edinburgh. Fergus was going on, driving through the night for an engagement the next day in Birmingham, and so he took her to Bruntsfield and parked down the street from her bedsit so they could make their passionate goodnights under anonymous windows. Jenny was wary of offending her landlady; she was uncertain of her rights and did not wish to find herself homeless before the end of term. Fergus watched from the window of the van until she was safely at the door, and while she fumbled with her key he backed the van discreetly down the street.

Jenny's landlady was a highstrung Welsh woman and their relationship was strained. She was not old, grey-haired and cosy as Jenny had expected, but young and married with small children. Her husband's work had taken her away from friends and family. She was isolated, over-worked and perpetually short of sleep. She said, archly ironical, 'You wouldn't think a woman

183

with just two children and a house to look after would have much to do, but I have.' Jenny missed all the irony. She nodded pityingly and moved, oblivious, about her own affairs. She was an abysmal tenant. She left clutter on the stairs, hogged the bathroom, wasted hot water. Worst of all she habitually came in late and woke the sleeping babies and went to bed to the faint accompaniment of infant howls and adult curses. In years to come she would do penance for her sins, and remember in shame. Then, she blundered on in selfishness, wandering off to her classes beneath the nostalgic and envious gaze of the abandoned drudge.

'*I* was at university too,' her landlady said once, angrily.

'Were you?' Jenny answered with innocently crushing disbelief.

The key rattled in the lock and the door clunked open. 'Oh shit,' Jenny said as a light came on. She attempted to creep unnoticed up the darkened stairs, but another light joined the first and she stood blinking against it, peering up to the landing.

'Is that you, Miss Conti?'

'Did I wake you, Mrs Jones?'

'No. Not this time. This time, for once, I was awake.' In the distance a baby began to wail, but was ignored. 'Miss Conti, this is simply not good enough.'

'I'm sorry,' Jenny cried, half apologetic, half petulant. 'It was a long drive. We've been all the way to the Isle of Skye.'

'I don't care where you've been or who you're with.' Her narrow pretty face looked sour. 'What your parents think, I just don't know,' she added gloomily. 'But that's your business, I suppose.'

'Yeah,' said Jenny belligerently. 'It is.'

'Very well.' The landlady waved the side of her hand. 'Don't come to me when you're in trouble . . .'

'I wouldn't,' Jenny was outraged. 'If it's all right with you I'd like to go to bed.'

'You can't.'

'Huh?' Jenny stared, wearily disbelieving. If she was going to get thrown out, she'd hoped at least it would be in the daylight. 'Can't I stay here any more?' she said. She felt her confidence sag. She was tired, keyed up with emotion, and missing Fergus dreadfully already.

'You can't go to bed because there's someone in your bed. The *person* you gave your spare key to, to be exact.'

'I didn't . . .'

'Don't lie about it, Miss Conti. She's *here*.'

'Elizabeth?' Elizabeth had her key so that clothes, books, common property could be borrowed and returned.

'*I* don't know her name. She just came. This is my home, Miss Conti. My babies are here. I can't have perfect strangers . . .' But Jenny barged by her, up the curving stone stairs and into her room. Behind her, Mrs Jones shouted, 'I suppose you'll want that man here next?'

'Elizabeth?' Jenny said. She switched on the light. A large backpack sat in the middle of the rug and a figure, fully clothed, sat up on her bed. She was sleepy, jet-lagged, her short black hair tousled over squinting eyes. She grinned lop-sidedly, 'Hiya, kid,' she said.

Anne was on her way to Paris. She had stayed on almost a year in Binghamton, without Jenny. In that time her itinerant business had found roots in a small store front, and expanded into a general emporium servicing student needs; favourite articles of clothing, as well as the jewellery; joss sticks, statues of the Buddha and other esoteric deities; posters; and the rebellious accoutrements of the drug culture: hashish pipes, the ubiquitous cover-all-sins sunglasses, silver marijuana leaves to hang defiantly on neckchains. She never sold drugs, under or over the counter, or used them herself, but the paraphernalia surrounding them was but another form of fashion. She moved easily amongst the devotees of the drug culture, knowing their rendezvous, their contacts, their hours and venues. Too easily, as it turned out. A rumour of an imminent bust set toilets flushing campus-wide, and disgruntled pot-heads searching for a scapegoat. Suspicion centred on Anne. She knew everything and did not indulge. Rumours grew gloriously; from simple informer, she became in days a federal plant, a spy among them, one of the enemy. Her trade dropped to nothing. She was at first irritated, later exasperated, finally furious. Good sense told her to ride it out; the rumour would pass and the custom return. But indignation and disgust overrode her patience. She was sick of the whole scene anyhow, bored with the pretensions and the hypocrisy, of middle-class communists on the way to careers in advertising, self-deluding mystics, academic snobs. She knew they had turned on her chiefly because she was not one of them; she was working and they were above such materialist pastimes. She sold her stock to her assistant and the lease to a local man, packed her things, stopped briefly on the Island to see her family, bought a map of Europe and boarded a plane. She had a few hundred dollars and the confidence to travel until it ran out; a confidence rooted in the assurance that at any time, or in any place, when the need came, she could earn more.

'Why didn't you tell me?' Jenny said.

Anne shrugged. 'I thought it would be fun to surprise you.'

'I might have *been* here, if I'd known.'

After the initial delight of sisterly greeting, which had sent her landlady retreating in sentimental confusion, Jenny floundered into sudden resentment. Her new life with Fergus was private and emotionally full; she hadn't room in it just yet for Anne.

'Yeah,' Anne agreed. 'I thought I was going to be sleeping on the street or something. I went to that Student Centre place . . .'

'Refectory,' Jenny corrected.

'And nobody knew *where* you were. It sounded like they hadn't seen you in years.'

'They hadn't. It's the first week of term. We've all been on holiday. Anyhow, you found me.' Jenny was guiltily off-hand, her guilt directed less towards Anne than her education. It was Wednesday. Term had begun on Monday, a fact she and Fergus had managed to ignore.

'Well, I found your friend Elizabeth.' Anne paused. 'Where *were* you, anyway?'

'Didn't she say?' Jenny said, lightly.

'She grilled me for identity, and when I finally dug out my *passport*, she accepted I was your sister and gave me the key. She was pretty vague about you.' Anne rubbed her hair with the flat of her hand and stared, blearily suspicious, at her sister.

Jenny smiled to herself. Of course. Elizabeth: so wonderfully British when she chose, so very like her mother, all reserve and discretion. She said, still lightly, 'I was in the Highlands, with a friend.'

Anne found out about Fergus soon enough. Jenny was too proud

186

of him to keep him a secret long. And she really hadn't any need. But once Anne knew, her family were involved; whatever lay in the future for Fergus and herself was no longer private, and the intimacy of the honeymoon was over. Anyhow, she had no choice. She had promised to join him in Liverpool for a special gig at the weekend.

'You're leaving already?' Anne said, after her second night sleeping on Jenny's floor. 'You just got back.'

'I know. But I promised this friend . . .'

Anne looked briefly hurt but rallied quickly. 'Hey kid, I'll come with you. I've got a week before my Paris flight. I'll see some of the country.'

'It's just Liverpool,' Jenny said uneasily.

'I've never seen *any* of it,' Anne said. She stopped. 'Your friend won't mind, will she?'

Jenny sighed. She felt, for the first time ever, older than Anne. 'Gee, you're dumb,' she said.

Anne liked Fergus. She liked him a lot better than any of Jenny's student friends, both here and at home. She certainly liked him better than Tim. He was a man, not a boy with, despite his theatrical panache, a solid practical streak with which she could identify. He treated her with respect, because she was older, because she was independent, like himself, and mostly because he was clearly desperate to be liked by Jenny's family.

'He's real nice,' she told Jenny, who waited nervously for her judgement.

'He's Catholic,' Jenny added helpfully.

'Nobody's perfect,' said Anne. She narrowed her eyes. 'Christ,' she said, 'don't tell me we're back to Vatican roulette.'

Jenny turned red. 'No,' she said, looking away. 'But it wouldn't matter. He wants a baby anyway.'

Anne sat down on Jenny's bed, amongst the scattered articles of her clothing that she was repacking into her rucksack. She was moving out of Jenny's room to forestall the wrath of the Welsh landlady, and into a corner of Elizabeth's Tollcross flat. She leaned back against the wall. 'Oh, terrific,' she said.

'And so do I,' said Jenny, with a sweet and unbudging smile.

Anne spent the weekend in the company of Elizabeth while

Jenny went away with her lover and, because of that, the week in Scotland became almost a year, and Anne never got to Paris at all. She liked Elizabeth for the same reason she liked Fergus; she was real, living in the real world, interested in the things that interested Anne. She dressed well, and enjoyed what money could buy, and was weighed down with none of the fashionable asceticism of so many of Jenny's friends.

They were both willing to partake of menial work for the immediate benefits gained, and the essential difference between them – the wealth that Elizabeth sprang from and to which she could easily return – was not immediately relevant.

Elizabeth was playing at work as, the previous year, she had played at study, but her frivolity made her bold and cheerful and a willing partner to Anne's inventiveness. By the Sunday night they had resolved to found some glorious joint enterprise, and three days before Anne's intended departure for France, they found their opportunity.

Elizabeth was shopping for clothes. A lunch-time of flirtation with a group of young architects at the Laigh Coffee House had won an invitation to a weekend on the Isle of Mull. Elizabeth was delighted and, as usual, since such occasions rose with happy frequency in her life, she had nothing new to wear. A dismal sortie through her wardrobe in the Tollcross flat resulted in a fit of depression, an urgent telephone call home for further funds, and an advance on Princes Street. She took Anne along because she realized already that Anne had a better sense of fashion than anyone she knew.

Princes Street was not encouraging. The grand old establishments reeked tweed and good taste, the newer boutiques showed racks of identical trouser suits and mini-skirts in lifeless Crimplene. 'Oh why aren't I in London?' Elizabeth moaned. They veered off, over the North Bridge and into the Old Town, hunting amongst the smaller, more esoteric shops.

Tartan tinselry engulfed them on the Royal Mile. They retreated, shop by shop, down its length, stopped for tea, set out again, and were on the verge of surrender when Elizabeth halted in front of a window, pointed triumphantly and said, 'That's what I want.'

It was an Indian shop with brass plates, inlaid wood tables, and embroidered cushions scattered amongst a display of carved ebony elephants. The windows were smeared, the display dusty, the door held a 'Closed' sign that someone had forgotten to turn, since there were customers within. Anne located the bright splash of cloth that Elizabeth had indicated.

She said, 'That's a bedspread.'

'Oh, pooh,' said Elizabeth.

She turned to leave, but Anne said, 'Wait a minute,' pushed the door gingerly, and stepped inside. The shop was dark and cavernous, cool, and smelling of incense and tropical woods. It reminded her faintly of her own in Binghamton. She fingered a display of Indian bangles and earrings, stroked a cluster of bright silk scarves. Elizabeth followed her cautiously, looking around with refined distaste.

'They don't sell clothes,' she said.

Anne said, 'Wait.' She jingled a set of brass chimes to get attention, and a man came out from behind a curtain at the rear of the shop. He was dark and foreign.

'No, no,' he said. 'No skirt for English lady. Only sari.' He went to a shelf and took down a folded bolt of bordered silk.

'It's beautiful,' Elizabeth said.

'No good for English lady,' he said. But Anne reached for it and took it from his hands. She unfolded two lengths and wrapped them swiftly around Elizabeth's shoulders, looked critically, and took it back, handing it refolded to the shopkeeper.

'I can't wear a sari to Mull,' Elizabeth said.

'That one.' Anne pointed. 'That light blue.'

He handed the second sari to Anne, curiously, and she took it, and Elizabeth, to a mirror by the window. She draped it expertly around her, nipping it in at the waist with one hand and layering a swathe of silk deftly across her throat. 'Well?'

'It's gorgeous, but it isn't a dress, Anne. It's just cloth.'

'How much?' Anne asked the shopkeeper, and when he gave her an answer she said, 'And that bedspread? How much is that?'

In the street, Elizabeth was still protesting. 'They're beautiful, Anne, and I'm sure I'll do something with them, but what about Mull? So far I've got a sari and a bedspread and it's nearly five o'clock.'

'You have a cocktail dress and an evening skirt. Wasn't that

189

the order?' Elizabeth stopped on the cobbles of the Royal Mile, clutching her parcel. A light had dawned.

'Anne, you don't for a moment imagine I'm going to *make* them?'

'*We* are.'

'Anne, that's ridiculous. I can't *sew* to save my life.'

Anne laughed. 'This isn't sewing,' she said, tapping the parcel. 'It'll take about ten minutes. God, anyone can do this. We'll just have to persuade Jenny's landlady to lend us her machine. That'll be the hardest bit, I bet.'

Elizabeth was still standing forlorn in the shadow of Holyrood. 'Anne,' she said firmly, 'you simply don't understand what it's like to be *totally* inept. You Americans are impossible.'

Elizabeth was not, as it turned out, quite as totally inept as she had imagined, although Anne was forced to admit she came really very close. But it didn't matter. Anne had skill enough for both of them: Nonna had seen to that. Anne had grown up knowing that the best and most beautiful clothes she possessed were the ones that Nonna had made and, later, the ones she made herself. The fashioning of a simple sheath dress from a few yards of sari silk, and a fringed tapestry skirt from an Indian bedspread, was the easy work of an afternoon. Elizabeth went off to Mull with two Anne Conti originals in her case, more than pleased with her bargain. Anne stayed behind, returned to the shop at the foot of the Royal Mile and bought a dozen each of the saris and the bedspreads and went out looking for a sewing machine of her own. When she found it, she cashed in her Paris ticket to pay for it, and brought it home in a black Edinburgh taxi to Elizabeth's Tollcross flat.

Jenny was married to Fergus O'Brien on the anniversary of the day she arrived in Scotland. In the year that had passed neither she, nor her sister, had yet returned home. Jenny made a desultory effort to complete her university year, for the first time in her life barely scraping through her exams. Her funds and her visa were both rapidly expiring; she stretched the first and managed a three-month extension on the second. When the date of her expected return drew too close to ignore, she collected a mountain of British silver and telephoned home. Anne and Elizabeth stood beside her, feeding in the coins and, over a crackly

190

line, haunted by the echoes of her own voice, she told her parents that she was not coming back at all, but staying on in Scotland as Fergus O'Brien's wife. It never occurred to her to ask permission or even consult them in advance. With the supreme selfishness of people in love she simply cut herself free.

They made no real argument; they were in little position to do so. She was far away, and their only potential allies were on Jenny's side. Anne was backing her loyally, and so, indeed, was Grannie. Grannie was a fervent believer in marriage. Besides, she liked Fergus. He was Catholic and Glaswegian and she regarded him as one of her own. Jenny's parents capitulated without a fight. Their own lives, circumscribed by Joseph and now by the ill-health of Jenny's and Anne's grandfather, were too harried and limited for them to exercise any authority over her. Their only request, that she come home first and marry later, was financially impractical. As she talked, Jenny tried to conjure a picture of the house, her parents, Joseph; but the distance, the different time zones, and the vividness of her own new life came in between. The picture was blurred and remote, and as she hung up the phone it shimmered bravely for a moment and then faded with the echoes of the transatlantic line.

'Are they happy?' Elizabeth asked.

'Sure,' Jenny said lightly. 'They're really thrilled.'

Anne made Jenny's wedding dress. It was a splendidly romantic concoction of Indian silks on a medieval design, and Jenny looked wonderful in it. By the time of its creation Anne had already taken the lease on the Grassmarket shop, and she did her sewing in the back rooms there, rather than in Elizabeth's crowded flat. In the front of the shop, racks of long skirts, smock blouses and kaftans testified to her industry and seamstress's skills, and those of the two young Edinburgh girls she employed, part time, to help out. Students, and the Edinburgh theatrical set – actors, musicians, dancers – provided their custom, almost from the moment she opened her doors. She had not the money to advertise; for the first two weeks there wasn't even a sign over the shop door because it hadn't a name. People found her still. The colours within were brilliant against the drab light of Edinburgh, and she fed the air of exoticism by burning incense in little clay pots. Anne, Jenny and Elizabeth debated long and hard over the choice of a name, Jenny and Elizabeth leaning towards popular songs, current films, famous people, for inspiration.

'Sure,' said Anne, ' "Maggie's Farm" sounds great. But in two years it will sound dated, in five, ancient, and in ten no one will remember what it was about. I want something that will make sense in twenty years.'

'Twenty years!' Elizabeth cried, despairing. 'Could you bear to be still running a shop in twenty years?'

Anne smiled. She said, 'Yes. I could. But in twenty years I'm not going to be running a shop. In twenty years I'm going to be running ten.' She called it Anne Conti, and painted a sign with flowers in the corners in red and cream. When she hung it over the door, she said, '*That* will last.' Then she shrugged, 'At least as long as I do, anyway. After that, who cares?'

Jenny was married in Glasgow, in the church her grandmother attended. Unlike her mother, she remembered to post the banns in her own parish in Edinburgh, and to organize flowers and a simple meal. It was a modest wedding, attended by Fergus's fellow musicians, a sprinkling of her student friends, Elizabeth and, as her maid of honour, Anne. From her Grannie's house she telephoned home as a married woman for the first time. The line was bad. She shouted her greetings. Her parents shouted congratulations. The words tangled up and muddled with each other.

'How's Joseph?' Jenny shouted.

'What?'

'Joseph. How's Joseph?'

'I can't hear. Wait, I'll get your father . . .'

'It's all right. Just kiss Joseph for me.'

'What?'

'I love you,' Jenny cried.

'The line's dead,' her mother's voice said, clearly. 'I can't hear anything.'

'Mom?' Jenny said.

'Jenny?' Her father's voice came on to the phone.

'Dad?'

'Nothing. I'm getting nothing.'

'Mom, can you hear me?'

Her parents' voices came solemnly, chanting together. 'If you can hear us, have a wonderful marriage.'

'I love you,' Jenny cried, impotently, into silence. 'I love you all.'

She waited sadly until they gave up and then slowly put down the phone. Fergus said, 'Call again. We'll pay your Grannie.' Jenny shook her head.

She said, 'There's nothing . . . we've said all we have to say.'

They drove north, for their honeymoon, in the Bedford van, stuffed with backpacks, hiking boots, tent, and all Fergus's musical gear. They had a week together, alone in the hills, and then, without returning to Edinburgh, set off on the road. Fergus had engagements in Aberdeen and Dundee, and then in England. While they travelled they lived out of the back of the van, sometimes sleeping in it as well. Before she left, Elizabeth and Anne argued fiercely with Jenny that she remain in Edinburgh while Fergus travelled, finish her university course and take her degree.

'What for?' Jenny said.

'The Future,' said Elizabeth ominously.

'Fergus is my future.'

'Supposing he scarpers,' Elizabeth said.

'What?'

'Scarpers. Runs out on you. Buggers off. Men *do* that, Jenny. Some of the positively *nicest* men . . .' She smiled encouragingly.

'Fergus won't,' Jenny said, with so great a confidence in her love that she needn't even get angry.

'Other things happen.' Anne was cautious. 'You should have something, just in case . . .'

'*What* other things?'

'He could die, Jenny,' Anne said bluntly. 'You know, a car crash or something. He's on the road all the time.'

Jenny looked serene. She said, 'What would it matter then? I don't want to live without Fergus.' The absolute certainty comforted her, just as it made her content to be now all the things that frightened her: rootless, itinerant, financially uncertain, an urban gypsy travelling beside her wandering man.

XI

Jenny O'Brien sat cross-legged, heavily pregnant, in the sun-baked dried grass of a Rhode Island field. She wore a high-waisted flower-sprigged smock and ropes of multi-coloured beads with which the child on her lap played happily. Jenny was pink-cheeked from the sun and her long hair was crowned with a garland of Black-eyed Susans. Her bare feet were calloused and dusty and she covered them with the flounced hem of her dress as she leaned her unaccustomed weight against the fence at her back, closed her eyes and let the music soak, like sunlight, into her bones. It was her last Newport, she knew, and she wanted to remember it just like this.

A few feet away, Fergus was playing the Northumbrian pipes for a circle of eager young musicians. The lonely, alien sound drifted across the hot fields like a breath of Northern wind. Jenny felt a shiver of homesickness for Britain. Other kids, carrying guitars slung over shoulders, neck downwards in the fashionable way, entered the enclosure, casually joining the workshop. As they settled in the circle around Fergus, they glanced involuntarily at Jenny: the glances were curious, respectful, even a little awed. They knew she was not one of them, not a student or a groupie, but someone set apart, on the inside, within the honoured circle where everything happened. Jenny knew because they were herself four years before, when she came to Newport with Tim, moved among the crowds, stood packed together for the big concerts and glimpsed Dylan and Baez far, far away, tiny dots on the stage.

Now, she was in the centre, or, if not in the centre, as near to it as she was ever likely to come. She had learned that even fame had its hierarchies and that Fergus and his friends were still as awestruck by their own idols as the kids with the guitars were of them. Though Fergus's idols were unexpected. They were not the epic heroes of her generation, but other, older figures, whose fame was more subtle. Some had names she had not even heard. Fergus sought them out, the hill-billy stars, the Appalachian ladies, the city loners and work-worn black men from the South. He sat at their feet as the college kids sat at his, and Jenny was proud.

Jenny stood and walked across the enclosure with her queenly, pregnant gait, hand on the small of her back, her long dress trailing in the dust. Angus stumbled happily after her. She was aware of eyes upon her and knew she was at the zenith of her being: sun-washed, fecund, filled with nature's power. There was no one she would rather be.

Newport was the climax of Fergus's American tour. Afterwards, Jenny was going home for the first time since her marriage, bringing her husband and her little boy to meet her family. They would all be together again under one roof: herself, her mother and father, Joseph, and now Fergus and Angus too. Even Anne would be there, having carefully coincided one of her own infrequent returns.

It was Anne who drove to Greenport to meet them at the ferry, piling them and their rucksacks and guitars and teddy bears into their father's old car. Fergus filled the front passenger seat with his long body, stretching his dusty bare feet out in front of him, leaning curiously out of the open window, pointing at things. He loved America. He couldn't get enough of it. And he loved most of all the things he would have hated at home: fast-food restaurants, gaudy billboards, noise, lights, clutter. He was on holiday from his own sensibilities. Somehow, in America, nothing counted.

Angus fell asleep on Jenny's lap. She sat holding him quietly, suddenly afraid of what she would find as they drove the well-known way. Everything looked the same; startlingly unchanged in the time she had been away. Her parents' house sat at the end of its short walk, plain, ordinary, achingly familiar.

Jenny eased herself out of the car and passed Angus to his father. Fergus draped him over his shoulder and offered her his hand. She grinned and stood up, heavily, revelling in her temporary clumsiness. The hot air hit her like a soft wall. She drank it in, and with it the late summer smells of dust, hot tarmac, cut grass, barbecue smoke. Home. Sounds drifted from neighbouring yards: children's voices, a distant radio, dogs barking, a lawnmower; the outdoor sounds of American summer.

The two mimosa trees had grown tall and tossed pink tufts of blossom among their lacy green leaves. Rippling shadows crossed the grass. Jenny noted beds of flowers. Her father had taken to gardening now that he had given up most of his work. She walked reverently up the concrete path, her husband following behind. The screen door opened. An old man came out, shaded his eyes, peered and then smiled joyously. He came down the two steps in a quick, shuffling gait, holding out his hands. They were shaking as they reached for her, and she realized the old man was her father, not her grandfather as she had thought for a wild, disconcerting moment. Because, of course, her grandfather was dead.

He reached her, embraced her, laughing and patting her stomach. They both stared at it because it was suddenly hugely funny and that way they could avoid each other's eyes. She could not believe how old he had become. 'Where's Mom?' she asked, but her father was turning to greet her husband and to exclaim over his first grandchild. She was glad then that Anne was there to shepherd the introductions, because suddenly she wanted only to see her mother, who had not come out to meet her. She found her in the living-room, standing beside her brother's chair, just as she was on the day Jenny left.

'Mom,' she cried.

'Here's Jenny,' her mother said. She did not look at her but at Joseph, and Jenny mastered the need to run into her mother's arms and knelt down instead beside her brother. He had changed. She was not sure how. She reached for his hands but they were involved with each other, the fingers entwined. His face, lolling sideways, was turned half away. She reached to touch it but her mother stopped her.

'He's frightened by strangers,' she said.

Jenny couldn't believe it. She said, angrily, 'Since when?' And thought bitterly, *So now I am a stranger*.

'He doesn't see many people,' her mother said. 'He's not used to it.' She leaned over. 'Are you, pet?' she murmured. 'He'll get used to you when you've been here a while,' she added with a professional cool.

Jenny was filled with a desire to clasp her brother and to will him to acknowledge her, but she did not dare. Her voice sounded crisp and strained when she said, 'I'm hardly a stranger. I'm his sister.'

'You can't expect him to remember that,' her mother said.

Jenny thought, *She's punishing me. I went away and she's punishing me*, and then was ashamed of her childishness.

'Of course he can't,' she said, and she reached her arms around his chair to her mother who at last stepped forward, her face lighting, and fell into them. They hugged, but the big firm bulk of Jenny's belly held them half apart and they laughed and pointed at it and Jenny said, 'There's always *something* between us, isn't there?' They laughed again and she realized suddenly what had changed in Joseph. He was silent. The coos and gurgles and chortles, even the girning, had ceased. He was silent, his hands folded into each other, his blind eyes still, no longer wandering in their search for glimpses of light. They stared or did not stare into nothingness. *He's not here any more*, she thought. She felt the baby within her stir, and clutched at her stomach for comfort in her moment of grief.

Jenny's visit was meant to last five days. In the end it lasted nearly three weeks, not because anyone was particularly enjoying it, but because of the momentous thing that happened while they were there. It was, Anne thought afterwards, about the only good thing to come out of their return home. If, of course, it *was* a good thing at all.

Anne had returned to the States six weeks before, looking for a property for her first American outlet. She had two of the ten shops she had promised Elizabeth, the Edinburgh original, and the new, splashy and renowned Carnaby Street Anne Conti. Her trade had grown hugely in three long years of hard work, and the nature of her business had changed. She no longer sewed kaftans in a back room, nor took any part in production. She bought in all her stock from new, young designers. Buying was her best talent; buying and assessing the mood of street fashion. She spent her most productive days sauntering about London, watching what people wore. Her eye was on the young and the daring, the lovebeads and kaftans and military jackets; ironically on the people who dressed like Jenny. From them she drew her ideas, ideas which, modified, made wearable and less outrageous, sold to the broad base of people for whom she catered: the shopgirls and boys, the young married women, the more conservative students, who wanted fashion but lacked the confidence or imagination to create their own. Gradually, as she selected her designers, weeding out those who proved less popular, adding new ones who suited her line, the Anne Conti look emerged: colourful but not gaudy; startling but not outrageous, or even truly daring.

No new idea appeared first in an Anne Conti shop: her customers had not the nerve for new ideas. A feature writer in one of the slick magazines cattily, but accurately, described the Anne Conti look as 'fashion for the woman who thinks she's in the know'. Anne's staff were outraged, but Anne was quietly satisfied. Her customers didn't read the slicks. They read *Woman* and *Woman's Own* because that was what they could afford. At least, just yet. They were not wealthy yet. But they would be wealthy, one day, when their new careers were firmly grounded, their babies grown into school children, and their earnest ideals scattered behind them like so many faded flowers. When that time came, Anne would be there with them, at their service, and they at hers.

Coming to the States was her first big gamble. Edinburgh was easy. She had nothing to lose but a plane ticket to France. London was only slightly trickier. She had borrowed against the Edinburgh shop, but had good reason to be confident. She knew the British fashion scene. London, in spite of Elizabeth's woeful longings, was not light years from Edinburgh. But America – New York – was another planet.

'But you *are* American,' Elizabeth said. 'You must understand them.'

'I've been away three years. That's a century in the States.'

Elizabeth remained baffled, but Anne was shrewdly aware how different Americans were, how demanding of quality and variety; how impatient, even as she had been impatient with the Edinburgh of 1966 in which she could not buy a proper pair of jeans. The post-rationing wait-patiently-for-better-times mentality had never existed in the States. And Americans were conservative as well, a fact that Elizabeth, never having lived there, could not believe.

'Look at you,' Anne said, pointing to Elizabeth's tight little skirt riding just three inches below her butt, so short that she wore her knickers, frilly and lace trimmed, over her tights to enhance the inevitable view when she bent down. 'You couldn't dress like that in the States. There aren't any mini-skirts in New York.'

'But the *British* are reserved. Everyone knows that.'

'Until you let your hair down or roll your skirts up. Then you're about as reserved as your grotty seaside postcards, all boobs and bums.'

'How extraordinary,' Elizabeth said with the vague air of wonder she used for subjects of distaste. She remained unconvinced, but Anne knew she was right. Assessing the American market, and choosing the right place to launch herself upon it, was a venture fraught with dangers. She could lose it all, like she lost Grandpa's restaurant and the store in Binghamton. She had to get this right.

She had not the finances, nor the nerve, to attempt Manhattan. She was looking instead at the fashionable east of Long Island, where the artists and theatre people had their summer homes. For America she was shifting up-market, moving beyond the price-range of students in sandalled feet.

In the week before Jenny and Fergus arrived from the Newport Folk Festival, Anne found her venue, a white clapboarded bow-windowed shop fronting the sun-baked brick sidewalks of East Hampton. It was perfect, and what made it more perfect was that its real discoverer was not Anne herself but her school friend Marion, who, having won her Liberal Arts degree from Bryn Mawr, now worked for her father selling real estate. She had been seeking a site for Anne for three months, since Anne wrote to her from London, and finding it was her first major career success. Anne took it as a good omen that her newest venture should be launched by her oldest friend. Indeed, and ironically, by her two oldest friends. Marion's partner in the search was Greg Forsyth, graduate in law from Brown University, and trainee in her father's practice, a pleasant, unassuming young man who in another, distant world, had abandoned Anne Conti on the night of her junior prom. He was also Marion's lover and fiancé. Anne's bitter forecast had come true. Though no one was more surprised than Greg and Marion.

They had fallen into each other's company gradually over their university years, drawn together by their parents' friendships, social gatherings, common interests. In Marion's final year they began to date. He worked for her father during law school vacations. They sailed together, attended Yacht Club events, swam and played tennis. Common background formed common ground. Friendship became fondness and moved towards love. But always the strongest tie between them was Anne. They both missed her fiercely: Marion because she never replicated the friendship they had known, and Greg because he was still in love with her.

In the earliest years Greg took Marion out primarily for the opportunity to talk about Anne, to reminisce, to hear her name on someone else's lips, and to learn, by transparently unsubtle questioning, where she was now, what she was doing and with whom. Marion was a fount of information because she had never relinquished her relationship with Anne's parents. She saw them every school vacation and, when she began working for her father, dropped in at least once a week, drank tea with Louise and played with Joseph. When she had private things to share she shared them, as she always had, with Anne's mother, not her own. She told them about Greg.

'He's an idiot, waiting around for her. Anne's not coming back for anyone. Certainly not for him.'

'He's never forgiven his parents for making him do it.'

But Louise Conti had not forgiven the misery of her daughter's prom night, and had no sympathy. 'Anne was the first thing he wanted and didn't get. That's all that's wrong with him.'

Marion smiled and acquiesced but she was sorry. She liked Greg. She even loved him a little. But she was neither a doormat nor a fool. One steamy August night, after a barbecue at his parents' home, he drove her back to the little second-floor apartment above the law office that she rented at minimal rates from her father. He kissed her goodnight, as he always did, but this time the kiss was less formal, more sensual, and followed by a second. His hands, usually brotherly upon her shoulders, wandered down her back, and one slipped cosily on to her butt.

She removed it, briskly, and stepped back. He closed the distance, kissed her again. 'I love you,' he muttered suddenly, and he nudged her towards the wooden stairs. His face in the moonlight was softened with yearning. He had drunk too much, a rare occurrence.

'You don't love me,' Marion said. 'You love Anne Conti. Remember?' She stared at him, annoyed, turned and ran up the stairs and slammed the wooden screen door.

After that he didn't talk so much about Anne. And he started treating Marion differently: asking her out with more deference, taking her to nicer places, looking at her as they shared dinner as if he had not really seen her before. Which perhaps, with his cherished memory in between, he never had. He began to compliment her on her looks and he grew jealous of the attentions she had always received from clients and friends. It took him a year to win her favour, and by the time he did he was as much in love with Marion as he had ever been with Anne, though he doubted she would ever fully believe him.

When they got engaged, with a lavish party at the Yacht Club, it was only Marion who mentioned Anne.

'She said I'd do this,' she said thoughtfully.

'Who said?'

'Anne.'

He looked pained. He had buried the Anne ghost. 'Anne said you'd marry me?'

'She said I'd get you for myself. The day I tried to warn her about the prom. I couldn't believe it. I couldn't believe she could be jealous of me.'

'Do you think she will be?' Greg said.

Marion watched him wisely. She knew exactly what Anne felt. She had called Anne in London a month before, the day he proposed. 'Have you forgiven him?' she asked. 'I couldn't bear to be married to a man you hate.'

When Anne spoke, her voice was almost too quiet to hear. 'Yeah,' she said slowly, 'I've forgiven him.' And then, much louder, 'But you tell him from me: if he tries a shit-assed thing like that on you ever, I'll string him up by his silver-plated Forsyth balls.'

Marion smiled at her fiancé. 'I'm sure she'll be just a *little* jealous,' she said.

They met her together, at JFK, when she flew in from London. Anne and Marion ran into each other's arms, and Marion's young Ivy League lawyer stood in the background with Anne's luggage, scuffing his feet like a pimply-faced sixteen-year-old kid, waiting to drive them home.

Anne found the house grim. In the years since she and Jenny had left home it had become, perhaps inevitably, less a family home than a hospital ward. Joseph's bed had been moved into the living-room to avoid the difficulties of transferring him from room to room. Now physically, as well as emotionally, he centred the house. With no one else there, it hardly mattered anyhow. Strict routines had developed, and hardened in isolation. The influx of returning family – first Anne, then Jenny and her husband and child – was disastrous. Anne had stayed only a few days before realizing that her presence, far from being the happy treat for her parents that she had hoped, was an exhausting trial. She had gracefully slipped out of the way, moving her things into Marion's little apartment.

Her mother was tearfully apologetic. Her father begged her to stay. Both were visibly relieved when she left. She was still close enough to visit them every day, play with her brother just long enough not to upset him, and slip away before meals or bathtime or the visit of his physiotherapist, all of which were best organized by her parents. She had tried, and failed, to help. They had coped too long without her; it was beyond their capacity any longer to share their trials. She left with a mix of relief, guilt and grief: glad to be out of the oppressive heat, the smells, the tense, repetitive voices of her parents coaxing her brother through his grim day, but miserable to be shut out, by them and by him, a stranger now in their world. In the three years that had passed, all the laughter and good moments seemed to have gone from their lives. Marion said, 'It can't go on, but none of us knows how to make it stop.' But it was neither Anne nor Jenny who found the way, but Fergus O'Brien.

Anne had always liked her brother-in-law, but those hot late summer days on Long Island, he won from her gratitude and love. He brightened the gloomy household with his cheer, charmed her parents with his music and storytelling and, most of all, won her mother's heart with his utterly unfeigned devotion to Joseph. He played with him, carried him around, and sat for an hour or more at a time with Joseph's ungainly body sprawled across his lap while he read, or talked, or sang. Fergus loved children and Joseph was simply another child; he saw right through the damaged husk to the untrammelled infant soul within.

'You're so great with him,' Anne said gratefully.

'Ah, he's a good lad. Aren't you, Joe?' Fergus locked his big muscular arms around Joseph, rocking him like a baby. Joseph hummed to himself. He had begun crooning again, since Fergus had come.

'He's a wreck,' Anne said. 'He's far worse than ever before.'

Fergus continued rocking her brother. He began to sing, softly, in Gaelic. Then he said, 'I'll tell you one thing, love, he's the soundest soul in this house.' Anne laughed, a deep rich laugh, but Fergus looked at her solemnly. 'I'm not joking, love.'

Anne stopped laughing. She looked at him, and Joseph, carefully, and then she turned her face away. Behind her turned head, she heard his soft voice.

'Bejesus, Anne, it's not for me to be saying it, but this is a madhouse. It's killing your Dad and driving your poor Mam around the twist. And it'll not be doing this lad much good either.'

Anne turned abruptly back. 'Who are we to criticize?' she demanded fiercely.

'I'm not criticizing, love. I'm telling you what I'm seeing. I'm telling you what's in front of your face, as plain as day for you to see as well.' And then, quite suddenly, Anne saw it too, and wondered ever afterwards why she had not seen it five, even ten years before. But the answer was obvious: neither her parents, nor herself, nor Jenny, nor even Marion could see because they were all part of it. Only Fergus, the stranger among them, saw with the sad clarity of a stranger's eyes.

Anne took a deep breath and stood up. Fergus watched her, waiting. 'I'll talk to Jenny,' she said.

But that was not easily done. There was no privacy in the tiny house. And Jenny, pregnant and trammelled with Angus and his needs, was rarely out of it. She was either in the kitchen, trying to prepare food for her son around her mother's own preparations of meals for the family and for Joseph, who was as complex in his requirements as Angus. Or she was closeted in the small bedroom that had once been hers and Anne's and into which Fergus, herself, and the baby were all awkwardly crammed. Or she was struggling to wash Angus's clothes in the brief spells when the sink and the washing machine were not occupied with those of her brother.

Angus, strong-willed and highly strung, took one look at Joseph upon arrival and screamed in terror, a scream which recurred instantly whenever their paths crossed. Jenny coaxed and Fergus cajoled, but he was not to be won. The initial embarrassment subsided in a stony-faced stand off between Jenny and her mother, each fiercely protective of her own unhappy child.

It was the last straw that broke the back of the visit and made it an endurance trial. Jenny gave up even trying to help her parents as they shuffled about, manoeuvring Joseph from bed to table to bath, straining against his weight, working themselves with determined co-ordination through the rigid pathways of their day. She gave up even wanting to help. Her brother rejected her, stiffening his limbs if she even attempted to touch him, and wailing for her mother who hovered, watchful and distrusting, only inches away. Jenny felt reduced, maimed, turned from adult woman and mother to her own childish, useless self, with Joseph snatched from her arms on his christening day. She turned to her own baby for comfort, hiding with him in the bedroom or spiriting him out to the tiny backyard where he played disconsolately in the heat and she sat watching him, miserable and alone. But eventually she had to bring him in, and then inevitably they met Joseph and the howls began again.

Her mother tried awkwardly to help and made it worse. 'Here, pet,' she coaxed, crouching in front of Angus as he clung to Jenny, wrapping himself in her skirt. 'Come meet my Joe. He's a good boy, too. Just like you.' She held her arms out, beguiling, 'Come to Nana. Come to your Gran.' Jenny saw her as Angus saw her, a tense stranger with lined face and faded housedress, hands in pink rubber gloves from washing clothes. God knew how he saw Joseph. 'Come on, pet, he's not going to *hurt* you, silly.' Jenny heard the tension in her mother's voice, and Angus heard it too. He wailed and shrieked, struggling free, burying his face between Jenny's knees.

'Give up, Mom, it's not working.'

'He's just making a fuss. You pay too much attention.' Her mother caught Angus's arm, pulled him back; and suddenly Jenny was tugging too, and the boy in the middle shrieked louder. Behind them Joseph began his tuneless moan of discontent.

'*No*, Mom,' Jenny said sharply. 'He's terrified.'

'Why should he be terrified? What's there to be terrified about?'

'Oh, Mom, please.'

'Is Joseph a monster or something?'

'Mom, he's a *little boy*.'

Her mother crouched down again at Angus's level and turned him firmly towards her. 'The trouble with you,' she said looking right into his wet, brimming eyes, 'is you're spoiled.' Her voice was grim.

Jenny shouted, 'He's not spoiled. He's eighteen months. It's natural for him to be shy.'

'Of course it's not,' her mother snapped. 'Such a fuss. *You* never carried on like that. Any of you.'

'Oh no,' Jenny said, 'we were perfect. All of us.'

She looked savagely at Joseph in his chair. Her mother's only response was to bend down again over her son and whisper, 'You're a spoiled, naughty boy.'

Angus held his hands up to Jenny in hysteria, and she bent and lifted him up on to her hip.

'How can you be so rotten to him?' she cried. 'He's your grandchild.'

'I know,' her mother said stiffly.

'I thought you hadn't noticed,' Jenny said, and then she ran, awkwardly with her burden, into the tiny hot bedroom, and sank down on the camp bed that Fergus slept on, and wept. She sat for a long time, sobbing and clutching Angus to her, and hearing whispered voices just beyond the door. The whole thing had been heard by everyone – her father, Fergus, Anne – in the living-room but a few feet away.

When the door opened, she expected Fergus, and braced herself for his gentle and infuriating admonishment. But it was Anne. And Anne was not gentle at all.

'Oh well done, kid,' she said, her voice acid with sarcasm.

'She started it. It was her. Go talk to her about it.'

'You selfish cow.' Angus, who had quietened, opened his

mouth in a resentful square, preparing to recommence. 'Don't even try it, little pig,' Anne said. Jenny gasped, but Angus closed his mouth, studied Anne, and then slid down from the camp bed and began playing with a wooden car on the floor. Jenny watched, amazed.

'You do let him get away with things,' said Anne. 'He's not a bad little squirt, though, for all that.' She smiled a little, watching him.

Jenny cried suddenly, 'Oh God, Anne, it's so awful here. I can't stand it. I'm going crazy trying to keep him quiet and out of her way, and away from Joseph, and then she goes and pushes them together . . . I'm leaving. I'm going right now.'

'You do and it's the last you'll ever see of any of us. I mean it, Jenny, and I'll make it stick.'

Jenny sat hunched over on the camp bed, her arms wrapped around her swelling body. Her eyes, reddened from crying, met Anne's. 'It's all right for you. You go home to Marion's when you've had enough. But I'm stuck here.'

'Oh yeah. You're stuck here. For a week. Then you go back to Scotland and *they're* stuck here for the rest of their lives.'

'That's not my fault.'

'Oh grow up, Jenny. Who's fault it is doesn't fucking matter. What matters is that they're in the middle of it and the least we can do is help. Not make it worse.'

'But that's just it. I've tried to help. I've tried since I got here and they won't let me. They won't let me *near* him. They've got him all shut up to themselves and everything I try to do is wrong . . .' Jenny was whimpering again.

Anne said, 'Look, kid, you can't just piss off to Europe and get married and come home and expect to find it all the same. You're grown up now.' Anne's voice was patient, as if she were explaining it all to Angus, who indeed watched with round blue eyes exactly like Jenny's when she was little. 'You can't expect them to run around being Mom and Dad to you still.'

'But they *are* my Mom and Dad. And yours too. And they never were any different. There never was time for me or for you. It was all him. Always. It was always, always him.'

Anne was silent. She stepped back from the camp bed, carefully stepping over Angus's line of toy cars. She walked to the window of what had been their bedroom, looking out at the view of crab grass, split rail fence and driveway. The shrubs were bushier, the two strips of concrete of the drive seamed and cracked, the wood of the fence weathered grey with age.

'Nothing changes,' Anne said.

'It's not for me,' Jenny said. 'It's for Angus. Even if she never has time for me, I want her to have time for him. It's not parents for me I want. It's grandparents for my children.' Jenny's voice was controlled now and thoughtful, as if she had just made a discovery.

Anne turned back from the window. She ignored Jenny and sat down gracefully on the floor, one long leg outstretched, the other folded under her. She was wearing cuffed white shorts and her legs were tanned and slim. She held her arms out to Angus and, after a moment's hesitation, he clambered up into her embrace. He began to show her the car he was holding, pointing at the wheels and saying his word for them. She nodded, spinning the wheels one by one with her finger. Then she said, 'I thought that you'd understand at last, now that you're a mother too. I thought it would be a bond between you and her. But it's just the opposite, isn't it?'

Jenny watched Anne playing with her child in that easy, big-sister way she had. She was jealous, suddenly, of the readiness with which he went to her.

'She never wanted my help,' Jenny said fiercely. 'She wanted him all to herself.' She straightened up and added earnestly, 'If she had shared him from the beginning, then we could all help her now. But she never did. And she never will.'

Anne set Angus down among his toys and stood up. Once more she walked to the window and stood looking out at the small, plain yard. 'She's going to have to, Jenny,' she said. She paused, and then turned to face her sister. 'Fergus and I are looking for a Home.'

They found the Baytree Center at the end of the week. The search for it had been a conspiracy between Anne and Jenny and Fergus, Greg and Marion. Even Marion's parents were involved. Only Joseph's parents were excluded. Anne hated doing it that way, but Fergus insisted upon it.

'Some of these places are grand and some are bloody awful. If your poor Mam sees a bad one once, she'll never let him go, no matter what we find.' And, having viewed six establishments scattered across the Island, Anne was forced to see that Fergus was right. When they found the Center, Greg and Marion checked out references, interviewed parents, vetted the staff, both openly and underground through personal connections in their social network. When they passed the Baytree Center on for Anne's approval, she went with Fergus to see for herself. It was clean, orderly, efficiently run, and the staff were kind. She could not fault it. On the way home, she pulled her father's car over to the side of the road, switched the engine off and sat weeping in front of the steering wheel. Beside her she heard Fergus's soft voice.

'It's a fine place, Anne. They'll be good to him there.'

'I know,' she said, and then she cried fiercely. 'Oh, hell, Fergus, why couldn't he have died before it ever had to come to this?'

He did not answer at once, and the question hung in the hot air inside the car. 'That's a question for God, love,' he said finally. 'Not for me.'

'Oh, screw God,' Anne said. Fergus shrugged sadly. Anne found Kleenex in her handbag and carefully mopped her face. She re-did her mascara and lipstick, watching herself in the rear-view-mirror. Then she put her things away, restarted the car, and drove them home.

On the day Joseph was to enter the home, the whole family gathered. They drove to the Baytree Center in a convoy of two cars: Anne and her parents and Joseph in one; Greg, Jenny, Fergus and Nonna in the other. Marion stayed at the house and looked after Angus for Jenny.

Joseph was not disturbed by the journey to the Center. He was accustomed to being taken, on occasions, to clinics or hospitals and placed in strange beds. As long as his mother was there too, he was content. There was no way for him to know that this time was different, final, and that this night Louise would not be there.

Everyone else knew, but there was no time to think about it. Their arrival at the Baytree Center was busy with staff introductions, form-filling, domestic details. A kindly nurse listened attentively as Louise listed Joseph's favourite foods, his small amusements, his bedtime routine. Anne wondered if the attentiveness was genuine or professional posture, to be abandoned once they were safely out the door. She hoped for the first; feared the latter more likely.

Joseph was taken to his new room: they tried to make a party out of it, admiring everything, tucking possessions into cupboards, decorating his side of the room with cherished toys. Jenny was reminded disconcertingly of her first day at college, the same forced jollity patching over homesickness and fear. The room was shared with one other boy, a thin, tiny creature hardly bigger than a six-year-old, though they were told he was nineteen. They attempted to introduce themselves but the boy remained curled in his cot, apparently unaware of them, crooning secretively and sucking his thumb. Anne found him alien and repellent and realized that that was how Joseph would appear to anyone but themselves, stripped of the mask of individuality that their love cast over him. Suddenly she needed to leave the room at once and get far away.

It was time to go, anyway. They were all lined up, waiting. But their mother was still fussing about Joseph's bed, adjusting sheets, tucking corners in, and did not seem to notice. Eventually the supervisor came and gently placed herself between Louise and the bed, and with bright, cheerful smiles, led her away.

That September evening – still, dark, the air full of the singing of crickets and the whine of mosquitoes – the Conti family sat out on the patio of flagstones in a circle of Adirondack chairs: Anne, Jenny, their father, Fergus, Marion, and Nonna. It had been a hot day, as hot as any in summer, but the air cooled quickly and smelt of Fall. In the distance there were voices of other families sitting in their own backyards, but the house behind them was silent. Jenny got up and moved towards it.

'Where are you going?' Anne said.

'To check on Angus. OK?'

'Yeah. Sure.'

She left and they were silent once more. Nonna spoke then, her voice quavery, 'He was so good. Wasn't he, Mike?'

There was a pause, and then Mike said, 'Yeah, of course he was, Mom. He's a good boy.'

'Hardly a peep out of him. Still, he'll miss you. You could tell that . . .'

'Nonna, would you like some coffee?' Marion said quickly.

'I don't think so, dear . . .'

'Come on. Let's make coffee and bring some of that cake through. You give me a hand, OK?' Marion was helping Nonna up out of her chair. Nonna shifted her weight forward and rocked up on to her feet. She still wore high heels but she teetered on them, and Marion put a cautious hand under her elbow. Nonna had grown old since Grandpa died, and she no longer worked in the restaurant. She talked more than she used to, and repeated herself a little, but she still dressed with care. Anne watched them go out.

'That Marion,' her father said. 'She's a wonder.'

Anne nodded.

Jenny came back and settled in her chair. 'I keep expecting the phone to ring,' she said.

'It won't,' Anne said quickly. 'They're professionals. They'll handle anything that happens. It's not the first time they've had someone like Joe.' It startled her, even in saying it, the realization that there were others like Joseph out there. He had always seemed their own unique fate. The Baytree Center, and the other places she'd seen with Fergus, had shown her otherwise.

'It's the first time for Joe, though,' said Jenny.

Fergus took her hand. 'He'll get used to it, love. It's like going to school for the first time, or off to university. Everybody leaves home sometime. It's just the same.'

'No, Fergus,' Mike said. 'It's not the same at all. Nobody goes to school when they're a year old. And that's all Joseph is; he's just a baby, one, maybe two years old. At that age, they don't know anything. Only you, and they trust you. They trust you.' Quietly, sitting back in his wooden chair, he began to cry.

'Dad,' Anne whispered, anguished. 'We *had* to. You know that.' She watched her father cry and was filled with grief. This was her doing. Fergus was the catalyst, but she was the force behind it all. She had used all her persuasive skills, honed in business, all her sharp wits to make it happen. She organized the place for Joseph. She broke the news to her parents. She countered their arguments, one by one, with sure logic. She battered them down with a barrage of insistence from every quarter, organizing friends and family, even their old doctor, Tom Walsh, in one united front. She won Nonna to her side, and eventually even her father, until at last her mother stood isolated, surrounded by them all. And then she wore her down, working on her exhaustion until she had no arguments left.

And so, Anne had won. Joseph was in the Baytree Center, and her mother was lying in an unlit bedroom staring in silence at the ceiling. It was a necessary victory for which Anne would never forgive herself.

Beside her Jenny too began to cry. Anne sat, rigid, staring into the darkened backyard. The outline of Joseph's pool was black against the dim grass.

Her father said, 'I think maybe I'll go see your mother.'

'Leave her, Dad,' Anne said. 'She needs time alone.'

Her father fidgeted. He lit a cigarette, smoked half of it, ground it out on the flagstones. He was restless, lost without the burden of Joseph to fill his day. A thin child's wail arose from the house. Fergus got up, but Jenny was ahead of him.

'I'll see to him,' she said quickly, and she went in, glad to be away from the dark circle, the mosquitoes, the unspoken accusations. In the house she met Marion and Nonna with a tray, coffee cups, the cake. Nonna was more cheerful having something to do, and they went out past her and switched on the back door light. Jenny watched for a moment, the circle of moths by the door, and then went into her bedroom. Angus was already asleep, his brief misery forgotten. She thought of Joseph and tried to picture him curled in the same contentment in his clinical cot. The thought twisted, and she saw him crying for his mother as Angus cried for her, but fruitlessly and without hope. She smoothed the thin blanket over the hump-shape of her sleeping son and walked quietly from the room. Outside, through the screen of the back door, she heard voices and the sounds of china and silverware. She listened and then turned away from them, inwards, to the darkness of the house and her mother's bedroom door.

Jenny tapped lightly on the door, heard nothing, tapped again. There was still no answer, but she turned the knob slowly and pushed the door open. 'Mom?' She stepped within. The room was at the front of the house, and the light of the streetlight flowed through the slats of the venetian blinds. Jenny stood until she could see and then moved towards her parents' bed. 'Mom?' she said.

'I'm all right, Jenny.' There was a pause. 'You can go back to the others.'

Jenny waited, and then said, 'Can I come in beside you?' Her voice sounded childish and she realized she was repeating a phrase, forgotten, from her babyhood when, frightened by dreams, she begged entry to her mother's bed.

'Sure, pet.' The response too seemed from memory. 'In you come.' Her mother was holding up the edge of the loose blanket she had thrown over herself. Jenny sat on the bed and then lifted her feet up and slid her awkward shape across it until she lay next to her mother. They were silent for a long while. Then her mother said, 'He'll be fine, Jenny, won't he?'

'Sure, Mom.'

'It's a lovely place. So bright and airy. And did you see those pictures around the walls of his room? Up high, you know, what are they called?'

'The frieze?'

'Yes, that's it. A frieze. I always wanted a frieze for his room here. It makes a room so cheerful, don't you think?'

'I've got one for Angus, in the flat. Zoo animals, but it's an alphabet too. I figured he'd learn from it.'

'Never too soon for them to learn.'

'We'll take it with us when we move up North.'

'So your little girl can have it too.' Jenny felt her mother's hand reach across her big stomach and rest there. 'Oh. A kick. Your little girl kicked me!'

'What if she's a little boy?'

'A girl. You're carrying high.'

Jenny laughed. 'That's what Grannie said . . .' She stopped.

After another little silence her mother said, 'About Joseph? When I was carrying Joseph?'

'She said "a boy" because you were carrying high.'

'A girl. You've forgotten. A girl high, a boy low.' She paused. 'Anyway, it doesn't matter. As long as it's a fine healthy baby like Angus, who cares?'

Jenny shivered. Her mother's hand stayed resting on her stomach. She said in a low, careful voice, 'Don't worry, Jenny, it won't happen again. We've had our turn.'

Jenny nodded in the darkness, and then she turned heavily on the bed and reached for her mother who reached for her in

212

the same instant. They clasped each other tight and her mother sobbed, 'Oh Jenny, they've taken my baby. They've taken him away.' Jenny held her while she wept. She felt large and strong, and her mother in her arms was bone-thin and frail. They lay there for a long while until Jenny was aware that her mother was sleeping. The baby in her womb was quiet too. Jenny lay awake, her lips moving silently, saying her prayers.

XII

In April 1977, the Anne Conti shops had their tenth anniversary. There was a big advertising campaign, the launch of a new line of leisure wear, and widespread media attention. Anne toured her British shops, congratulating staff and giving interviews, and held celebrations at each of the American stores: East Hampton, New Haven, and New York. There was a lengthy article in Edinburgh's *Scotsman* newspaper which brought letters of congratulation from old friends from her early days, and a nice little write-up in *Time* in a feature on successful women. Anne cut it out to send to Jenny, but then changed her mind. She never knew how Jenny would take things any more.

Anne tried to arrange a family celebration in New York, but it proved impossible. Nonna was unwell, and Anne's mother would only come if she could arrange the timing around her twice daily visits to Joseph at the Baytree Center. In the end she couldn't, and Anne's father, grown nervous in old age, chose not to travel to the city without her. They apologized profusely in a telephone call. Anne accepted graciously and then spent the rest of the day trying to shake the inordinate depression that settled around her. David took her to dinner and was sweet and consoling, and the next day, on his advice, she invited Marion Forsyth to lunch at the Four Seasons. And so, as often before, the only one from home to share her triumph was the one who was not family at all.

'This is wonderful,' Marion said. 'It doesn't even feel like me.'

'Oh, come off it. You went to places like this even when you were a kid. I was always jealous as hell.'

'No we didn't, Anne. Not really. Maybe it seemed like it, but

214

we didn't. We went to posh places on the Island, old and stuffy. But not this. Besides,' she added wistfully, 'it's so long ago. It's been ages since I've been out anywhere. Greg's always working, and it's so hard to find anyone you trust to sit. And Susan gets hysterical if she wakes up and I'm not there. You know what it's like with kids.' She looked up, but Anne, aside from sympathetic, looked comfortably blank. Marion sighed. 'No, you don't, I suppose. Well, take it from me, it's macaroni cheese with one hand while you feed the baby with the other. God, I haven't had a dress on in months. Just jeans and a top with milk dribbles on the shoulder. You know that red outfit I bought from you in November? I haven't worn it yet.' She looked around again, and then down at herself, and carefully brushed a speck of lint off her pink linen suit. 'Heaven,' she said.

Provincial, Anne thought, regarding the suit. It was a professional, not a personal judgement. But it surprised her. Marion *was* provincial. Suburban. A Long Island matron. And why not? And yet, she wondered, would that have been her, but for the disaster of her prom night? She tried to picture herself with husband and children, a station-wagon at the elementary school, clubs and committees, gardening and the PTA. But it was impossible, a road not taken. 'How's Greg?' she asked, politely.

'Boring,' Marion said. But she smiled, and then she looked sideways as if someone they knew might, inconceivably, be watching, and she dropped her voice. 'But I've been hearing stories about you.'

'From my mother, no doubt.'

'She said there's a New Man. She wouldn't tell me anything else.' Marion looked faintly offended. 'She made it a real secret.'

'She doesn't know anything else,' said Anne.

'So there *is* a new man.'

'Oh, yes.'

Marion studied her seriously. There were so many men in Anne's life. Somehow this one sounded different. She leaned over the perfect white linen of the table, 'So, are you going to tell me about him?' She was conspiratorial and giggly, and Anne giggled back, and suddenly they were two girls at a drug-store soda fountain, in spite of the wine waiter in immaculate black, pouring champagne.

215

'OK,' she said. She spoke almost shyly. 'His name is David Rosenfeld . . .'

'Jewish?' Marion asked. She looked surprised.

'I'd rather think so,' Anne said drily. There was a pause in which Anne grew annoyed.

But then Marion said, 'I guess the religion thing doesn't matter much any more.'

'What religion thing?'

'That's what I mean,' Marion said quickly. 'Go on, tell me about him. Where did you meet him?'

'At Fifty-Seventh Street. He was shopping with his wife.' Marion's eyes opened wider at the word 'wife', but she said nothing. Anne said, smiling, 'I thought, "I wonder why she stays with him . . . her so glamorous and him, this plain, dumpy little man" . . . I remember, I offered him a *chair* . . . he pulled himself up to his full five-seven, sucked in his little paunch . . .' She laughed warmly, remembering, a girlish laugh, hands over mouth. Marion had never seen her like that. Never, not even when they really were girls.

'I think you're in love,' she said.

'You're damn right I am,' said Anne.

Marion looked intensely serious. She said, 'What does he do?'

'He's a writer,' Anne said lightly.

'Of what?' Marion's eyes were narrow, her fingers restless, playing with her glass.

'What is this, the third degree? Are you my mother or something?'

'Anne, if you're serious about him . . .'

'If I'm serious, what? Will he be able to support me? Christ, who cares? I can support *him*.'

'He might not like that, Anne.'

Anne looked exasperated. 'Good God,' she said. 'I think that's the least of our worries.'

'Yes, probably,' Marion said, unnervingly. Anne looked at her hard, remembering a lifetime of conversations that led into pitfalls, with Marion.

'What are you getting at?' she said.

'How old is he, Anne?' Marion said, as if she had not spoken.

Anne shrugged, 'Forty-five. Forty-six. He's just had a birthday.'

'Forty-six. That's thirteen years older than you.'

'I can count.'

Marion didn't answer. She turned to her plate, delicately lifting pink slivers of salmon free of bone. Anne watched her belligerently. Marion said, 'First Jenny, then you. Sometimes I think you both are looking for father substitutes.'

'Spare me the analysis,' Anne said sharply. 'The truth is he's a brilliant lay.'

'You always get crude when you're uneasy about something.'

'I'm not *uneasy* about anything. I'm just a little bit less than thrilled to have my private life picked apart . . .'

'It's really getting to you, him being married, isn't it?' Marion looked up from her lunch and met Anne's startled eyes. She looked down again. 'So what's going to happen?' she said.

'He's getting a divorce.'

'Because of you?'

'No, not because of me. Because of his wife. Because he's lived for twenty years with a selfish woman who doesn't love him.'

There was a long silence in which Marion finished the last of her salmon, laid down her fork, and delicately patted her lips with her napkin. She sipped from her champagne and said, 'So it's nothing to do with you. Nothing at all.'

Anne thought carefully before she answered. When she did, her voice was calm. 'You know, not long ago my father told me that a week after Joseph went into the Center, if someone had told him he'd have to take him back again, he'd have gone out of his mind. And yet he lived with that, uncomplaining, for all those years. You can stand a lot of things when you can see no alternative.'

'And you're David's alternative.'

'Yes. I am.'

'Lucky David.'

'Lucky me.'

Marion paused suddenly, puzzled. 'But Anne . . .'

'What?'

'If he's divorced . . . I mean, you can't marry him, can you?'

'Why not?'

'But you people . . . Catholics don't divorce . . . that hasn't changed.'

'I wouldn't know,' Anne said angrily. 'I haven't been inside a

217

church for fifteen years.' It was a lie. She'd been twice. To bury her grandfather, and again, for the same reason, for Grannie in Scotland last year. But that was all.

Marion shook her head, smiling. 'Sorry, I kind of believed that old thing. You know, once a Catholic . . .'

'Always an asshole? No. Not me, sweetheart.'

'So it *does* bother you, then?'

Anne crumpled up her linen napkin and threw it on the table. Marion looked uneasily around the cool, airy room, where voices were as soft as the play of the fountain. A real Anne Conti temper would go down here like a ton of bricks. She said, hastily, 'Never mind. Look, how's Jenny? I haven't heard for ages.' She smiled engagingly. Anne retreated, only reluctantly, from her anger.

'Up to her knees in goat shit, I imagine.'

'I guess I'm not going to get a straight answer.'

Anne relaxed. She sighed slightly. 'No, she's fine I suppose.'

'You don't sound too convinced.'

'Well she *says* she's fine. She *says* she's deliriously happy.'

'Well,' Marion said, 'maybe she is. Why shouldn't she be, anyhow? She's got two lovely kids and a helluva nice guy for a husband . . .'

'Marion, it's the pits, that place. When I was up there after Grannie's funeral I couldn't believe it, Jenny living like that. It's better than at the beginning. I mean, at least they have electricity and water, thank God. But still no heating, no carpets, no *furniture* really. And the kids in the weirdest clothes that Jenny makes. Fergus stomping around in rubber boots smelling of sheep . . .'

'And Jenny?' Marion was smiling gently.

'Jenny in the middle of it, in woollen skirts down to her ankles, her hair in pigtails, a child apparently permanently fastened to her hip . . . baking bread, shelling peas, *spinning wool* . . . did I tell you, she has a spinning wheel by the fireplace? It looks like something out of the frontier.'

'Happy?'

'Ecstatic. If you can believe her.'

'And why can't you believe her?' Marion said.

Anne leaned back from the table and looked around the room. Two men at the far side of it had stopped eating to look at her. She was wearing a plain black suit from one of her favourite designers, no jewellery, very little make-up; little effort and not a lot of expense, just style. She smiled, pleased with the effect she was creating for reasons of professional rather than personal pride. She said to Marion, 'She was on the Dean's List two years running at Harpur. Her English professors were falling over themselves. And now she's content to milk goats?' Anne shrugged. 'Nobody *chooses* to live in that kind of deprivation.'

'Maybe she doesn't see it like that,' said Marion.

'How else can anyone see it?'

'An adventure. Back to nature. They're not the first.' Marion leaned forward, urgently, 'She's not you, Anne. She has different values. She always had.'

'Oh, not you too,' Anne said sourly.

'What?'

'All this anti-materialist hippie crap. Jenny and Fergus and the Brave New World. I can't stand that superiority.'

Marion shook her head. 'They're not superior,' she said. 'Just different. You can't stand anyone choosing to be different. It was always impossible to argue with you.'

They glared at each other, and Anne was ashamed, allowing her treat for Marion to degenerate into one of their old, girlish rows. She said quietly, 'Yeah, I'm sorry. You're probably right.' Then after a pause added, 'Frankly, I wouldn't mind so much if it wasn't all such an obvious disaster.'

Marion looked serious, like she had when questioning Anne about David's prospects. Financial stability was dear to her heart. 'Is it?' she said cautiously.

'Look,' said Anne. 'They've had the farm since Sarah was born – what is it now – seven, eight years. You accept at the beginning that things are going to be rocky while they get established, learn the ropes, make a few mistakes. But for how long? After all this time it's as chaotic as ever. There's always *some* disaster hitting them: some sheep disease, or the weather, or some calamity. Whenever you talk to them, things would have been great this year *except* . . .' Anne waved her hand, dismissing it. 'Meanwhile, they're losing money all the time. Fortunately, or maybe unfortunately, Fergus had quite a lot to start with. But they're going through it.'

'Is he still singing?'

'Almost never. He's not interested. All he wants is to be a farmer. And not just a farmer . . . they've got to make everything they use, everything they wear, like they're in some dry-run for Armageddon. Only there's one thing they can't seem to make, and that's money. I don't think Jenny realizes. She's pretty stupid with figures.'

'Jenny? She had straight "A's" in math.'

'She had straight "A's" in everything. It doesn't make the slightest bit of difference out in the real world, apparently. Anyhow, she's too busy milking her goats and spinning her fleeces. She leaves it all to Fergus the Genius.'

Marion looked unhappy. At last she said, sorrowfully, 'I don't get you. I thought you *liked* Fergus.'

'I *love* Fergus. He's a terrific husband and a great father. But as a farmer and a business man he makes a great folksinger.'

Marion smiled. She drank the dregs of her coffee and then said suddenly, 'And what about your David? Will he be a terrific husband and a great father?' Her eyes were narrow and shrewd.

Anne said, calmly, 'He *is* a great father. His children adore him.'

'What about *your* children?'

'Mine?' Anne said. She tried and failed to sound unsurprised by Marion's question. An image came to mind, from years ago, of Jenny in her long dress, a bare-assed Sarah under one arm, wiping snot off Angus's grizzling, mud-splotched face. 'I never thought we'd have children of our own,' she said calmly. There was a silent unease in her voice when she added, 'I'm sure he wouldn't want to.'

'And you?'

Anne laughed, heartily, 'Not in a million years.'

David met her again for dinner that night. He met her most nights when she was in New York, and they went out, to a restaurant or the theatre, and then afterwards to his apartment or hers. David's was a shabby place in SoHo. Everything in it was either borrowed, or cheap and temporary. He had left all he owned in the family home in Connecticut.

Anne's was a one-room studio on Seventy-Ninth Street. She had taken the lease when she opened the New York store. It was expensive, and expensively furnished. As much as any place, it was her home, though she still spent weekends on the Island with her parents as frequently as her schedule allowed, and she travelled so much that she was only sporadically there anyhow. Several times each year she went to the UK to oversee her interests, which extended to four shops in three cities: London, Edinburgh and Oxford. In Edinburgh she stayed with Elizabeth, now married to the young solicitor Gordon Fraser, and usually managed a quick trip north to the hillcroft on Loch Ness-side to see Jenny and Fergus and her nephew and niece. She found those visits trying. She was physically uncomfortable in their cold and primitive house. The children, who seemed to do little but argue and cry, tried her patience after a week of concentrated work. And Jenny's airy placidity amidst it all irked her tremendously. The relief when she flew home from Prestwick, back to central heating and toilets that flushed and floors that were covered in wool pile rather than dust and biscuit crumbs, was immeasurable. She felt guilty, but only a little. Jenny's smug self-satisfaction did not invite sympathy.

Anne was working in the office upstairs at Fifty-Seventh Street when David came. One of the sales assistants brought him through. He took her to a quiet French restaurant he had known for years and over dinner he asked about her lunch with Marion. He had deep brown eyes that focused on whoever he was conversing with as if they were the only person in the world.

'Marion thinks I'm father-fixated on you.' She was joking, but he responded seriously.

'Are you, do you think?'

Anne rested her chin on her palm and looked straight into his solemn eyes. 'And she's worried about your prospects.'

Again David nodded thoughtfully. 'It sounds like she's not very happy about us.'

Anne laughed. 'Marion worries about me,' she said lightly. 'She thinks she's my mother.'

'I see.'

'Don't look so solemn. I'm joking.'

'I'm thinking about what your *mother* will think.'

'*She* doesn't worry about me,' Anne said. She had meant it light-heartedly, but it came out sounding so vehement that she felt obliged to qualify. 'She doesn't worry about Jenny either,' she said lamely.

'I find that hard to believe. Even Sharon never stops worrying about the kids.'

Anne felt that uncomfortable little lurch that came whenever he mentioned his wife, but all she said was, 'It's different in our family. Once Joseph came, anyhow, there was never any time . . . Joe concentrates the mind wonderfully.' David looked sad and she said briskly, 'We all understand.'

'I bet you didn't then,' he said.

Anne didn't answer. She looked down at the table in front of her. They had finished their coffee and were waiting for the bill.

They had had another coffee and brandy at her apartment when Anne remembered. 'Oh God, what time is it?' She peered at her watch in their dim and romantic light. 'I meant to call my sister. It's my brother-in-law's birthday.'

'Ten o'clock,' David said.

Anne added hours quickly in her head. 'Shit.'

'What time is it there?'

'Three A.M.'

'Do they go to bed late?' David asked helpfully.

'Hardly. They'll be getting up in a couple of hours. Oh never mind. It doesn't really make any difference. I can always wish him a late one tomorrow.' She shrugged, put down her brandy, climbed on to the sofa beside David and curled up against him, her head on his shoulder and her feet tucked up beneath her like a little kid.

Jenny woke first. It was just after four, but it was already light. Through the open window she heard a sweet flood of birdsong. The room was as cold as winter. She snuggled in under the downy, and turned so that her spine rested against the warmth of Fergus's back. Contentment flowed through her. She began saying her leftover prayers. When she was done she turned slightly to see the clock. It was still frightfully early but they were in the middle of the lambing and Fergus, who had finished his last round five hours earlier, would need to be up for the next. Downstairs, in a paper carton by the Aga, an orphan lamb waited for its baby-bottle of milk. Jenny steeled herself to rise in the cold air, but then relaxed. Jut five minutes. She closed her eyes, savouring the last peace before the chaos of the day.

In her mind she pictured the children in their beds. Angus sprawled on his back, arms and legs sticking out from the rumple of covers; Sarah curled in a tight, protective knot. She broadened the picture to include themselves in their room and, downstairs, the dogs in their baskets, the lamb by the Aga, cats dotted around like afterthoughts. Her mind reached up to the heavy slate roof, resting so simply on its firm pine trusses, plain, clean, protective. She felt wonderfully safe, and the feeling dredged up a memory of childhood when, in the earliest years, before Joseph was born, she would lie awake waiting for her parents to return from the theatre, for the babysitter to leave, and for their steps to sound softly on the carpeted hall outside her door. Then after a while the house would be silent and she would lie picturing herself and Anne, her Mom and Dad, and the roof over them like a blessing.

Jenny felt her mind waking up faster than her body, and as she lay she began to plan out the design of a knitted dress for Sarah in her blue and violet home-dyed wool. She made all Sarah's clothes: wonderfully colourful patchwork skirts, striped jumpers and socks, tasselled hats. When the children were really little she dressed them both like a rainbow, in fantasy clothes. But Angus grew rebellious. He patterned himself after the older boys at the village school and demanded his hair cut short. He slopped about the house in a maroon nylon track suit with white striping down the legs, but for school he insisted upon the traditional uniform of grey Crimplene trousers, white shirt, blazer and tie. He refused to wear anything Jenny made any longer.

She acquiesced, but sadly. The memories of his earlier complaisance drew her back to the comfort of the baby years, the years in which children were simply what you made them, without the disruptive influence of school and peers. Even television encroached upon them now, though on Fergus's insistence they had none of their own. Angus saw it at friends' houses, lingering hungrily over it when it was time to go home. Likewise, all the private rules about homegrown food, the ban on sweets, the exile from their house of guns and tanks and Action Man toys, came, in the end, to nothing. Fergus muttered about moving out, further west, out to the Islands, where life was still pure and uncorrupted. Jenny listened patiently. She knew it was hopeless; even the Islands had television.

'St Kilda,' she suggested drily. 'Last inhabitant forcibly shipped out in 1930. Rocks and guillemots and seals.' But they didn't go.

Another baby, Jenny thought hungrily. *Time for another baby*. It was a frequent thought, growing more frequent in recent months. She let herself contemplate it for a few moments of uninterrupted pleasure: the infant wail in the house, the smells of talc and sour milk, the secret sensuality of nursing. Then deliberately she changed the picture – broken nights, nappies, leaking breasts – to talk herself out of it. It didn't work. They couldn't afford a baby. She knew that. They couldn't afford the two children they had. *You can always afford one more,* her old Highland neighbour had once said. She thought about the masses of hungry Chinese, starving Africans, the human flotsam of Calcutta. But they seemed far away.

Jenny turned, folding herself around Fergus's back, reaching her arms around him. He stirred and she kissed the back of his neck and fumbled with the buttons of his pyjamas. He woke up with a start, sat up, peering at the clock.

'Christ, Jenny, not now. I've got the lambing.' She sighed, smiling slightly, and sat up as well, swinging her feet out on to the cold board floor. There was always tonight.

By the time Fergus had come in from the lambing, Jenny had finished her chores. She did them all in a concentrated blur: feeding dogs, cats, stock. Milking. Letting the goats out on to the hill. Making the porridge and the tea. She fed the orphan lamb with one hand, leaning over its box, extending the bottle towards it while she stirred the porridge with the other. It sucked desperately at the bottle the way in the fields the lambs sucked like lampreys at their mothers' teats.

'Poor Mom,' she said aloud as it tugged backwards, nearly jerking the bottle from her hand. After, it curled up and went to sleep like a dog, its chin on its small perfect hooves. They were such perfect creatures, refugees from church windows and Bible stories. When Fergus and Jenny were newer to the croft, they fell in love with all the orphans and let the children make pets of them. But that nearly always ended in disaster. Most of the time, they sickened and died. And the few who survived grew up unsheep-like and bold and were a nuisance about the place ever afterwards. Now, Jenny fed them out of duty, uninvolved. The children had grown bored of them, anyhow.

After, she went to stoke the Aga, opened the fire door, poked about in the ashes with the bone-handled poker and reached for the coal scuttle. It was frustratingly light, an inch of dross on the bottom. Jenny sighed. She turned to the log box and lifted the lid. A pile of bark sat on the bottom. 'Oh, damn it,' she said wearily. She closed the firebox door, lifted the scuttle, and went out of the door, angrily kicking out at a chicken scratching in the middle of the path. In the coal shed, she set the scuttle down. She leaned against the door, her hands thrust in her pockets. A few loose coals were scattered on the floor. Fergus had been promising to order more for weeks. Like a fool, she had left it to him.

Jenny was long past leaving many things to Fergus. Anything that really mattered – animal feed, the vet – she took care of herself. Fergus's intentions were splendid but his organization was diabolical. 'Oh for Pete's sake,' Jenny said aloud. 'Surely you could remember coal.' Wearily she returned the scuttle to the kitchen and trekked out to the woodstack with martyred determination. Wood and coal were Fergus's job. She was not meant to carry either; but somehow she always did. If, of course, there was wood or coal to carry. Today, there was neither. The cut stack of logs had dwindled to half an armful, enough to feed the Aga for a morning at best. Jenny gathered them up in a fury, damp, from the bottom row of the stack, and alive with grey beetles. Beside the stack lay a healthy pile of birch lengths waiting to be cut. She had glared at them for weeks, whenever she went out for wood. She had asked Fergus a dozen times, but the pile remained as it was, the big circular saw silent. Jenny stamped into the house, dumped the wet logs in the log box and stuffed three into the ashy fire within the stove. Ash flew up, scenting the room. She shut the door, latched it, and sniffed. There was another smell, burning.

'Oh *shit*,' she shouted, slamming the porridge pot off the hot-plate. Angrily she stirred it, coming up with blackened sheets from the bottom which she flicked out on to a plate and dumped into the dog's dish. By the time Fergus came in it looked like porridge again, anyhow. She saw him through the kitchen window, carrying a dead lamb by its feet, a wet bundle of wool. He laid it down, outside the door, waiting for burial. She felt sad for him. There had been so many dead lambs this wet, cold spring. She decided not to mention the Aga until after breakfast. But as he came through the door he wrinkled his nose and said, innocently, 'You burn something, Jenny?'

225

'Yes I fucking burned something.' He looked surprised, wide-eyed. 'I burned the fucking porridge while I was out getting coal. And wood. Only there wasn't any.'

'Oh shit,' said Fergus.

'Precisely.'

'I'm sorry, Jenny.'

'You're always sorry.' She waved the porridge ladle, splattering grey lumps on the hot plate. They sizzled and smelt awful. 'What's the point in being sorry?'

'I'll go and cut some.' Fergus stood up and Jenny slammed the porridge into the bowl.

'Oh don't be stupid. Have your breakfast. But don't say anything about how it tastes.'

'I won't, Jenny,' he said meekly. He sat, drew the bowl towards himself and began to eat. 'It's really quite good,' he said.

Jenny whirled around from the Aga, pointing the ladle at him like a weapon. 'Don't you humour me,' she said.

He ate the rest of his breakfast in silence. Upstairs she heard the children stirring and began getting out their boxes of Crunchy-Nut Corn Flakes and Rice Krispies. They never ate porridge. They never ate anything that was good for them, or cheap. Jenny felt resentment rising within her towards them, Fergus, everything. She stamped about the kitchen, laying plates out, slopping milk from the big dairy can into a jug, shoving dogs out of her way. Fergus took the hint.

'I think I'll cut some wood,' he said, standing up, sliding his empty plate towards her. She took the plate without saying anything. He went out of the door with a chastened look, like the collie dogs into their baskets. Upstairs she heard noise; an authoritative shout from Angus and then the predictable howling wail from Sarah. In moments they were thundering down the stairs to confront her, in mid-argument. As usual Angus, in half buttoned grey shirt, grey trousers and socks and no shoes, was bristling with righteous certainty. Sarah wore only her knickers and undershirt. Angus held his striped school tie in one fist and was yelling something incomprehensible and filled with accusation. Sarah continued to wail.

Jenny said, without turning from the sink, 'Get dressed and eat your breakfasts. You'll miss the bus.' She used her goat-milking voice, calm and imperturbable.

Angus shouted, 'Well, she shouldn't use my school tie, should she?'

'I didn't,' Sarah cried before resuming her wail.

'She did. She made a belt out of it. It was on her doll. It's *ruined*.'

'You'll miss the bus,' Jenny said.

'Well, it's not my fault. It's Sarah's fault.'

Jenny whirled around. 'Get upstairs and get dressed,' she shouted.

Sarah shrank away and whisked out of the door. Angus stared right at her.

'That's right, side with her.'

'I'm not siding . . . get out!'

'Fine,' Angus said. 'I won't wear a tie. I'll get thrown out of school. You'll have to come and get me.' Angus was good at dramatic sequences leading to ever more horrific consequences.

'Out,' Jenny shrieked. 'Out, out, out.'

Angus stayed, glaring at her until the precise moment when she lunged for him, and then scuttled out of the door, eluding her hand. '*It's not my fault*,' he shouted down the stairs. His sense of justice was flawless. Fergus called him 'The Jesuit'.

Jenny sagged against the kitchen table. She couldn't believe she had seriously contemplated having another child. It was all chaos: the house, the croft, children, everything. Outside she heard the familiar homely mutter of the petrol-driven woodsaw, and the whine of the circular blade, punctuated by the swift wail as Fergus fed through the lengths of birch. Her anger waned in a wave of satisfaction. She lifted the lid of the hotplate, slid the kettle across, and took two mugs down from the shelf.

The children crept warily down into the kitchen and settled themselves in front of their plates. While she ladled instant coffee into the mugs, she was aware of a wordless squabble over the cereal packets, but ignored it. She poured boiling water over the coffee powder, slopped milk into both cups, and stirred sugar into one for Fergus. Then she lifted his mug and carried it out of the back door and around the back of the byre until she could see him working at the wood. She waited until he came to the end of a length and had bent to gather up the cut sticks, and then she shouted, in her conciliatory voice, 'Coffee?'

He looked up. She lifted the mug. He grinned, sheepishly, as he always did when they'd had a row and it was over, regardless of who was at fault. 'I'll be in in a minute,' he said. He lifted one more birch length from the pile and turned back to the saw.

Jenny turned back to the house, went in and set Fergus's cup down again, took a sip from her own, and automatically took her place behind Sarah at the table, and began brushing and braiding her long hair. It was thick and lush, like Fergus's; the sort of hair Jenny had always yearned for. As she braided it, she listened with pleasure to the whisking sound of one strand crossing another, remembering Anne's friend Marion, long ago, sitting on a kitchen stool with her mother braiding her long, honey-brown plaits, Jenny watching enviously.

'You lucky thing,' Jenny said fondly, and Sarah grinned all over, thrilled by her mother's envy. Outside, the sound of the saw blended with the rhythm of her plaiting: her work and Fergus's work melded together. Jenny began to sing, softly, one of his old songs.

'Oh stop, Mom,' Angus said, brutally. 'You sing terribly.' Jenny stopped, embarrassed. As she did there was a sharp bang from outside and a ringing clatter as if the saw had hit an exceptional knot. Then it was silent. She imagined it had broken down, as it frequently did. It was old and needed servicing, something else which Fergus had forgotten to arrange. In a moment he would come stomping in for his coffee, fuming as he always did when machinery failed him, and it would be her turn to comfort and placate. She sent Sarah off to find her shoes and began slapping together sandwiches for their lunches, with Angus watching and making complaints. 'Not *that* cheese. The one from the shop. I *hate* goat's cheese. My friends say it smells. That's too much butter. *No* lettuce.' She obeyed, like an automaton, rather than argue. When the sandwiches were finished and wrapped in greaseproof paper and packed, with an apple and shop biscuits, into the plastic lunch boxes, she realized that Fergus had not come in. Nor had the saw restarted. Fergus's coffee sat cooling with a milk scum on the surface in the middle of the table. She sighed, picked it up, stirred it briefly to disperse the scum, and tramped back out of the door.

She called Fergus from the corner of the sheet-tin porch, and when he didn't answer she set the coffee cup down on the low wall and walked resignedly out to the byre. She did not see him.

228

The motor of the woodsaw idled lamely, unattended. She stared at it. It looked odd and forlorn. The circular blade had vanished; in its place was only a thin triangle of metal, like the last petal of a plucked flower. In the next moment she glimpsed a flash of sunlight on the old larch tree that propped the woodpile. She stared again, and saw another petal of the metal flower, buried inches deep in the weathered wood by the force of its flight. In the same moment in which she realized what had happened, she saw Fergus.

She did not panic or cry out or run away, because the rational, detached part of herself saw that there was no purpose. There was no one to hear her cry, nowhere to run to, no need to panic or to hurry, because it was all over already.

She stepped closer, looked carefully for as long as she could make herself look to be absolutely certain, since already mad ideas were flitting through her head that what she was seeing could not possibly be real. But the sound part of her knew it was. She knew there were rituals, that people in such a state were always covered; but she had no cover, no blanket, no coat. She knew she was going to the telephone to call someone official; probably the doctor, or maybe the police, although there was nothing for either of them to do. In the seconds that passed as she stood there, two things intruded on her mind; the abandoned petrol engine of the woodsaw, still running, and the great streaks of blood splashing the wood stack. Slowly she stepped around Fergus and closed the throttle on the engine. It muttered into silence. There was nothing she could do about the blood. She turned to go, and then she heard the children, sounding far away, though they could surely not be further than the back door.

'Mom. *Mom*! Where are you? We need our bus money. It's coming.' Angus in his turbulent indignation. And then higher, Sarah squealing, 'My gym shorts. You forgot my gym shorts!'

She froze. The part of her that was just Jenny alone, lost and terrified, felt a great scream rising within her; but the other part, the part that was mother, was in control.

'No dear,' she shouted to Angus, because he, bossy and determined, would be in the van. 'Don't come here just now. Go back in the house.'

'But Mom . . .'

'Now, Angus. In the house. Now.'

She was walking back, shepherding them before her before they could turn the corner of the byre and see what she had seen. She was alone. She would be alone forever now.

When the phone rang in her New York apartment, Anne lifted it off the hook at once, before she was truly awake. The machine was off, as always at night, in case her mother needed her. She squinted against the dim light slipping in soft bars around the heavy curtains. Automatically she noted the hands of her bedside clock, glowing greenly. She was certain it was about Joseph.

'Hello,' she whispered, as David stirred beside her.

'Anne?'

'Yes. Who is it?'

The voice, far away and thinned by static said again, 'Anne?'

'Jenny, is that you?' There was a small, somehow affirmative sound, like a little sigh. Anne looked again at the clock. 'Jenny it's six A.M.' Her voice was sharp. David woke beside her, looked sleepy and surprised.

'I know. I waited . . .'

'Jenny, what's wrong?'

'Fergus is dead, Anne.' Her voice was flat and tired, as if she had been saying the same thing over and over again and had lost appropriate expression.

'Oh my God.'

David sat up. 'What is it? What's wrong. Is it Joseph?' Anne rested her hand on his arm. He heard her say, 'Oh, God' twice more, then, 'Yes, Jenny. Yes. I'll call you back when I've told Mom.' She put down the phone. 'I'm going off to Scotland,' she said.

They didn't talk until after the funeral. There was no time, no solitude. The house was full of people: Jenny and Fergus's friends, people from the Social Services, the local police, the family doctor. Jenny, in the super-calm of deep grief, coped beautifully. Anne resented the noise, the talk, the mass of strangers, though Jenny seemed to welcome them. Anne resented Jenny's friends even more. There were so many of them, which surprised her, and they claimed the sort of intimate understanding of Jenny that Anne felt to be her own right. Even

Elizabeth, who had travelled up with her from Edinburgh, annoyed her slightly with her thoughtful confidences. When Anne protested, 'I know, I'm her sister,' Elizabeth answered vaguely, 'She's very different now.'

Anne retreated to looking after the children. She took charge of them, since everyone else, including Jenny, seemed to have forgotten them. Jenny accepted her help without either objection or obvious gratitude. She seemed to expect it, as she seemed to expect her friends' loyal attentions and willingness to arrange all the essential details for her. She treated bereavement as a special physical state, like pregnancy, that allowed special privileges. She sat among family, friends and strangers, weeping openly, without apology. She had no sense of privacy or of shame.

On the morning of the funeral, Anne took the children for a walk. She felt remote from children, having had limited contact with them. To bridge the gap, she extrapolated downward from adulthood rather than upward from babyhood as parents do, and therefore treated them like siblings, younger versions of Jenny herself. She miscalculated age, and expected more of them than the years allowed. Usually they rose to her expectations. Sometimes it all broke down in mystification.

Sarah puzzled her most. Sarah looked like Fergus; so much so that looking into her eyes wrenched at Anne's insides. But aside from looking like him, she was not like him at all, but was instead a sturdier, prettier version of Jenny, full of her deep dreamy moods and religious certainties. 'You can't see my Daddy,' she announced virtually on Anne's arrival, 'because he's gone to heaven.' She seemed as sure and as essentially uninterested as if he had gone to the shops.

'I don't think she cares,' Anne confided in Elizabeth.

Elizabeth shrugged. 'Children don't,' she said.

'But she loved her father,' Anne persisted unhappily.

'Sure. But they don't take it that seriously. They really believe all the rubbish we tell them about God and everything, so they're happy enough. When my grandmother died I was most miserable because we'd been promised a trip to the Panto – it was Christmas – and now we weren't going to get it. And I really loved my grandmother.'

'But this is her *father*.'

'Look,' said Elizabeth. 'Count your blessings. What do you want, to have her howling her heart out?'

'Maybe she is, inside.'

Elizabeth smiled her pretty, brittle smile. 'Inside, she's probably wondering what's for tea. You Americans. You always have to analyse.'

While they were walking, Anne said quietly to Sarah, who was noncommittally holding her hand, 'Do you miss your Daddy?'

'Mmm,' Sarah said, revealing nothing. She stopped and pointed. 'Look,' she said. 'That sheep has foot-rot. That's why it's eating on its knees.' She sounded wonderfully authoritative. Anne looked. The sheep's hooves were curled and misshapen. It knelt on bent front legs and nibbled at the grass, crippled and distorted, but somehow unperturbed.

'Does it hurt?' Anne asked.

Sarah shrugged. 'You can't tell with sheep,' she said.

'It's not one of *our* sheep,' Angus said. Then they got in a fight about whose sheep it was. Anne wondered how they, or anyone, could hope to tell; or how indeed Jenny and Fergus's sheep could be isolated from the others out in the wasteland of bracken-ridden grass and heather moorland in which they roamed. The fences, where there were fences, were old and sagging, with half-strung wire broken in a dozen places. Like the byres, the inner fields, the garden, the house itself, everything was crumbling in disrepair. There were signs of effort in disparate places – a weeded segment of garden, a line of bright new pine fence posts, a sheet of fresh tin on a roof – but it was all dwarfed by the immensity of the task, overridden by the sheer stubborn inertia of the land. Anne felt grieved for Fergus who had struggled gamely, if foolishly, to salvage something that was clearly beyond repair. Except, of course, with money. Money could fix anything, but money was the one tool Fergus and Jenny religiously scorned. Anne shrugged. She could have told him eight years ago. But he wouldn't have listened then. And he surely wouldn't listen now.

'I'll have to do the lambing now,' Angus said. He looked worried.

Anne felt sorry for him. 'Of course you won't,' she said.

'But who will do it?'

'Someone. Someone else.' Anne felt ignorant and useless. She had no idea what you did for lambing, even.

'Mom can't do it,' Angus said.

'Why not?'

'She's a woman.' He was calmly scornful. Anne's pity for him evaporated.

'Women can do lots of things,' she said sharply. But she didn't want to talk about it any more because it brought to mind all the things that were going to need doing, and the rising panic in her when she tried to imagine Jenny doing them all. 'Come on,' she said. 'We'd better go back and get dressed.' She walked on, ahead of them, wearied by the incongruities of their conversation. Behind, she heard them playing at some game among themselves. She found it hard to believe they were going to bury their father in half an hour.

Anne felt worst of all in the church. She sat next to Jenny who was weeping but serene, and watched with dismay, like a returning traveller who finds revolution has swept his country in his absence and rendered everything incomprehensible. She was lost, uncertain of the responses, or of when to stand or kneel. She found the new liturgy graceless and uninspired. She took no comfort from it, or from any moment of the mass or the procession to the graveside, where Jenny leaned on her frightened little boy's shoulder and threw roses into the dark ground where they left her husband. Anne thought, *That is all, that is all there is, and all the rest is lies.* As they rode back in a procession of cars to the house, she herself in one driven by Elizabeth's husband Gordon, she thought, *A week ago, he was like us. Next week, we could be like him.* The thought filled her with terror. She wanted David. She wanted to curl up on his knees and be held.

Jenny held a gathering of friends at the house after the funeral; a wake, really. It was actually quite jolly. People relaxed and laughed and joked. The children ran around snatching at food, and the dogs, excited by strange people, barked playfully. Jenny seemed high with spiritual joy after the funeral mass. She talked about Fergus only in the present tense, and she wore one of her bright flowing dresses and poured wine for her friends. She had left all the preparations – the food and drink – to Anne and Elizabeth, and in the middle of it she went out like a bride from

233

her wedding party and left them on their own. Anne found her sitting alone in her bedroom, in Fergus's rocking chair, silently crying. 'My life is over,' she said.

Anne sat down slowly on the bed. It was a big old bed, rumpled and unmade; and it made her think of her sister's intimacies with her husband, and she was ill at ease. She said warily, uncertain how to interpret Jenny's change of mood, 'Of course it's not. It can't be. You've got the children anyhow.'

'I wish I hadn't.'

'Jenny . . .'

'I don't want the children. I want Fergus.' Anne thought she would cry again, but instead she began to talk in a hurried, high voice.

'I had made him this jumper for his birthday. It was real nice, blue with like a Fair Isle yoke in green and turquoise. It looked terrific on him. He put it on after he opened his presents and wore it all day. And then the next day he put it on again when he got up. He really liked it.' Anne cringed inside, knowing what was coming. 'So he was wearing it when it happened, and of course it was all cut up . . . I keep thinking about sitting in the evenings, knitting that jumper . . .' She sat straight, upright, dry-eyed. Anne got up slowly and crossed the room and stood behind the chair and tentatively reached around to hold her arms around Jenny. Their hands fumbled together and held, and they stayed there, both looking out of the bedroom window to the distant rainy hills.

Anne stayed with Jenny for three weeks, much more time than she could spare. She made telephone calls to her managers and buyers, reversing the charges, awkwardly doing business at long distance. She called David almost daily, saying all the things she could not say to Jenny and the children, her worries over them, the farm, the pressing financial difficulties. Only David was understanding. Everyone else simply wanted her home doing everything they depended upon her to do. Even her mother, as sorry as she was for Jenny, sounded faintly impatient with Anne for staying so long away.

Jenny and her mother seemed to have a secret union of understanding, as if true grief had matured Jenny in a hurry, wiping away all her resentments. She never asked if she would see her mother; on the telephone they talked about the children, and about Joseph, their one common bond. To Anne, Jenny said, 'She couldn't help, anyhow. No one can. I have to do this alone.'

Anne left her alone much of the time. She helped around the house, at first awkwardly and later with more skill. She cooked and cleaned and got the children ready for school. She left the animals to Jenny. She seemed happiest with them, anyhow. But she got wood in, and coal, and did sensible things like seeing what was in short supply and finding phone numbers and ordering more. Jenny signed cheques without looking at them. Anne paid for most things with her own British cash. Jenny did not notice. Anne realized quickly that she had little idea what things cost, or who paid for them, or when. It was clear she had left all that to Fergus, and was as ignorant and as trusting as a child. It was also clear to Anne, after a brief, frustrating survey through the chaos on Fergus's desk, that it had been a terrible mistake.

Out of compassion, she waited as long as she could before confronting Jenny with her financial situation. Secretly, she hoped Jenny would raise the subject herself, would come to her for help, but in the end, with only two days left of her stay, she realized it was not going to happen. By that time, she had quietly gone over everything in Fergus's accounting book, his bank books, his private papers. She examined them with the fastidious disinterest of an accountant, painfully aware of both the intrusion of privacy and the necessity. She waited until the children were in bed and Jenny had come in from her evening chores. She made coffee for them both and then sat across from her sister at the kitchen table.

'Do you know how much money you have?' she asked baldly.

Jenny looked pained and uncomfortable. 'Not exactly,' she said eventually.

'All right,' Anne said slowly. 'Let's try another tack. Do you know how much you owe?'

Jenny looked puzzled. 'Do we owe somebody?' she said.

Anne sighed.

'What's the matter?' Jenny asked innocently.

Anne said, 'I'm wondering where to start.'

'I thought the solicitors were going to do all this,' Jenny said.

'Solicitors,' Anne said, 'will handle the will and make everything legal, and make sure you and the children get what's rightfully yours. They'll charge you for it too,' she added. 'But they won't find money that isn't there, or pay bills you can't cover. Jenny, I think you're going to have to sell the farm.' She had decided to hit her with the hardest bit and work back.

Jenny said only, 'Never. I won't leave here.' Her eyes were bright, her face determined. 'It's my home. I'm never leaving my home for anyone ever again.'

Anne, poised to protest, drew back. Instead she said softly, 'OK, let's see what we can do.'

She had already realized there was only one thing to do. The hard part was going to be getting Jenny to realize it too, and to accept that if she was going to keep her home she must sacrifice her pride. She could have one or the other, but not both.

'I won't borrow money from you,' Jenny said. Her vehemence, in her present emotionally-battered state, surprised Anne. She had expected stubbornness, but not such determination, nor such anger. The argument went on all the next day, in low voices and broken by interruptions because it was a Saturday and the children were home, hanging about and listening. Anne remembered herself and Jenny lurking in the same covert, ostensibly uninterested way to eavesdrop on adult argument. The last thing she wanted was to panic them with fears of penury.

It was in the children, however, that she found the key to Jenny's resistance. 'If you won't take it for yourself, then take it for them. I've a right to give them money; I'm their aunt. And you have a duty to accept.'

Jenny got angry then, and tearful, and Anne knew she was near defeat. She lashed out suddenly. 'You're happy about this,' she said. 'You've proved your point. Everything you've always done was right. Everything Fergus and I did was wrong. It's just the same as always. You're enjoying this.'

Anne looked at her coolly for a long while. At last she said, 'I'm right about the children. I do have a duty towards them. And just as well too because if I didn't I'd go back to New York right now and leave you to get out of this mess yourself.'

'Good. Go on. Piss off.'

Anne sighed, 'Yeah, sure.' She had her back to Jenny and was sitting at Fergus's desk, writing out a cheque. 'Look, Jenny,' she said as she turned around, 'it's lovely not to need anybody at all. It's everybody's childhood dream. The day you don't need this any more, pay me back. In the meantime, it's for the kids.'

She held the cheque out for Jenny, who took it grudgingly, looked down, and when she read the figure looked up with wide, round eyes.

'I can't take this,' she said.

'Jenny,' Anne said patiently, 'that's the bare minimum that will get you out of hock. Believe me. Fergus had the Midas touch in reverse. Poor lovely idiot.' She ran a hand across the papers she had left in unaccustomed tidiness, and very gently she scattered them into a semblance of the chaos of before.

XIII

Jenny made her first return payment on the second anniversary of Fergus's death. It was ten pounds, a minuscule percentage of what she owed, and totally symbolic. She enclosed it in a pretty card and tucked the card into the interior of the package she was sending to Anne, the contents of which were symbolic too.

When Anne opened it in New York, she found, wrapped carefully in white tissue, an ankle-length evening coat of hand-crafted wool in four shades of lavender and blue. On the card her sister had written, 'The first shearing of my first lambing: spun, dyed, designed and knitted by me. This one thing at least I did alone. Love Jenny.'

Anne wore it that evening, over a black jersey dress, to dinner with Sandi Lang and her husband Josh. It was a social occasion, not a working one, but Anne knew Sandi well enough to understand that business was never far from her mind. With satisfaction she caught Sandi's admiring sideways glances at the coat throughout the meal. Before coffee they went off to the Ladies' Room together to refreshen make-up and escape from Josh's lecture on the economic ills of the city. Anne seated herself on a plush chair in front of a mirror and saw, in its reflection, Sandi's shrewd brown eyes sweeping her voraciously. Sandi leaned over and lifted the edge of one intricately worked sleeve.

'And where did you pick *that* up?'

'Oh. This? It's nice isn't it?'

'Are you playing games with me? Is this another one that Petra gets in East Hampton and I don't see?'

'I've *never* done that to you.'

'Sure you haven't.'

'It's a different clientele, Sandi,' Anne said soothingly. 'The Hamptons are very arty.'

'And New York is frump-town? Where'd you get it, Anne?'

'Actually, it's an original.'

'No kidding.'

'And a one-off.'

'Anything done once can be done twice for enough money.'

'Not this.'

'Why not? Who's the designer – Leonardo da Vinci?'

'My sister.'

'You're joking.'

'No. Why should I be joking?'

'Your *sister*.'

'Yes. Jenny.'

Sandi leaned back, one hand on her solid hip, studying Anne and the coat through narrow eyes. 'I thought she was some kind of earth-mother hippie.'

Anne gave her a calculated look of offence which won an instant apology. Then Sandi said, placatingly, 'I don't suppose she'd be willing to do one or two for me. I'd make it worth her while,' she added hastily. 'I could charge a small fortune for that.'

Anne stood up and turned around briskly, the way her models did on the catwalk, feeling the garment flow easily with her body. She shrugged prettily, 'I don't know. She's very busy . . .'

'I'm talking a *lot* of money.'

'Money doesn't mean much to Jenny,' Anne said sweetly. 'You know what these hippies are like.'

When Anne telephoned Jenny the next afternoon, she heard the panic come into her voice in response to her question.

'I can't do it.'

'Why not?' Anne said smoothly.

There was a flustered silence and then Jenny said quickly, 'I haven't the time.' It was the good, tried, true excuse for everything, from school sports' days unattended, to social invitations ignored, to cleaning the windows, or mending clothes. No one could argue; she had so much to do with the croft and the children. But Anne was unimpressed.

'You always say that,' she said. 'And you always have time in the end.'

'Only because I never stop running,' Jenny cried, indignant. 'I never rest.' Anne said nothing, waiting in silence. Jenny's voice turned brisk. 'Anyhow, I can't do it,' she said. 'They wouldn't be good enough to sell in New York.'

'I wouldn't have *asked* if I thought they weren't good enough,' Anne said plainly.

'Yes,' Jenny whispered, the panic returning, 'I know.'

'Well,' Anne told David, six months later, 'It worked. Sandi's getting her first order at the end of the month. I may take them back with me if I have the time.' It was September, and Anne was dining with her lover on the eve of her departure for her autumn trip to Europe.

'You're a wise cookie,' David said. He smiled, but Anne did not.

'Only about other people's lives,' she said.

David looked down at his plate. After a long while, he said, 'I haven't made much of a job of this, have I?' He laughed wryly. 'If I was so lousy at being married, you'd think maybe I'd be good at getting divorced.'

'It isn't just you,' Anne said quietly. 'I don't think either of us is very good at this.'

David sat back, studying her for a long time. Then he spoke, slowly, trying out his words with care. 'I seem to feel that whatever I say I'm going to fall into some cliché that a thousand men have used before me. A thousand not-very-nice men. So what, do I lie, or tell the truth?'

'Let's try truth, and then maybe go into lies when things get rough.'

'OK. We'll try truth. I want, with all my heart, only that I should be divorced and married to you. I want it more every day, and now the days are turning into years. And after these years, I'm no closer to making it happen than I was on the day I first decided it. So, I move out, fine, but what happens? The toilet leaks and she needs a plumber and she calls me. So, am I a plumber? No. But I'm her husband and I have called the plumber for twenty years. So I call the plumber for her. Then Julie has an asthma attack, and so of course she calls me. Am I a

240

doctor? No. But I'm Julie's Daddy and for fifteen years I sat up with her, I drove her to the hospital, I held her hand and promised her she wouldn't die. Then Danny fails English. So she calls me. Am I a teacher? No. But for twelve years I've made the rules and made them stick and done the homework with my son. And for all of this, does she love me? No. She hates me, because she depends on me and she hates depending on me. So when do I serve her with divorce papers? When the plumbing is leaking, when the child is ill, when the school is angry? It is never the right time to leave.' He held his hands out, palms upward.

'When *is* the right time to leave a marriage?' Anne asked. She heard coldness in her voice and so did he.

'Anne, I am not making up lies. This is the truth. So what does it mean, I'm a weak man? I should maybe put down the phone and let her cope? She *can't* cope. That's why she's depended on me for everything all these years.'

'My sister Jenny depended on Fergus for everything. Now he's dead and she's coping fine. She has to.'

'So I should die maybe?'

Anne laughed softly. She said, 'It might solve your wife's problem. It wouldn't solve mine.'

He took her hands across the table. 'Anne,' he said, 'do you think I'm leading you on?' He sounded serious and worried.

Anne said, 'No. Not me. But you're leading her on. And most of all you're leading the children on. Unless,' she said slowly, 'unless of course, you're going to go back.'

There was a long and, to Anne, ominous silence. David let go of her hands. He said, looking down at his own on the table, 'That's what they want, of course. The children, I mean. All the time, since I left. Whenever I see them they look at me like they're waiting for something, a present, maybe. And that's the present. That's what they're waiting for.'

'It would be kinder,' Anne said, 'to tell them the truth.'

He grew agitated, shaking his head, and said, 'You don't understand. It's so black and white to you. You don't know what it's like with children.'

Anne stared at him. She bit down hard on her lip to keep from saying anything. She felt her hands tightening into fists. Then her anger overwhelmed her and she raised the fists and slammed them down on the table linen, so hard that the silverware and

241

glasses jingled and diners turned to stare. 'I'm so sick of this,' she whispered hoarsely. 'I'm so sick of people telling me I can't understand anything because I don't have children. Jenny . . . you . . . you'd think children were another species. They're just small people. They can't be that different. And I can't be that much of an incompetent because I haven't any of my own.'

'Anne,' he pleaded. 'Please. Please don't be angry. It's just that if you *had* children . . .'

'But I don't. And I won't, will I? I'll just be screwed about by married men and left to grow old alone.' She stopped, startled at her own words which seemed like someone else's. She put her hands up slowly to her mouth, then dropped them, brushed down her skirt and gathered her purse and her coat and stood up. David stood up also, mortified.

'Anne,' he cried, anguished.

'I'm not leaving you,' she said quietly. 'Don't get upset. I just want to be alone to think. There's no point in us being together when we're like this.'

He stood watching her, hands clasped in front of him like a chastened child. She leaned across the table and kissed his cheek. 'I'm flying tomorrow night. I'll call you from the airport to say goodbye. When I get back, maybe we'll have a better talk.' She smiled a little, then turned and walked briskly out. Heads turned in the restaurant to watch her go.

Anne went out to the Island early the next morning, and spent the day with her parents before flying to London. In the afternoon she went with her mother to the Center to see Joseph. Her father stayed behind, watching a ball game on television.

'He hasn't any energy,' her mother said. 'Going to the Center exhausts him. I tell him to see the doctor but he ignores me. He says he's sick of doctors.' Anne nodded. She could see why. She pictured him sitting with his can of beer in front of the black and white set, falling asleep in the dull bits, his pinched, grey face set in deep, tired lines.

'I imagine the ball game's as good as a doctor,' she said.

Joseph was having a bad day. Everyone in the Center seemed to be having a bad day. It was a hot, fierce September morning with summer hanging on by its claws to the dying year. The air in the place was thick with humidity, rank with hospital smells.

The sound of children wailing fretfully came into Joseph's room through closed doors. The blinds were drawn against the heat, and the room was murky with suppressed light. Joseph whimpered when his mother spoke to him, and touched his hand. He seemed filled with a vast discontent. They brought him water, food, a toy. Nothing interested him. The boy in the neighbouring bed hummed tunelessly.

The hour of the visit seemed endless. Anne sat at the end of Joseph's bed and studied him dispassionately. He had lost individuality in the years he had been in the Home; he no longer seemed her kin. She tried to remember the fierce love she had once felt for him but it seemed to belong to another child in another life. He was a stranger; a bent, tortured, unfinished attempt at humanity. *If I leave here and never see you again, what difference would it make to either of us?* she thought.

'He's so good,' her mother whispered. 'Even in this heat. He's so good.'

'Yeah,' Anne said. She got up and walked up to the head of the bed, and ran her hand over his hospital-cropped hair. 'He's not a bad kid.' She paused. 'I liked his hair longer,' she said.

'Well. They have to cut it short. It's hygienic.' She smiled, leaning over her son, and Anne, watching her, smiled too. 'You'll tell Jenny about him?' her mother said.

'Of course,' Anne said.

'It's so long since Jenny has seen him. I wish she could. He was always so fond of Jenny. Jenny was so good with him.'

Anne felt hurt creep in. She said, 'She wasn't any better than any of the rest of us.'

'Oh, but she was. Jenny had her special thing with Joseph. She always had. But she's motherly of course. She's such a good mother. Poor Jenny . . .' Her voice broke suddenly.

'Jenny's all right,' Anne said, as much in anger as to comfort.

'Oh, I know. But I do worry about her.'

'You're wasting your time,' Anne said sharply. 'Jenny will be fine. Jenny's a survivor.'

'I wish I could be sure.'

'She's a survivor because she looks after Jenny,' Anne said. 'She survives by keeping vast amounts of territory to herself. She shuts out anything she can't cope with. Like Dad being ill, or

243

Joseph in this place. She cloaks it all with religion . . . "crosses to bear".' Anne paused, warily. 'She's like Grannie,' she said.

'Sounds fine to me,' her mother said, lightly. She was stroking Joseph's face over the safety bars of the bed, smiling gently to herself.

'It's fine for her,' Anne said. 'It's the rest of us who get the raw deal.' She laughed, to soften a little what she had said, and added, 'We're Martha and Mary. I do all the work and she sits at the feet of the Lord.' Her voice was strong and without self-pity.

Her mother looked up and the smile was more pronounced. 'The better part?' she asked. Her eyes were sharp.

Anne looked straight in them and said, 'It's things like that that made me leave the Church.'

Her mother shrugged and turned away. She looked over her shoulder to the grey bars of light behind the venetian blind. 'Oh, it takes more than that if you really have faith,' she said.

Elizabeth had warned her, but the changes in Jenny's house, and in Jenny, still startled Anne. It had been almost a year since Anne had last visited her sister. A planned trip in the spring to help her over the anniversary of Fergus's death, as she had done the first year, had had to be abandoned when their father's high blood pressure sent him into the hospital. By the time he was out, the summer season was upon Anne. She kept in touch with telephone calls, but they gave an incomplete picture. She was unprepared for the activity, the determination, and the sheer vigour of Jenny's new life.

Jenny never stopped moving. They could rarely talk because there was always someone coming in. Angus, who talked through anything they said. Or Sarah, an odd, emotional child, prone to sudden, inexplicable tears. Or the workmen; there were always workmen in fixing something. Or the old man who helped out on the farm. Or the dogs. Anne couldn't understand why Jenny needed so *many* dogs.

'Just four,' Jenny said. 'Two for the sheep. One in charge and one coming on. And Honey who's Sarah's. And then the terrier, Beetle, because my friend Fiona's bitch had pups and I helped her out.' Jenny had ticked them off on her fingers, along with their justifications. She glared at Anne, defensively. 'Other people have dogs.'

'Not quite so many,' Anne said. She wanted to add, 'Other people have money to feed them', but knew that was dangerous ground. Money was not something you could talk to Jenny about.

Which was a pity, because money was something with which Jenny was proving herself surprisingly clever. Not in the way Anne was clever; she had no entrepreneurial spirit, no cool-headed eye for business. But she had a certain shrewdness, born perhaps of desperation and fed by a determination to recoup the ground Fergus had lost. She made good use of what treasures and talents she had. She expanded her henhouse and now sold eggs as well as supplying her own needs. She increased her herd of dairy goats. She found a market in friends, neighbours and local hotels for the homemade cheese her children so assiduously scorned. Her beautiful hand-knitted jumpers and cardigans, which Sarah and Angus now both refused to wear, were bought up greedily by friends and even strangers. She hung a sign on a fencepost at the turn-off to her driveway – HAND KNITS – and a surprising number of summer tourists found their way to her remote door.

Then of course there was her contract with Sandi Lang. Anne had offered to take the completed garments back to New York, but she had been with Jenny for over a day before Jenny even mentioned them. When she did, it was shyly and with a nervous diffidence.

'They're in my workroom. I'm not sure they're good enough.' She made no move to show them and Anne had, herself, to suggest it. She followed her sister into the room at the back of the house where Jenny kept her wool, her wheel, and her vegetable dyes. The room was a surprise. Unlike the rest of the house it was neat and tidy. The floor was bare wood and carefully swept; it was the only room in the house forbidden to both children and animals. Carded fleeces lay in mounds in a heavy woven basket. On wooden shelves were skeins of wool in a rainbow of soft colours. There was a cork board with drawings pinned to it. Anne stared at the sketches, realizing they must be Jenny's.

'I didn't know you could do all this,' she said honestly.

Jenny didn't answer. She was standing nervously by a pine

table upon which, neatly folded, were the four coats she had promised Sandi. Anne reached to lift one in her hands but Jenny hovered nervously in her way. She said in a quick, breathless voice, 'I know you set this all up for me. I just want you to know that you can back out now if you want. I won't mind if you tell me they're awful, or anything.' She gulped and paused. 'I only do this for fun.'

Anne was studying the coats, searching details of seams, collars, edgings. She tugged the knit out over her hands, examining stitches. Finally she turned to Jenny.

'The colourways are lovely. I'm not sure the wider sleeve is a good idea. It might be hard to wear. I *love* the border. It must take forever to do.'

Jenny nodded. Anne said, 'In that case, leave it off the next lot. And by the way, who supplies your buttons?'

'What?' Jenny said.

'The buttons. Who's your supplier?'

Jenny looked blank and then said, 'Woolworth's?'

'Woolworth's.'

'It *might* have been that little sewing place on Union Street.'

Anne sighed. 'I get the point,' she said. 'I think, maybe, we're going to have a little talk.'

The little talk lasted for two days. It was the first of the many Anne would have with Jenny as her knitwear business grew from am imaginative idea to a career. In some ways it was the easiest of all those engagements between Anne's determination and Jenny's stubborn will, because on that early occasion Jenny was still malleable and uncertain enough to be swayed into compromise. Later, as Jenny's confidence grew and with it her rigidity, Anne left dealing with her to Sandi Lang. At the end of the two days Anne had instilled in Jenny something of the need for the conventions of sizing, pricing, continuity of design and colours, as well as the real necessity for the increased production made possible by mechanization. Reluctant and suspicious as a nineteenth-century Luddite, Jenny agreed to investigate the possibilities of buying in spun wool, and investing in a knitting machine.

'You can still do the hand stuff occasionally,' Anne comforted. 'But only for something really unique.'

Jenny looked sad.

246

'Cheer up, kid,' Anne said lightly. 'We're going to make you rich.'

'I never wanted to be rich,' Jenny said.

Anne sighed. 'Tough shit,' she said. 'You'll just have to put up with it, I guess.'

Anne was pleased and somewhat surprised to have reached agreement during her visit. It had not been easy. Reasoning with Jenny was never a pleasure, and doing it against a background of arguing children, yelping animals, demanding workmen and sundry other interruptions was difficult in the extreme.

The workmen were there to repair the roof, something Fergus had neglected for years with the result that there were ominous damp patches infecting ceilings and walls. Jenny, with more courage than money, had employed professionals all over the house and the croft to finish the jobs that Fergus had started and start the ones he'd never begun. There was new tin on the byre roof, new plumbing in the kitchen, new flooring in the dairy. She had found an ageing handyman to maintain the place in between major assaults by contractors and to do the heaviest work of which she was physically incapable.

Anne was impressed. The house and outbuildings certainly didn't look immaculate, but they had an air of well-being, as of a patient in convalescence rather than one on a death-bed, as before. While they talked and, as always, Jenny worked, the two workmen came down off the roof, made comments and suggestions, asked Jenny's permission for further work and, to Anne's surprise, listened carefully to her replies. They looked at her with respect, and something else as well: a touch of admiration bordering on desire. They smiled and joked with her, and one of them touched her arm lightly as he went out. To Anne they were indifferent, stepping coolly behind a barrier of anonymity and class.

'You get on well with them,' Anne said.

'Oh, they're really nice. They're so helpful.'

'I bet. He's got the hots for you.'

'What?'

'The one you were talking with. He wants you in bed.' Jenny's eyes widened and went round. She looked shocked but not entirely displeased.

'Don't be silly. He's just a nice man.'

247

'There's nothing *wrong* with it, Jenny.'

'Of course there is,' Jenny said quickly. She blushed girlishly, and looked with her two mouse-brown pigtails, utterly too young to be either a widow or a mother. 'He's probably married,' she said. Then, before Anne could reply, Jenny was saved further embarrassment by her son and daughter barging into the kitchen full of loud argument. Anne stepped quietly aside, annoyed as always with Jenny's abrupt dismissal of her when the children intervened. She could never accustom herself to the willingness of parents to parcel their lives into brief moments of child-free privacy constantly broken by interruption.

Of the two, it was Angus, hard-working and helpful, and clearly Jenny's mainstay, who annoyed Anne most. He did without question a man's share of work, but he had taken upon himself, with it, a man's authoritarian self-confidence. He asserted a father's rights of domination over his younger sister, and occasionally even over Jenny. He could be quite scornful of her abilities and of her mistakes.

'Where did he get this macho crap?' Anne demanded.

'From school.' Jenny's voice was mild with an undertone of resignation. 'They're all like that.'

'He wouldn't stay like that if he was living in my house,' Anne snapped.

'You don't understand,' Jenny said.

'It's not fair to Sarah,' Anne said belligerently.

'Oh, Sarah's all right.'

Anne didn't pursue it; in part at least because Sarah seemed to have an easy life. She drifted about the house, rising late and staying up late, reading and painting and drawing. No one seemed to expect any work from her and she herself appeared happy to keep it that way. But Anne liked her. She was quiet, and quirkily amusing, and undoubtedly talented. She was moody, but her moodiness resulted only in long, secretive withdrawals which did not trouble anyone.

She was shy with Anne, but after the second or third day of Anne's stay, she began coming into her room, staying at first only for a quick question, later for longer times. She lay on Anne's bed and read the copies of *Vogue* and *Cosmopolitan* that she had bought for the plane. She rustled through the guest-room wardrobe, eagerly investigating Anne's clothes. Her fingers were deft and quick, exploring fabrics and details. 'These are beautiful,' she sighed. 'Are they from New York?'

'Mostly,' Anne said. Sarah rolled over on the bed, and held one of Anne's cashmere sweaters against her face. She moaned softly. Then she sat up.

'My Mom hasn't any clothes like this,' she said. She was suddenly as scornful as Angus. 'She hasn't any *real* clothes at all.' She looked at Anne wistfully. 'I wish *we* lived in New York,' she said.

That was the beginning of the argument, though Anne didn't realize it at the time.

'Surely,' she said to Jenny over breakfast, 'it would do her good. It wouldn't have to be long; just a couple of weeks or so.'

'No.' Jenny stared into her porridge bowl, eating small hurried mouthfuls without looking up. Anne was baffled. She was hurt as well. She had considered an offer of a holiday in New York for Jenny's daughter really quite generous, in both money and her time. She had expected gratitude, not vigorous rejection.

'She'd love it, Jenny. I don't understand why . . .'

'She's too young.'

'They have escorts on the planes. Or I could even come and get her if you *really* want.' Anne paused. 'Though there's hardly any need. I see youngsters like her travelling all the time.'

'Not like Sarah. She's . . . she's too shy. She'd be terrified.'

'Well,' Anne said angrily, 'I suppose if you're going to tell her she will, she will. Come on, Jenny, don't be so protective. It would be great for her. Make her grow up, expand her horizons. *See* something for God's sake, other than sheep and fields.'

'You city people are all the same.'

'*What*?'

'You all think what you have is so much better, so important. Country children are different. They don't need all that glitter and junk. They have *real* values.'

'As far as I can see,' Anne said coldly, 'Angus has the values of a male chauvinist pig and Sarah's only expressed point of view was that she wished she lived in New York.'

'She didn't mean that. You don't understand her. You don't know what children are like, the things they say and don't mean.'

'Jenny.' Anne spoke so quietly that Jenny looked up startled.

'I've met children. There *are* children in New York. As a matter of fact I'm very likely going to be stepmother to two of them, whom I know very well indeed and love very much.'

Jenny stopped eating. She looked up, her eyes deeply hurt. 'I don't know about any of this,' she said. 'You've never told me about this.'

'You never asked,' said Anne. She was conscious how cold it sounded, and was sorry. If bereavement had made Jenny self-centred in the past, she could hardly be blamed. And more recently, and for her own reasons, Anne had kept her involvement with David Rosenfeld to herself.

'Maybe you should tell me about it now,' Jenny said stiffly. 'Only if you want to, of course.'

Then, naturally, there was no avoiding it. Anne told her of her three-year affair with David, of David's two children, Julie and Danny, who spent weekends with them in the city and, briskly and without emotion, of David's wife. She found herself recounting it all dispassionately, as if it were the cause of a stranger. She was aware of leaving out the portions that made her uncomfortable. Jenny listened sitting very upright, her head tilted slightly to the side, her gaze just to the left of Anne's shoulder. When Anne finished she turned her head and met her eyes. She said, 'There's only one thing I want to ask. How do you imagine those children *really* feel about you?'

Anne, who expected questions about David, was taken aback. She gathered her emotional resources and said calmly, 'I told you. They love me. And I love them.'

'Oh sure,' Jenny said sourly, 'I bet they just adore you.'

'Yes. They do,' Anne shouted. 'And why shouldn't they? What's wrong with me? Why shouldn't children love me?'

'Children love their mother,' Jenny said.

'Sometimes.'

'Always.'

'*Not* always. Sometimes their mother is a selfish, childish bitch.'

'His words?'

'*No*. My words.' Anne struggled to control her anger. She said, when her voice was calm again, 'He's never said a harsh thing about her. Never. In all the time I've known him. No matter what she's done.' She paused and said more quietly, 'He's never said a harsh thing about anyone.' She felt near to tears, as if she had betrayed David somehow in her floundering to make Jenny understand.

Jenny said then, disarmingly, 'He sounds like a nice guy.' Her voice was very soft, and it drew from Anne a torrent of emotion.

'Oh, Jenny, he's such a lovely, lovely man. He's a lovely man who's done his best for twenty years with a marriage that was wrong from the start. He made *one* mistake. He chose the wrong woman when he was twenty years old. And he's paid for it and paid for it and paid for it. He's tried everything, counselling, therapy, expensive holidays . . . he's turned a blind eye to three affairs. What more can anyone ask?'

'Fidelity,' said Jenny.

'You're joking.'

'Not me. The Church. The Church isn't joking.'

Anne got up from the table. She walked away, still holding her coffee cup, and stood looking out of the window at the cobbled yard. She said, 'That has nothing to do with us.'

Jenny shrugged. She remained sitting for a while, and then she got up too and began clearing her place and those of the children who had gone off to school. She piled things in the deep ceramic sink and, with her back to Anne, asked, 'What will Mom and Dad say?'

Anne turned about angrily. 'How should I know?' Then she paused and said, 'Mom probably won't give a damn. She hasn't been to mass in years.'

'And Dad?'

Anne stared at her sister. She felt weak suddenly against the strength of Jenny's certainty and a part of her was filled with outrage. She wanted to cry, *Who are you to challenge me over them? I've stayed with them, cared for them, worried over them. Not you.* But instead she waited until she was once more coolly in control and said, 'Look Jenny, I'm not a Catholic. That's all over for me. The whole breast-beating, cross-carrying lot. He's getting a divorce and I'm going to marry him.'

It was late November, and in the tree-shaded gardens of the New England hotel where Anne Conti and David Rosenfeld were sharing a weekend away, the fall colours had already faded to brown. But the air was still warm and soft, and an Indian summer haze hung over the distant wooded hills. They were seated at a

251

table for two on the wide, white painted verandah, enjoying a leisurely Sunday lunch. It was something that Anne had always hoped they would do often, once they were married. Now she knew they would do it only this once, and that they would not marry at all. Had she still believed in God she would have been bitter with him for granting her secret wish in the act of taking it away. Godless, she was simply resigned.

David asked her yet again if her lunch was all right. She smiled and nodded. He was not talking about lunch, but about life. And it was not all right, and he, and she, both knew. But it was easier this way, to be pleasant and gentle and enjoy the thin autumn sunshine, and then, as the evening grew dark, get back in his little MG sports car, and drive home to their separate lives. They would leave the canvas top down and enjoy the cooling air, knowing that too would be the last time for both of them. He was selling the car on Monday. It, and the SoHo apartment, both part of his brief single life, were now surplus to requirements because on Monday he was going home.

'Will I still see you?' he said, shyly now, as if they were strangers. 'I mean, just for lunch maybe, now and then.'

'I won't be in town that much,' she said. 'I'll be running most things from East Hampton now.'

She was moving back to Long Island. Marion and Greg Forsyth were looking for a house for her in the Hamptons – where they lived, perhaps. It was not because of David, nor in retaliation for his defection, but because her father had died, three weeks before, not long after her return from Scotland, and her mother and Joseph were now alone. The crisis in her life coincided with that in David's neatly, as if by some higher power intended. That was how Jenny would see it, she knew.

Jenny did not return to bury her father. The children, the farm, her distant, complicated life, stood between. She talked to her mother for an hour on the phone and had mass said for her father's soul. Their mother placed the mass card prominent among the others on their father's old piano and showed it proudly to everyone who called. As often, the few attentions of the daughter at a distance seemed somehow to outweigh the many of the daughter at hand.

Anne did everything else. All the funeral arrangements, the dealings with lawyers, the insurance, the painful partings with her father's clothing and possessions. He had died of a stroke in the middle of the afternoon, in his armchair before the television. Anne's mother returned from her visit to Joseph to find him there, with the ball game still playing on. She had been very sensible and controlled, calling the doctor for confirmation and allowing the next door neighbours to come in and make cups of tea. Late in the afternoon, Anne found a message on her answering machine, rang home, and learned what had happened. When she rang Jenny to break the news, she found with a dismay she did not really understand, that her mother had called Jenny first.

'I guess,' she said to David during that strange, timeless weekend in New Hampshire, 'I expect first notice of things because I'm the oldest. I expect first place. There's no reason really. She has a perfect right to prefer Jenny. We're both adults now. We've both proved what kind of people we are; it's all settled. And if it turns out that Jenny's more her kind of person than me, why not?'

David smiled. He said, 'The hardest lesson in life is that parents have preferences. But they aren't always the preferences we imagine. Julie is sure I prefer Danny, because we get on so well, and she and I fight whenever we meet. But, and God forbid he should ever find out, he's never meant to me what Julie has.' He reached and patted her hand. 'So don't be too sure Jenny's her favourite.'

'Oh, she's not,' Anne said at once, startling him. 'We both know that. First and forever there's Joseph. All Jenny and I ever fought for was second place.'

Now, second place or third, Anne was going home. She knew that was what she was doing, even though there would be an expensive and luxurious house on the Island which she would call her country place, and even though the New York apartment would remain for the necessary days spent in the city. She was going back, to take over her father's role as supporter and head of the family, to take upon herself the responsibility for her mother and for Joseph, for as long as that might last. David understood because he was going home, himself, to do the same.

His crisis began when Anne was in Scotland, and he weathered the first of it alone. He allowed her a day to recover before making her party to it. They met for dinner, her second night at home, after she had returned from the Island and the obligatory visit to her parents with Jenny's gifts and regards. He found Anne cheerful and approachable, in spite of the tension of their last meeting. In a way, it made it worse.

'There's a problem with Sharon,' he said, as soon as they had ordered. He said it so lightly that Anne misunderstood.

'Tell me what else is new,' she said.

'No. I mean it.'

Anne stopped smiling. She sipped from her water glass and said quietly, 'She wants more money.' That had happened often enough before.

'No,' David said. 'It's a problem with her health.'

Anne sighed. Sharon had produced health problems coincidental with every move closer to her that David had made.

'What is it this time?' she said wearily.

'She found a lump.'

Anne put her glass down. 'What do you mean?' she said.

'She found a lump. In the breast. She went to the doctor.'

'Oh Christ,' Anne said. 'Well, what are they doing?'

'They've done it. They do these things very quickly.'

'What, David? Is it malignant, or what?'

'Oh yes. They've taken it away. They've taken it all away. You know.'

'Oh Christ.'

'They say she should be fine. It was little. Like a pea, they said. And they took, you know, the glands and things. So they're doing radium treatment, just in case, but they're very optimistic. She's going to be fine.'

Anne felt herself sweating, dizzy. She was tired still from the journey. She said, 'Oh, David. I'm so sorry. I hope everything . . .'

'She's fine,' he said. 'She's going to be fine.' She looked up then, into his eyes, and saw to her amazement that he was crying, silently, and she knew precisely what he must do and what she must do.

Oh damn her, she thought. *Damn the bitch. Why now?* But she said, aloud, only, 'I understand.'

And so they were here, in a hotel for honeymooners, saying goodbye. It was difficult to talk. Finality weighted their words. Jests were forced, and endearments made hollow by the imminence of parting. They talked about the food and about the view.

254

Anne teased David for breaking his diet and ordering dessert. He did not laugh.

'What does it matter now?' he said.

She was sharp. 'What does it matter? It matters for you.'

But he shrugged, and she saw how quickly he would grow old now, with no reason to stay young. Solemnly, while they waited for coffee, he said, 'You'll always be the best thing in my life.'

'That's something, anyhow.' She heard how hard it sounded. But she was angry, because his words were so trite. She knew he talked in clichés because he was a man without guile, and the true language of the heart, universal and familiar, was unoriginal. But still, she wanted poetry to treasure in the days alone when she would remember this.

'I mean it,' he said, hurt. She told herself, *Don't ruin it. Don't get petty and small.*

'I know.' She took his hand across the table, twining her own with his short stubby fingers. She was fiercely aware of the gold wedding ring he had never ceased to wear.

He said, 'I should say, "I hope you find someone nice." But I'm not saying it.'

She laughed softly. 'You needn't worry. I imagine I'll always stay single. I think it's my natural state.' He looked sad, but she smiled brightly. 'I'll grow old and crusty and become Miss Conti to everyone. The formidable Miss Conti. I'll be a dragon.' She laughed again, envisioning herself grey-haired, hard-mouthed, beautifully dressed like an ageing French matron, ruling her empire with a rod of iron. 'Everyone will be terrified of me.'

'The formidable Miss Conti,' he said softly. 'I like it.' He paused and then said, 'Why aren't you Ms? I thought all career women were Ms.'

She laughed again. 'Too old. I was born too late for that. When Jenny and I were young, being liberated meant going to bed with men.' She looked down at their joined hands. 'We were so proud of ourselves. Our brave new world. What a bunch of patsies . . .'

'Anne . . .'

'Don't feel sorry for me. I warn you.'

'I'm envious,' he said.

She thought, *How easy for you. You'll always have someone.* He thought, *How easy for you. You'll be free.*

Anne went upstairs to put her overnight things in her case

while he settled their account. He put the bill on his business credit card where his wife wouldn't see it and joined Anne at the front of the hotel. She was standing alone amidst piles of brown leaves beneath a bare-branched maple. She looked like a fashion plate, in brown, belted trousers and a cream sweater, her short black hair shining in the sun. He stood and watched and his mind closed on the image like the shutter of a camera. And then it was over and she was still standing alone, a beautiful, elegant woman, no longer his.

XIV

'Fifteen years,' Anne said to Marion. 'He's been in there fifteen years.'

'It can't be that long.'

'Jenny was pregnant with Sarah. Sarah would be a Freshman in high school if she was over here. Fifteen years. When we put him in there I thought he'd last one.' Anne shrugged. She turned her pina colada around in her hand, drawing marks with her finger in the water-beading on the glass. It was a hot beautiful July day and they were lying side by side on beige-cushioned deckchairs beside Anne's pool. Marion's three children, in bathing suits of bright colours, were chasing each other across the wide green lawn, shouting and laughing. They turned in a ragged line and dashed back to the poolside.

'Wipe the grass off your feet before you go in,' Marion shouted. There was a combined bright splash as they hit the water together, ignoring her. 'I'm sorry,' she said.

'It doesn't matter. The filter catches it.'

Marion kept watching her children.

'Relax,' Anne said. 'They're having fun.'

'Everything's so perfect here,' Marion said worriedly. 'I hate when they mess it up.'

'God, what does it matter?' Anne said. 'It's just grass and flowers anyway.'

Marion glanced across, surprised. 'You sound a bit fed up. Something wrong?'

'Oh, just the usual. Sandi on to me all morning about something she feels I've neglected her over. And Stephen moping about in East Hampton, refusing to get the winter line under

257

way because he's had a fight with his boyfriend. And Mom. And Joseph. And Nonna. The day before yesterday I spent two hours at the Center with Joseph and then an hour in the evening with Nonna at *her* loony-bin. Sometimes I think I should be in one myself.'

'You're a good person, Anne,' Marion said.

'Oh the shit I am. I do the bare minimum, I promise you.'

Marion smiled. Around her eyes white crow's-foot lines marked her suntan and there were grey strands in her heavy bun of golden-brown hair. She made no attempt to disguise her age. *Why should she?* Anne thought. *Happily married. Three growing children. Why fight to stay young?*

Marion stretched herself lazily, contented. 'I should go,' she said.

'Don't,' Anne said. She glanced at her watch as casually as she could. 'There's lots of time.' There wasn't. She had promised to pick her mother up at four to take her to the Center. They found Joseph was better natured in the late afternoon, when the worst of the heat was past.

'You sure?' Marion said.

'Yeah, fine.'

'Do you go every day?'

'Monday, Wednesday and Friday. I leave the rest to her. And of course, when I'm in town or travelling she has it all. But I can't help that,' she added briskly. 'I have to work.'

'I think you're terrific,' Marion said.

'Far from it. Anyhow, you see him almost as much as I do, and you're not even family.'

Marion shook her head. She sat up and shouted at her boy, Gary, who was tugging at the branches of the big lilac beside the deck.

'Relax,' Anne said. 'It needs pruning anyway.'

'Not by that horde. God, Anne, I don't know why you invite us. You must breathe a big sigh when we go.'

Anne laughed. 'I don't really,' she said. She knew she would miss them when they went and was conscious of dragging the visit out, detaining them as long as she could because the pool and the lawn and the gardens would seem so empty when they had gone.

'Do you ever see David Rosenfeld any more?' Marion asked. She said it with elaborate casualness.

Anne answered mildly, 'Almost never.' She lifted her sunglasses slightly, her eye on the pool and Marion's youngest daughter, Anna, the one Marion had named after her when it looked clear she would never have children of her own. 'That's good,' she shouted, as the child dog-paddled across the shallow end, buoyant with blue and white arm-bands. 'I saw his daughter Julie at a party last month. She's at college upstate somewhere. New Paltz, I think. We had a nice talk.'

'They're still married?'

'I didn't ask.' Anne sat up and called to the children, 'Hey, you lot. There's ice-cream in the freezer if you want some.'

'We'll have to go,' Marion said. She looked at her watch and then back to Anne. 'What about the nice doctor at the Center?'

'What about him?'

'So you *are* still seeing him.'

'I might be,' Anne smiled. 'I might not, also.'

'You are,' Marion smiled broadly as well. 'Defensive as ever. Affairs are *allowed*, Anne. Everybody's having them. I might have one myself,' she giggled, but Anne was sharp.

'We're *not* having an affair. So if anyone's said . . .'

'*No* one. For heaven's sake, take a joke.'

'Look, he has an important position there. We have a professional as well as a personal relationship. There's medical ethics and all that.'

'All *right*. I'm not telling the world.' Marion sat up, faintly hurt. 'You sure are sensitive. Besides,' she added, 'I don't think medical ethics extending to the patient's big sister very likely.'

Anne sat up as well. She removed her sunglasses and said seriously, 'Of course not. But I have to deal with the staff there whenever there's a problem with Joseph. I have to deal about his treatment, about money, about everything. It changes things if they all think I'm screwing around with the medical director.'

'Which you're not of course,' Marion said calmly.

'Which I'm not.'

Marion looked up. 'I believe you,' she said. 'Would you like to?'

'Like what?'

'To screw around with him.' She grinned sweetly, managing

to be wholesome and bawdy at the same time. Anne lay back in the sun and drew her long sun-tanned legs up and wrapped her arms around her knees.

'You know,' she said, 'if I weren't the randy cow I am, my life would have been a helluva lot easier. And different. The answer is "yes, of course". And the answer to the next question is "no, we won't". We haven't time for it, if you can accept that for an explanation. We each have too much on in our own lives. He's got two children he's raised on his own since his wife died. He's done a great job too and it hasn't been easy. He reminds me of Jenny, actually. Jenny in reverse. It isn't exactly a ball for a woman, but it's tougher if anything for a man. And he's got his work and . . .'

'And what have you got?'

'You're joking.'

'No, I'm not,' Marion said. The children had gathered near and she sat up again and shouted, 'Look kids, go get the ice-cream your Auntie Anne said you could have. And then get dry and changed because we have to go.' When they had run out of hearing, she said, 'What's at the end of it for Anne? When Joseph is gone. He will go, one day. And Nonna. And even your Mom. What's there for you?'

'Jesus,' Anne said. 'You're a real bundle of tact today. Right, so I'll be an old maid with no family, OK? Any other salient points you'd like to make? Like my hair will go grey and my teeth fall out? Jesus.'

'Anne,' Marion said gently. 'I'm saying it now because now's the time to do something about it.'

'Oh, thanks a lot. What do you suggest I do? Ditch my Mom and Joe and run off with a billionaire?'

'No,' Marion said. Her voice was very patient. 'No. I'm not suggesting that. But it would be possible to just be a little more self-regarding. A little more certain of your own rights. You could do all this and still carve out a bit of life for yourself. I'm sure you could.'

'Are you? Well you try it. Christ, I haven't time for anything some days. I can't even change my fucking Tampax without *someone* interrupting . . . my secretary, or Mom, or Sandi or . . . oh screw, Marion, you can't understand.' Marion was silent. Anne said more reasonably, 'Look, I do have something of my own, you know. It may not seem important to you, but I have got these little clothes' stores in New York and London and Paris, and *some* people actually think I have a sort of career . . . there *might* be a future in that.'

'People with careers marry.'

Anne got up and flung her sunglasses down on the deckchair. The children were wandering back out on to the lawn with their dishes of ice-cream, but she made only a token effort to restrain her voice.

'Some *don't*,' she whispered hoarsely. 'Some try, and find that everybody they meet is a jerk, or gay, or married, or all three. I really maybe did want to get married once. But it just so happened nobody asked. Nobody who was free to ask, anyhow. That's the way the cookie crumbles. Some of us get lucky and some of us get left on the scrap heap.'

'Anne,' Marion cried, her face twisted in real anguish. 'I'm not saying that. Everyone knows you could have married if you wanted. You just didn't want hard enough . . .'

Anne smiled. She stood with her hand on her hip, her head back, her gaze up to the roof of her big house. She began to laugh softly. She came and crouched down beside the deckchair where Marion was sitting, large and kind and baffled. 'Do you remember the playground, at the elementary school? And the sandbox we used to walk around while we talked? And the grey teeter-totter? And beside the teeter-totter there was that merry-go-round thing that when we were little we never used because the big boys made it go too fast?' Marion nodded, uncomprehending. 'Well, that's the marriage game. It's OK if you get on at the beginning, because the thing is moving slow. But once you let the littlest time pass, it's too late. The merry-go-round goes faster and faster and you can't jump on, or off, without getting hurt. So the little kids, and the ones who came late just stand at the edge and watch everyone else's fun. I'm forty years old, Marion, just like you. It's not going to happen now. I've missed my ride on the merry-go-round.'

'Look,' said Elizabeth. 'Let's face it. Life is a balls-up. Marriage. Motherhood. Domestic bliss. It's all one big disaster area. The only sensible people are the ones like your sister who avoid the whole chaos entirely.' It was one of her sweeping statements of

261

commiseration that were meant to end a conversation she was finding tedious. Jenny O'Brien had arrived two hours earlier and they were still sitting in the big kitchen of Elizabeth's Georgian house, Jenny's luggage in a circle around them, dissecting the significance of the sudden desertion of Jenny's children. Jenny had come for the annual Edinburgh Craft Fair laden, as in years before, with paper cartons full of knitwear. It had become a tradition that she stayed with Elizabeth and Gordon during the fair, and until now Angus and Sarah had joined her, helping out with her stall, and in their spare time taking in museums and galleries and big city treats with their mother. Only this time they had, in Elizabeth's words, 'baled out'.

'I'm afraid the children couldn't make it,' Jenny had said breathlessly when Elizabeth met her at Waverley. As they loaded the cartons and Jenny's battered rucksack into Elizabeth's estate car, Jenny explained, 'Angus feels there's some reading he should do before he starts his course at Cambridge. And Sarah is very involved with her painting . . .' She had thought out the little speech carefully, having not wanted, for a variety of reasons, to quote either of her children correctly. What Sarah had actually said was, 'Oh Mom, it's so boring. I just stand around all day while you talk to your friends. All those ghastly people in organically grown sandals.' The rest of her protest had involved Elizabeth's children, Annabel and Victoria, who were supposed to be her companions in Edinburgh, and whom she referred to as 'a pair of toffee-nosed prigs'. Jenny certainly wasn't repeating that. As for Angus, he had been more generous and somehow, inexplicably, more hurtful as well. 'Of course,' he said with a weight of duty on the words, 'if you really *need* me, I'll come.' That was when Jenny had blown up. There had been a large, unpleasant and tearful fight that was not fully resolved even in the morning when she left. Angus drove her to the train with the hang-dog air of a failed husband. And so she was here, feeling oddly naked without her offspring, lying to her closest friend.

'They would have loved to have come if they could,' she said, appalling herself. Elizabeth lifted Jenny's rucksack with bemused distaste, holding it at arm's length as she dropped the shapeless heap of battered canvas behind the dog-grate of the car. It was

262

the same one that had accompanied Jenny and Fergus in the old days on the road.

Elizabeth smiled wisely. 'My two bale out on me all the time too,' she said helpfully. And that was the beginning of the discussion that was still continuing now. Elizabeth had little tolerance for problems that refused to be resolved because people were not facing facts.

'The perfectly ghastly thing about children,' she added, 'is that they climb up you like drowning men to get into adulthood and, when they've made it, they kick you under with their last step. There they are, young and beautiful and having a ball, and *you're* left behind, fat and sagging and covered in stretchmarks. Too bloody tired to have fun even if anyone wanted to have it with you. Which is hardly likely.' She sighed, and looked as if she actually believed what she was saying, which Jenny knew of course, was impossible. Elizabeth was slim as a model, twice as beautiful as either of her daughters, and looked young enough to be their sister. Her husband clearly adored her and was always trying to get her into bed at peculiar moments. Jenny heard them giggling in odd corners of the house whenever she came to stay.

'I don't feel that way at all,' she said stiffly. 'I loved being married. And I love being a mother.'

'Well, you could have fooled me,' Elizabeth said testily.

Jenny looked sheepish. She glanced around the kitchen, taking in her heaps of luggage, their cold tea-cups, the clock on which two unproductive hours had passed. She said, 'I'm sorry. I didn't mean to go on about it. It's just that I'm disappointed. I just expected they'd want to come with me.'

'Why?'

'Because they always did.'

'Sounds like a perfectly good reason to expect them not to,' Elizabeth said flatly. 'They're growing up. They're getting sick of you.' Jenny looked so devastated that Elizabeth softened it by adding, 'My two can't stand me. They think I'm a *total* bore. They much prefer the au pair. And their *father* of course,' she added sourly. 'But then, they're girls. What can you expect?'

'It's different for us,' Jenny said stubbornly. She paused. 'We're very close.'

Elizabeth chose not to take offence, perhaps because Jenny sounded so sad.

'They'll grow up anyhow,' she said gently.

Jenny was silent, fiddling morosely with her tea-cup. Then she burst out, suddenly, 'It's so unfair. I worked so hard for so many years. And finally I got everything – the house, the croft, the family – just the way I wanted it. We did everything together. And now it's all falling apart. They're not interested in the croft or the animals any more. Sarah doesn't spin or knit any longer. They both leave the garden to me, even the bits they started for themselves. And Sarah's so strange. She hates all the things I make and wears awful black skirts and things from the chain-stores. She's cut all her hair off and she puts this glop on it.'

'Hair gel,' Elizabeth said knowingly. 'There's half a ton of it upstairs. What about Angus?'

Jenny stiffened. At last she said in a small voice, 'I don't understand Angus. All he's interested in is money. He actually says so. He keeps coming up with schemes to get rich. Last week he told me I should try for planning permission to put a couple of bungalows in the field next to the house.'

'Sounds a good idea,' Elizabeth said sharply. Her eyes lit. 'Gordon would help . . .'

'I don't want a damned bungalow beside my house,' Jenny cried. 'It would ruin everything. The view, the privacy . . .'

'You'd make a bomb.'

Jenny glared at her.

'I don't know why I'm telling you this,' she said coldly. 'We've always disagreed about this sort of thing. You're just like Anne. And so is he. That's what Angus is like. Though I can't see why he should be. Fergus and I were never like that, either of us.'

Elizabeth smiled wryly, 'I think it's generation, not genetics, that makes children what they are.'

'Well if it is,' Jenny said belligerently, 'I don't *like* this gener-ation. They're *proud* of things we'd be ashamed to admit. Greed and selfishness and . . .'

'I think they're more honest,' Elizabeth said lightly, 'that's all.' She stood up and cleared the cups from the table, but left them on the draining board for the au pair to load into the dishwasher. 'They're all like that,' she said. 'My two are a total disaster. Thank God for the nuns at that school, is all I can say. At least they get *some* discipline there. Children are little pigs. All of them.' She reached down to lift Jenny's rucksack but Jenny still sat, unmoving, by the table.

'I'd love another,' she said dreamily.

'You're mad.' Elizabeth put the rucksack down and stared, open-mouthed. 'I don't believe you said that.'

Jenny shrugged. 'Never mind,' she said. She smiled to herself, a sweet smile.

Elizabeth sat down again with a weary sigh. 'I think you've gone off your chump,' she said evenly. 'The *only* thing one can say for children is at least they do eventually grow up and get civilized. It takes long enough. But now, when they're finally about to clear off and leave you in peace, to even contemplate having another . . . good God.'

She looked genuinely appalled, and Jenny shrugged again. She never could quite understand how Elizabeth managed to find child-rearing such hard work, bolstered as she was by au pairs and boarding schools. She said, 'Well, maybe it's different for you.'

Elizabeth shook her head, unbelieving. She watched Jenny seriously for a long while and then said, 'If you really *mean* that, I think I have to point out to you that you're lacking one basic requirement.'

'Money?' Jenny said mildly. 'I've always managed without that.' She felt a little smug. Angus on his way to Cambridge, Sarah top of her art class. Surely she'd proved herself with them?

'A man, Jenny,' Elizabeth said firmly. 'Remember? Man? Two to tango and all that.'

Jenny laughed softly. 'I'm just dreaming,' she said. 'I always imagined if I wanted another baby, some bloke would father it for me willingly enough. Wrinkles and stretchmarks notwithstanding.'

Elizabeth looked shocked. 'I thought you were very devout and all that,' she said.

Jenny just waved her hand, laughing again. 'I'm only joking,' she said. But Elizabeth was regarding her with a new shrewdness.

'That's it, of course,' she said. 'That's what you need. That's exactly what you need.'

Jenny sat up straighter. 'A new baby?' she asked, surprised at Elizabeth's concurrence.

'Of course not, you idiot.' Elizabeth smiled triumphantly. 'A man.'

The mornings were slow at the Craft Fair. Most of the main buyers came in after lunch. Jenny arrived early, however, and set up her stock. She was not good at displaying it. Anne had tried to show her how to drape garments for the best dramatic effect, and to arrange colours in attractive sequences, but Jenny did not learn. She said she lacked artistry, but knew it was really lack of confidence. She was reluctant to draw attention to herself. 'You're trying to *sell* something,' Anne insisted. Jenny nodded morosely and still set out her wares as if by accident, ready to pack them and flee at a moment's rejection.

The man on the next stall seemed to share her uncertainty. He laid out his silver bracelets and earrings and brooches in a jumble of plain boxes. Some were stacked three deep, hiding their contents. The sign above the stand was hand-painted. In slightly smudged letters it read: Simon Hamilton, Silversmith. The man was young, and nervous, with glasses and a flop of yellow hair over his forehead. Jenny felt sorry for him and smiled once, encouragingly, and he broke out in a happy grin.

Later, she was a little sorry. He became attentive, helping her set up her stall, coming over in quiet spells to admire her work and to chat, bringing her paper cups of instant coffee. Although he was doing nothing more than be pleasantly sociable, she was uneasy. She was so accustomed to having the children as a buffer between herself and men, ensuring only the most decent, unromantic attentions from them, that bereft of their company she was as shy as a schoolgirl. She blushed and stammered and then felt silly because he was such a young man that imagining he entertained a romantic interest was undoubtedly self-deluding and ridiculous. Thinking that, she was saved by her mother-instinct and became protective and helpful.

He told her this was his first craft fair; that he had a degree in law and had worked for a conglomerate in London, but was abandoning money and security to work with his hands in the North. It pleased her. She said, wistfully, 'When I was young, everyone was doing that.'

He looked at her oddly. She didn't notice, but added, 'Now, not even my children understand.'

266

He was cautious. He said, 'How many children have you?' It was a carefully neutral question. He made no reference to her marital status though as she answered she was aware of his glance crossing Fergus's broad gold band that she still always wore.

'Oh, just two.'

'How lovely.'

She looked up, surprised. 'Do you like children?'

'Oh, I love children.' His enthusiasm was genuine, but he was suddenly shy. 'I have some little cousins, but I don't see them very often because my parents are divorced.' He went silent, reddening, started to explain about the hard feeling within his father's family, and stopped awkwardly. He swallowed and asked, 'What age are your children? Are they boys or girls . . . ?'

'A boy and a girl,' Jenny said. Normally she was proud to talk about the children, but just then, feeling estranged from them, she would rather not. 'Eighteen and fifteen,' she said briskly. 'Angus is starting at Cambridge next term. Sarah's still at school.' She hadn't noticed he was staring, faintly appalled.

'I thought they'd be little children,' he said. Jenny looked up, surprised at his mistake and his disappointment.

He said, 'You must have married very young.' It was perhaps a compliment, but in his awkwardness it came out much as a criticism.

'Not that young,' Jenny said.

'I mean you look very young.' They stared at each other. The conversation lurched and became significant. 'You look very nice,' he said.

Jenny only told Elizabeth about Simon Hamilton on the last day of the Craft Fair, when she was already preparing to go home. She told her in passing, by accident, and was immediately sorry she had done so.

'What man? You didn't tell me about a man.' Elizabeth was as sharp-eyed as an over-eager mother.

Jenny, annoyed, said, 'Oh, for God's sake. He was just a nice bloke on the next stall. He helped me set mine up when things were quiet.'

'Was he attractive?'

Jenny paused, thoughtfully. 'I suppose so.'

Elizabeth glared at her. 'Didn't you even look?'

'Elizabeth, he was really young. Maybe twenty-five.'

'So?'

'*So*? Elizabeth, that's only seven years older than Angus. You can't seriously expect me to be interested in a man that age?'

'But you are interested. It's obvious.'

'Of course I'm not.'

'Anyhow, what's age to do with it? If you fancy the bloke and he fancies you . . .'

'He doesn't, I'm sure. And I don't. And anyhow, it would be disgusting. I'm so much older. It would be cradle-snatching.' Jenny's mouth tightened primly with distaste. Elizabeth said, 'Did you give him your address?'

'Of course I didn't. He was just a nice, friendly bloke. That's all.'

'Idiot,' Elizabeth said.

'Yes.' Jenny was still prim. 'I suppose I am.' She did not tell Elizabeth that although she had definitely not given Simon Hamilton her address, he was moving North in September and had taken special care to give her his. Elizabeth didn't need that kind of ammunition. Jenny said instead, 'Look, you'd better understand, I'm really not interested in men. I have no intention of getting married again. I've got all I want with the croft and my work, and the children . . .'

'You don't have to *marry* anyone,' Elizabeth broke in brittly. 'I just thought a little romance in your life might be good for you. It might keep you from *dwelling* on things.'

'I don't *dwell* on things. I'm very busy. You have no idea what my life is like. How could I fit a man into it? What would the children think?'

Elizabeth looked surprised. 'It doesn't matter what they think. You're hardly going to *ask* them, are you?'

Jenny blinked. She knew instinctively that if such an occasion arose, that was precisely what she would do.

Elizabeth said with authority, 'You make it a *fait accompli* and then they just have to stick it. It's none of their business anyhow.'

'We're a family. You don't treat family like that.'

'They'll do it to you fast enough when the time comes.'

Jenny was uncomfortable with that. 'That's not true,' she said.

Elizabeth shrugged. 'You're the one who's been moaning on

about family desertions all week.' She lifted Jenny's old rucksack to take it to the waiting car downstairs. As she did, she said casually, 'Have it your way. But trust me on this one. All this sacrifice will have precisely one effect. They'll feel frantically guilty every move they make away from you, and they'll end up hating you for it. Life's a pig, Jenny. Grab what you can while you have the chance.' She hoisted the old sack over her arm and strode gracefully down the echoing stone stairs, Jenny following meekly behind.

That was July. By the time Anne arrived in Edinburgh *en route* to Paris in September, Elizabeth was brimming with gossip and opinion regarding Jenny and Simon Hamilton. She launched into the subject with enthusiasm at the first opportunity, as soon as dinner was finished and they had retired at last for coffee.

Elizabeth had a different standard for Anne Conti than for Jenny O'Brien. Evening meals were always dinner in the dining-room, with candles and silver, not pot luck about the kitchen table with the au pair. She imagined such efforts rather wasted on Jenny. Also, there was always a man across the polished rosewood for her guest's amusement. The current offering, Lachlan Stuart, directed an art gallery on George Street. He could be counted on to look nice, talk amusingly, and go lightly on Gordon's claret. What further arrangements he chose to make with Anne were his own business; Elizabeth had done her bit.

Lachlan Stuart watched, faintly morosely, while Elizabeth brought the meal to a close, handed her husband the port decanter from off the sideboard, and escorted Anne out of the room. Gordon himself looked no less disappointed. 'I say, couldn't we just be informal since we're all old friends? I haven't seen Anne for a year.'

Gordon was always a bit of a problem during Anne's visits. Although he was quite oblivious of Jenny, treating her like one of his daughter Annabel's friends, he made a great fuss over Anne's arrival, taking time off from work to meet her train, carrying her matching Gucci luggage faithfully himself. Hanging about the kitchen even, while Elizabeth prepared dinner. 'No chance,' Elizabeth said tartly. 'She's mine. Amuse yourselves.'

When she had settled herself in front of the coffee table in the upstairs drawing-room, where the au pair had set out demi-tasses and a silver pot filled with a burnt-smelling brew, she said, 'Gordon fancies you of course.' Anne shook her head and laughed awkwardly, but Elizabeth nodded firmly. 'He's thoroughly potty about you.' Her voice was mild. Then she grinned wickedly. 'Now, let me tell you what little sister's been up to while the cat's been away.'

Anne listened, without comment and with little expression. She was aware that Jenny's love-life was being presented as a source of entertainment, and although she suspected that Elizabeth would use anyone's personal affairs, even her own, in the same way, she still resented it. 'Actually,' Elizabeth concluded, 'the whole thing's a bit of a mystery. Jenny hasn't a clue about making herself attractive. She's no beauty but she *could* make the best of herself. But she doesn't. She never has. I can't *quite* imagine what it is he sees . . .'

Anne could not disagree with Elizabeth's judgement on Jenny's lamentable lack of style, but she refused to show accordance.

'Jenny has her own look,' she said vaguely. 'And maybe that's not important to him, anyhow.' She paused and said uneasily, 'She must have *something* special. At that age, he could have his choice.'

Elizabeth looked faintly offended at Anne's refusal to play. She shrugged coolly. 'I imagine he's something of a twit,' she said. 'Though he *looks* nice enough.'

'You've met him?'

'Just for a moment. They were on their way to London . . . Can you imagine, Jenny leaving Cold Comfort Farm for a solid week . . . it *must* be love. Anyhow, she had business in Edinburgh and they were taking the sleeper down that night, so Gordon and I joined them for drinkies in the NB.'

'The sleeper?'

'Oh *separate* sleepers. Jenny made quite sure I knew that. She's a hoot.'

'I don't suppose it will be separate sleepers forever,' Anne said quietly. Inexplicably, she thought of Fergus, with a deep sense of hurt. 'I suppose it was bound to happen some time.'

'Oh, but it wasn't. To hear Jenny, this was the last thing she intended.' Elizabeth shrugged again. 'Lucky for some.' She made the small twist of her mouth, secretive and sour, that meant she was temporarily fed up with Gordon. 'She *says* they're just friends of course,' she added, sententiously.

'Maybe they are,' Anne said. 'You can't be sure.'

'Oh, I can,' Elizabeth said. Anne raised an eyebrow. Elizabeth leaned close. 'I have a lot of experience in this,' she said. 'You see, you may think that Edinburgh is the epitome of provincial restraint, but I promise you it's not.'

'A hotbed of sexual intrigue?' Anne said, laughing.

'Emphasis on "hot" and "bed",' Elizabeth returned at once. 'Half my friends are indulging at the moment. And if old Gordy doesn't shape up soon, I might just join them. But that's not the point. The point is, I can recognize the signs. The first thing a woman does when she begins an affair is drop all her women friends. No more lunches, no coffee mornings, no cosy chats over G and T's. Female solidarity crumbles at the first intrusion of a wayward phallus.' She sat up straight and poured more coffee for herself and Anne. 'Jenny was a good friend. She always kept in touch. I haven't heard from her now since she left here in July, except to say she was passing through with her brown rice Lothario, and *that* was less being social, than showing off.' She sniffed. 'If they're not in the sack yet, they will be soon enough.' She looked morose, and then abruptly dropped the subject. 'Anyhow, tell me about *your* Mr Wonderful,' she said.

Anne smiled to herself. Her mind was still on Jenny and Simon Hamilton, but she said for Elizabeth, 'Oh, he's simple enough.'

'I thought there were all *sorts* of complications.' Elizabeth made a mimicry of disappointment. 'I thought Aunt Elizabeth was going to be called upon to sort everything out.' She sniffed again, but this time with good nature.

'Oh hang in there. You probably will.' Anne paused, a little reluctant to talk, but aware that Elizabeth was waiting eagerly. She said slowly, 'You see, at our age, *nothing* is really simple. You don't just have an affair like when we were young . . . you and some guy and a lot of bed. Now you have a *relationship*; you've been married, or he has, and he has kids, or you have, and there's an ex-wife and alimony, or,' she paused briefly, 'a dead wife and memories, which may be worse. There's one time only to do things simply, and that's when you're both nineteen. At my age, you need a UN delegation to Geneva just to make a date.' Elizabeth laughed loudly. She passed the box of mints to Anne, and then got up and listened briefly at the door for any sign of the men.

271

'Tell me,' she said, returning. 'Any treaties yet?'

'Several. All compromise of course, like any good politics.'

'On both sides?'

'Mostly on mine.'

Elizabeth looked severe. 'Not a good start,' she said.

Anne shrugged unperturbed.

'It has to be,' she said. She grinned, suddenly. 'Unilateral disarmament. I relinquish Christmas and New Year; those are for the children. I relinquish wearing red which is my favourite colour but was also hers.'

'You gave up *your* favourite colour because he asked you?' Elizabeth shouted.

Anne glanced nervously to the door. 'Of course he didn't ask me,' she said, dropping her voice. 'He said I looked lovely. And that she did, too. And then I saw the memories in his eyes.'

Elizabeth absorbed that doubtfully. She crumpled her mint envelope briskly. 'Right,' she said. 'No holidays. No red. What else?'

'A lot else,' Anne said quietly. 'All the portions of an adult heart that are already occupied. There's no way to avoid that at our age.'

'Jenny has.' They looked at each other and a small smile passed between them. Elizabeth sighed.

'Well,' she said. 'If he's rich, handsome, and absolutely fantastic in bed, I suppose I might give up Christmas and the odd red dress. What about those children? Are they little beasts like most American brats?'

Anne smiled. It was the sort of remark that used to cause fights when they were young, together, in Edinburgh, but she had long since given up hope of changing Elizabeth. She said lightly, still smiling, 'Leaving out any slight national prejudices, no. They're lovely girls.'

'Do you see a lot of them?' Elizabeth's eyes were narrow.

'Quite a lot.' Anne grew quiet. She drank from her coffee, the cold dregs at the bottom of the thin china cup, and nibbled at another mint. 'Frankly,' she said, 'I try to limit it a bit.'

'Ah, hah. As I said. American brats.'

'No,' Anne said patiently. 'No, very lovely young American girls. The oldest is a little like Julie Rosenfeld.'

'*Who?*'

'Julie. The daughter of my friend David.'

'Oh. The Jew.'

Anne restrained herself until her voice would again be friendly and calm.

'Yes,' she said clearly, 'David. David's daughter. I still see her . . . she's like a sort of distant daughter to me as well. Very distant . . .' Her voice went thin. 'I don't think I'm prepared to go through all this again with any more children until I'm sure it's permanent. I'm a hard bitch, but some things do hurt.' She was crying.

Elizabeth stared. 'Good God,' she said. 'I had no idea. You've not gone broody too?' She looked so comically suspicious that Anne laughed. She quickly and carefully blotted her eyes, hearing the deliberate shufflings and coughs of the two men coming up from the dining-room.

'Well, if I have,' she said, 'there's not much point.'

XV

In July, Bob and Anne took a beach house on Fire Island for a month. It seemed faintly silly to Anne, considering that each of them had comfortable homes within easy reach of the Southampton shore, but it did provide an opportunity to live together, if briefly, as a family, without anyone making any irrevocable step. It was a significant occasion, and they were both aware of its importance.

Anne expected the longest four weeks of her life, but at first it went very well. She had been wary of such a long period away from her mother and Joseph. Although it was not far, ferry schedules and packed summer roads precluded quick returns. But Bob was persuasive and Anne found that after a day or two the hot, lazy, sun-soaked atmosphere of the beach crept over her, made her relax and even forget. After a few days she was not even thinking of them; her mind no longer touching down at points throughout the day that echoed Joseph's routine, her mother's visiting hours. She wondered if this was what happened to Jenny, responsibility fading and finally dissipating with distance and time.

'I could really forget about him. I really could,' she said, alarmed, to Bob. They were lying side by side on a broad beach blanket, up near the dunes, facing away from the ocean but listening to its steady soothing roar. 'Does that happen ever? Do people just go away and forget and never come back?'

He turned on his back and lay looking up at the immaculate sky, blazing with heat. He laid the back of his hand over his eyes and said, 'It happens. Not often, but it happens.'

'It could never happen to her,' Anne said.

'No. Not to her.' They lay quietly, their fingers entwined. Occasionally Bob sat up and stared, squinting into the white sun until he located Robin in her black bikini among the crowds.

In the afternoons, when Robin went back to the beach after lunch, Anne and Bob made love quickly in the sticky heat behind their bedroom door, windows shut to contain any muffled sound. When they had finished he was clumsy in his haste to dress and return to the beach again and his daughter, the role of protective father forgotten briefly in the heat of sex, reviving instantly afterwards. Anne was resigned. The nights were no better, waiting and waiting for the last sound, the last click of the refrigerator door, the darkening of a last light before they could turn into each other's arms. As often as not, exhausted with sun and heat they fell asleep first and awoke, disappointed and unsatisfied in the morning, with Robin already laughing on the deck, splashing their window with the garden hose.

'It was easy when they were babies,' Bob said, and then bit off the words midway, as he always did when the present suddenly stumbled disastrously into the past.

In the evenings they sat around the kitchen table of the rented house and played family games: gin rummy, Trivial Pursuit, Monopoly. They turned the lights low and, one night, when cool Canadian air broke the stifling heat, even lit a small, sweet-smelling wood fire in the free-standing stove that centred the living room. Robin played with ferocious determination, mopping up hotels and putting everyone out of business. Anne kept to her side of the table, watching more than playing, feeling detached and removed from them, shut out innocently by family in-jokes, and private emotional codes. Often, she went to bed early to leave them comfortably alone. Those were the hard nights; lying in bed trying not to feel lonely, trying to be generous of heart and not be hurt or resentful of their total self-sufficiency. Having feigned tiredness she felt obliged to feign sleep as well, but it was hard to sleep. Peals of childish laughter broke the silence and, when they were quiet, there were other sounds in the night.

The beach house, expensive as it was, was still crammed in beside dozens of others; in any other place the clutter of wooden cottages would be a shanty town. Here every square inch was worth a fortune, and privacy amongst the boardwalks and beach plum and poison ivy was almost unattainable. Anne lay awake listening to strangers talking on the hot air that drifted through the screens. In the next house, separated by only a few yards of stunted holly and white oak, there was a new baby. In the daytime it slept in a play-pen on the decking, sheltered by tents rigged from yellow and pink blankets. At night, invariably it cried, a high, bleating young animal sound, like the lambs in Jenny's fields.

Robin complained about it every morning. Bob teased her, evoking her own infancy, and she just moaned louder, confident in adolescent disgust. But the cries, which annoyed her so, tormented Anne. She tossed and turned, fighting the urge to rise from her bed and sneak out to comfort it in the darkness. In the morning she hung about the nearside of the deck, hoping to be there when the mother came to feed it, and perhaps to speak, to make friends, and at last be offered a chance to hold it in her arms. When she woke to its hungry wail in the grey dawn hours her virgin breasts tingled as if they would fill with milk.

When Robin said, each morning, 'Did it wake *you*, Anne?' rubbing her eyes ostentatiously and glaring at the neighbouring house, Anne always said, 'No.'

After the first week, they found people they knew vaguely among the other summer residents, and invitations came to share drinks and barbecues on other decks in the evenings. Robin, too, found friends on the beach and began to drift away. Anne and Bob had time to themselves. They read, made each other iced coffee, talked endlessly.

'It's so great,' he said. 'It's so great having this freedom, not needing to be there all the time, or always find someone to cover when you're not.' He became quite jubilant, envisioning the future opening up before them. He began to plan things they would do together: a European trip; a winter vacation in Vermont – she would learn to ski. They would camp in the Rockies. He and his wife had had a vigorous, outdoor courtship, wholesome and adventurous. But then of course the children had come. Anne wanted to tell him about the baby and how it made her feel, but could not find the words.

Then Mandy came, with her new husband John. It was a continuation of their usual habits. Since their wedding in Septem-

276

ber, the family had expanded rather than diminished. Mandy still chose to spend most weekends in her father's house.

The cost of the beach house was formally split three ways, though Anne suspected that Bob had also paid John and Mandy's share. He had told Anne of their plans cautiously, leaving room for objections. Anne did not presume to object. Fortunately she liked Mandy, a bright, cheerful girl who, having taken on the role of surrogate wife – cooking for her father and helping to raise her younger sister – could not be blamed for finding it difficult to relinquish.

'In time, she'll let go,' Bob confided, speaking more in hope than in knowledge, and Anne wondered if it would happen before her young husband wearied of his slightly secondary role. There was no danger of that yet, however. They arrived off the ferry twined like teenagers in each other's arms, their eyes full of the dreamy exclusivity of lovers. If anything they seemed more intimate than on their wedding day. They watched with secret smiles as everyone busied themselves loading their luggage on to the traditional red wagon that came, as transport, with the house. They set off, Bob and Anne and Robin coddling the overloaded wagon along the boardwalks, Mandy and John following, whispering together, behind.

On the beach Mandy sat in matronly reserve for half an hour, watching her sister and her father play in the surf. Then, quite suddenly, she got up and ran down the sand, splashed into the creamy foam, flinging her arms around her father's neck. Her husband stood up and trotted patiently down the beach to join her. Anne watched Bob swing her easily in an arc, and set her down in the bright surf. She was a little jealous, but also pleased; pleased at his delight in his daughter, and at the sight of him. He had a nice body, a little slack around the waist, but not much. He played tennis and squash, cycled and jogged. Sun-tanned, his hair freshly washed, he looked fit and young even beside his son-in-law, and he moved with a surer, more confident grace.

John was thin and awkward, and his shoulders, white from working indoors, were burning pink in the sun. He reminded her of Jenny's friend Simon, even to the repetitive gesture of brushing back a loose forelock of hair. The comparison filled her with confusion. She rearranged herself on her beach towel and returned her eyes to Bob, trying suddenly to envision what he must have looked like when they were both as young as Mandy and John. A gawkier, leaner-faced version of him arose in her mind, minus his funny little bald patch, and without the lines of care and thoughtfulness that she loved. A real Jock probably, she decided: flat stomach, brown muscular thighs, even as a boy. Like Greg Forsyth; though Greg had grown a paunch and his hair was receding. She ran an alternative life in her head in which they met and married young, had children, and were now drifting comfortably together into middle-age. That would be fine then, if these two girls were her own, and child-rearing something she was quite ready to put behind her. She put her head down on her arms, listening to her own breathing muffled against the sun-tanned skin, and letting the sun soak into her bones. The sounds of the beach, quintessentially summer, drifted a little further away. *This is enough*, she told herself. *Be content*.

At dinner, John told them. They had planned it between them, evidently, because they kept glancing back and forth at each other until he quite suddenly rang his knife against his glass, stood up self-consciously, pretended to clear his throat, and said, 'Um, we have an announcement to make.' He looked at her and she nodded, vigorously, in support. 'Mandy and I, I mean, she . . . we're having a baby,' he said. 'She's pregnant.' He looked wildly towards Bob, with an expression midway between pride and apology. Robin shrieked and stood up and flung herself at her sister and while they embraced Bob also stood, slowly. He patted his son-in-law's arm gently. Anne saw that his hand was trembling. He stepped away from the table so that he could approach his daughter, and she freed herself from Robin's embrace, moved towards him, and then they both stumbled into each other's arms.

Later, they sat out together on the deck, with candles burning to keep away the mosquitoes, and watched fireflies twinkling green and blue in the dark undergrowth. They talked for a while and then grew silent as the slow, soft rhythm of the surf crept over them. Bob lay stretched out on a lounger, with Mandy curled up beside him, her head on his shoulder. John sat on the decking, leaning his head against his wife's leg. Robin got up and went inside to read. In a little while Anne followed. Behind her, she heard Bob call her name.

'I'm fine, darling. I'm just going to wash my hair.' She said it lightly, even gaily. She would not ruin his special evening for anything. Inside, she dutifully showered and shampooed her hair, and stood in front of the bathroom mirror, and towelled it dry. Carefully she checked the roots for any intrusive grey, and then combed it easily into place. Mosquitoes hummed around the small damp room. She put out the light and went through to the bedroom. She closed the door and undressed in the dark and got into bed. Outside on the deck she still heard the soft murmur of voices, far away, as if they belonged to strangers. She turned her face into the pillow and silently wept.

The surf rolled in, muted and soft, and rolled out again. Anne lay awake, unable to sleep, counting each swell. At times the sound drifted away, and she felt herself nearing the release of unawareness, but something, a voice, a moment's laughter, the chime of a glass, drew her back each time. She opened her eyes. There was almost no light in the room anyhow. She closed them again and she dreamed without realizing she had fallen asleep. She was in her old room, in the old house on Long Island. Jenny was beside her in the bed because something had frightened her in the dark. Joseph was in his room, crying and crying. Far away she heard the sound of applause in the theatre that meant the show was ending. She lay waiting. The crying continued and no one came. She must go to him, but she could not move.

Then suddenly she was awake. The applause was swallowed by the soft roar of the surf. But the crying went on, sharp, jagged, newborn wails. 'Joseph,' she cried, sitting up. A light flicked on. Bob was beside her, alert, though he had been asleep.

'Darling? What's wrong?'

'Nothing. A dream. That's all.' He peered at her, eyes narrow in the brightness of the light. The light filled the room, driving away the sounds beyond, of the surf, and of the infant wailing in the neighbouring cottage. Their world was intimate and contained. Bob sat up in the bed. He was wearing pyjamas in case he went out in the night and met his daughters. He turned to look at her more carefully.

'You've been crying,' he said. 'Your eyes are red.'

Anne turned away. 'When did you come to bed?' she asked quietly. He looked at his watch.

'Half an hour ago. You were asleep. I didn't want to wake you.'

She nodded her head, still not looking at him. 'What's wrong, Anne?' he said, and she could not hide from him further. She turned, buried her face against his shoulder and sobbed, 'I'm so happy for her. Really. But I can't stop thinking, why can't it be me? Oh God, what's wrong with me? Is it my age, my hormones? Tell me, can you?' She drew back from him, shaking her head in self-disgust. 'I'm so ashamed,' she said.

'You want a baby.' His voice was calm, medical, as if they were strangers. She recognized that already as his line of retreat. She fought for restraint, for caution, but failed.

'I want a baby so much, so much . . .' she whispered. 'I can't bear it any more.' Again she hid her face against his shoulder. He reached around her and turned out the light, and gently lay down, holding her, all the while, in his arms. The darkness enclosed them, and the night sounds, but the baby was no longer crying. The dim hiss and thunder of the surf surrounded them and she lay comforted by his body beside hers, but aware, all the time, that he had said nothing at all.

The first Sunday after the shearing was finished, Jenny and Simon climbed the hill on the moor above her house. She felt self-conscious in the new leather boots he had bought for her, her familiar mud-spattered wellies left behind. The hill-walking was Simon's idea. Jenny was faintly scornful of it. She had taken on the attitude of her crofting neighbours, that the hill was a place for hard work, not sport. But she went anyway, with a lover's tolerance, and then perversely dragged her children along as well, in the end, to everyone's annoyance.

Sarah floundered through the heather, begrudging each step, making herself overtly clumsy, as if she had not grown up here and run happily wild over the moorland when she was little. Jenny glared at her, but Sarah pretended not to see. Over her thick socks and walking boots she wore a long, silky skirt with a fringe of tassels that entangled with brambles and sprigs of juniper. Her hair stood straight up, five inches from her head, dyed dead black and splashed with red and blue. She had plucked her eyebrows into a thin, wry line. Jenny thought she looked hideous, but Simon, who liked Sarah, defended her.

'She's a gothic,' he explained, as if her daughter had become part of some alien tribe. 'They're all right. Art students, drama students, you know . . . they're like hippies really.' He paused, 'She's like you.'

'Hippies were never ugly. That's ugly. And it's all so artificial.' Jenny recoiled in distaste. 'We were never like that.'

'She's you if you grew up in the eighties,' he said gently. 'Inside, she's you.'

Jenny shook her head, unconvinced. But she was glad of his loyalty to Sarah. It was sweet, touching. And it was good for Sarah. Adolescence had been hard for her, without her father. Angus had risen to it, taking on early manhood, but Sarah seemed lost, without a ready role to assume and without a man around to ease her into an understanding of sex. She was at first prickly and uncertain around Simon, but later relaxed and joked and teased with him, even flirted a little in her awkward, sharp-tongued way. The question of his age had never arisen. He seemed to her, with his jeans and broad leather sandals, as old as her mother; comical, but kind.

It was always more fraught with Angus. The age gap was narrower, and Angus's perceptions sharper. Simon was ill at ease with Angus, swithering between boyish companionship and avuncular authority, neither of which were well received. Still, the essential clash between them was not age but personality. They had little in common, and little to like about one another. Angus was too eagerly trying to become the sort of person that Simon had fled the south of England to escape. Any discussion became a political debate, and any debate an argument. Jenny found herself forever dashing between them, an emotional sheepdog, tugging them this way and that, keeping them apart. And yet they were quite capable of joining forces and turning on her, in a sudden up-swelling of male superiority, demolishing any viewpoint she put forth. She liked such moments, although she was invariably the loser in them, because they gave her hope for her family which mattered far more to her than any idea.

On the hill Angus slogged upwards at a brisk pace, head down, intent on outstripping Simon. A rugby player and an aggressive skier, he was proud of his strength and youth and confident of victory. But Simon proved a greater challenge than he imagined. His light, seemingly unmuscled body was stronger than it looked, and his long, shambly legs covered ground with steady ease.

Soon they were hundreds of yards ahead, moving upwards at a half run. Jenny plodded on behind, listening to Sarah moan.

'We're not going to the top, are we?'

'I think that's the idea.'

'This is ridiculous. What are we doing this for?'

'Because it's fun.'

'You never thought so before. You always made fun of hill-walkers.' Jenny ignored her. Children had unbearably long memories and were utterly intolerant of any adjustment of viewpoint. 'We're doing this because of Simon,' Sarah said.

'Yes,' Jenny said. 'Is that so awful?'

Sarah was silent. 'I don't like you changing because of Simon,' she said finally.

'I'm not changing because of Simon,' Jenny said, denying it foolishly enough because, put that way, she didn't like the sound of it either. Sarah took that as the transparent untruth it was. Jenny said, placatingly, 'People have to *adjust* to each other when they're . . .'

'When they're what?' Sarah cut in, piranha-quick.

'Friends,' Jenny said coolly. 'When they're friends.'

'You have lots of friends. You don't change for them. You don't change for Elizabeth. You disagree about everything and you're still friends.'

Jenny felt herself hedged into a corner, her escapes expertly cut off. Only this time Sarah was the sheepdog, she the wayward lamb.

'It's different between a man and a woman,' she said, resignedly. She scrambled over a small ledge of rounded rock and waited while Sarah hiked up her silky skirt and climbed clumsily up after.

'I don't want it to be different,' she said.

Jenny sat down wearily on the ledge of rock. She stretched her legs out in front of her and studied the alien boots, still shiny with newness. She said, 'What don't you want to be different?' She felt trapped by the conversation, as if all its exchanges were dictated and set.

'Us. The family. It's all changing.' *It's over. The family. It will never be the same again.*

'Nothing's changing,' Jenny said soothingly, but Sarah answered instantly, anguished, 'It is. It *is*.' She whipped her

282

head around, the stiff, false hair flicking over her forehead. 'I don't want it like this. I don't want Simon around all the time.'

Jenny looked out over the heather hill, the falling fields, the band of birch trees along the line of fencing, and below, to the distant roof of her house, dull slate grey in the sun.

'I thought you liked Simon.'

'I *do*. I do like Simon.' Sarah shook her head in frustration. 'I just don't want him to change everything.'

Jenny decided to be practical. 'He hasn't changed *every*thing, Sarah. We've just gone hill-walking. Once. That's all. I think you're making rather a lot . . .'

'I don't want you to marry him.'

Jenny laughed aloud, almost in relief. 'Good God, girl, if that's what you're worrying about . . . I have no *idea* of marrying him. And I doubt he has any idea of marrying me. For heaven's sake, we're just friends.' She laughed again, relaxing.

'But you're not just friends,' Sarah said at once. 'There's more than that. There is.'

Jenny looked at her coolly. She remembered Elizabeth and said carefully, 'If there *is* more, Sarah, and I'm not saying there is, it's my business. Not yours. It's no one's business but Simon's and mine.' She closed her mouth firmly and awaited rebellion, but Sarah only looked bewildered.

'But Mom,' she said. 'You *have* to marry him.' She paused. 'Or stop going to mass, or something, anyhow.'

'Sarah.'

'I hear you at night, Mom. I'm not a little kid.'

'Sarah, whatever you *think* you hear . . .'

'You don't even go to confession.'

'Sarah! It's not your affair if I go to confession or not. It's between me and God.'

'It's mortal sin. You shouldn't take communion unless you go to confession.'

Jenny sighed and looked away. When she looked back, Sarah was staring at her with intent, hurt eyes. Jenny began softly, 'Sweetheart, it's never so simple as that.'

'Yes it is. It *is* simple. There are rules and we all obey them. *You* know that. That's what you always taught me. You can't just turn it around now that it doesn't suit you.' She stood up, tugging her foolish skirt free. 'You think you're so superior to

283

everybody, but you're just a bloody hypocrite like all the rest.' She gave the skirt a last angry yank and stormed off, leaving a trail of ravelled silk threads across the heather.

'Sarah, you don't understand . . .' Jenny called impotently.

Sarah turned once, still walking. 'Oh yes I do,' she shouted. She started to run, and now that she had reason to, outpaced her mother with little difficulty. She was sitting cross-legged by the stone cairn, head down, picking at the threads of her torn skirt, when Jenny reached the summit of the hill.

Simon and Angus were there, off to one side, laughing and joking about something. They looked hot and sweaty, and had taken off their shirts and were standing with them flung over their shoulders, like towels, and Jenny was annoyed with them suddenly, secluded in hearty male companionship, oblivious to her daughter.

'I beat him,' Angus said, when he saw her. But Simon was grinning also, and Jenny knew he had not been beaten by much. Rivalry seemed to have drawn them together. They strode around the hill-top possessively and then jointly levered a big stone free and added it to the cairn. Pebbles shifted and trickled down to rest at Sarah's feet. She ignored them, busying herself braiding three of her skirt tassels into a lumpy plait. Jenny sat down near her, but not close enough to intrude, and looked out over the view of moorland, hills and the loch. She could still just make out the red tin roof of the dairy, although that of the house itself was obscured by a clump of trees. She tried to see it as Simon meant her to see it, anonymously beautiful, but familiarity intruded. Her eye was drawn to the line of fencing that needed mending, the rusty roof of the barn that should be replaced, the insidious green of encroaching bracken eating away at her pasture land. The big, ancient hills retreated and her view narrowed to the few tiresome fields that were hers. They reproached her for sitting in such a useless place, so far from her work.

'We'd better go,' she said.

Simon and Angus still led on the way down, their strides lengthening subtly until they were again racing each other. Jenny walked stolidly, making no attempt to keep up. Sarah paralleled her course, deliberately far enough away that they could not talk. Jenny concentrated on her son and her lover walking on before her. Once they stopped, where a burn cut through the deep heather, and she could see them wrestling with each other in a half-hearted attempt to push each other in. They puzzled her. Men seemed never able to negotiate any emotional ground without some physical violence. She heard their shouts and laughter, boyish, like two brothers. She tried to imagine Angus with his own father at this age, but it was impossible; they remained locked in her memory, a man and a little boy, divided forever by a chasm of age.

'Sarah's not happy,' Jenny said. She was sitting at the kitchen table, an old newspaper spread before her, on which she was cleaning hill boots: hers, Sarah's and Angus's. Simon sat across from her, his own boots, finished, on the bench beside him. The labrador, Honey, sat with her chin on his knee and he rubbed her ears as he watched Jenny.

'What's wrong now?' He spoke in a measured tone meant to convey concern, but Jenny heard impatience instead.

'Us,' she said bluntly. 'We're what's wrong.'

Simon made his little reasoning pause. 'In what way?' he asked. 'In what way are we wrong?'

'She knows we go to bed.'

'Oh.' Simon's voice was cautiously light. 'Tell me,' he said slowly. 'How does she know? Did you tell her?'

'Of course I didn't tell her.'

'No, Jenny, not "of course". You might have told her. It might have been quite reasonable to tell her.'

'She heard us making love.' Jenny blushed suddenly as she said it, surprising herself and him.

'I see.' He lowered his head and sat staring at his long, mobile fingers. After a while he said, 'What is it about our making love that upsets her?'

'Oh for Christ's sake, Simon. Stop being so obtuse. Her mother's screwing around. She doesn't like it.'

Simon's head came up with a jerk. 'You are *not*,' he said sharply, 'screwing around. You're having a love affair.'

'What's the difference?'

'If I have to tell you that . . .'

'I mean, what's the difference to her?'

Simon leaned back on the bench, his eyes closed thoughtfully. The dog, disconcerted, moved away and settled by Jenny's feet.

Simon said, 'Don't you think, if we talked to her, she could be made to see the difference?'

'No.'

'Jenny, you're not even trying to help.'

'I know my daughter.'

'Probably not as well as you think you do,' Simon said at once.

'Better than you do, anyhow.'

Simon sighed. He stood up, lifted his boots off the bench and set them on the flagstone floor by the back door. A cat came and curled around his leg and he lifted it and petted it, absently. 'Jenny,' he said. 'I may not be a parent. Yet, anyhow. But I have been a child. An unhappy child in an unhappy house. I know how children think.' He was still stroking the cat, but looked now steadily at Jenny. She looked away.

'She thinks I'm a bad Catholic,' she said.

'Is *that* all?' Simon asked sharply. He clutched the cat harder in his surprise, and ignored its struggles to get away. It turned its head suddenly and sank teeth into his wrist. He shouted and dropped it from chest height, and it thudded solidly on four paws and walked stiffly away.

'They're not pillows, Simon. If you're going to pay them attention, it has to be full attention.' *Like children*, she wanted to add. Instead she said, 'In a Catholic household it's a big issue.'

Simon was standing in the middle of the room, sucking blood from his bitten wrist. 'Wash it,' she said, with routine sympathy. He went to the sink and ran cold water over his arm for a long time. When it was done, he dried it carefully with the dish-towel and said thoughtfully, 'I never think of this as a Catholic household.' He actually meant it as a kind of soothing compliment, but Jenny rounded on him at once.

'Why not? What's not like a Catholic household about it?'

He ignored her flicker of anger and said calmly, 'I don't know. A certain openness, liberality. A willingness to let other people have their own opinions.'

'And that's not Catholic?'

'Jenny, I like your household. I like the way you raise your children. Most of the time, it's terrific. I wish *I* had had a family like this.'

'But not a Catholic one.'

'Jenny, don't make a barrier of this. You know it doesn't mean that much to you . . .'

'What?'

'Oh, I know, you go to mass on Sundays and you say grace at meals but it isn't the be-all and end-all of your life for God's sake.'

'For God's sake,' Jenny said firmly, 'Simon, it is.'

They stared at each other in blank incomprehension. Eventually he walked back to the table and settled in his place across from her. She was carefully working saddle-soap around the eyelets of Sarah's walking boot. The boots looked new, like her own, but Sarah had had them for years. They were bought for a school hostel trip and used rarely since. Simon said, 'Why are you doing that?'

'Because it's dirty.' Jenny looked up and shrugged.

'I mean, why are you doing it for her? Why isn't she cleaning her own boots?'

'Oh, don't pick on her just because she's annoyed with us.'

'No, Jenny. Not because of that. Because it's a perfectly reasonable expectation. She's nearly eighteen. Can't she clean her own boots?'

'She can,' Jenny said evenly, setting the boot down and picking up its mate. 'And she won't. And the leather will dry out and be useless.'

'So? It would serve her right.'

'It might. But I'd still have to pay for new ones.'

Simon flung one hand up in disgust. 'That's what's wrong, Jenny. That's where the problems really lie.'

'In Sarah not cleaning her boots?' Jenny laughed.

'In you not making her. In you letting her remain a child when she should be becoming an adult. No wonder then, when she meets an adult situation, she responds like a child, a spoiled little girl wanting to dominate your life.'

'She thinks I should marry you,' Jenny said. She did not add, *or leave the church*. She watched Simon's face, perversely enjoying his consternation. To her surprise, his shocked look was replaced by one of interest.

'Does she?' he asked. Jenny shrugged. 'Is that what she wants?'

'I'm not sure it's what she wants,' Jenny muttered, sorry she'd led herself into this.

'But Jenny, she's probably right. It's probably what she needs . . . some assurance . . . stability.'

'For God's sake, Simon, there's nothing un*stable* . . .'

'Children are conventional, Jenny,' he said in his irritatingly wise voice. 'They like their parents to be conventional too.'

'Crap. My parents were wonderfully unconventional . . . until Joseph came, anyhow . . . and I loved it. It was the thing I missed most.'

'They were *married*, Jenny.' He paused. 'I'm sure it's what she wants. That's probably why she raised the whole thing.' He leaned forward over the table. Jenny looked away. He reached to touch her face. 'Is it what *you* want, love?' he said.

'Of course not,' she said briskly, having the awful feeling that he imagined she had arranged the whole conversation as a ploy for a wedding ring. But when she looked at him he was not relieved as she expected, but bitterly hurt. In haste she said, to mend what damage she could, 'Well, we certainly wouldn't decide such a thing just to placate *Sarah*, would we?'

Jenny stood up in confusion, and then busied herself carrying Sarah's boots to the door where she set them down beside Simon's. She stood for a moment, with her back to him, looking out of the low kitchen window at its homely view of sheds and stone walls. The July light was still strong at ten-thirty, and there was a blue glow over all, giving beauty to familiar things. She loved it. It was unique to Scotland – there was no light like this at home – and it made her think of her early years here with Fergus, and Angus, just a baby. When she turned back to face Simon, the memory slipped heavily into the past. Though Fergus's ghost sometimes confronted her out in the yard or up on the hill, it seemed to have lost its grip on the house. She found it hard even to envision Fergus within the kitchen; as if he had never been there. Simon was watching her steadily. She returned to the table and sat on her bench, and lifted the first of Angus's boots. She ducked her head to avoid Simon's remonstrating look, and began to soap them carefully.

'I *like* doing this,' she said, defiantly. 'I like looking after things, and looking after people.' She raised her head, expecting argument, but found he was staring at her with eyes filled with devotion.

'You're so beautiful,' he said solemnly. 'So strong and

pure . . .' He turned his face aside while Jenny just stared in amazement. Simon looked back, and said curiously, 'Is that why you and Anne don't get on sometimes? Was she jealous of you a lot when you were young?'

'Anne! Jealous of me?'

'I mean, she's very nice looking too,' he said hastily. 'But she's rather ordinary . . .'

'Anne?' Jenny laughed. 'God. Love is blind.'

It was late that night before Sarah finally drifted off to bed and Simon and Jenny felt free to do the same. They were all tired by then, and Jenny was irritable with Sarah for her procrastination and with Simon for his too obvious need to make love. Guilt and resentment, her two familiars, threatened to ruin the night, and she struggled hard to overcome them, smiling too kindly on her lover, undressing with a play at eroticism she did not feel. His arms were around her before she was halfway into the bed.

'No, wait,' Jenny said, drawing back stiffly, and then sitting up again. Moonlight poured through the undrawn curtains and she saw Simon's outline against it as he propped himself on one arm and then sat up as well.

'What is it, darling?' he said. His voice was smooth and patient, but she sensed irritation hovering at its edges.

'I heard something.'

He leaned forward, his knees drawn up and his arms linked loosely around them, his head bowed. 'I didn't,' he said. There was the trace of a sigh, suppressed.

'She's still up,' Jenny said.

'Jenny, you're imagining things. I didn't hear anything.' But she knew he had not the fine-tuned ears of parenthood, trained for years to capture the slightest sound.

'She walking around. She's gone downstairs for something to eat. She'll be back up in a minute.'

This time Simon's sigh was audible. 'Jenny, since she knows anyhow, what are we hiding from?' He touched her arm, slipped his own around her. She could not see his face but imagined it, softened about the mouth, and the eyes narrowed in the hunger of sex. His love-making, though skilful, still betrayed his youth in its eager desperation. He gently pressured her downward towards the bed and she threw her arms up and pushed him away.

'No!'

'All right. All right.' He moved clumsily in the bed, shifting himself away from her, and swung his legs over the side.

'Don't be angry.'

'I'm not angry, Jenny. I just don't understand you.' She realized that Simon had never, ever admitted to anger. Only confusion, or hurt. She remembered Fergus losing patience with her in the difficult days when Angus was small, and flinging her shouting on the bed, making love to her against her protests and leaving her exhausted, satiated and at peace. *Be a man*, she thought, angrily, and then turned the anger inward: *What am I asking for, rape?* She said, to placate Simon, 'It will be easier when she goes to college.' She felt at once a great pang of remorse towards Sarah, as if she were turning her own child out into the cold. She stifled it and said, 'It will be easier when they are both away.' She knew that Simon looked forward to Angus's returns to Cambridge with the same eagerness with which she awaited his homecoming. She understood why, but it hurt desperately all the same, no less because he hid his feelings scrupulously.

But Angus was not the problem, anyway. He was different from Sarah, not just older, but more sophisticated by nature, and at the same time more reserved. What had passed between her and Simon could not have eluded him, and yet he had absorbed it without comment or conflict. He had learned already the British habit of compartmenting emotions and shutting them away, out of sight. She could never discuss her lover with him, as one day she knew she would with Sarah, but with him she would also never have the need. He disappeared gracefully at just the right moments; maintained the foolish pretence of the guest room, in which even now Simon's small case was lying; learned not to pass too late by his mother's bedroom door. But Sarah. Sarah haunted the hallways like a ghost.

'It's like doing it with a nun in the house,' Jenny had confessed to Elizabeth.

'Tell her,' Elizabeth replied, 'that nuns go to bed at eight.'

Nuns might, but Sarah didn't. Simon stood and put on the light, fumbling for his dressing-gown to cover his nakedness. Jenny sat up blinking, pulling down her old-fashioned frilled nightdress. 'She'll be in bed in a moment. We don't have to sit up.'

'I'm finding it a little difficult,' Simon said reasonably. He looked lost, like a man looking for a cigarette, only he didn't smoke. 'I think we ought to talk,' he said.

'All right.' She was relieved, thankful that Simon was, unlike Fergus, a very verbal man, who could soon be diverted, even from passion, into conversation.

'I think we have to confront Sarah,' he said. 'Both of us. We have to sit down with her and talk it through. We have to bring it out into the open.'

An image crossed Jenny's mind of herself, Sarah, Simon, sitting at the breakfast table talking about sex like some terribly liberated American family in a new, racy sitcom.

'She'd flip out,' Jenny said.

'Okay. So she gets a little upset . . .'

'Not upset. Hysterical. I mean it, Simon, she's a very sensitive, very emotional . . .'

'Very coddled little girl.'

'If you like,' Jenny said coldly. 'But I'm not shocking her to pieces just to please you.'

'Oh really, love, that's going *way* over the top.'

'No it's not, Simon. You don't know her. You keep thinking you know her because she talks about pop groups and bloody hair gel with you, but there's more to fatherhood than that. Sex and Sarah . . . Look, I went through the whole prescribed thing. No birds and bees crap in our family. She had it all, from two years old. All the straight answers, the anatomically correct picture books, the whole bloody scene. Bloody is the word for it. When she started menstruating she hid all her knickers in the cupboard for a week before she'd tell me. OK, so I've ballsed it up and she's wacko and suppressed and God knows what . . . but I did my best. And now I use my judgement. She doesn't want a knickers-down heart-to-heart with the three of us, for sure.'

'On the contrary,' Simon said. 'It might take something like that to make her realize.'

'Realize what?' Jenny glared at him, and Simon sat calmly on the edge of her bed, just turning his head towards her.

'That it's time to grow up. You've given enough of your life to raising them, Jenny.' He turned his body and reached and took her shoulders in his hands. He said, seriously, 'You've a right to some time of your own.'

But I don't want it, she thought wildly. Aloud, she said, 'I know that. But I don't see what the rush is about.'

Suddenly he was intent with urgent emotion. 'Jenny, if there's ever going to be time for us, for *our* family . . .'

'What family?' Jenny said, pulling back. 'Wouldn't *they* be our family?'

'Of course they will. Of course.' He buried his face against her neck. 'Oh Jenny, Jenny. Please have my baby. Please.'

XVI

Jenny's first thought when Anne told her she was pregnant was of Simon and her first emotion was anger. She knew at once how Simon would react and imagined already the calf-eyed devotion with which he would regard Anne; the look of recrimination he would turn on herself. She felt betrayed, as if her choices had been suddenly and unfairly narrowed. *How can* you *do this to me,* she thought. And there was something else: resentment at her old territory of marriage and motherhood summarily invaded by her sister, an illogical flash of jealousy. Then at once she was filled with shame at her own selfishness. They still stood there, at the edge of the wet moor, beside the dripping wire fence: Anne muddy and breathless from her impetuous striding over the drenched heather; Jenny tense now, watching her, uncertain what to do. At last she said softly, 'Does he know?'

Anne blinked. 'Who? Bob?'

'About the baby. Does he know?'

'Oh Christ.' Anne had gripped the top wire of the fence in order to step over it, and now she leaned back for a moment on her heels, her arms outstretched, smiling slightly. 'He's a *doctor*, Jenny. Besides, I've a new spare tyre around my middle and tits like Jayne Mansfield. *Any* man would know.' Jenny glanced at her quickly.

'You don't seem to show.'

'I do show. I've just camouflaged it well. That's my job. Concealing life's little indiscretions with the designer's art.' She laughed softly. 'Elizabeth guessed anyhow.'

'Did she?' Jenny's eyebrows went up and she glanced again at

Anne as she scrambled over the fence. 'I didn't. But then, Elizabeth always imagines the worst.'

'Maybe she didn't regard it as "the worst" anything,' Anne said sharply.

Jenny only nodded a knowing head. 'Elizabeth would,' she said. 'Was it that, then?'

'Was it what?'

'One of life's little indiscretions?'

'If you mean a mistake, yes.'

Jenny stopped, still holding the fencepost she had used for support. She looked carefully at her sister. 'But how?' she cried. 'At your age. And with a *doctor* . . .'

Anne shrugged. 'Who knows? My periods were a bit screwed up. I thought it was menopause. I got a little careless.' She shrugged again.

Jenny was quiet. Eventually, she said, 'You know, when you told me, you looked so, I don't know, sort of *proud* of it, that I almost thought it was deliberate. Though I couldn't imagine you actually wanting a baby, still . . .'

'Jenny. I *want* this baby. Don't you ever say I don't want this baby.'

Jenny, who had been searching for her car keys, stopped in confusion, her hand still thrust into the pocket of her anorak. 'I'm sorry. I didn't understand. I just thought somehow we were talking about a problem. I think it was the way you brought it up after talking about Joseph and all that.' She turned to face Anne, smiling hesitantly. 'So, do I congratulate you? Are you getting married, you and Bob? Or are you just going to live together, once the baby comes . . . ?'

Anne was aware of Jenny being consciously fair-minded, leaving room for any stretching of convention that might be asked of her. She said softly, 'Oh Christ, Jenny, I wish I knew.' She buried her face in one hand. She heard the noise she made, like sobbing, but there were no tears and, in a moment, the contortion of her features passed. She turned towards the car, opening the passenger door. 'Let's go home, kid, eh?' she said.

As soon as they got back into the car, Anne knew she had lost the diamond Bob had given her. She had just shrugged out of the old anorak, shaking the water off it, and brushing the yellow dog hairs from her sweater and trousers when, touching her

294

throat, she found the necklace gone. She tossed the jacket into the back seat and felt quickly around her neck for the chain. It was not there; not tangled in her hair, not caught in the soft rolled collar of the sweater.

Jenny, her face averted, started the engine.

'Wait,' Anne said.

Jenny looked up slowly, her hand still on the key. 'Do you want to talk some more?' she said softly.

'No, it's not that,' Anne said. 'I've lost something. She was still searching, plucking hastily at her garments, knowing already she would not find it. 'Oh damn,' she said sadly.

'What is it?' Jenny turned to face her. She switched the engine off. 'What did you lose?'

'A necklace,' Anne said. Her voice was flat. 'A little diamond . . .'

'A diamond!' Jenny shrieked.

'Just a small one. On a chain.'

'You've lost a diamond,' Jenny whispered, open-mouthed. She started peering around Anne, in the car, as if she might see it somewhere.

'Oh for God's sake, Jenny, it's not that important,' Anne said, partly to reassure her sister, but more because Jenny making such a fuss about it, had instilled in her too a feeling of awesome significance about the loss.

'It must be terribly valuable,' Jenny said, continuing pawing at the upholstery of the car in a desperate search.

'No. I mean, yes, I suppose it was. I don't know. It was a gift. It was Bob's Christmas present.' Suddenly tears welled up as she reached instinctively to touch it, the way she had been doing since the plane.

'Oh, Anne,' Jenny said. 'How awful.' She sat staring miserably at her sister, but then was caught up in a diligent frenzy of searching, as if the loss had presented her with exactly what she craved: something simple and tangible that she could easily remedy. Something utterly unlike the dilemma that Anne had revealed a few moments before in the pouring rain.

'We won't find it,' Anne said hopelessly but, borne along a little while yet by the intensity of Jenny's helpfulness, she too kept looking.

'Maybe it fell inside,' Jenny suggested. Anne patted her chest, checked inside her bra. It wasn't there. She knew it wasn't, anyhow. She knew exactly where it was: out in that forsaken wet hillside, amongst sodden grass and sheep droppings and a million, million raindrops, shining identically.

'We won't find it,' she said clearly to Jenny.

'Don't give up. We can keep looking.'

'It isn't here. It's not *in* the car. I lost it out there.' She waved a hand towards the steamed-up windows, the hill beyond. 'We'll never find it.' Still, Jenny did not give up, but got out of the car and searched around in the mud of their footprints until Anne was eventually sick of the whole thing, wanting only to leave the wet miserable roadside and resign herself to her loss.

'It's just a bit of jewellery,' she said firmly, as Jenny reluctantly climbed back into the driver's seat. 'Nothing unique. Thoroughly replaceable. My insurance will quite likely cover, anyhow. It only matters at *all* because Bob gave it . . .'

'Sentimental value,' Jenny said, starting the car.

'We aren't sentimental people,' Anne answered at once.

Jenny looked straight ahead, through the sweep of the wipers, and pulled the Subaru back on to the road.

As they jounced up the rough driveway to the house, rougher and more pot-holed than Anne remembered it, Jenny said, without turning her eyes from the track, 'Ask St Anthony.'

'What?'

'To find the diamond. Ask St Anthony.'

'Oh grow up,' said Anne.

Simon was waiting for them outside the door. Tall and lanky, he stood with his hands clasped together in front of him, still like a shy professor. But there was something new that Anne recognized at once, the self-assurance of belonging. She felt again a flicker of sorrow for Fergus. Having not shared the years and depth of Jenny's mourning, she found it difficult to share in the healing that had occurred.

'You remember Simon,' Jenny said, as Anne climbed out of the car. She was blushing girlishly. Anne shook Simon's hand. He was deferential towards her; respectful, carrying her case, opening the door for her. Jenny followed easily behind, and when in the doorway they hugged and kissed, Anne felt suddenly old. She stepped wearily inside the house, finding at once a kind of lethargy settle upon her at the sight of the familiar and shabby furnishings. Nothing changed here. Nothing was ever painted, or redecorated. Carpets worn down to their backing still remained; even the worn spots were familiar. Anne remembered all the nights she had shivered in an unheated bedroom here; all the days she had wandered aimlessly about, wrapped in alien woollens, looking for somewhere to get warm. The depression that had come upon her with the loss of the diamond settled and thickened. *Grow up*, she said, now, to herself. *It's just a hunk of stone, don't ruin the visit over it.* But in the tremulous emotional state of her pregnancy, she could not forget it, nor master the feeling. The lost diamond had already become what she feared it would: a bad omen for the visit, for Christmas, for everything.

In the big, draughty bedroom she always used, she unpacked her clothes, hanging them carefully in the free-standing old-fashioned wardrobe. It smelled of lavender; a mass of the dry pale flowers hung upside down from one of the brass clothes-hooks. She imagined herself emerging smelling like an ageing vicar's wife. Sleet rattled against the big window. She stood against it, feeling the damp cold creeping through the glass, looking out on the grey mist, the grey heather, the grey sheep. She pictured Bob and Robin in the bright sun and snow of a New Hampshire winter, and yearned to be with them with the passionate desperation of a child. Then the door banged open, and Angus was there.

'Hi, Anne.'

She turned, surprised, slightly offended by the assault on her privacy, and yet warmed by the sight of him. He was big like Fergus and filled rooms in the same comforting way. He dressed with the reassuring tweedy cosiness of the British upper classes, which to Anne translated into preppy conservatism. He looked like the young men who came into Anne Conti shops and lounged around on straight-backed seats while their girlfriends tried on clothes. It seemed impossible that he was Jenny's child.

'Hey kid,' she said. 'You look real good.'

'So do you.' He grinned, with the new confidence that had grown on him in his Cambridge years. She grinned back. Unlike Simon, he made her feel young. He crossed the room boldly and kissed her cheek. *You've been around since I saw you last,* she thought. She returned the kiss. 'My glamorous Auntie,' he said wryly. 'How you got into this family, I'll never know.'

She smiled. 'I don't know. You're not doing so bad yourself.'

He grinned, deprecatingly, but glowed underneath with pleasure. 'Mom's made tea downstairs,' he said.

In the kitchen, Jenny and Simon were arguing. Anne stopped discreetly at the doorway, but Angus just shrugged and walked on in as if such arguments were of little importance. Uneasily, Anne followed. Jenny glanced up, acknowledging her presence, and turned back to her lover.

'Did you at least think to get a telephone number?' Jenny was quivering with frustration.

Simon, patient, smiling slightly, said, 'Telephone? Really, Jenny.' He laughed softly. 'I doubt they use anything so mundane as a telephone. They probably only communicate by angelic revelation.' Angus laughed, and Jenny turned briefly to glare at him.

'You both seem to find this very amusing. Well, I don't. And what about you, anyway? Didn't *you* at least have the sense . . .'

'Jenny, this is unfair,' Simon said, hurt.

'Don't look at me.' Angus raised both his hands in innocence. 'I don't know what this is about, even. I've just come in. I've been mending your *fence*,' he added, with something of his old childish demand for justice. Jenny glared again, but decided to believe him.

'Sarah's called,' she said. 'She's not coming home.'

'Never?' Angus said, awed.

'Don't be ridiculous. Of course not "never". She's just not coming home tonight. Or something like that.' She turned away.

Anne thought she looked frightened. She wanted to ask what had happened, but did not dare. But Simon, seeing her watching, explained carefully, 'Sarah has some religious friends that she goes out with. Evangelists. She just called to say she was going to spend the night with them . . .'

'She's not *allowed* to spend the night . . . that's the deal. She can go out with them all day. At night she comes home.' She turned back to Simon. 'You knew that,' she said.

It was an accusation and Simon bridled under it. '*I* can't tell her what to do, Jenny,' he said. 'I'm not her parent.' He watched her, reprovingly, and Jenny turned away.

Angus said, 'He's right, Mom. It's your fault, really, letting her go with them. We told you . . .'

'Oh right,' Jenny shouted. 'It's always my fucking fault. Everything is.' She turned to the Aga, lifted the big kettle and poured boiling water into the tea-pot, angrily, splashing it across the counter. When she set the kettle down, she took a rag and rubbed the counter vigorously, drying it, and then dried her hands with quick angry twists of the cloth. She turned back to them, looking as if she would throw the cloth at someone. But Anne's presence restrained her. She shook her head, dropped the rag on the counter. 'I'm sorry,' she muttered.

They drank their tea in awkward silence. Angus tried, for a while, to jolly everyone along with grins and cheery comments, but then he too gave up. Anne remembered Fergus teasing around Jenny's moods. She found something fatuous and child-like in the male desire to derail female anger with ill-timed humour. When Angus's last attempt failed, Anne said, 'Is this a Catholic group, Jenny?'

'Hardly.'

'Jenny wouldn't *mind* if it were a Catholic group,' Simon said, sourly.

'Oh yes I would,' Jenny answered, 'if Catholics behaved like that. Only they don't.'

'It depends on how you look at it,' Simon said quietly.

Jenny gave him a bitter look.

Angus said, 'They're Jesus-freaks. Full of that born-again crap. Mom's right. They're a menace.'

He reached to pour himself more tea, and opened his mouth to explain the Saints to Anne, but Jenny said quickly, 'Angus, did that guy call for you again?'

'What guy, who?'

Jenny sighed. 'Somebody called this morning before I went out. I couldn't find you.' She paused, watching the unease cross his face. 'He said his name was Matthew.'

'Oh shit,' Angus said softly.

'What?'

'Nothing. What did he want?' His voice was cautious.

'He didn't really say,' Jenny lied. She paused, and added, 'He said you'd know what it was about.' She was still watching him, and now Simon and Anne were watching too. 'Do you?' she said.

He looked away. 'Yeah. I mean, I might.'

'I think you'd better call him, Angus,' she said.

'Yeah, sure.' He looked around the kitchen, avoiding her eyes. The swagger and confidence had left him and he sagged boyishly in his chair. After a while, he got up, nodded to everyone, and left the room.

'What was that about?' Simon asked.

Jenny stood up and poured tea. 'I haven't the slightest idea,' she said.

They were at dinner when the telephone rang. Anne had cheered herself by changing her clothes, refreshing her make-up, and digging out the gifts she had brought, which now rested on the low table before the living-room fire, waiting to be opened and exclaimed over after the meal. Sarah's present – leggings and a knee-length sweater from the Anne Conti teen line – waited discreetly out of sight in Anne's room. Sarah was not mentioned again, and the meal was pleasant and relaxed, or at least as relaxed as any meal in Jenny's house could be. There were all the usual interruptions, as Jenny leapt up to let dogs out, cats in, check the latch on the henhouse, retrieve forgotten and now burnt components of dinner from one of the Aga's three ovens.

'I'm a lousy cook,' Jenny said cheerfully. Simon denied it loyally.

'It's better than college,' Angus said, smoothly cryptic.

'Telephone,' Jenny called from where she bent over the oven, poking ruefully at a darkened mass in an ovenproof dish.

'I'll get it,' Simon said, rising to go, but Angus jumped up instantly, brushing by him and was out of the door before Simon had fully straightened up. Simon shrugged and settled back down, patting the head of the black and white sheepdog that sat watching him throughout the meal. He looked like the master of the house, except that he sat on the long bench, midway down the table. The big carver in which Fergus had lounged was where Jenny sat. She had taken it over in the early days of her widowhood, just as she had taken his side of the bed, worn his too-large shirts, even dabbled at playing his guitar, as if, bereft of

300

him, she sought to become him herself. That had passed, but she still slept where he had slept, and sat at the head of her table. The place that Simon had found was neither Fergus's nor hers, but modestly his own, halfway between honoured guest and subservient child.

Jenny put her burnt offering on the table absently, her eyes on the door through which Angus had gone. While Anne and Simon talked, she sat listening, hearing only a murmur of a voice through the closed door. When Angus came back, he was smiling broadly with relief.

'What was it?' Jenny asked.

He shook his head. 'Just someone called Marion, for Anne. I told her you'd call back after dinner,' he added airily.

'Christ,' Anne said. She stood up, trying to hide both her concern and her irritation with Angus. She said quickly, 'I'll just call now. Get it out of the way.'

Jenny watched her, uncertainly.

Angus said, 'She's not expecting it. I wouldn't bother to rush.' He shrugged as Anne hurried past him and out into the hall.

The telephone was in an alcove in the broad wood-floored entrance-way. There were piles of books and papers on the shelves below it, and a rickety lamp which Anne turned on. She dialled the international code and then Marion's home number from memory. Marion lifted it on the first half ring.

'Anne? Oh, thank God. I tried to tell him I had to talk with you, but he wouldn't listen.' There was a pause. 'Who *was* that?'

'My nephew. He's all right. He was just being grown-up,' Anne said in apology. 'What's happened?' There was another pause that dragged out into what seemed an interminable silence. 'Joseph?' Anne whispered.

'He's had this sort of fit.'

'Oh God!'

'I don't think it's *too* serious.'

'What does Bob say?'

'Bob's not here, Anne.' Marion's voice betrayed her surprise. 'He's in New Hampshire.'

'Of course. Of course.' She fought back an impotent and irrational anger at Bob for being on vacation when she needed him most.

'That other doctor . . .'

301

'Nussbaum.'

'Yes. The one your mother doesn't like. He saw him. They seem to think it was some viral thing . . .' Marion's voice trailed off. 'Anne, I fought with myself about telling you. I know it's so pointless and I hate messing up your vacation. But I knew you'd want to know.'

'Shall I come home?'

'No.' Marion sounded suddenly vehement. 'No, for God's sake, Anne, why should you? What can you do anyhow? He's in an excellent place. He's surrounded by professionals. And it's probably nothing anyhow. A false alarm.'

'What about Mom?'

There was a long silence. Marion said quietly, 'As you'd expect. Look, Anne, she's been here before. And, anyhow, I'm here. I'm not you and I'm not Jenny, but I'll do at a pinch.'

'You're wonderful,' Anne said. 'I don't know how to repay you.'

'Try malt whisky,' Marion said with her soft laugh. 'Go back to your dinner. I'm sorry I disturbed you.' She started to say goodbye but Anne stopped her.

'No, wait.' Anne paused, while Marion waited, and then she asked, 'Have you checked my machine?'

'Yesterday. Just the usual . . . lovesick suitors, enraged creditors . . .'

Anne's voice remained serious. She said carefully, 'I'd like you to check it again when you can. There might be a message from my clinic. Probably a Ms Dawes.' She paused again. 'I want to be sure to get it,' she said eventually.

'Is there something wrong, Anne?' Marion's voice was suspicious.

Anne said quickly, 'No. Nothing. Just routine.' She said goodbye quickly before Marion could ask any more.

Anne returned to the dinner table and sat down in silence. They all sat watching her: Jenny, Simon, Angus. She looked at them each, and then let her eyes settle on Jenny. 'That was Marion,' she said. 'About Joseph. He's had a funny turn. They've treated it. She doesn't want me to come.'

'Is it serious?' Simon asked.

Anne said, still looking at Jenny, 'With someone like Joseph everything's serious. All the time. That said, he's made thirty-five like that.'

'Do you think he's really all right?' Jenny said tentatively.

Anne shrugged. She said, 'I have no real reason to think otherwise.' She paused. 'But if you want an honest answer, I think this time he's on the way out.'

'Oh God,' Jenny said. Her small, plain face crumpled slightly at the chin. She sat staring straight ahead. Angus looked at her, and back to Anne. He shuffled around in his chair in ill-ease.

'Mom?' he said, plaintively, as Jenny still stared, blinking back tears. 'Does it matter that much, Mom?'

Then Simon reached and took Jenny's hand. 'I think, love,' he said, 'you have to regard this as the blessing it is.'

'He has no faith,' Jenny said. 'He has only reason, and good sense. You can't deal with something like Joseph with common sense.' It was early morning, and she was working in the vegetable garden, doing winter chores: turning the ground over, gathering up dried pea vines, making a bonfire, on which she tossed the tired remnants of summer. She liked the winter-clearing best of all the year's work; it was clean, uncompromising. 'He actually said to me, "There's not really a person there, surely, is there?" Can you imagine?'

'Yes,' Anne said, 'I can imagine.'

Jenny stopped in her work. She looked shocked. Anne said, 'You haven't seen him for years.'

Jenny bent hard over her spade, lifting a sticky clod of black earth and throwing it down, slicing it again and again with the steel edge.

'He's still Joseph,' she said stubbornly.

'Yes. He's still Joseph. Whoever that is.'

'He's a person, Anne. He has likes, dislikes, feelings, preferences, sorrows, needs . . . what else is there?'

Anne was silent. She stood at the edge of the garden, wearing a heavy borrowed anorak. Somehow, she never remembered how cold it was in Scotland and never brought the right clothes. She was shivering anyhow, standing still, watching Jenny work.

'Sometimes I think we invented him,' she said. 'Like when we were little and we used to play Monopoly with a piece for Joseph.

And we took turns deciding whether he'd buy houses or rail-roads.'

'He always ended up with Mediterranean Avenue,' Jenny said, laughing. 'I remember. Whatever happened, whoever was playing, Joseph got Mediterranean Avenue.'

'Sure he did,' Anne said. 'It was cheapest. Nobody wanted it.'

Jenny flung another clod of earth from her spade. She straightened her back and looked directly at Anne. 'Look,' she said, 'at least he *got* something. He was the youngest. The youngest always gets palmed off with what nobody else wants. It happens with normal kids too.'

'Normal kids,' said Anne, 'have the option of leaving the game.' She drew up the hood of the anorak, tightening it around her face as the wind gusted. 'Anyhow, you're the one who would have dealt him out from the beginning, if you had the chance.'

Jenny leaned over her spade, her boot kicking it into the ground. 'That doesn't mean I don't love him now. That's what Simon can't understand. I love him anyhow.'

'So do I,' Anne said. 'And it's got nothing to do with *faith*.' She said it bitterly, annoyed at Jenny's neat divisions of the world between believers and heathens. 'I haven't any faith either, any more than Simon.'

'Of course you have,' Jenny said.

Anne sighed. She leaned against a post, watching the quick flames of the bonfire burst upwards, consuming each new offering and dying to ashes at once in the cold wind. She said, 'You cannot conceive how arrogant that sounds.'

Jenny laughed, placidly.

Anne looked coldly at her and then quite suddenly stepped closer, over the broken ground. She laid the flat of her hand over the anorak, midway down her body. 'What about this, then?' she said, just above a whisper. 'Is this a person then?'

Jenny looked surprised at the abrupt change of subject. She smiled, slightly bemused. 'Of course,' she said.

'You're sure.'

'Of course I'm . . . oh, for Christ's sake, we're not going to have one of those damned pro-Life, pro-Choice debates.'

Anne repeated, 'But this is a person. Even if I have another Joseph in here.'

'You haven't,' Jenny said flatly. 'If that's what's getting at you,

304

forget it. I went through this all the way with both of mine. Don't torment yourself. It's not going to happen to you.' Her voice wavered between the sharpness of annoyance and the softening of compassion. 'We all think we're the centre of the universe when we're pregnant, but babies are born all over the world every moment and almost all of them are perfect. Yours will be too.'

'I'm forty-three.'

Jenny straightened up from her digging. She brushed the loose strands of grey-brown hair out of her eyes; the same gesture Anne remembered from childhood. 'I know,' she said quietly. 'Lots of women have late babies these days. You'll have had your amnio . . . they'll tell you if anything's wrong. But there won't be.'

'What if I haven't?'

'I don't understand.'

'What if I *haven't* had it done?'

'I don't understand, Anne. Why not? Are you too early still or what?'

Anne turned away. 'Maybe I don't see the point,' she said elusively.

'You don't see the . . . oh for God's sake, Anne, this can't be *you* I'm hearing. You're an intelligent, informed woman, not some dumb sixteen-year-old. But here you are pregnant by mistake at forty-three . . . by a *doctor* of all people . . . and now you're not even taking the basic precautions to see everything's all right.' She stood with one hand on the handle of the spade, the other flung out in a gesture of despair. 'What's with you? And what's with *Bob*, for Christ's sake?'

'Oh don't worry about Bob,' Anne said crisply. 'He's one hundred per cent in agreement. If I'd known how wonderfully in agreement you'd be I might have stayed in New York.'

'Anne?'

'I'm going to have this baby, Jenny. No matter what.' Jenny stared in silence. Anne said brittly, 'Well, don't look so shocked. That's what the Church would want, isn't it? Three cheers for the good old faith.'

'Don't throw the Church at me, Anne.'

'You've been damned well throwing it at me . . .'

'Anne, I've learned to live with the Church. Maybe I break a lot of rules, but I've stayed in there. It's more than you've done.

So lay off.' She glared at Anne with deep, hurt anger. But then almost at once, the anger transmuted into sorrow. She said softly, 'Well, whatever you do, it *should* be all right.' She stopped, prodded at the earth with her spade and said, almost under her breath, 'And if it isn't, at least it will be an only child.'

The wind, gusting, blew Anne's anorak hood down, exposing her ruffled black hair. Unthinking, she lifted the hood again with one hand, her eyes still on Jenny. From the beginning, she had assumed that regardless of what happened between herself and Bob, this baby would be the only one she ever had. She said, 'What's that got to do with anything?'

Jenny looked straight into her eyes. 'There won't be anyone else's lives to screw up.'

'Crap!' Anne shouted. Jenny started to speak, but she just shouted louder, 'Crap! Don't give me that. We've been through this and I'm not buying it. He didn't screw anyone's life up. Except maybe Mom and Dad's and I'm not so sure about that. He didn't screw my life up. And he didn't screw yours up either. What's wrong with your life anyhow, what are you complaining about? Are you going to blame this,' she swept her hand in a dismissive arc around Jenny's tattered fields and steadings, 'on *Joseph*?'

She was sorry she had said it at once, sorry to, in a careless moment, reveal the despairing scorn she tried always so hard to conceal. The hurt bloomed in Jenny's open childish eyes.

'I didn't mean this,' she said with dignity. 'I love this.' They stared at each other across their perpetual divide. 'This,' she said, 'is my escape. This is what I built to repair all the damage . . .'

'Fuck it!' Anne shouted. 'Damage. There wasn't any damage. You were a bright, happy child. You were intelligent, loved, and successful. You were *brilliant* at school and brilliant at university and if you chose to throw it up and get married . . .'

'Throwing it up and getting married was the first sensible thing I ever did. The first *real* thing. The first thing I ever did for *me*.'

'Garbage,' Anne said.

Jenny was calm. 'No. Not garbage. Anne, did you ever think *why* I was so great at school?'

'You had brains.'

'Maybe. But so had you and you failed everything. I was brilliant at school because I worked my ass off. I drove myself

306

every day of my childhood. I sat up until eleven and twelve doing every ounce of homework that the other kids didn't even bother to look at.'

Anne looked at her coldly. 'Big noble you. Nobody made you do it. And you got your rewards.'

Jenny suddenly spun around and flung the spade she was holding so it clattered against a garden post and fell flat on the ground.

'Yes,' she whispered hoarsely, 'I got my rewards. I got my shiny gold stars on top of the paper. And I took them home and then, if I was lucky, and Joseph wasn't howling, I got my mother to *notice* me. And when Dad came home he maybe stopped before shutting himself in that blasted music room . . .'

'He was *working*,' Anne shouted.

'Yes. And I was growing up. And nobody fucking noticed me at all.' She gasped and buried her face in her hands. Behind them she murmured, 'You had Nonna. She thought the sun shone out of your ass. I had nobody. Except at report card time, and parents' nights when one of them got away and came in to be proud of me. And graduation. And when the Dean's list came out with my name on it. Only by then, she was so wrapped up in him she didn't even notice that. My biggest brightest shiny gold star.' She laughed, bitterly, and Anne said with her voice shaking, 'She couldn't *help* it. She hadn't time.'

Jenny let her hands slip from her face, and straightened, raising her head. She looked surprisingly calm and mature, a streak of mud on her cheek.

'I know,' she said coolly. 'And I love Joseph anyhow and I always did. And none of that fixes the hurt.'

Later, in the car, driving to town, Jenny said bluntly, 'Does Bob want this baby?' They were alone, or she would never have spoken. Angus had gone in early with Simon in Simon's car: Simon to go to work, and Angus to shop for a new suit. It was Jenny's Christmas present to him; a sum of money she regarded as desperately large. He had accepted it gratefully but she could see the disappointment in the amount. Talking to Simon she had raged about it. 'What does he need a *suit* for? We went to university in jeans and sweatshirts. Fergus never owned a suit in his life.' Simon, in his persistent fairness pointed out that Angus was *not* Fergus, the eighties were *not* the sixties, and Cambridge was neither Edinburgh, nor Harpur College. All of which she knew. It didn't help her ravaged purse any.

Now, she and Anne had agreed to meet both of them for lunch, and she was ashamedly grateful that Anne would, as always, pick up the tab. Anne was wearing a simple draped jersey dress and, for the first time that morning, Jenny had noticed the tiniest pregnant bulge, though she doubted she would have recognized it without foreknowledge. Anne sat, somehow remote from the shabby interior of the car and from Jenny herself, still dressed in the jeans and jumper in which she had been gardening. Eventually she said, 'He wants the baby. Conditionally.'

'Conditionally?'

'Conditionally upon its being whole and well and perfect.' Anne made a small grimace. 'I've got my orders. He doesn't want any botched jobs.'

Jenny said at once, indignantly, 'If you put it like that, you make him sound like a bastard. He's not a bastard. He's a good, compassionate man. If he's reluctant to raise a damaged child, well, who would know more about that than him?'

We might,' Anne said softly. 'But never mind,' she sighed. 'I know I'm not being fair.' She looked out of the window. 'I don't think I want to be fair.' After a little while she said, 'He was devastated at first, when I told him I was pregnant. Or rather,' she laughed softly, 'when he told me.' When she spoke again, it was with loving, intimate gentleness. 'He knew my own body better than I did. He's such a caring . . .'

'But he didn't want a baby.'

'Of *course* he didn't,' Anne said. She had done one of her about turns and become briskly defensive on Bob's behalf. 'He had two daughters of his own, practically grown. He had just crawled out from under twenty years of parenthood, the last five *solitary* parenthood with all the restrictions that imposes. He was looking forward rapturously to at last having some freedom. Aside from that, his oldest daughter is about to make him a *grandfather*. Is that any time to start all over again with diapers and sleepless nights?' She laughed heartily, but Jenny, her thoughts her own, said softly, 'I'm not sure.'

Anne gave her a quizzical sideways glance but didn't learn much. She said then, 'Well, Bob was sure.'

'You said "at first". What won him round?'

Anne turned again to look out of the side window. She said, with her face thus averted, 'Love. Pride. Men all have that. Decency. He realized I had a just cause. He knew how desperately I had *wanted* a baby.' She looked back to Jenny. 'You know, he is so damned fair-minded. It never even occurred to him that maybe I had cheated. Got myself pregnant deliberately and pretended it was an accident. And yet, I had every motivation.'

'Did you?' Jenny said curiously.

'What?'

'Cheat. Did you cheat?'

Anne lifted her chin, proud and, in profile as Jenny saw her in a quick glance, terribly beautiful. 'You don't know me,' she said.

Jenny said gently, 'Don't be offended. If it were me, I might have cheated.' She laughed, with a rare self-awareness. 'My moral sense has always been a bit negotiable.' She added then, 'Was it a just cause, Anne?' She had her own reason for asking.

Anne said only, 'He thought so. Anyhow, it had happened. And he accepted it. It's a lot, too, another twenty years of parenthood. He'll be sixty-six when it's Angus's age. Not much mountain-climbing time left then.'

'But he accepted.'

'He accepted twenty years. What he can't accept,' she said with laboured slowness, 'is the *possibility*, remote though it obviously is, of a life sentence. Like Mom and Dad.'

They were passing the place along the single-track road where, on the journey from the airport, they had stopped to walk and Anne had lost her diamond. Jenny slowed the car slightly, as if in doing so she might catch a glimpse of the lost treasure. She said, 'Did you ask him?'

'What?'

'Did you ask St Anthony?' She shrugged towards the wintry hillside. Anne stared at her for a moment to see if she was serious.

'Oh, don't be insane,' she said, exasperated.

'Just *ask*,' Jenny said calmly.

Anne waved an angry hand towards the rolling miles of heather moorland and yellowed grass. 'It's just impossible, Jenny. There's no way in a million years we're going to find it out there.'

'Don't hem God in with your own limitations.'

'Screw it, Jenny, you make me sick.'

'*Just ask*.' Jenny was grinning, unperturbed. Anne stared bleakly out of the window until Jenny began the descent off the hill to where her road joined the main one to town.

'Look kid,' Anne said softly, 'take some advice from someone beyond the fold. If you want to hang on to God, don't ask for anything bigger than he can handle.'

She expected Jenny to be angry, but Jenny laughed instead, swinging the long car expertly around the hairpin bends.

'Small miracles,' she said, laughing still.

They split up in town. Jenny had appointments and chores: the bank, her accountant, a woman on the High Street to whom she supplied knitwear, the usual monotony of the household shopping. Anne had her traveller's duties: postcards and souvenirs for family, friends and staff. She spent the morning selecting scenes of hills, lochs and rivers; boxes of shortbread, miniatures of whisky, scarves and neckties in tartans and tweeds. A lot of it was hideous but she knew what people expected and was meticulous about matching gift to recipient. She brought out her Gold Card in one of the best woollen shops and signed the slip happily for the most perfect cashmere pullover for Marion. For Joseph she found a white plush Scottie dog in a red and green kilt, an appalling bit of kitsch. She pictured his little therapist rubbing the soft fur against his face, and then setting it up on his locker for visitors to admire. She was quick and efficient in her purchases, making immediate decisions, having everything wrapped and packed away even as she was paying. By eleven o'clock she was done, and set off in search of a café in which she would sit with a cup of coffee, writing 'Best wishes, Anne,' on two dozen cards.

She did not know the town very well. She was usually there with Jenny and Jenny had her own favourite places to which she led guests by circuitous routes and in a flying hurry. Rather than seek one out from muzzy memory, Anne settled for the only eating place she had seen in the big shopping mall, a bakery franchise that served sandwiches and salads of typical British mediocrity. She was standing at the self-service counter, awaiting her turn, when she saw Angus, just outside the open entrance. She turned and stepped back, relinquishing her position in the queue of women shoppers, thinking to invite him in. But, absorbed in something he was studying in a neighbouring shop window, he did not notice her upraised hand. She stepped out of the café and approached him in the central arcade of the mall. He looked up, startled.

'I was just stopping for a cup of coffee,' she said. 'Care to join me?'

He smiled, glad to see her, but also preoccupied. 'I'd love it, Anne, but I'd better get on. I've not got very far yet.'

She noticed he was empty-handed; indeed his hands were thrust rather forlornly in the pockets of his cord jacket.

'Not finding what you want?'

'This place is hopeless,' he said. 'All fusty old country gent stuff, or else cheap rubbish for the kids.' He clearly did not regard himself any longer as a kid. Anne smiled, remembering a long-ago Edinburgh in which she sought a stylish dress for Elizabeth and ended making it herself. Maybe the revolution hadn't quite reached this far north.

'I think you'd have better luck down south,' she said mildly. 'Why don't you wait until the beginning of term?'

'Well, of *course*,' Angus said companionably, as if he was aware of being in the presence at last of someone who understood things. 'Anything worth *having* is down south. But, quite frankly, it's all a bit beyond my range. Cambridge prices are OTT, at the best. And I'm afraid Mom has a pretty fanciful idea about what things cost even here. She's still living back in the sixties . . . do-it-yourself tie-dyes and flares. *You* know.' He laughed conspiratorially, but Anne drew back slightly from associating herself with his scorn.

'Your mother does very well. But she hasn't a lot to spare.'

'I *know*,' Angus said, irritated. 'Look, I'd better be off.'

She didn't want him to go, unhappy, with his meagre Christmas present in his pocket. She took his arm and pointed towards the shop window he had been studying. It was a branch of one of the vibrant new chains that had swept across the country in recent years, and seemed to make a fetish of exquisite window displays and interiors that were ninety per cent empty space.

'What about that?' she said.

'Which? The brown with the check? I was looking at it. It's way over my limit.'

311

'Not the brown. The grey at the back. That's lovely and it's a very fair price.' She spoke authoritatively, judging cut and fabric with a professional eye.

'I've never worn grey. I always wear brown.'

'Start now. Grey is your colour. You'll look too tweedy in the other. Listen to your Auntie Anne, she knows what she's talking about.' She said the last lightly, with humorous warmth.

'I'll bet you do,' Angus said, respectfully. He was eyeing the grey suit with brightening interest.

'Go try it.'

He hesitated. 'Yeah, just a minute.' He turned away from her. She realized what he was doing and pretended fascination with some detail of the window display. In the glass, in dim reflection, she saw him surreptitiously opening his wallet and carefully counting bills. She felt a pang of sympathy: he reminded her so much of her young self, struggling in Binghamton and Edinburgh, counting her savings down to pennies. But not just herself, all the young; the crowds of kids who hovered about the entrances of her own shops, came in, fingered racks of garments, tried things on and left empty-handed. They tugged at her heart; they always did. It was for their sake that she hunted around to find at least some lines of decent, wearable fun clothes at reasonable prices to fill out the 'Think Young' corners of Anne Conti. And conversely they were the reason she resisted the move towards 'In-House' credit cards with their too-easy temptations to buy. She loved them, the kids with their foolish dreams, because she knew them so well, and knew too that for the rest of their lives they would be haunted by larger and larger versions of the same sad fantasies . . . the yearning need of *things* that turned adults into vulnerable children still. She also knew that all the ascetic lectures of a lifetime wouldn't change that.

She saw Angus replace his wallet resignedly in his pocket and turned to face him. 'Well?'

'I'll go and find something in M&S,' he said. 'I saw something on sale that ought to do.' Anne smiled gently. She again slipped her arm beneath his elbow, turned him around and marched him into the shop. Her Gold Card was nowhere near its limit, yet.

* * *

At lunch, in the wine bar, Angus showed the suit to his mother and Simon. He was very proud of it, and Anne had directed him firmly not to lie but, on the other hand, not to volunteer any unnecessary information about how he made up the shortfall in the price. She was relying on Jenny's notorious fogginess over figures to ensure that the truth did not come out. Jenny admired the fabric, complimented the choice of colour, and kissed her son in response to his warm 'thank you'. Anne had had her kiss earlier, at the check-out counter of the shop. Simon beamed happily, pleased that the issue was settled and everyone was content. Only once, as Angus carefully folded his treasure away, did Anne catch a glance from Jenny that warned her that all was possibly less than well.

They parted company again after lunch. She had a small jousting match with Simon as they both reached to pay a bill, but she had years more expertise at such matters, and quickly outfoxed him.

'You're very kind,' he said.

'Not at all,' she said briskly. 'I'm having a free holiday with you and Jenny. This is the least I can do.' He looked pacified, his pride comforted. She only hoped she'd manage the same with Jenny over the suit.

Out in the street, she was glad to be on her own, with nothing pressing to do until they met again for tea at four. The meal at which, in her new delicate state, she had picked cautiously, still lay with some unease on her stomach. She decided to walk it off, circling the few squares of shopping streets and wandering off down by the river. She watched gulls, visited an art gallery, bought a small print, browsed over some rather nice local pottery, and was making her way back into the centre of town when she came upon them.

They had gathered in a small open area between two rows of buildings, an old street, pedestrianized by a row of bollards at one end and turned into a mall. There were half a dozen of them, all young, quite well dressed, nondescript even in the ordinariness of their clothing. The exception, if any, was a young girl with spiked dyed black hair who stood with an armful of leaflets at the edge of the pavement, handing them to anyone who passed. Directly behind her a large banner, strung on poles

313

and held at either end by two of the young people, proclaimed:
JESUS IS LORD

The two holding the banner – a boy and a girl – were singing the chorus of a song. The verses were sung by the star performer, as Anne chose to regard him, a handsome, alert, fair-haired boy who was telling a story in song, illustrating it with quick, clever drawings on a large blackboard set up in the street. It was a kind of parable involving an unhappy Christian, journeying through an obstacle course of Lustful Temptations, Material Pleasures, False Prophets; Bunyan up-dated with hypodermic needles, automobiles, pop-stars. Beside him, a fixedly smiling girl strummed relentlessly at a guitar. Anne stopped, in the casual way of a person with time to waste, and watched.

The handsome boy sang on, verse after verse, simplistic but smoothly rhymed, and his wandering Christian dutifully abandoned one by one the pleasures of life, among them his girlfriend, his mother, his father. The chorus chanted happily, even the black-haired punk-girl with her leaflets joining in:

> You know not the time,
> You know not the day,
> Turn to the Lord,
> Turn to the Way.

The song was jingly, irritating. Anne shrugged, half-amused, half-annoyed, and turned to go. As she did, the light fingers of a slender hand touched her arm. Instantly she whirled around, furious at the invasion of her private space. It was the girl with the leaflets. Anne relaxed, reaching to accept one and dismiss the child. But the hand still held her, and she wondered if a contribution was expected.

'Look, I'm not religious,' she said sharply.

The girl's voice was soft and hopeful, 'Auntie Anne?'

'I met Sarah,' Anne said that night at dinner. She said it as casually as possible, but still got the reaction she had feared. All three of her dinner companions froze in a mime of amazement, knives and forks held in mid-air.

'You *met* her?' Simon said.

Jenny's surprise turned immediately to exasperation, 'Anne, for God's sake, why did you wait till now to tell me?'

314

Anne shrugged and tried to look unperturbed. 'I hardly thought . . . I forgot actually. I mean, she was standing there with her group in the middle of the High Street in full view . . . I sort of thought you'd have run into her as well. I don't see how you missed her,' she added.

Angus said, 'Did she say when she was coming home?'

'No, actually . . .'

'Anne, this is ridiculous,' Jenny said sharply. 'You *know* we've been worrying about her. You *know* I have no way of contacting her. And you *saw* her in plain daylight. Why on earth didn't you come and tell me *then*? When I could have gone and talked to her.' She put her cutlery down on her plate and leaned back from the table, her forehead resting on the nervous fingers of one hand.

Anne felt remorseful, but still not about to give Jenny the truth. She said, 'Well she seemed so perfectly normal and happy . . .'

'What was she doing?' Simon asked.

'Singing. Singing and handing out leaflets. I've got one some-where.'

'Singing,' said Angus in his 'let's-be-sure-I've-got-this-right' voice.

'Yes,' Anne said, looking right at him. 'She was singing a sort of hymn and giving these things out. If you get my handbag I'll show you.'

'We've seen them,' Simon said with irritation.

'Did she say anything?' Jenny asked.

Anne paused. 'Yes. Well, we had a little chat.'

Sarah, your mother and brother are worried about you.

These are my mothers, my brothers.

When are you coming home?

This is my home.

'Did she *say* anything?' Simon asked.

'Nothing of any consequence.' Anne looked around the table and gave a small smile. 'They seemed pretty OK, the friends she was with. I wouldn't worry too much.'

But they weren't listening to her. Angus said to his mother and Simon, 'Look, just let me go up to that place they've got and haul her out of there.'

Jenny kept her head in her hand. 'First of all, we don't *know* she's there.'

315

'Where else?' Angus demanded.

'They may have other places,' Simon said reasonably. 'They're all quite young. They probably have homes of their own. She could be staying with any one of them.'

'She could bloody disappear,' Angus said. There was a silence. Jenny let the hand slip from her face. She was white, pinched. 'We should go and get her while we still have some idea where she is. Before they decide to take her away somewhere.'

Anne broke in quickly, 'Angus, your concern is very sweet, but she looked to me like a young lady quite in control of herself. I don't think anyone's *taking* her anywhere.'

Simon said, 'I wouldn't be *too* sure about that.'

Anne looked up. Jenny, she knew, was panicking, and Angus was filled with brotherly outrage, but from Simon she expected sense.

'Do you think we should do something?' she asked quietly.

'I'd give it a week,' he said, 'and then I'd report her missing and call in the police.'

Jenny stood up and looked from Simon to Angus, to Anne and back to Simon. She said, 'She's hardly *missing*, Simon, if she's singing Alleluias in the middle of town.'

After dinner, Anne and Jenny did the washing-up together and Simon and Angus slipped quite readily into the role of non-working males. Jenny didn't mind. She wanted Anne to herself. When they were alone, she said without preamble, 'She doesn't want to come home, does she?'

'Not yet.'

Jenny sighed. She said then, 'I do understand your loyalty to her, but I would have preferred if you'd had the decency to tell me right away. I'm not quite the idiot you think I am. Whatever you, or Sarah, might imagine, I wasn't about to tear into her and her friends and drag her out by her hair. I have a little more sense than that.' She looked coldly at Anne and then looked away, 'I would have liked very much to *see* her.'

'Christ, Jenny, you saw her yesterday. And I *told* you she was all right. She was fine. You've really got to loosen up. Cut the apron strings. She's *eighteen*.'

'She's eighteen and in trouble,' Jenny returned. She looked back to her sister. 'I don't really expect you to understand.'

316

'Yeah, yeah. I'm just the wicked stepmother who eats children for breakfast.'

'No,' Jenny said with a small smile, 'but you're an indulgent aunt who always thinks she knows better than their mother what's good for them.'

'That's not true.'

'I saw the price tag on the suit, Anne. I didn't give Angus *near* that amount.'

Anne sighed. She had only partly imagined she would get away with it, but she hadn't thought to be found out so thoroughly, and at once. She said quietly, 'Do you know, Jenny, what he said to me? I mean after we'd bought it, and he'd said thank you. As we were walking out of the door, he said, "I can't believe it's really for me." Jenny, it meant *so much* to him. I didn't realize myself, until then, how much it had meant.' She turned and took Jenny's small shoulders in her hands. 'And it was so easy for me. Can't I help out?' she smiled sweetly. 'Please?'

Jenny hesitated and then pulled free. She turned away. 'You're trying to turn him into your kind of person.'

'Face it, kid,' Anne said sharply, 'he already is.' She felt a surge of anger, but suppressed it. 'Look, it's nothing to do with me. It's the times he lives in. Our moms and dads wanted jackets and ties and they got sandals and long hair. You want sandals and long hair and you're getting jackets and ties. Rebellion is the most reliable convention of all.'

'It's not what he looks like. It's the attitude. The attitude towards money.'

'Sure. He wants it. Like the rest of the world.'

'Like *some* of the rest of the world.'

'Oh right, Saint Jenny the Barefooted.'

'Look.' Jenny whirled about. 'Let me tell you this. If you think you can buy them, you're probably right. But it's only because they're young. They'll see through you one day, I promise you.'

'They'll see through us all, one day,' Anne said. She paused calmly. 'It's called growing up.'

Anne was alone in the house when Sarah came home. The first five days of her vacation had passed; she had begun to mark off on a mental calendar the days until her return. The trip, on the whole, had been a mistake.

She did not entirely regret it. It was good seeing Jenny, good getting to know Simon. It was even good to feel her defensiveness about Fergus slip gently away, and his memory fall more firmly into the past. All those things could only have happened here. Nor was being here in any way worse than Christmas at home without Bob; a Christmas that, like so many before it, would centre by necessity on a hospital bed and Joseph. She thought of her mother there, alone, without guilt; she rationed guilt carefully, too much of it merely curdled love. But the main reason for coming had proved a false hope, and in that way the visit was a failure. She had come, for the first time ever, for solace from Jenny; and she had got none.

Anne sat curled on a sofa in Jenny's living-room, before a fire that she steadily stoked to keep the cold at bay. The two tall windows, in the front wall and gable end, rattled with each gust of the wind, and the jug of dried garden thyme on the sill of one rustled slightly in the draught. The room, like all the house, was impossible to keep warm. The best one could hope for was a singeing heat on shins and hands while bending over the hearth like over a campfire. *How does she live here?* Anne asked herself yet again, wrapping the tartan rug that decorated the sofa around her shoulders, tucking her legs up under her, tighter, like one of the cats. Each morning she woke stiff from sleeping in a shivering knot. She had rearranged the sitting-room while Jenny was out, dragging the sofa nearer the fire, building a little wall of cushions on it, shifting a lamp in closer for light. She felt like a nomad, pitching a tent in an alien land.

It was the first morning since arriving that she had to herself. Simon was away. He had gone away the previous morning and not come back at night. Jenny seemed neither surprised nor perturbed, so Anne assumed it was a normal arrangement. She had been unable to grasp the complexities of their relationship; whether they were *actually* living together, or just trying it out, like herself and Bob on Fire Island. Or indeed whether the affair was waxing, waning, or simply steady on some carefully negotiated plateau. It seemed quite stable: they never fought; although arguments, mostly over Sarah, were frequent. That they were inevitably reasonable she credited to Simon, since she recalled Jenny as a high-strung and passionate fighter in her marriage to Fergus. On the whole, she regarded this as an improvement;

certainly easier to live with for everyone concerned. Jenny still fought with Angus, but that was to be expected. They had nothing in common and every reason to clash. Anne imagined that if Sarah were there she would fight with her mother as well, and secretly considered her absence something of a relief. In fact, she was only slightly ashamed to admit she was finding everybody's absence this morning something of a relief.

Jenny was up on the hill with her dogs and a neighbour, gathering a mutual herd of sheep together for reasons that remained obscure to Anne. Angus had gone skiing with school friends. And so she was alone, and for the first time the house had actually become what she had, from New York, imagined it to be: a place of solitude and peace, a sylvan retreat in which she might carefully think, plan and order her troubled mind. If, she thought wryly, she didn't freeze to death first.

There was no epiphany. She had all the morning alone, but the only realization that grew out of solitude was that she had been beguiled by a cliché: that one went to strange surroundings and found revelation. All she had found here was loneliness, the feeling of being an outsider that was familiar enough from her summer with Bob. Simon, Jenny, Angus, even Sarah, even in their angers, were still a family, a unit, and she was outside it. *The story of my life*, she thought, without rancour. It was the unavoidable reverse of the privacy she had cultivated and treasured. And, ironically, she only felt it at times, like this vacation, when she was not alone.

She stretched her feet out on the couch, warmed now by the mature glow of the fire, and yawned lazily. The rain pattered against the window, and she was almost cosy, and then quite suddenly she felt an airy flutter within her. *Oh shit, not again.* She had been sick once this morning, like most mornings, and once was surely enough. But the feeling did not grow and become nausea but simply went away. And then it recurred, definite, unique, and somehow pleasing. She sat up and looked down at her body. *Hey you*, she thought. *It can't be you already.* The flutter came again, and she stared, enchanted and amazed, as if expecting the infinitesimal thing to be visible. 'Well, hello,' she said, aloud.

Outside she heard the sound of a vehicle approaching the house, bumping and clattering its way up the long, rutted drive.

She was sorry. She wanted more time to herself with her discovery. Jenny would be unimpressed; she would say dismissive, matronly things about it only being wind pains. She had the whole baby thing wrapped up; she was a pro and Anne just an amateur playing at her game.

But it wasn't Jenny. She heard, instead of the familiar heavy slam of the Subaru door and the yapping of emerging sheepdogs, a long rasping creak of something heavy sliding. Then young voices, male and female, and then the sliding sound repeated and the noise of the vehicle pulling away. Angus, back already? The skiing abandoned for storms, or someone's broken leg? She shrugged, sitting up, imagining the worst. She was wary of this business of flying down snowy hills that Bob so enthused over. *Great*, she thought, envisioning Angus in a plaster cast, on crutches. *Just what Jenny needs*. But it wasn't Angus, either.

The door banged open then, and then the sitting-room door too, and Sarah walked into the room. She looked fresh-faced and pretty from the wet, cold air, and the wind had flattened the grotesqueries of her spiked hair so it flopped almost becomingly over her forehead. He eyes were bright, glowing.

'Where's Mom?' she demanded with the instantaneous need for gratification that made the adolescent so like the infant.

'She's not here. She's out with the sheep and somebody called Donald Ian.'

'Oh.' Sarah looked faintly devastated.

'Can I help?'

'Is Angus here?'

'No. He's skiing.'

'Simon?' she asked, a little reluctantly.

Anne shook her head.

'Sorry,' she said, feeling lamely insufficient. 'Just me.'

She expected Sarah to walk out in unexplained disappointment the way Robin might, but instead she paused, appeared to think something over, and then suddenly brightened her face into a determined, almost aggressive smile, the same smile she had used while urging her leaflets on uninterested passers-by.

'God must have intended this,' she said.

'What?' Anne said, thinking she had misheard.

'That it be you. God must have intended me to reveal it to you.'

320

'Intended *what*?' Anne said. She stood up, regarding Sarah with narrowed eyes. She was wary of Sarah. She was even more wary of God. 'What?' she repeated suspiciously. 'Reveal what?'

Sarah's smile was sweet and serene. 'The coming,' she said, 'of the rapture of Our Lord.'

XVII

' "Grace," ' Simon read aloud. ' "The undeserved salvation of God." ' He held the dictionary open on his outstretched palm, and walked about the room, musing upon it like an actor upon a script. Jenny laughed. She was crouched on the floor over the paper box of Christmas ornaments, delicately retrieving them while Angus and Anne did solid practical things with the tree and the red and green metal stand.

'What's that in aid of,' she said, still laughing. Jenny loved Christmas; the homely familiar tasks that transformed their ordinary lives into a glitter of celebration. She felt warm and secure, as if nothing could undo her happiness.

'Us,' he said. 'We're supposed to be praying for it, according to Sarah.'

Jenny shrugged. 'That's nothing new.'

'It is the way *Sarah* tells it,' Angus said sharply.

'Not really.'

'Oh come on, Mom. You mean *we're* all expecting to get whisked off to heaven *en masse*, leaving nothing but our dirty knickers on the ground?'

'I mean we're all expecting salvation,' Jenny said. She did not look up from the box where she was carefully untangling a garland of tinsel. 'And I don't think that's precisely what Sarah means either.'

'Don't count on it,' Angus returned at once. He stood back from the tree and gingerly released his hold on the slender trunk, watching it sway uneasily. 'You insist on giving those people credit for intelligence which they just haven't got. It's not helping the situation.'

'Neither is sarcasm,' Jenny said.

'Where *is* Sarah?' Anne asked. 'She's good at this kind of thing. Where's the artist when we need her?'

'Upstairs, praying,' Angus said sourly.

'Yes,' Jenny said, getting up, carrying the tinsel garlands, carefully separated, to the sofa, where she draped them, one by one. 'Probably.' She turned deliberately to Anne. 'Sarah doesn't approve of Christmas trees, I'm afraid. The Saints say they're pagan.'

Anne nodded, cautiously, not knowing whether to take Jenny's calm at face value or expect an explosion.

Angus said, 'Oh for *Christ's sake!*'

'They *are* pagan, of course, Angus.' Jenny had returned to the box and was lifting out ornaments and carefully laying them on the lid. 'We've all just chosen to ignore that.' Angus glared at her.

Simon said, 'Actually, the ancient Church was very wise about things like that.' He was in one of his expansive, live-and-let-live-moods. 'They adopted all sorts of pagan rituals and holy places to pacify the people.'

'Comfort,' Jenny said softly. 'Not pacify. Comfort.'

Simon shrugged. He said, 'Same difference.' But of course it was not. Jenny left her garlands and crossed the room to the bookshelves where Fergus's stereo sat amongst her rows of university texts. The stereo was the most expensive furnishing in the house; the one remnant of his music days when such things mattered and he had money to pay for them. She carefully withdrew her favourite old Christmas record from its worn sleeve and set it on the turntable. The music poured gently into the room. Anne made a last adjustment to the tree-stand and stepped back and gave the cut and braced Scots pine a firm shove. It bounced but returned to a steady vertical. She brushed dust from her hands and said, 'There. That will hold.' She turned back to her sister who was untangling the string of coloured fairy lights. 'You're taking this remarkably calmly,' she said.

'What?' Jenny was humming tunelessly along with the recording.

Anne watched her suspiciously. 'Your daughter's private apocalypse.'

Jenny laughed. 'Well, she's either right, or she's not right.'

'*Mother*,' Angus said, 'It's just *crazy*.'

'What's crazy, Angus? The Second Coming?'

He shook his head, exasperated. 'Of course not. But not like *this*. Christmas Eve and everyone suddenly lifted bodily into heaven. It's so *hokey*.'

'Not everyone,' Jenny said mildly. She had found the one loose bulb that had broken the circuit and now, twisting it, was rewarded with a merry flash of green, blue, yellow and red.

'Oh no, of course not. Just Sarah and her bloody Saints.'

'And us too,' Jenny said generously, 'if we accept God's grace . . . That's why she's praying so hard. I think it's very sweet of her.' She smiled, irritating Angus further.

He said, 'Shit.'

'You believe in the Assumption, Angus?'

He glowered but did not answer. Simon said, 'What's that, Jenny? I've never understood.'

She answered without looking at him, still checking and tightening the little light bulbs.

'The belief that Mary the mother of God was taken bodily into Heaven. She didn't die . . . she was just taken up . . . it wasn't necessary for her to die.' She looked up from the lights.

Simon was staring at her, his jaw slack. '*Jenny*. You don't believe that?' He sounded reproachful.

Anne said quickly, with a bright smile, 'Yes she does, Simon. That's Catholic doctrine. Amazing, isn't it?'

'But *you* don't, surely?' He turned to her as if seeking reassurance.

'I don't believe any of it, Simon,' Anne said briskly. 'My bit's easy.' She took the end of the lights from Jenny. 'Shall we string these first?' she said.

Simon watched her unhappily. Eventually he said, 'I don't understand how the two of you could be raised the same and come out so differently.' Anne and Jenny looked at each other and both shrugged. 'I mean coming out *believing* so differently.'

'I asked the wrong questions,' Anne said.

'Like?' Simon looked hopeful, as if her questions might prove to be the same as his, and they would find a solidarity.

'Like, why we were always meant to be *thanking* God all the time.' She looked not to Simon, but to Jenny for a response.

324

'For his Grace,' Jenny said. 'Our undeserved salvation. The love that wants nothing in return.'

'Fine,' Anne said. 'But it all presupposes our being here in the first place. I don't understand why we should be grateful to God. We didn't choose to be here.'

'He chose. That's what we're to be grateful for.'

'Should Joseph be grateful?' They stared at each other through the prickly branches of the pine, each holding a clump of unlit lights.

'Low blow,' Jenny said, 'but yes.'

'Jenny,' Simon interrupted. 'That's simply not something any thinking adult can believe.' Jenny stared at him through the branches of the tree. She was ominously quiet. And then suddenly she dropped the string of lights, leaving them dangling, the bulbs clunking against the wooden floor. She stepped away from the tree.

'Right, Simon. Let's hear it then. What do thinking adults believe?'

He hesitated. 'Well, it's not easy . . .'

'No, no. Come on. Let's have it. The creed according to Simon Hamilton. I'll have a go . . . We believe in, well not exactly *God*, as such, but some sort of superior, well, not a *being* actually, but a force perhaps . . . obviously not personified or anything, but a general *aura* of goodness. And of course Jesus *wasn't* obviously God Incarnate or anything like that, but he was probably the greatest humanitarian *teacher* there's ever been . . . and if all the so-called Christians would stop fighting over him and just try to be good and kind and sympathetic and *nice* to each other then the whole world will be just hunky-dory. Forever and ever. Amen.'

Simon looked at her coldly. 'I don't have to take this, Jenny,' he said, and walked out.

Jenny watched him until the door closed behind him. She looked startled, but not particularly perturbed. She returned to the tree, carefully circling it with wire and bulbs.

'That wasn't very fair,' Anne said. She was watching from the far side of the room. Beside her, Angus had become inordinately involved with the record collection, seeking something intently, his head down and his face turned away. Jenny looked absently towards the door through which Simon had left.

'He really pisses me off,' she said.

'Why? Because he doesn't believe exactly what you believe?'

Jenny finished adjusting the lights. She stretched the plug end to the socket beside the hearth and switched it on, nodded approval and switched it off.

'Because what he believes is such muddled nonsense and he *thinks* it's so rational.'

'More rational than the Assumption and the Virgin Birth.'

'Anne, I don't make any *claims* to rationality. Simon is so busy patronizing me, he never sees the intellectual mire he's in himself.'

Anne listened, standing in the centre of the room with her hands on her hips. 'Christ, Jenny,' she said finally. 'Of all the dumb things to argue about.' Jenny looked up. 'You've got a good thing going here . . . a really good thing . . . and you're going to ruin it fighting over this nonsense.'

Jenny shrugged, irritated. 'That's not what we're fighting about,' she said. She picked up a garland of tinsel and turned away.

Later, Anne cornered Simon in the kitchen. 'Then what *are* you fighting about?' she asked. While the music played faintly on the far side of the house, he worked determinedly over the Aga, the sink, the kitchen counters, trying to ignore her. He had taken off his pullover and hung it over the back of a chair, and with his sleeves rolled up was washing, scrubbing and tidying the leftover mess of their supper. He was efficient and practical and somehow pleasing to watch. 'Come on, Simon,' she said, 'What's going on?'

'I don't think I want to talk about it,' he said. But he sat down, laying the dish-rag, neatly folded, on the table before her.

'Of course it's none of my business,' Anne said. As always, she was dodging a little from emotional revelations, even those she had sought. He sat watching her, and after a while he smiled, slightly. He looked very gentle.

'How do you feel?' he asked.

Anne looked up, startled. 'Me? I'm fine. Why?'

But he kept smiling. 'I'm so glad for you,' he said. She drew back slightly, momentarily puzzled. Then she quickly realized and said, without surprise, 'Jenny's told you.'

'We don't have any secrets.'

'No. No, of course not.' She looked up, meeting his eyes. She wondered if it were true about the secrets, or whether he deluded himself.

He said, 'I hope you don't mind.' He was so considerate that she said, 'No, of course not,' again. Then she smiled slightly and added, 'I imagine you'd have guessed soon enough, anyhow, with my morning sprints to the john to throw up.'

'It *was* a little obvious.'

He was really much more man and much less boy than she had thought. He was attractive as well. She softened and said, 'It must seem pretty ridiculous to you, a woman my age . . .' She laughed at herself but he leaned forward and lightly touched her hand.

'It seems wonderful to me.' His voice was rich with longing.

Anne said, softly, amazed, 'Oh my God. You too.' She laughed and he was hurt.

'Why should it be funny? It's not just women who want babies. Men want them too.'

He looked at her, clear-eyed and young and so irrevocably of another generation. She shook her head, apologized, was only partly forgiven. Tentatively she asked, 'What does Jenny say?'

He shrugged and looked away. 'We haven't really talked that much,' he said.

Anne knew what the fight was about then, and knew also that it was more serious than joustings over God.

'He wants a baby,' she said to Jenny. They were alone in the living-room with the newly decorated tree. Simon was still in the kitchen, carefully taking down all the big platters and tureens that would be needed for Christmas dinner, washing and drying them. Angus had gone back to his books and Sarah still remained closeted in her room. Jenny was tying lengths of green velvet ribbon in loose bows on dozens of red candles. Christmas, Anne realized, must cost her a fortune. She finished the bow she was constructing before she answered.

'Of course he does,' she said. Anne had expected a feigning of surprise or, at the least, argument. She sat slightly disconcerted and then Jenny said, 'So do I.' Anne stared and Jenny's mouth quirked in a small, involuntary smile.

'Well,' Anne said eventually, 'I guess there isn't a problem then.' She was faintly mystified, but also slightly relieved. She realized suddenly that she liked Simon and liked Simon and Jenny together and did not want to see it fall apart.

'Of course there's a problem,' Jenny said. The smile was gone. She paused. 'It's a lovely *idea*, Anne. But it's just impossible.' Her voice was flat, final.

'Why? Why should it be impossible? You're younger than me. You're brilliant at mothering . . .'

'Am I?' Jenny asked sourly. She shrugged and tilted her head back to indicate the upstairs of the house where her children were. 'I don't seem to be doing too great a job at the moment.' Before Anne could argue she said hastily, 'Not the point, anyhow. I haven't *time*, Anne. I'm committed already to Angus and to Sarah.'

'But they're growing up. They'll be leaving home.'

'They don't stop needing a parent just because they're living somewhere else. It doesn't *stop*, Anne. It goes on and on . . . money, or emotional problems, or religion . . . even if they were married, I imagine it might still go on.'

Anne thought suddenly of Bob, lying on the deckchair with Mandy curled against his shoulder, his son-in-law sitting on the decking beside him.

'It has to stop sometime,' she said.

'Yeah. When I'm a hundred and forty probably. I don't *mind*, Anne. I like it even. And I'm looking forward to all sorts of things . . . seeing them married, grandchildren . . . but there's not time or room for a baby, not just the ties and limitations, there isn't room for the *emotions*. I can't be counselling young adults and playing nursery games at the same time. There just isn't enough of me to go around.' She stopped and looked down at her candles. 'I thought I could,' she said slowly. 'I thought for a while it was just what I should be doing. But then I met Simon and I realized it was all a fantasy.'

'It's not a fantasy for Simon,' Anne said.

'No.' Jenny turned restlessly away. 'No. I suppose it's not.'

Anne persisted, urgently. 'Doesn't that matter? Hasn't he got rights too? You've had your family. Simon has none. He's a young man. He has a right to children.' She paused and drew a breath and said carefully, 'Don't you think that if you continue this relationship, you owe him a child?'

Jenny shook her head sadly. 'A child is a gift from God, an undeserved gift. No one owes anyone a child.'

Anne nodded. She sat with her arms around her body, leaning her head back against the sofa, dreamily. 'It must be sad to be a man,' she said.

In the morning, Anne went hill-walking with Simon. She borrowed Jenny's boots and expressed delight in the surprisingly pleasant day. It was a pretended enthusiasm; she felt sorry for Simon, who had been trying to interest someone in his expedition since breakfast.

Jenny was busy icing her Christmas cake, with Sarah sitting at the kitchen table beside her, reading her Bible. Angus was still in bed. While Anne sat on the long bench beside the table and tied her boots on, Sarah interrupted her mother three times to read out sections, all of which Jenny absorbed with a nod and a thoughtful lick at the icing spoon.

'Do you want a pair of thick socks? You might need socks to fill them up.'

'I've got bigger feet,' Anne said.

Jenny thought of Anne's long, slender brown feet, when they were children on the beach; her own feet, white and pudgy beside them.

'*But of that day and hour no one knows, not even the angels of heaven, nor the Son, but the Father only,*' Sarah read.

'I've got gaiters,' Simon added. 'You can borrow my gaiters.' He waved something, canvas and mud-encrusted. Anne shook her head. From upstairs, Angus's voice, sleepy and faintly belligerent, shouted, 'Mom? Where's my blue shirt?'

Without turning from her half-iced cake, Jenny answered, 'In the ironing basket.'

'*For as in those days before the flood they were eating and drinking, marrying and giving in marriage..!*'

'Simon, find Anne that old Barbour that Elizabeth left here, will you?'

'Mom, you're not *listening.*'

'Yes, I am, dear. *So will be the coming of the Son of man.* I've read it, Sarah. About a hundred times.'

'Then why don't you *listen* to it?'

Jenny put her icing spoon down and laid her palette knife

gently across the top of the bowl. She wiped her sticky, sugary hands on her apron. 'Sarah, if the angels and our Lord don't know when it's to happen, I don't see why I should.'

'But I'm *telling* you. It's happening now.'

'So you say.' Jenny picked up the palette knife and drew a smooth line across the wet, shining cake. Simon sat down on the bench beside Sarah. He rolled his thick woollen socks up over his trouser legs and wrapped the canvas gaiters around his ankles, zipping them carefully as he spoke.

'It may seem very immediate to you, Sarah, but it might be worth considering that *every* generation has suspected it was living in the last times. There's a sort of psychological dependency on the idea. It saves us having to imagine the world going on quite successfully without us. Besides,' he added, tying the top of the second gaiter, 'it's terribly convenient. Living in the shadow of the Apocalypse also saves us from having to actually *do* anything about the world.'

'You don't understand. You're laughing about it, Simon, and your immortal soul is at stake.'

Simon stood up and straightened his jacket. He looked embarrassed. 'Yes, from your point of view, I suppose that's true.'

'Oh Christ, are we on to this again,' Angus said, emerging from the corridor in his jeans and T-shirt. He crossed the kitchen and began rooting around in Jenny's overflowing wicker ironing basket. He had woken up a bit and grinned his troublesome grin. 'What I can't understand, Sarah, is why *this* Christmas? It's so dashedly inconvenient.' He had shed his Scots accent and made his voice archly Home Counties. 'At the very least, it could wait until I graduate. I'm sure I could face the Apocalypse far better with BA Cantab after my name. Gets one into the *right* sort of after-life, don't you know.' He crossed the kitchen again with his wrinkled blue shirt over his arm, lifted a banana from the fruit bowl on the table, peeled it quickly and took a quick, insolent bite, grinning at his sister.

'*In those days,*' Sarah said, '*two men will be in the field: one will be taken, the other left. Two women will be grinding at the mill: one will be taken, the other left.*' Her face was white beneath her sloppy cascade of black hair, and her thin, perfect lip trembled.

'And two men will be working upon the Stock Exchange, and one will be taken, and the other will stay behind and corner the market in brimstone.' He grinned again at his sister and walked out, munching his banana.

'I can't save him,' Sarah said. 'He's my own brother. And I can't save him.'

'I think he has to *want* to be saved,' Jenny said gently. 'Would you like to lick the bowl?'

Outside, as they walked away from the house, up the muddy track that led to the open hill, Simon said to Anne, 'That girl is seriously disturbed. We need professional help.'

'Jenny doesn't seem too worried,' Anne said.

'Jenny isn't facing facts.'

The track petered out, became two low indentations in the heather, still leading upwards, and then vanished entirely.

'It was a peat road,' Simon explained. 'But no one cuts peat here any longer.'

'Didn't Fergus? That sounds just the kind of thing he would have done.'

Simon said, 'I think he did for a while. But it takes forever and then you have to do things to dry it. It's back-breaking and it doesn't even burn that well. It's so much easier to get coal. And, in man-hours, cheaper.'

'I don't think,' Anne laughed, 'Fergus ever thought about man-hours.'

Simon turned to look at her for a quick moment as they slogged up the hillside, and then turned away. 'I didn't know Fergus, of course,' he said.

'He was a good man,' Anne answered. 'She loved him.'

'Yes, of course. I'm sure she did.'

'It doesn't matter, Simon. It's all over now, anyway. She loves you now.'

He stopped walking. He turned around, his hands in the loose pockets of his climbing jacket. It was bright purple and green, extraordinary colours, out of keeping with his character.

'Do you think she'd ever marry me?' he said.

Anne watched him carefully. The wind was blowing his blond hair all over his face, but he was too intent on her answer to brush it aside. She said, 'Is that really what you want?'

He did not answer at once, but when he did his voice was confident. 'Yes. That's what I want.'

'She's a lot older than you, Simon.'

He laughed, and sounded slightly irritated when he spoke. 'I wouldn't think that would even come up between you and me. I mean, it's totally obvious, and it's also totally obvious that I don't mind.'

'What right have you not to mind?'

'What?' He narrowed his eyes, uncertain.

'You sound like you're doing her a favour. Like being older than you is some kind of disability. Something you should forgive.'

'Oh, come on, Anne. I didn't say anything like that. I mean simply that it doesn't matter to me about the age difference.'

'But it *does* matter to you. You say you love her, but you want her to change. You want her to be your young wife. You want her to have your babies. You're not *accepting* that she's a middle-aged woman with grown children.'

'That's a bitchy thing to say.' He brushed his hair back with one quick angry gesture, taking his annoyance out on the winter wind. 'I'm amazed at you, saying a thing like that. I'm glad Jenny isn't here to hear it.'

'To hear what?' Anne almost smiled.

'To hear you calling her old. My God, she's younger than you.'

'I didn't say old, Simon. I said middle-aged. She *is* middle-aged. So am I. And there's absolutely nothing wrong with it. Nothing.'

'I don't see her that way,' he said stiffly.

'I know. You see her quite differently. You see her without half of what makes her what she is: her sense of responsibility, her dedication to her children, her very real commitment to her faith.'

'Oh, come off it. You feel the same about that as I do.'

'Oh no I don't, Simon. You don't know me at all.'

He hunched his shoulders up into his puffy jacket and turned away. She turned also, following his gaze. Down below them she could see the grey strip of winding tarmac road running by Jenny's house, and the paler beaten earth of the driveway. As she watched, a long, silver-grey car approached, slowed and turned on to the drive. It crept towards the house, easing its way over the potholes and ruts.

'Who's that?' she asked curiously.

'I don't know,' he answered. He was watching intently. 'I can't tell from here. It's too far.' He still watched. 'It doesn't look like anyone I know.' He looked concerned, protective, and Anne said gently, 'Do you want to go down and check it out?'

He thought for a moment, then shook his head. 'Jenny can handle it,' he said.

'Yes,' Anne said quietly, 'Jenny can handle most things.'

After a while, Simon said, still watching the car and the distant house, 'I really do love her, Anne, whatever you think.'

'Oh, I know that.' She paused. 'And I'm glad. I want you to marry her, Simon. But I want you to understand the terms.'

He turned towards her, his face open and warm with gratitude. 'I'd marry her on *any* terms,' he said.

'Including no children of your own?'

He made no response at first, but then he narrowed his eyes and nodded agreement. 'Yes. Including that.' He started to walk upwards again. He went quite quickly for a while, as if escaping her and her questions. But then he stopped suddenly and waited for her. 'I'm sorry,' he said. 'I shouldn't be rushing you. Are you all right? Is this too much for you?'

She had come up to him and he was bending towards her, concerned and compassionate, almost fatherly. She laughed. 'I'm fine. I think I'm getting into the good time. Jenny tells me there's a good time in the middle. Anyhow, I feel great.'

'We won't go to the top,' he said. And in spite of Anne's protests, they didn't, but turned around, upon his insistence, halfway, and went down. On the way back to the house he said, 'You're really lucky, you and Bob. Having the whole thing just happen to you, by accident. It saves all the hassle and the arguments and, in the end, I'm sure you'll be thrilled.'

Anne stopped beside the gate to Jenny's field, while Simon painstakingly unfastened the wire that held it shut and swung it open for her. As she watched him, her hand fumbled with the thin chain around her neck, the replacement for the one that had held Bob's diamond. Upon it was a tiny gold St Christopher that Nonna had given her years ago and which she never wore but always carried in her purse. Now she was wearing it because her throat felt sadly naked without the lost gift. She said as she stepped through the gate, 'It's not really as simple as that.'

The grey car sat in front of the house still when Simon and Anne came down from the field. It was a Volvo estate and, in spite of a liberal splashing of mud down its sides, looked very new.

'Somebody's rather posh,' Simon said.

'One of Jenny's friends?' Anne had long been accustomed to a surprisingly wide social span among Jenny's acquaintances; there were as many like Elizabeth and Gordon as there were like Jenny herself.

'No one I know,' Simon said.

It was no one Anne knew either. When they entered the house she heard a voice, thinking for a moment it was Angus, the Home Counties accent again put on in mockery. But when they stepped into the kitchen where Jenny and Angus sat, she realized that the voice belonged to the stranger sitting with them and the accent was real. He fell silent as they entered. Anne saw a slender, handsome boy dressed conservatively in pleated wool trousers, pullover, Harris tweed sports jacket; he was small, beside Angus, and in some subtle control of the room. Everyone stood as they entered and for a moment no one spoke. Then Jenny swept back her hair with a nervous hand and said, 'This is Matthew Aitken. A friend of Angus's. From college.' The boy stepped forward and shook her hand and Simon's as names were exchanged. He was charming and well-spoken and the only occupant of the room not obviously thrown off-stride by their sudden entrance.

'Do you live near here?' Anne asked, since no one was saying anything.

'Surrey,' he said, still smiling.

'You're a long way from home.' She wondered if he'd come all that distance to see Angus. It seemed unlikely.

He said, 'House party in Ross-shire. A bit of a bore but I told my father I'd attend. One or two people he wanted me to meet. Thought I'd run over and see Angus for the afternoon. Have you been walking?' Anne nodded. 'How splendid,' he said. He looked quickly to Angus and Jenny and they both looked away. 'I was just going, actually. Promised everyone I'd be back before the evening's revelry.' He grinned, looking younger, and Anne wondered if the antique manner were genuine or some sophomoric act. He kept it up, however, as he made his farewells. They all followed him to the door where he thanked Jenny for the tea he had consumed and then said abruptly to Angus, with

334

a slight raising of one hand, 'I'll be in touch.' There was something dimly unfriendly in the way it was said. Angus did not answer. They all stood in the cold air while Matthew Aitken climbed behind the wheel of the silver-grey Volvo, fastened his seatbelt carefully, and started the engine. He backed the long car awkwardly up to the edge of the house and, before turning it, gave them all a little wave. Then he brought the wheel around and drove away, bumping and lurching down Jenny's rugged drive.

Back in the kitchen, Anne sat on the end of a bench and began unlacing her boots. Simon sat at the other end, doing the same. He began to tell Jenny about their walk; how far they had gone, the red deer hind they had seen, the four stray sheep beyond the fence. Halfway through he realized that Jenny was neither commenting nor listening. Anne looked up, aware that the silence between her sister and her nephew had gone on unreasonably long.

'Are we interrupting something?' Simon asked.

Jenny shook her head. Anne watched Angus standing, head down, at the corner of the room, like a small child in trouble. She said clearly, 'That was nice of your friend to come all that way to see you.'

'Yeah,' Angus said.

'No,' Jenny said sharply. 'It wasn't nice of him.' Her voice was so uncharacteristically bitter that even Sarah looked up from her Bible at the table where she had sat reading throughout, and watched her mother in surprise.

'Mom . . .' Angus raised his hands, placatingly, then clenched them into fists and turned away. He thudded one fist with restrained force on the kitchen counter. 'What the hell am I supposed to say?'

'Nothing,' Jenny said. 'Absolutely nothing. There is absolutely nothing you can say.'

'Mom, I . . .'

'I don't want to hear it,' Jenny shrieked. 'You're *sorry*, I suppose. A lot of use that is.'

'Would it be all right if someone told me what's happened?' Simon asked. 'Or do you want to be alone?'

Jenny looked up, anger flaring in her eyes, but then she turned her glance aside and said quietly, 'Oh, you might as well know.'

She looked more aggressively towards Anne. 'And you too. You'll find out soon enough.'

'Mom, I'll handle it,' Angus protested, impotently.

'How the *fuck* will you handle it?'

He snapped around, his hands still in fists. 'Look. I screwed up. I know. But I *will* handle it. I'll get a job. I'll leave my course and get a job.'

Jenny waved his words away wearily. 'Oh don't be childish,' she said. 'I'll have to do it. I'll sell something.' She sounded hopeless. 'I'll sell the car.'

She looked up to Simon and Anne. Simon said warily, 'Jenny, you can't live here without a car.'

'Then I'll sell the house,' she shouted. Then she calmed down abruptly and said, 'Angus owes that pretentious little shit two thousand pounds.' She nodded towards the door. 'That's what he so nicely turned up here to collect. Two *thousand* pounds.' She looked around and half-smiled and then whispered, 'Oh Christ,' and covered her face with her hands.

'*What?*' Simon said. Angus muttered, 'Well, not exactly . . .'

'*Yes* exactly.' Jenny's head came up. 'You owe him two thousand pounds and he wants it back. Now.' She looked straight at Angus and he turned to avoid her gaze, looking to Anne and to Simon and even to Sarah for help. His eyes were wide and innocent, and filled with tears.

'I said I was sorry,' he mumbled, and then he backed away from them and ran quickly from the room. His steps thudded heavily on the stairs and in a moment they heard the slam of his bedroom door.

Anne turned to her sister, but before she could speak, Jenny pointed a forefinger at her and said fiercely, 'Don't. Just don't you dare.'

She stood facing Anne a moment longer and then lowered her hand and walked quietly around the table until she stood behind her daughter. She put her hands on Sarah's shoulders. Sarah raised her eyes from her Bible, looked over her shoulder to her mother and smiled. The smile was sweet, caring and confident. She said clearly, 'It doesn't matter, Mom. Not any more.' She smiled again, in encouragement, and Jenny leaned over and gently kissed her stiff black hair.

* * *

336

Anne found Angus still in his room. She knocked softly on the door and after an illogically long time he said, 'Come in,' in a muffled voice. He was sitting on the edge of his unmade bed when she entered, forlorn and boyish. His eyes were red. She went in and sat beside him, noticing as she did the suit she had helped him buy still hanging on his door, too new and cherished to be put away. She wanted to embrace him, but refrained and tried to make her voice businesslike and brisk.

'How did it happen?' she said.

'Everyone was doing it,' he answered defensively. 'All my friends. The market was rocketing. You could make a lot of money really fast. Some people I know did really, really well.'

'And others got caught.'

'Yeah. Others got caught.' He faced her suddenly, his hands extended before him. 'Look, Anne, I got *that* close. I mean, if I'd sold a week earlier, everyone would be congratulating me and I'd be buying everybody terrific presents.' She smiled sadly. 'I got so close.' His voice broke in a muffled sob and he stopped speaking. When he began again he said, very quietly, 'All I wanted was to make a decent bit of money and get us all out of this hole we've always been in. Not just me. All of us. Mom, Sarah. Even Simon. He's a great guy, Simon. He's really great to Mom. I was going to get him this fantastic pair of climbing boots . . .'

Anne said gently, 'When I got my first real pay cheque from my grandfather, I bought presents for everybody: Jenny, my Mom and Dad. And I bought the dumbest thing for my brother Joseph. I bought him these bright yellow and green surfer's swimming trunks. To wear in his swimming pool.' She laughed and he looked up and smiled. 'I spent every penny of that dumb cheque.'

'You're not like Mom,' he said gratefully. 'You understand.'

'Maybe,' Anne said, abruptly cool. 'But I wouldn't understand being dropped two thousand pounds in the shit any better than Jenny.'

'That wasn't what I intended,' he said hopelessly.

'I guess not. What did you do, use up your grant and then borrow?'

'Everybody was doing it. I mean two of my friends borrowed from their fathers. They didn't have grants of course . . .'

'No. And they had fathers with money. Who may be pissed off but aren't likely to foreclose.' She paused, studying his bowed head, the lank hair, like Jenny's. 'When do you need it?' she asked.

'Now.'

'He's not getting it now,' she said baldly. 'How long can you get him to wait?'

Angus shrugged. 'It depends on his father. He's not really a bad bloke, in spite of what Mom said. It's not *his* fault.' He paused. 'It's mine. It's my fault.'

'I'm going to give you the money, Angus.'

He looked up. Gratitude warred with despair. 'She won't let me take it. I know she won't.'

'I think she may when she sees my terms.'

A small hope dawned and, with it, a small wariness. 'What are your terms?' he asked.

'Very simple. You finish your course and take your degree. And then you come to work for me.' He stared at her, his mouth open.

'*That's* your terms? You give me two thousand quid and a job to walk into when I graduate?' He laughed. 'If that's your idea of punishment . . .'

'It's not my business to punish people, Angus. And you haven't asked what job I'm giving you.'

The wariness returned, but was overridden by his genuine relief. 'Oh Christ, I'll do anything. And I'll pay you back. As soon as I'm earning . . .'

'You won't pay me back out of what *I'll* be paying you,' Anne said sharply. She stood up and looked down at him, smiling slightly. 'You are going to work as a storeman in my London warehouse. You'll haul racks of dresses around and on good days you'll drive a delivery van. You won't be able to afford to live in London, but I'm sure you can find a little flat out on one of the commuter lines. My shop assistants manage. In fact, lots of people manage. People who don't have good degrees from Oxbridge, and rosy futures in the City. And you'll manage too. And after a year, which is all I'm asking, you'll have some idea how most people your age are going to live the rest of their lives. Then you can go back to the real world and get rich.' She grinned devilishly. He drew a deep breath and swallowed hard.

'I guess you are like Mom,' he said.

'No,' she said reasonably, 'Jenny distrusts success. She's convinced that money is essentially evil and people who have it are in some kind of moral danger. I don't agree. I like money. And I like having it. I'm not ashamed. I've worked for it. I pay my taxes and give my bit to charity. The rest, I enjoy. But,' she turned easily, leaning against the tall window pane, 'it doesn't really matter much to me. *That's* how Jenny and I are the same. It's just a game, Angus. It's a game she doesn't want to play, and I do. But it's just a game. I know Jenny thinks I'm an awful materialist, but she's really wrong. I don't care a lot for things. I have a nice house and decent possessions, but that's only reasonable. If you can afford good things, why not? But that's not what I work for.'

'What *do* you work for?' Angus sounded puzzled.

'Fun.' She smiled. 'If you really want to get rich, Angus, you can't *care* too much. You can't be too greedy or too much in a hurry.' She stepped closer to him. 'Do we have a deal?' He stared at the floor and then looked up to her, grinning slowly. He offered his hand.

'Hi, boss,' he said.

XVIII

The Saints came before dawn on Christmas Eve. Once again, Jenny returned from her milking, cold and half asleep, and found them there. The dogs flung themselves in bounds about the big red van, barking uproariously. Three young people stood before it, smiling the Christian smile. 'We've come for Sarah,' they said. Jenny recognized them as the same three who had come the week before.

'Oh good God,' she said. 'Don't you people ever rest?'

'*He who keeps Israel will neither slumber nor sleep,*' said the boy, Mark. The two girls nodded in unison.

'So I gather,' said Jenny. She watched them silently a moment longer and then said, 'Sarah's in her bed. You'd better come in.' Shifting the milk can to her other hand, she walked towards the house. After a few steps, she realized they had not followed. When she looked over her shoulder they were in a sort of huddle, talking quietly amongst themselves. She remembered that none of them had entered her house before and wondered if it offended one of their rules. 'It's warmer inside,' she said.

They turned to face her, united as a threesome again. 'You follow the Pope?' Mark said. He smiled when he said it. Jenny smiled back.

'More or less.' They looked hesitant and she smiled more broadly. 'I doubt he's actually *in* here,' she said.

They stared at her and Mark even grinned. They went into their huddle again and then he straightened up and said, 'It's all right. We'll come in.'

'Thanks a lot.' Jenny walked away without looking at them, leaving the door open behind her. She had set the milk can on the table and was ladling some, fresh and creamy, into bowls for the cats, when they appeared warily at the kitchen door. 'Come in,' she said brightly. She decided to be normal and hospitable. 'The kettle's on. I'll make some tea.' They stood looking carefully around. She was suddenly very aware of the crucifix over the kitchen door, the Palm Sunday crosses pinned to a cupboard.

'What a friendly kitchen,' Mark said.

'I like it.'

'I can see why Sarah's so happy here.'

Is she? Jenny thought. She said nothing.

'She's finding it very hard to leave.' His eyes met hers, as if they were sharing a confidence; as if he was looking to her for help. She was unnerved.

'Well there isn't any need for her to *leave*,' she said. The kettle was whistling on the Aga but she did not move towards it. Her eyes were locked on his, disturbed by their deep blue honesty.

His voice changed, '*Henceforth there will be five divided, three against two and two against three . . . father against son and son against father, mother against daughter and daughter against her mother . . .*'

'Mom?' Jenny's eyes broke from Mark's and she looked up to see Sarah standing in the doorway. She was in pyjamas and a bathrobe and looked sleepy and confused. Then she saw the Saints and said, 'Oh! You're here.'

Mark held out his hand to her and the two girls smiled encouragingly, but Sarah did not move.

'Sarah,' he said gently. 'It's time to come home.'

She did not answer. No one spoke and the sound of the steam from the kettle became unbearably insistent. Jenny turned and slid it off the hot-plate. She stood with her back to the room, her hand yet on the black handle, waiting.

'Mom?' Sarah said.

'You must do what you wish.' She did not turn. She heard a shuffling of footsteps and then the door closing. When she looked around the room was empty. Overhead, she heard the creak of floorboards in Sarah's room and imagined her hastily dressing, flinging her few things into a rucksack. She poured herself tea and sat down with it at the table. She was sitting there when the footsteps sounded again on the stairs, hastily running. She fought with herself not to run out, to intercept and to argue. After a while she heard the rough van engine start, and the vehicle move noisily away. She began to prepare in her mind what she would say to Simon and Angus, and to Anne. The door opened again and she looked up, bracing for the first assault. It was Sarah, small and somehow defiant. She came to the table and sat down. 'Is there any tea left?' she said.

Jenny got another mug and as lightly as she could, she said 'Well, is that done with now?'

Sarah sipped her tea. When she looked up from it she smiled the Christian smile.

'The work of the Lord is never done,' she said.

Jenny sagged on her bench. She felt wearied out by inconsistencies. She said carefully, 'Why didn't you go with them then, Sarah?'

'Because my work is here.'

'Here.'

'With you. And with Angus and Simon. And with Anne.'

'And what work have you to do with us?' Jenny did not hide her sarcasm. Sarah made no response to it. She smiled again.

'To bring you to the saving grace of God.'

Jenny sighed. 'And how,' she asked patiently, 'are you going to achieve that?'

'By asking you to take Jesus Christ into your heart as your personal saviour.'

'Back to that,' said Jenny. Sarah said nothing. 'What,' Jenny began cautiously, 'if I were to say I already have.'

'Have you?' Sarah's face brightened.

'I've been baptized. I've been confirmed. I go to mass.'

Sarah turned away, disappointed. 'It's not enough.'

'Who says?'

'John 3.3. *Truly, truly I say to you, unless one is born anew, he cannot see the kingdom of God.*'

'Sarah, that can be interpreted a dozen different ways . . .'

'No.' She leaned intently over the table, her hair bouncing with the sudden movement. 'No. One way. There is only one way. You must say it. You must take Jesus Christ. You must be born again.'

'By water. In baptism.'

'No.'

'I go to church. I live a Christian life. Why must I say this formula . . . ?'

342

'You don't love God,' said Sarah.

'How the *fuck* can you say that, you arrogant little . . . ?'

'*If you love me, keep my word.* You don't keep His word. You swear, you drink, you break all the rules.' She paused and added in a quiet voice, 'You and Simon break *all* the rules.' Jenny sat back on the bench, holding her tea-mug in both hands.

She said softly, 'That's the whole thing, Sarah, isn't it?'

'No.'

'I know I break rules, Sarah. It's hard to live an adult life and not break rules. God understands.'

'If you take Jesus for your saviour, He'll help you.'

'Just like that. I just say the words. That's all.' Sarah nodded eagerly.

'It's very simple.'

'It's beautifully simple,' Sarah said joyously. 'You just say it, once, and you're saved forever and when the rapture comes you'll be taken up to the Lord.'

'Marvellous.'

'Will you? Will you say it?'

Jenny nodded. Sarah waited eagerly. Jenny said, ' "I believe in one God, the Father, the Almighty, maker of heaven and earth." '

'Say it, Mom.'

' " . . . of all that is, seen and unseen." '

'*Say* it.'

' "I believe in one Lord, Jesus Christ . . ." '

'Oh Mom,' Sarah cried, despairing. '*Say* it. Just say it. That's all.'

'Sarah,' Jenny said, turning her tea-mug in her hands, 'I am.'

Sarah flopped her head forward into her hands. 'You're all so *stubborn*,' she said.

Jenny got up and took the box of porridge oats from the cupboard and began making breakfast. When the telephone rang she glanced up with surprise.

'That's hideously early,' she said. 'Will you answer it, pet?' Sarah looked at her hopelessly for a moment longer and then swung her legs over the bench and padded in stockinged-feet away.

Anne was asleep. The knocking on the door only gradually

intruded, first as part of an intricate, changing dream, then as the instrument of awakening. Then she heard the high, young voice calling her name and sat up. At once the nausea climbed her throat. Her breasts felt taut and sore and she held her arm against them as she cautiously got to her feet.

'Just a minute, sweetheart, I'm coming.'

'Telephone, Auntie Anne.' She found the borrowed woollen robe that she had spread across the bed for added warmth and pulled it on. When she opened the door, Sarah was standing there in jeans and a faded sweatshirt that said Benetton across the front. She said, 'Sorry to wake you. It's from America. Some kind of a clinic.'

Joseph. 'I'll get it, dear,' Anne said. She fought back the nausea and ran quickly down the cold wooden stairs in her bare feet. She glanced at her watch as she lifted the receiver. Eight o'clock. One P.M. in New York. Too early for a social call. Besides, she was expecting none. She had spoken to her mother yesterday, Marion the day before. Once again she expected Bob's voice, until the female tone on the line reminded her he wasn't there.

'Ms Conti.'

'Is it about Joseph?' she said.

'Sorry, Ms Conti. I don't understand.'

'Is that the supervisor?'

'This is June Dawes from the Bayside Clinic.' The nausea returned, a compelling wave, driving words into retreat.

'One moment,' Anne whispered. Her mind lurched from one dimension to another; from Joseph to herself. *I'm not ready*, she thought. *Not like this.*

'Are you all right, Ms Conti?' the voice asked.

'Yes, of course.' She pictured the woman, tall, heavy, a Long Island housewife doing part-time work as a medical receptionist. She would not think about time zones, or latitudes, or that Anne was standing in a freezing Scottish farmhouse in the pitch dark of a Highland December morning. 'It's just a little early here,' she said. She was apologetic, as if by being very nice, she could keep ill fortune away.

The voice was brisk in response. 'I have the results of your amniocentesis here, Ms Conti, and I'm telephoning you at this number, as you requested.'

344

'Of course,' Anne said. Her heart fluttered. The sickness rose higher.

'Is there someone with you?' The voice gentled.

'I'm in my sister's house,' she said.

'Very well. I'm afraid we do have a Down's Syndrome indicated, Ms Conti.' The voice sweetened. 'I'm really sorry.' *Oh Christ, Christ. What have we done? Why us again?*

'Are you there, Ms Conti?'

'I'm here.'

'I understand you will be returning next week. We are here of course to provide any advice or counselling you need. Shall I make you an appointment?'

Anne said, 'No. That won't be necessary.'

'You're quite sure . . . most people . . .'

'I'm sure.'

There was a brief, slightly awkward pause and then June Dawes said hesitantly, 'I must point out, Ms Conti, that looking at your dates, if you are considering a termination, there is some urgency.'

Anne said, 'Thank you. I'm not considering a termination.'

'I see.' There was another pause, and then the voice on the line changed, dropped something of its official reserve and said, 'Ms Conti, did you suspect? Some women somehow *realize* something is wrong . . .'

There's nothing wrong with my baby. 'No,' Anne said, 'I didn't suspect.' There was a distant sigh. Anne said, kindly, 'You know these calls are very expensive.'

She expected the woman would take the escape route offered, but she didn't. Instead her tone grew warmer, more personal, and she said in a breathy rush, 'Ms Conti, they are *lovely* children. So loving . . . it's their special thing. Their saving grace, if you know what I mean.'

'I know.'

The woman sensed Anne's slight withdrawal. She said, 'Well, I'll let you go now. Is there anything . . . is there anything else I can help with?'

'Yes,' Anne said, 'Yes there is. Is it a boy or a girl?'

'Oh!' The woman's voice was suddenly brightly happy. 'Oh, of course. You have a little daughter,' she said.

Anne thanked her and put down the phone. The nausea, held

345

in check by willpower only, became relentless. She clutched the borrowed robe about her and ran up the bare wooden stairs. In the cold bathroom she retched miserably, and when she was done, straightened up, washed, and went through the quick, sure routine of making up her face. It was minimal, but never neglected. When she appeared twenty minutes later at Jenny's breakfast table, dressed in wool trousers and an Aran knit, she looked well-groomed, alert, and ready for the day. Sarah and Jenny were arguing over religion, but they stopped when she entered. Jenny studied her face.

'What *was* that?' she said. 'Sarah said Bay*side* Clinic . . . it wasn't the Center?'

'No. It wasn't the Center.'

'That's a relief.' She smiled but the smile faded into puzzlement. 'What was it then, at this hour?'

'Nothing. Just my medical building. They had some mix-up about appointments.'

'They called *Scotland*?'

Anne shrugged, as she seated herself on the bench beside Sarah, absently stroking the collie that had come out from under the table to greet her. 'Silly secretary. She must have taken the number off my answering machine. Obviously she didn't know international from next door. Some of the girls they find these days . . .' She laughed softly and Jenny laughed also and it was over. She had got through it, unscathed.

It was just the three of them at breakfast. Simon was still asleep, and Angus, who had worked late over his books, would not likely be down before ten. Jenny was already beginning her Christmas cooking. Anne resisted the guilty need to offer help. She said, 'I'm going walking, if it's OK. Can I borrow your boots again?'

'Alone?' Anne nodded. Jenny laughed, 'Christ, Simon must have infected you with the bug. He'll be proud of you.' She was mixing a vast bowl full of breadcrumbs and herbs for stuffing the big turkey that hung in the larder, locally grown, freshly plucked, and too realistic for Anne's taste. 'My boots are in the shed.'

Anne tied them on quickly before Simon could appear and offer to join her. In ten minutes she was out in the sharp, wet air, Elizabeth's old Barbour wrapped tightly around her. The wind was blowing hard and the sky was full of big tattered

346

clouds, pink still from the hesitant winter sunrise. She began walking quickly out of the farmyard, through the gates that led to the hill, the boots splashing through puddles and sliding in mud. There was so much mud. Her strongest memories of Scotland were mud. Somehow, today, in borrowed footgear and with no need to remain clean, the mud became less of an offence and more of an amusement. She began walking through the puddles rather than skirting them. Children did that. She was caught by a memory of herself and Marion, really small, pre-Joseph, indeed, plodging happily through the sandy puddles on the old drive to Nonna's house. And Marion's children doing the same one rainy day in her own yard. She conjured up a small person walking beside her, dawdling behind, splashing, dragging sticks to make lines on the ground. She quickened her step, out on to the hill track, and left the small person behind.

The ascent of the hill was easy at the beginning and she was surprised how quickly she arrived at the point where, the last time, Simon had made them turn back. By now the sun was properly risen and, high up as she was, she caught its first early rays, deep golden in their low north angle. The air was sweet, almost mild. It did not feel like Christmas at all, and though there was snow on the faraway hills, the land around was green and lush. She thought of Bob and Robin in New England again, but now there was a new remoteness from them that had nothing to do with place or time.

Simon had been too cautious; the climb was not difficult, nor indeed very long. But men were like that. Pregnancy filled them with subtle horrors. They did not understand the tenacity of life; the eagerness of a child to be born. And this was a tenacious child. She knew already, knew before June Dawes and the Bayside Clinic, or before anything. There's nothing wrong with this kid; she's a fighter, all the way. On the summit of the hill her heart was pounding slightly, but her body felt good and strong. She found a dry rock, warmed by the thin sun, and sat down on it, near the cairn, looking out over hills, loch, pastures and forests.

She realized suddenly that she was further away from any other human being, at that moment, than she had been for years, perhaps forever. In the luxury of that isolation she rested her elbows on her knees, her face on the palms of her hands, and wept for a long, long while. When she was done, nothing had changed. Hills, loch, forests and fields remained. The heather moorland tumbled away from her down the long ridge she had climbed, extending for miles. She could see the road winding through it, and the little rise where Jenny had parked the car on the day of her arrival, where they had walked and she had lost Bob's diamond. She had been right to be devastated; it was a portent, after all. She twined her fingers in the chain of Nonna's St Christopher, the poor substitute.

Right you bastard, if you're out there, I'll accept this. But get your bloody St Anthony to find my diamond. She looked out over the infinity of heather and laughed softly to herself. She felt a flutter within, as if her daughter swept her womb with wet wings. She laid her hand gently on her stomach as she stood, with easy grace, and began the long walk down.

'Tonight,' Sarah said in a quiet voice. 'The Lord's hour.' She sat in Jenny's big chair at the head of the table. Simon and Angus and Anne were spread out along the benches, and Jenny was on her feet, darting about the kitchen preparing the meal. It was a plain pasta dish, prelude to tomorrow's feast.

'The Rapture,' said Simon, tapping his fork gently against the table edge. He studied her face with serious, compassionate eyes. Sarah nodded. She looked small and frightened in the big chair.

'You mean the end of the world,' Angus said. 'Armageddon. The whole shooting match.' His mockery had worn thin in frustration and now he was simply angry.

'No,' Sarah said plainly. 'That comes after. First, God will take his chosen ones from the world.'

'This is the dirty knickers left behind on the ground bit,' said Angus.

'He will lift us up on wings as Eagles,' Sarah said. 'Our bodily vestments will be left behind.'

'Sarah, what crap. Bodily *vestments*. Where do you get this stuff?'

'From Mark,' Jenny said. She was leaning over the Aga, trawling the deep oven for supper.

'The Saints teach me,' Sarah said, but Jenny said again, 'From Mark.'

She turned around and looked at Sarah. 'He's the one, Sarah.

Whenever you speak, I hear his voice. The girls are just puppets. It's Mark.'

'Well then, Mark is the bastard we need to get,' said Angus.

Both Sarah and Jenny ignored him. Jenny pursued, 'And Mark has told you it's tonight.'

'We all know it is tonight. It is the beginning. The Millennium.'

'Logically,' Angus said, 'if there were a millennium, it wouldn't be for another thirteen years, when we hit the big Two-oh. Or maybe,' he conceded laboriously, 'nineteen-ninety-six. That's what Nostradamus was supposed to have said, wasn't it?'

'Nostradamus was a Papist. He was deceived.'

'The calendar still stays thirteen years to go.'

'The calendars are wrong.'

'By the word of Pope Mark the First,' said Angus.

Simon said, 'The calendars *are* rather confused. It could be almost any time.'

Sarah smiled triumphantly and he added quickly, 'If it was going to happen. Which it's not, Sarah.' He said it gently, leaning forward like a conscientious school teacher. 'It's just an historical myth; just part of the great eschatological tradition of mankind. Doubtless there is some tribal need . . .'

'The world *is* going to end, Sarah,' Jenny said, setting plates out on the table. 'The argument is about when.' He looked up at her, his brow furrowed in a mix of hurt and confusion.

'Jenny, I've been trying to *help* Sarah,' he said. He looked across the table to Anne for support. She was sitting quietly, somehow apart from them. Her cheeks were pink after her walk in the winter air. Simon thought she looked very pretty, prettier than when she arrived. 'What do you say, Anne?' he asked. She smiled and, without looking at anyone, said, 'Looks like I just wasted three months setting up next summer's line.' She laughed gently, but Sarah clutched at her words.

'That's what I'm *saying*,' she cried triumphantly. 'You're all wasting time. Angus with his books and Mom worrying about money and Simon fussing because some design hasn't worked out. It's all *over*. We don't have to worry any more. We don't have to *do* anything. Just pray. And wait. And turn to the Lord. If you just give your hearts to Jesus, even *now*, you'll find your place among the chosen.'

'And if we don't?' said Angus sourly.

'The grace of the Lord be with all the Saints,' said Sarah. She sat unmoving at the head of the table, her young face pure with certainty. Jenny sat down at last, having served everyone and fed the dogs and cats.

'Who's coming to mass?' she said.

Jenny was surprised. She had expected a clear no from Sarah, a dutiful yes from Angus and, from Simon, a yes or a no according to his mood. The mood tonight was sentimental and traditional, and therefore he would go, sit quietly listening to the music and reading the missalette, like programme notes, during communion. She was grateful, particularly because he would drive on the long and likely icy road. They were all true to form. It was Anne who surprised her.

'Sure.'

'Really?'

'Why not?' She gave a pretty little shrug.

'Fine,' said Jenny, still doubtful. 'We'll leave at eleven. Dress warm.'

Jenny savoured midnight mass. It was one of the Church's best times, the icing on the cake; music and mystery, holiness and adventure. She liked waiting up late and fighting weariness. She liked the long and risky drive through the night, the road alien in midnight storm or starlight. When the children were little, Fergus would wrap them in blankets in the back of the car and they would sleep through the journey. Later, when she was first widowed, it was a test of courage to go out in an ageing car and chance getting caught by snow out on her lonely hill. Sometimes, when a blizzard was blowing or freezing rain coating the tarmac with a glisten of ice, she lost her nerve; mostly she leaned on God's mercy on His holy night. When they returned, the house, dark in their absence, would be awakened with untimely light, blazing out on to the hill. The fire would be rekindled and the table laid with wine and cake. They never got to bed before three, even when the children were young and would wake for presents and celebration at six.

That memory, of lost family warmth, haunted her as they set out an hour before midnight. She yearned sadly for Fergus and the earthy power of his faith that would have surely drawn wandering children safely into the fold. She worried through

Christmas mass; about Anne, who looked tired and queasy; Angus, restless and impatient as always; Simon, lest some aspect of the liturgy so offend his rational soul that he might stand up and begin arguing with the priest. And Sarah, most of all Sarah, at home alone with her strange new God.

She was glad when it was over and she could shepherd her family out, away from the candles and carols, back into the cold dark car. Simon drove steadily and surely, but it was still after two when he brought the Subaru bumping and swerving up the long drive, and the house at the end was dark.

'She's gone to bed,' Jenny said sadly. All the way home she had cherished a hope that they would arrive to find her daughter miraculously transformed to her old self; with the Christmas tree lights and the red candles and the glow of the fire announcing her return.

'Best thing for her,' Simon said. 'She'll wake up in the morning with all this nonsense behind her.'

'One up for old Nostradamus,' Angus said. As soon as they were through the door he bounded off with loping strides up the stairs.

'He's not going to wake her?' asked Anne.

Jenny smiled. 'He's just checking,' she laughed softly. 'Just checking old Nostradamus was right.' She was still laughing, busy setting out the Christmas cake and the glasses while Simon opened the wine, when Angus returned. He stood in the doorway and said in a low, uncertain voice, 'Mom, Sarah's gone.'

She stopped, with her hand still on the cake knife and said evenly, 'If this is a joke, Angus, you're in the shit.'

'It's not a fucking joke, Mom. She's not in her bed.'

'Christ,' Simon whispered.

'Is she anywhere else?' Anne said in her brisk business voice. 'Has anyone looked?'

Jenny dropped the cake knife on to the smooth white icing of the cake and ran out of the kitchen and up the stairs. Sarah's room, the light still on, her bed smooth, untouched. Angus's room; sometimes she slept there when he was away. She flicked on the light; the grey cat got up from the rumpled mess of his blankets and squinted its eyes against the light. Her own bedroom, full of her personal clutter, the bed roughly smoothed, empty. The guest room, Simon's case sitting foolishly on the

351

floor. The end bedroom, where Anne's things, elegant and neatly arrayed, filled the air with expensive perfume. The box room. Her heart was pounding; she ran, stumbling down the stairs.

Simon met her. His eyes looked odd and his voice was frantic with worry. 'She's not here, I've looked everywhere.'

Jenny pushed past him, into the living-room, the unlit Christmas tree garish under the bright overhead light. 'I've looked,' he shouted after her, but she had to look herself; the workrooms, the corridor behind the kitchen, the dairy. In the dairy, cold and smelling sharply of disinfectant, she stopped. Consciously she gripped her reason. *She's not a little child. She can look after herself.* She turned around and walked quietly back down the corridor and into the kitchen.

Angus, Anne and Simon stood together by the big table and the Christmas cake. Angus said with weary finality, 'That's it. They've come for her. We may never see her again.'

Simon stared at Angus, turned briefly to Jenny, and then looked away. She saw his patient, quiet hands tense slowly, as if by distant memory, into fists. He raised one and slammed it down on the table by the cake. Her car keys, still lying there, jingled.

'The bastards,' he said, and then he exploded in rage. 'The bloody bastards. Christmas Eve. Midnight. No one here. They come after a kid in her own home.' He opened his hand and then closed it over Jenny's car keys.

'Where are you going?' Jenny cried.

'To get that child back.' He strode past her, brushing Angus out of his way, and ran out of the door.

'Simon,' she shouted. She ran after him, Angus beside her. In the black night, Simon was already climbing into the driver's seat of the Subaru.

'You can't do this.'

'I bloody well will. I'm going up to that place to get her and I'll beat the fuck out of that little shit if he tries to stop me.' He slammed the door closed. Angus ran around to the passenger side.

'I'll come with you.'

'Stay with your mother.'

Angus hesitated. Simon started the engine and Jenny watched, astounded. Over her shoulder she heard Anne's light step across the frozen lawn.

'Jenny,' she said clearly. 'Simon. There's a light in the barn.'

Jenny turned from the car. She walked quickly away from the house until she could see the dark outline of the byre. Angus ran after her, and behind her she heard Simon open the door of the car, though the engine was still running. They came, together, to stand beside Jenny, where she still remained gazing quietly through the darkness to the dim glow that lit the one small four-paned window of her byre.

'Oh my God,' Simon said, chastened, 'I never thought of that.'

Jenny smiled in the darkness and shook her head.

Anne was sitting by the fire with a mug of tea when Simon came in from the barn. It was three in the morning. She felt giddy with tiredness. They were alone. Angus, wavering between relief and embarrassment, had retreated to his room after a brief impatient argument with his mother: 'Well, *let* her sleep in the barn if she wants. I don't see why *you* have to.'

Anne realized listening to him that he would grow into that sort of man who cared desperately for all the women in his life but never understood any of them.

'They're all right,' she said to comfort him. 'It won't hurt Sarah to spend the night there. It won't hurt your mother either.' She was about to add something about all the places and situations that Jenny and Fergus had slept in in their hippy days on the road, but restrained herself. It was an image of his parents' unfettered sixties youth he would find impossible to absorb. 'I'll bring them a cup of tea,' she added soothingly, and the familiar, British ploy worked.

'Those bastards had better not show up here again,' Angus said and stamped grumpily up the stairs. She laughed. She suspected they would not see Mark and the Saints for a while. Whisked to the bosom of Abraham, or enduring a humiliating tactical retrenchment – either way they wouldn't likely come here.

There was a glistening of snow on Simon's hair when he came in. It was his second visit to the barn and she could see from his face that it had been no more successful than his first.

'It's started to snow,' he said sadly.

'It won't snow in there,' Anne said. She got up to pour tea for him from the pot she had left on the hearth. She smiled. 'And they have sleeping bags and a duvet.'

'It's so bloody insane,' he said.

Anne shrugged. 'A little silly, Simon. But not much more than that.' She handed him his tea. 'How'd you get on?'

He grimaced, settling on the floor beside her and pulling his heavy sweater over his head. 'I'm not helping, Anne. I just don't understand.'

'I wouldn't worry about it.'

He leaned forward. 'Anne, I *would* worry. The child is disturbed. Whether it's the influence of these *pernicious* people,' his voice grated over the words, 'or something else. Something maybe deeper-seated that perhaps pre-dates *all* of this . . . the girl *is* firmly believing in this ridiculous idea. Her mind is unbalanced. And Jenny's allowing it. Humouring it perhaps, but allowing this fantasy, this *derangement* to continue when instead she should be calling in every ounce of professional help she can find.'

'Simon, Christians the world over believe in the Second Coming. What are you going to do, psychoanalyse the whole Church?'

He drew back slightly. 'Well of course, Anne. Of course they do. Or at least I suppose that's what they believe. In a sort of abstract way. But it's highly symbolic, surely? They don't actually believe this literal, farcical, carried off into heaven in the wink of an eye . . .' He stopped, his mouth working in distaste.

'Anyhow,' Anne said, 'psychiatrists don't make house calls on Christmas Eve.' She leaned forward. 'Look Simon, Jenny's not an idiot. *She* knows nothing's going to happen tonight. And by tomorrow morning, Sarah will know too. End of problem.'

'I *don't* believe so,' Simon said. 'I *really* don't. It won't stop here. She'll be back with those people. They'll dream up some story to explain why they had it wrong and in no time there'll be something else crazy she's wrapped up in.'

Anne poured herself another cup from the tea-pot and stretched comfortably in front of the fire. 'I remember,' she said dreamily, 'when Jenny and I and my friend Marion were kids in elementary school, there was this story that went round about how the Martians were going to come and take all the children

354

in the world away to Mars. It was supposed to happen at four in the afternoon, on a Friday in March. I can't remember the date. And you know, we sort of believed it. Marion and I thought it was terrific. We all sat around in the woods at the appointed hour, waiting for it, scaring the shit out of each other about what the Martians would look like. Then four o'clock came. Nothing. Four-ten. Four-fifteen. At four-thirty we all gave up and went to the candy store for ice-cream.'

'But you were kids, Anne . . .'

'Three kids' parents wouldn't let them come to school. I mean, they weren't the brightest parents, maybe, but they were adults. They'd heard about it in one of those newspapers, the *National Enquirer* or something, and well, you know. They played safe.'

'And is that what Jenny is doing? Playing safe?'

'No, Simon. Jenny's being a mother. Which in this case means playing along with a fantasy that a girl of a very impressionable age and nature has got herself locked into. I think she's very wise.'

'Irresponsible.'

'She knows her daughter.' He shook his head, irritated. 'Simon, when Sarah was eleven her pet lamb died. She sewed it a shroud. She buried it with a thoroughly blasphemous holy mass celebrated by herself, and she lay on its grave and wept every night for a week. On the other hand, when her father died, it didn't even seem to register. Who knows? Maybe it came out for the lamb, what she couldn't bring out for Fergus. Or maybe not. Whatever, she recovered. She *is* a very sensitive, imaginative, loving and caring child. She is also one hundred per cent a dramatist. I know, Simon. And so does Jenny, because she *is* Jenny.'

'Rubbish. Jenny's never been like that.'

'When Jenny first learned that my parents planned to put our brother Joseph in a Home, which would have made all our lives a lot easier, by the way . . . she kidnapped him.'

'She what?'

'What I said. She kidnapped him. She ran off with him out of his crib; he was maybe eighteen months old, or two, I forget. She ran off with a severely disabled baby and hid in the woods. I found her building some sort of wigwam thing. She was planning to live off the land like an Indian. In suburban Long Island. She had a thing about Indians.'

'How *old* was she?'

'I don't know. Eight or nine? Old enough to know better, you'd think, anyhow. But Jenny was always capable of believing extraordinary things. She still *does*, Simon.'

He looked incredulous. 'Like what?'

' "The communion of Saints, the forgiveness of sins, the resurrection of the dead and the life everlasting"?' She raised one eyebrow provocatively. 'The line between faith and derangement is pretty narrow, Simon.'

'Adults draw the line,' he said firmly.

'Faith is the province of children.' She smiled gently. 'The Lord's little ones.'

He looked up, confused. 'Are you a believer, Anne?'

'No. I'm an adult, Simon. Like you. That's our tough luck.'

He laughed, warmed by her including him in her circle. He said, 'God, I made a fool of myself tonight.'

'You? How?'

'Storming around like some macho goon. Threatening murder and mayhem. *God*,' he winced. 'Supposing you hadn't seen the light in the barn? Supposing I'd really gone *up* there, started a fight, *hurt* somebody . . . ?'

Anne shrugged, 'So? What of it?'

'*Anne*. It would have been disastrous. I hadn't a shred of evidence against them, and there I was about to start bashing people about . . .' He shuddered.

'So what?' Anne said again. 'It sounded a great idea.' She stretched, laughing lightly at the thought.

Simon stared at her. 'But Anne, it would have been so unfair. They hadn't *done* anything.'

Anne finished her stretch. '*Life's* unfair, Simon. Besides that little shit *does* need a kick in the butt. Why shouldn't you be God's chosen instrument of delivery?'

Simon was still staring at her, but humour quirked his mouth as if he had begun to suspect she was teasing.

'You know, Simon,' she said seriously, 'sense and reason go just so far in this world. Don't overestimate their value.' She smiled and added, 'Anyhow, you thrilled the pants off my sister. She'll be all over you when she gets you in the sack.'

'Oh, really not,' Simon said. 'That's hardly Jenny.' But he looked not entirely displeased. After a little thought, he said, 'You know, life must have been simpler when you could simply *do* things without always having to think of the consequences.'

'When was that?' Anne asked sceptically, but he answered almost at once, 'Oh, I don't know. In the sixties, maybe. I imagine it was like that then.'

'Christ,' she said. 'You make me feel old. Ancient history. The sixties.' He started to apologize, hastily, but she only laughed. 'No, anyhow. It was never like that. Or at least not for everybody. *Some* people always live like that.' She sat up, grinning like a rueful kid. 'Me for instance. And look where it's got me.' She made a comic gesture of expansion around her neat waistline.

He looked embarrassed and then laughed uneasily. 'Well? What's wrong with that? You're having a baby you want and marrying a really decent bloke. What more could anyone ask?' He sounded awkward saying it, as if the thoughts he had expressed were revolutionary and daring.

'I'm not marrying Bob,' said Anne. That took him aback, as she knew it would, but he rallied.

'Well, of course it's not necessary to actually *marry*.'

'I'm leaving him,' she said.

There was a silence. The room filled with the small flutter of the flames of the wood fire. Simon drew his knees up, sitting leaning against the leg of the sofa, and turned his head half away. In that position, without meeting her eyes, he said, 'I'm terribly sorry, Anne. I didn't know about this. Jenny didn't . . .'

'Jenny doesn't know either.'

He looked stricken. 'Anne, I had no *idea* anything was wrong. Jenny always talks about you being so happy . . .'

'We're happy.' He looked up then, lost and boyish. 'It's a contractual matter,' she said. 'I've failed to fulfil a contract.' He was floundering in confusion. She said quickly, 'I've done rather a bad job of this baby, you see. I've not got it right. I've made a balls-up as you say in this country.' Her voice was bright and brisk and he stared.

'What are you talking about, Anne? I really don't understand.'

'It's Down's Syndrome.' She paused. 'Do you know what that means? It's a mongol.'

He looked devastated. 'Of course I know what Down's Syndrome is,' he said miserably.

'Well. I've breached the agreement. Perfect goods. That was the contract.' He saw the edge of the brittle smile tremble but it did not break.

He took a deep breath. 'Are you telling me that this kind, decent, educated man . . . he's a doctor, right? This man is refusing to marry you because you're having a damaged child?' His eyes were narrowed with outrage; the new, angry and chivalrous Simon.

She laughed gently. 'Of course not.'

'Then what . . .'

'Come on, Simon. I can't *let* him marry me. You can see that. It's entirely unfair. He wasn't happy with this autumn fatherhood to begin with. It was an accident. *My* accident. And he accepted it. But I can't throw this at him. He didn't bargain for this.'

'Well, good Christ,' Simon shouted, 'neither did you. Who ever bargains for that?'

Anne smiled again, a private smile. She stretched out on the sheepskin by the fire, looking into the flames.

'You know, Simon, when you build a house of cards? You know what I mean?' She turned slightly to see his face, quickly trying to picture Simon Hamilton doing anything as pointless and trivial as building a house of cards.

'Sure,' he said.

'Well, you know how, no matter how high it gets, you never can manage to use the whole deck. And you *know* that. But still, you can never resist adding just one more card. And then, just one *more* after that. And then of course,' she propped herself on one elbow, 'then of course the whole thing collapses in a slithering heap.'

'I was never very good at things like that,' he said.

'I'm brilliant at them,' Anne said. 'That makes it worse. You get over-confident. You *have* to complete it. Well, I had the whole thing built, just about. Money, job, looks, I suppose, or so everyone tells me, great house, great apartment in the city, social life, *gorgeous* man, lovely step-children. I really could have stopped. But I had to have it complete. I had to have that last card.'

'You're punishing yourself.'

'No. I'm just taking responsibility. It was my house of cards.

And the only person who should have to pick it up off the floor is me.'

He sat staring at her, sadly, unable to speak, and the late night silence again enveloped them.

'You're going to tell Jenny?' he asked at last.

'No, Simon. You are. After I've gone.'

The barn was small, dark and cold. It was not at all like the big, airy wooden Long Island barn that had housed the theatre when Jenny was a child. It was a low stone building with earth and cobble floors. It was dry, particularly above in the half hay-loft, but it was never warm, and the stone walls were dank.

The goats were all penned at one end in their accustomed place, and they were quiet now, pale shapes in the dim light, adapted already to the peculiarity of human presence. Above, two hens made a burbling sound. They were her two renegades, the pair she could never trap into the orderly hen-house routine of their sisters. Instead they lived like brigands in the rafters, red-eyed, tawny-feathered, shitty-arsed, flapping up raucously when anyone entered, laying their eggs in treacherous abandon anywhere. Angus had suggested she wring their necks and cook them, but Sarah wouldn't allow it. Sarah had a weakness for useless follies; she was her father's daughter, at times.

Sarah was encamped at the opposite end of the barn from the goats, in what remained of the single, cobble-floored stall in which once they had kept the Jersey cow, Daisy. She was another of Fergus's brief, unsuccessful ventures. At first her copious creamy milk overwhelmed them; later recurrent mastitis ended her productive days. She stayed on for years as a pet. The children loved her buff, sloe-eyed gentleness, and long after she was gone, her corner of the barn was known as Daisy's stall. Sarah had spread out a bale of hay and, on top of it, her sleeping bag, in which she sat, knees hunched up, like a purple caterpillar. Her eyes were huge in a small white face, in the light of her flashlight. It was one of those lantern-shaped, car emergency lights that could be persuaded, at the flick of a switch, to flash a hazard warning of intermittent red. Twice already, Sarah had brushed the switch by accident, filling the barn with a pulsating ruddy glow.

Jenny looked surreptitiously at her watch while Sarah was busy

359

readjusting the duvet that they had tucked around behind their backs and over their shoulders. She said, 'I'm sure we could go in. They'll all be asleep. It will just be you and I, even in there.'

'If anyone will not receive you or listen to your words, shake the dust from your feet as you leave that house.'

'Sarah,' Jenny said gently, 'I received you. You know that.' But she accepted Sarah's determination to remain there, in the barn. Sarah read into that a grain of cautious hope.

'You really believe, don't you, Mom? That's why you're here. You believe it's going to happen.'

'Oh, I believe it's going to happen, Sarah. Not exactly as you say, perhaps, and not of necessity *tonight*. I mean, I believe it's a *possibility*, but I don't think it's likely.' Sarah turned away and looked into the dark shadows beyond the cast of the lamp. 'It might *be* tonight, Sarah. Or it might not be for a hundred thousand years. It's worth remembering that the apostles quite clearly thought it was imminent in their own lifetimes. We've *never* been much good at getting God's time span right . . .'

'You sound like Simon,' Sarah said. She tightened the duvet around her shoulders and kept her eyes on the battery lantern as if it were a camp fire. After a while Jenny said, 'When I was at college in the States . . . university . . . Auntie Anne was living in the same town. In an apartment, a flat. She had a job. She wasn't interested in university, but she used to come on the campus a lot, and hang around because it was comfortable and the food in the snack-bar was real New York food, not upstate food like in the town. Sometimes she came to classes with me just for fun. My philosophy class; she used to like to come and sit through that. The guy teaching it was very young, quite good-looking in a Byronic sort of way . . .'

'Did Anne fancy him?' Sarah said. She was still looking at the electric camp fire, but the question rang of normal adolescent curiosity.

'Oh no. Not Anne. Everybody else did though. He was tall and dark, and a Roman Catholic, which was a little unusual there. Everyone seemed to be Jewish. Anyhow, he was Catholic and he was having a *crisis of faith*. He was having an affair with a woman who was not a Catholic and he felt he could not marry her. It wasn't stopping him screwing her every night, but that's beside the point. He was a great romantic figure and we all angsted with him daily. Except Anne, who was not impressed.'

'What's this *about*, Mom?' Sarah said. She was getting bored, no longer seeing what the story had to do with her.

'Faith,' Jenny said. 'In the midst of this emotional crisis, he gave a lecture on the authentic voice of God, and how man was to recognize it. It would not, he suggested, be a silly voice. Or a cruel voice. It would not suggest that a man do something trivial and illogical, like for instance moving his family to California. Nor would it suggest evil, that the man should, perhaps, murder his grandmother. We all listened; it all made great sense. And then Anne stood up and said, "But he will say, 'Moses, take your people into the desert and lead them through the waters of the sea'. Or, 'Abraham, go up on the mountain and slay your first-born son.' " ' Jenny looked at Sarah. Sarah had dropped her expression of distanced reserve for a moment.

'What did he do?' she asked.

'What could he? Nothing. He said nothing at all. He just stared at us all and then Anne started laughing; and she'd been holding this bunch of wildflowers we'd picked on the way to class and she sort of threw them at him and got up and walked out.' Jenny paused. 'She could do that. She wasn't *in* the class at all.'

'What happened?' Sarah was hunched over her knees, her eyes bright, and almost mischievous. 'Did everybody laugh or what?'

Jenny shook her head, smiling slightly. 'Oh no. With Anne out of the room we all settled down and he got back to teaching us about the authentic voice of God.' She stretched her legs out towards the lamp as if it really was a fire providing heat. 'By the way, he married his girl friend who wasn't Catholic and they ended up having a bunch of kids. But that was after Anne and I were gone.'

'You mean he was like Mark, don't you?' Sarah said.

'No, love. He was nothing like Mark. What I mean is simply that distinguishing the authentic voice of God is the hardest charge we have. And anybody who says he's got it all wrapped up is riding for a fall.'

'Scripture is the authentic voice of God,' Sarah said. 'All that we ever need is right here.' She patted the Bible that sat beside her, like a back-country American preacher.

'Probably,' Jenny said. 'But wars have been fought over what it's meant to mean.'

Sarah hunched away from her, tucking herself forlornly deeper into her sleeping bag. It was past three, the lowest hour when all convictions ebb.

'I miss Daddy,' she said. Jenny looked at her with reservation. She had not heard Sarah say that before.

'So do I,' she said, eventually.

'You have Simon.'

It was curt, cutting. Jenny absorbed it without argument. When Sarah looked less angry she said, 'What do you miss about him, pet?'

Sarah shrugged. 'I don't know,' she said.

Jenny expected her to sink back into uncommunicative remoteness, but instead she said, 'Everything was so *certain* when Daddy was here. There was always enough money. The animals weren't always getting sick. You always seemed happy and not shouting at us and all. And things were, I don't know, *real*, solid. I believed in things then.' Jenny sat, bemused by the extraordinary fantastical tower of her recollection. Did she really see it like that? Were none of the stresses and struggles visible then or, simply, had she wished them away, banished them from her perfect memory? 'We used to go to church together, and I'd hear Daddy singing the hymns and it was like his voice was the centre of the whole church, everyone else's were just sort of attached to it . . .'

'He had a beautiful voice,' Jenny said, a little sadly.

'And I'd hold his hand when we went up to communion and it was, I don't know, *real*. It was real for you, too. You and Dad, you were married and you kept all the rules and everything was *clear*.' Jenny thought, *Do I tell her? Is believing this good for her or bad?* 'It was all so simple then,' Sarah said.

'Life's always simple when you're young,' Jenny said evenly.

'Life's simple now,' Sarah said. 'Or it would be, if you obeyed the rules. God is simple. Mark says God is the simplest thing in the world, pure love.'

'Sarah,' Jenny said, 'if God were simple the universe would be boring. It isn't, and He isn't. Wise men have spent lifetimes deciding what God is Love means. They haven't found out yet.'

'It's being like a little child,' Sarah said. 'That's what Jesus told us; to be like little children.'

'Another of His perfectly simple conundrums.' Jenny sighed. She was filled with the cold exhaustion of the small hours. 'I can't think about this now,' she said.

'After he was dead, I used to pray he'd come back.'

'Who?' Jenny sat straighter, her eyes narrowed.

'Daddy. That he'd come back from heaven, or out of the grave . . . I mean I knew it would mean a miracle, but I thought we were supposed to believe in miracles.'

'We are,' Jenny said.

'I prayed really hard, for days. For weeks. But then, something happened. It began to get scary. I mean, more time passed, and I was sort of used to him not being there. And also, I knew he was in the ground and his body would be . . . rotting, I guess. And I started to get these horrible ideas, that God would answer my prayers, but at the wrong time, when it was too late, and Daddy would come up out of his grave, but *too late*, with his body all, I don't know . . .' Her voice dropped to a murmur. In the chill of the barn Jenny felt rising deep in her memory the forbidden, shut out picture of Fergus ravaged by the spinning steel. She shook her head.

Beside her Sarah whispered, 'What happened to Daddy, Mom? What really happened?'

'You know.'

'You never told us.'

'I told you all you need to know.'

'Then it *was* awful, wasn't it?'

'Yes,' Jenny said. 'It was awful.'

Sarah curled up over her sleeping-bag padded knees. Her small face was in her small white hands. 'That's how I pictured him,' she whispered, 'coming back.'

Jenny leaned over her daughter. She said softly:

'Man's spirit will be flesh-bound when found at best,
But uncumbered: meadow-down is not distressed
For a rainbow footing it nor he for his bones risen.'

She stroked her daughter's cheek. There were wet streaks down beneath the fallen spikes of hair.

'What's that?' Sarah said.

'That's the resurrection, sweetheart. No clap of thunder. No lightning flash. No zombie act. Tomorrow or in a hundred thousand years.' *Forever and ever. Amen.*

When the thing that happened woke Jenny, she could not find the switch to the lantern, and so was trapped in deep winter darkness. It was already morning, in that the animals were stirring, awaiting her arrival for milking in their habitual way, even though she was here among them. She had slept for an hour, perhaps two. Sarah had slept first; suddenly curling up in her sleeping bag and putting her head down, like she would in infancy, in the midst of play, darting without warning into oblivion. Wearily, Jenny resigned herself to the rest of the night in the barn, plumped up a hay mattress beneath herself and lay down, wrapped in her own sleeping bag and a corner of the duvet. It was cold, and the stone floor soon intruded through the padding of hay. She slept without realizing she had, slipping from consciousness into a muddle of realistic dreams filled with the animal sounds of the barn. Then the thing happened, and she was awake.

At first she thought Sarah had called her, and she sat up quickly, saying, 'Yes?' Her hand brushed her daughter's huddled shoulder. Sarah did not stir, the hand too familiar to disturb the depth of her sleep. Jenny said, 'Who's there?' She reached in the tangle of hay and quilting for the lantern, brushed its cool metal side, fumbled for it, lost it again in the darkness. She sat up straighter and, aware that something was happening in the centre of the barn, in the rectangular area of open space that separated her from the animals at the other end, she scrabbled for the lantern more frantically until her hands, trembling, touched its smooth cylinder again. Her fingertips searched the cold metal for the extrusion of the switch, turning the lantern desperately, twice, three times in her hands. All the time she was aware that her need for it was growing less, that the murk within the stone building was retreating to its edges as the thing in the centre grew stronger. When it was strong enough that she could see her hands in silhouette against it, she gave up.

There was nothing there though, but a lightness. It had neither a source, nor a centre, but it suffused the stone floor, the rough wood supports, even the cobwebby rafters with a soft wash of blue. And yet when she looked directly at it, there was nothing she could actually see.

Moonlight. The moon had come out and was shining, somehow through the window, through chinks in the roof, filling the barn with light. She watched, faintly comforted by that rationale, waiting for the odd effect to disperse or reform itself into conventional lunar beams. Instead, the blueness intensified to a soft and vivid glow. Behind it, quite clearly, the animals moved about undisturbed.

'Sarah,' Jenny whispered, 'Sarah, look at this.'

'Jenny.'

Her body stiffened and she felt her heart jolt and begin to race. That was it. That was what had wakened her; not a dream nor the light, but a voice.

'Angus?' she whispered, without turning towards the sound. But it was not Angus's voice, though it was young, and male and intimately familiar.

'Angus?'

'Jenny.' She did not turn. The glow in the room brightened, but the voice was still behind her. 'Here's a light, Jenny,' it said. And she knew then she could turn, and see him, as she had always wanted to see him.

'I'm afraid,' she whispered, and she did not turn. The light softened and the edges of walls, beams, rafters blurred. Then quite suddenly there was nothing but the thick impenetrable winter night. Jenny found the switch of the lantern but her finger only rested on it for a moment, and then calmly and deliberately she put the lantern away. She lay down in the hay beside her daughter and listened to the rustlings of the goats, the burbling of the two renegade hens, and all the small nameless sounds of the night, none of which had stopped for a moment throughout the whole time. A barn cat whispered across the hay and found itself an unaccustomed nest between the two sleeping bags. She reached out into the cold air and rubbed it and went back to sleep, listening to it purr.

Simon made yet another pot of tea.

'Oh Christ, I'll be peeing all night,' Anne moaned. But she accepted the warm cup he poured gratefully. He had built up the fire and brought down two quilts for her to wrap around herself as they sat before it.

'I'm afraid there isn't much of the night left to worry about,' he said. Then he added, solicitously, 'Why don't you go to bed, Anne? You must be *extra* tired.' He smiled in the gentle, caring way he did whenever he referred to her pregnancy. 'If they need anything, I'm here.'

'You're a darling,' Anne said. She felt safe, and pampered, as if Bob were here. More so, even. Bob had a slightly blasé casualness about it all, courtesy of his medical expertise and Vicky's easy athletic childbirths. Simon was the sort of compassionate soul a pregnant wife could send out for pickles and ice-cream at three A.M. His very compassion inspired in Anne a brisk, no-nonsense rigour towards herself.

'There's nothing really *different* about me, Simon,' she said. 'I've just got this little hitchhiker tagging along.' She grinned cheerfully. It was all a bloody lie. She felt exhausted, ragged, worn out as never before. *Old.* The hitchhiker did her little fish-fin flutter. *Oh, you're all right, aren't you?* She was livelier at night. Nocturnal. Anne thought ahead to the fabled sleepless nights. 'Anyhow,' she said to Simon, 'I may as well get some practice in.'

He smiled again, sadly. He sat cross-legged on the wooden floor in front of the hearth, sipping his tea and staring into the flames.

'You're very brave,' he said. Outside there was a distant muffled noise, sharp, tenor, repeated twice.

'Oh shit,' Simon said. 'Honey.' The dog barked again, and then twice more.

'Where is she?'

'In the car. She's still in the car. Jenny was going to go back for her and let her out for a pee before she brought her in.' He got up quickly. 'I forgot all about her. Poor beast, she'll be frozen solid.'

'And crossing her legs,' Anne said. 'You going to get her?'

Simon nodded. He got up and stepped into his soft leather boots and pulled on his sweater before he went out. The barking grew to a happy, frantic crescendo, and then stopped. Anne heard the car door slam. Simon was a long while. When he came in the labrador was with him, padding hurriedly, blending in

366

beside his trouser leg, fearful of a resumption of its exile. Its tongue lolled in the excitement of its rescue. Its fur seemed beaded with a haze of dampness, as if the frost had been settling upon it.

'Here you are,' Simon said, sitting again by the fire, pulling the beast down on to the floor beside him, by its big, loose-skinned neck. It flopped, gloriously happy, big legs sprawling. 'Poor Honey. Poor deserted Honey.' He slapped its sides. Its tail thumped ecstatically. He ruffled the velvety folds beneath its collar, under its soft ears, his fingers working the golden fur expertly.

'She's in seventh heaven,' Anne said.

'What's this?' Simon said to the dog. 'What've you got here?' His long fingers had found something snagged in the wavy fur of her neck. He tugged, automatically, and then he peered at it, and tugged at it with more urgency. 'What've you got here, girl?' he said, quizzically. When it was free, he held it spread across his fingers, tufted with loosened buff hair. It sparkled like a line of frost beading, a hair's width wide. 'Anne, will you look at this?' Simon said, amazed. Anne looked. Looped across Simon's hand was a thin, delicate chain, pure, pale gold, and suspended from it, flashing back the light of the fire, one single perfect jewel.

'Oh shit,' Anne said. Her eyes were wide in the firelight as she reached for it. 'Oh shit, I don't believe this.'

She began to laugh, and then wrapped her arms around the dog's neck, clasping it in gratitude. She was still laughing and hugging the dog when the telephone rang.

Anne went alone to the barn. Outside it was dawn, although from within the house, with the lights on, it seemed still to be pitch-black night. There was a line of deep red across the southern sky. The rest was charcoal grey. Frost lay, thick and fantastical, on every stem and tassel of dried grass. She carried two mugs of tea which steamed in the cold air. Behind her, in the kitchen, Simon was riddling the banked fire of the Aga. She was no longer tired. Sleep and the desire for it had left her, and the hour since the telephone call had been spent in quiet alertness at the table in Jenny's kitchen. They had decided that an hour was long enough to wait.

The barn had a sliding door, painted a dull, peeling red, and it surprised Anne by working well, trundling quite easily on its metal runners, with only a small scraping rumble. It let a bar of grey light into the blacker dark within. At once, hens in the rafters cackled in response.

'Jenny?' Anne said. 'Sarah?'

'We're over here.' Anne had the door only partly open and she went through it sideways, holding the two cups. In the dim light she made out the outline of the wooden supports, the animals at one end, the darkness of the hayloft and, below, in the stall just to the side of the loft ladder, Jenny sitting calmly, still in her sleeping bag, her knees drawn up and her hands resting upon them. Her face was a white blur until Anne got close enough to see she was smiling sleepily.

'Happy Christmas,' she said. She stretched and yawned. Beside her, Sarah was just a curled lump under a rumpled white duvet.

'Merry Christmas,' Anne said. 'I brought you tea.' She lowered herself down in the straw and sat, still carefully holding both tea mugs. She handed one to Jenny. 'I'll put Sarah's down,' she said, and painstakingly found a nest for it on a cobble amidst the straw. 'No apocalypse this time?'

Jenny laughed softly. She snapped her fingers lightly and set her head on one side, 'That's the way the cookie crumbles. We'll just have to keep living.' She looked fondly down on her sleeping daughter.

'Simon's making breakfast,' Anne said.

'I'll have to milk first.'

'Yeah, sure.' The light had brightened and now Anne could see the four panes of the one window as a clear pale blue. She looked around. The goats moved about, white and restless. A hen had come down from the rafters and was scratching at the earthern portion of the floor. She looked back to Jenny and her niece. Sarah's face was lighted now, earnestly asleep, looking puffy and child-like, her cheek pressed against one hand. The comical black hair stood up straight on one side and was pressed flat on the other.

Anne said, 'When you're young you can sleep through anything. Even the end of the world.'

'It's a good way to be,' Jenny said. After Fergus had died,

when anxiety, or loneliness, or the memory of the steel blade and the blood-splashed wood became too much to bear, she would retreat to her bed and sleep whole afternoons away. It was only later she realized how fortunate she was to be able to do that. 'We're all great sleepers,' she said, laughing.

Anne said, 'Mom called this morning.'

Jenny looked startled. She said slowly, 'That wasn't just for Christmas was it? At this hour?'

'No. It wasn't.' Jenny looked at her again and she said, 'Joseph's dead. He died last night. Christmas Eve. Very peacefully, Mom said.' Jenny sat very still, in the sleeping bag, her hands folded around the hot mug of tea.

'Oh God,' she said. She looked very sad and very composed. After a while she said, 'Oh God,' again.

'You don't sound very surprised,' Anne said.

Uncumbered: meadow-down is not distressed. 'I'm not.'

'I suppose we were all expecting it.'

'Yes. We were.' Jenny still stared straight ahead. Her child-like blue eyes were very wide. Then she blinked quickly and turned to her sister. 'How's Mom?'

'As you'd expect.'

'Yes,' Jenny said. 'Yes, of course.'

'She wanted to know if you'd be coming to the funeral,' Anne said.

Jenny looked flustered. She set the tea down and brushed her hair out of her face with both hands.

'I don't know . . . I don't know if I can afford the fare.'

'Well I can.'

They looked at each other for a moment and then Jenny said, 'Yes, then. That would be nice. Simon can look after the animals . . . and everything.' She was alert now, climbing out of the sleeping bag, folding it carefully, all the time trying not to wake the sleeping girl beside her. She stopped then and said, 'Did she cry?'

'No,' Anne said. 'Not on the phone.' She paused. 'If you want the honest truth, I think she was a little relieved. She just sounded tired. She was busy already making plans and all, and in the middle she stopped and said, "When this is done I'm going to sleep for a week. A whole week." And you know, I thought, that's the nearest thing I've heard in thirty-five years to a complaint. That's the nearest thing.'

'She's a good woman,' Jenny said. She was rolling the sleeping bag, on her knees beside Anne. When she looked up, she saw the necklace, the diamond glinting softly in the grey light. Its chain was entangled with that of Nonna's St Christopher which Anne had neglected to remove.

'Anne,' she asked, reaching to touch it curiously. 'Isn't that it?'

'What?'

'The necklace you lost?'

Anne laughed. She patted it happily. 'That's it.'

'*How?*'

'It was on Honey. Simon brought her in last night and it was stuck to her fur.' Jenny stared. Anne was grinning still. 'It was in her bed in the car. I was *wearing* Honey's bed, remember? It was in that old coat all the while.' She caressed the thin chain lovingly, seeking the diamond riding its delicate loop of gold.

'You asked St Anthony,' Jenny said.

'Bullshit.' *My small miracle, brought to me on a dumb beast's back.*

'He's very good,' Jenny said. She was standing, drinking the dregs of her tea. She sounded like she was recommending a builder or a man to cut the lawn.

'Sure,' Anne said. 'I bet.'

She left her sister then to wake her daughter and attend to her animals and do all the things that did not change regardless of the importance of the day. Outside the light was stronger and the red line had spread and softened into a lovely pink over all the southern hills. A white spiral of fresh, hearty smoke rose from the kitchen chimney. There were lights shining in the kitchen, and upstairs. The dogs, let loose by Simon, were padding happily about the cobbled yard.

Anne walked around to the front of the house and stood in the frosted, overgrown garden. She thought of Bob, asleep in his ski hotel in New Hampshire, and of her mother, alone in the privacy of grief. Then she thought of Joseph, and the awful kitschy Scottie dog awaiting him in her luggage upstairs. *What he never knew he'd never have missed.* She smiled. 'Goodbye kid,' she said.

XIX

When Simon came home from the Harrogate Trade Fair, he ended up, almost at once, in Jenny's bed. It was partly celebration: their co-ordinated line of knitwear and enamelled jewellery had been a tremendous hit. His order book was full and they both had more work than they'd handle without employing outside help. He was very much the returning hero, and Jenny greeted him as such. It was also the simple randiness of separation.

They started in the kitchen, as soon as he brought his bags inside the door, and continued with happy abandon, undressing as they went, down the corridor and up the stairs. It was four o'clock in the afternoon, and wonderfully sensual to be lying in Jenny's big bed, under the airy weight of the duvet, naked in full daylight with the cold March wind blowing through the open sash.

And then, for the first half-hour, they did not make love at all, but simply talked. It often happened. Sometimes at night, they talked so much that they fell asleep without consummation and woke, disappointed, in the morning, facing the chores of the day. Today there was no hurry and they lay side by side, gently caressing and catching up on all the news. He told her of everybody she had missed by not coming to Harrogate, and insisted that the next trade fair would have to be hers. She asked after Elizabeth and Gordon with whom he had stayed last night, and told him that Angus had located a room in a south London flat that he *might* be able to afford for his year as an Anne Conti storeman.

'How's Sarah?' Simon asked. He was lying on his back with

Jenny beside him on her stomach, propped up on her elbows, looking down at him.

'Fine, I think. She's in some kind of play. Apparently she's got the lead role. There's some man involved, directing it.' She sounded casual, but he picked up the edge of concern.

'What man? Who is he?'

Jenny shrugged. 'Some theatrical bloke.'

'Oh great.' He sounded like a disgruntled father, and she laughed. She leaned over him, kissing his lips, her loose hair falling like two curtains either side of his face.

'Bob called,' she said.

'Again?'

'Hmmm.' She kissed him again.

'The same thing?'

'More or less. He's tried everybody. Marion. My Mom. Now me. I really feel for him. I'm sorry now I told him.'

'You *had* to tell him. Somebody had to.' He stroked her hair, thinking. 'Really, Anne should have told him. He had a right to know. I mean, being the father.'

'I imagine she would have told him eventually. He'd certainly find out. I guess she thought it would be easier to handle later.'

'She should marry him,' Simon said. 'She's being unreasonable. Stubborn. You should use your influence.'

Jenny laughed. 'I haven't got any influence,' she said. 'Nobody has any influence over Anne. Nobody ever had.'

He looked up into her face, admiring the wise, sharp lines around her eyes. He pulled her down on top of him and they lay quietly, touching from lips to ankles. She began to kiss him seriously. He stopped talking, his body stirring. Then he drew back. 'What about . . . ?'

She murmured something deliberately incomprehensible, and slipped her fingers behind his neck, drawing him closer. He eluded her, saying quickly, 'Jenny, you'd better get your cap.' She lifted her head and made a small shrug of her shoulders.

'I suppose so.' But she made no move.

'Jenny?' His eyes widened, a wary light brightening them. She grinned devilishly, running quick sensual hands down his body, under the duvet. Once more, he drew back from her, setting his hands against her shoulders to hold her away from him. She was amazed at his self-control. 'Jenny, are you sure about this? Do you mean what you're doing?'

'Oh Christ, Simon,' she laughed, 'act. Don't think. Just act.' He looked at her once more with serious concern, and then he too laughed, tentatively.

'Fine,' he said. 'Great.' He ran his hands around her shoulders and down the small of her back, on to her buttocks. 'Fine with me.' Then the telephone rang.

'Oh shit,' Jenny sighed. They fell apart. Their eyes met, and she said, 'Shall I leave it?'

'You can't,' he said, with gentle understanding. He lifted the receiver off the hook and handed it to her. Jenny half sat up in the bed, pulling the duvet up over her small white breasts. Simon stretched out languorously beside her. He heard her say, 'Sarah? Hello darling . . . yes . . . fine. No.' A pause. 'Not *too* busy.' He laughed softly, his hand before his face. She gave him a friendly swat. 'Well, I don't know, Sarah. I mean, I don't know the man . . . no. No, I don't imagine he gave you the part *just* because he fancies you.' Another pause. 'Well never *mind* what the others say, darling. They're probably jealous.' Another longer pause. 'Sarah, is there any *reason* maybe why everybody calls him "Jimmy Casanova"?' Jenny sat up straighter in the bed. She looked at Simon and shrugged. His eyes were narrowing. 'Well maybe it *is* all gossip, dear, but on the other hand . . .' She shrugged again, listened a while longer. 'Sarah, be reasonable, I haven't said anything against him. How can you say I'm just like all the others? I haven't *met* him, darling.' She ran a distracted hand through her long loose hair. 'For Christ's sake, Sarah, how old *is* he? *What*? Sarah . . . I . . . no I'm *not* being judgemental but seriously darling, forty-*seven*.'

Simon sat up straight, the duvet falling away from his tense young body. 'Give me the phone.'

She waved him away. 'Sarah . . . wait a minute.' She held her hand over the mouthpiece. Simon was trying to wrestle it from her.

'Cool down . . .' she whispered.

'A forty-seven-year-old lech . . . let me talk to her.'

'Sarah, Simon's here . . . yes,' Jenny sounded surprised. 'Yes, I'm sure he'd like to talk to you.' She looked back at Simon, her pale blue eyes startled. Her eyebrows made an upward curve.

'She wants to talk to you,' she said, handing him the phone. He took it from her and she slid down under the duvet and lay watching him.

'Hi, Sarah. What's this, hey?' There was a long, long silence while he sat up, eyes half closed, concentrating on the stream of Sarah's speech. Eventually he said, 'No, Sarah, of course age isn't everything. Yes, of course. Yes, your mother *does* understand that. But you have to admit she has got more experience in these things. No, I wouldn't call her rigid, Sarah. Morally *serious* maybe, but not rigid.' There was another pause. 'Well he might *be* a very nice man, but four marriages in forty-seven years isn't the *best* track record.'

He patted Jenny's arm while listening to Sarah's next speech, and laughed a little. 'No, dear. You haven't been silly at all. No, of course I'm not angry with you. No. She isn't either.' His voice gentled, and the replies became casual and monosyllabic as Sarah talked on. Jenny stretched and yawned. Outside, it was getting dim. Soon she'd have to get up, do the milking, make supper. Simon was lying on one side now, his back to her, listening patiently to her daughter.

She reached her arms around him, pressing her face up close to the back of his neck, her lips in his untidy, shining hair. When he said goodbye at last and hung up the phone, he turned easily into her embrace.

They had lunch in the Russian Tea Rooms. Anne thought her mother would enjoy the theatrical atmosphere; and Marion deserved a treat, a reward for the months of her devotion to Louise since Joseph's death. In the end, Louise spent most of the meal worrying about the cost. It could not be helped, Anne decided. The business of luring her back into ordinary life was neither easy nor quick. Even now she sat amidst the lushly gilded surroundings looking faintly lost, as if aware that she should be elsewhere. Three times Anne saw her lower her eyes surreptitiously to glance at her watch. That there was no longer any need to hurry was too obvious to be stated aloud.

She's like Grannie, Anne thought. *She looks like Grannie*. Small, pinched, wiry and tough, her face and hair grey, only her eyes, bright and bird-like, full of life. Over coffee she relaxed a little, began to admire the room, allowed Marion to point out famous

374

faces. She looked pleased, but not terribly impressed. She had an inner confidence, Anne realized, a pride. Again like Grannie, a pride in the way she had lived her life. *She was proud of him. He was an achievement.* Anne smiled. She had grown remote and yet maternal in her feelings towards her mother, as if this old woman was a stranger she could justly, and without cost to herself, admire.

It was only over coffee that they talked about it. She had thought, until then, that she would actually escape.

'Jenny called yesterday,' her mother said. 'She says I should talk to you.' And before Anne could put on her face a look of curiosity or surprise, she said, 'About Bob.'

Marion sighed. She gave Anne a commiseratorial look across the table. Anne sat, still smiling serenely, on the pretty bench. She was dressed in her favourite black; a maternity lunch dress with a white square collar and two smooth panels that adorned her neat pregnant bump. It was a great dress and she had been aware of eyes upon her as she was escorted through the room to her favourite table. It was the sort of dress that made every other woman in the room wish she was pregnant too. She sipped from her coffee before she answered, but when she spoke her free hand rose to fondle the diamond pendant that rested in the hollow of her throat.

'There's nothing more to say about Bob, Mom. We've been through it all.'

'Darling . . .'

'I mean it, Mom.' Her mother closed her mouth, looked side-ways to Marion for help. Marion, pink and contented from three glasses of wine looked upwards, chin on hand, seemingly oblivious.

'Darling, a baby is a very demanding change in your life. Even an ordinary baby. And this kind of baby . . . if I had had to cope with Joe without your father . . .'

Anne still smiled. She leaned forward and touched her mother's small tough hand. 'You'd have done gloriously, know-ing you. I wouldn't, but that's not the point. Mom, she's not Joe. She's her own young lady. She'll have some problems, but not Joe's problems. Ask Bob.'

'I *have* asked Bob. He's very concerned for you.'

'And he's also aware that my daughter is going to walk and

talk and play like any child. She'll go to school, probably a specialized school, but school anyway. She's not going to Harvard but that makes two of us. We'll be fine, Mom. Just fine.'

'Bob says they . . . these children . . . often have physical problems too.'

Not this one. Not this little tough. Aloud, she said, 'If she has, we'll treat them. We'll watch her carefully.'

'We?' Marion said. She spoke too quickly to hide the hopefulness in her voice.

Anne gave her a hard look but said only, 'Bob and I.' They both stared and she stared them down. 'We're not cutting off diplomatic relations. We're just not getting married.'

Louise looked sadly down at her hands. 'I suppose you know best,' she said.

'Yes,' Anne said sharply. 'I know best.'

She looked up and met Marion's eyes. Marion was sitting back in her chair, a handsome, sweet-faced woman with an old-fashioned bun of greying blonde hair. 'Anne *always* knows best, Louise,' she said with a small shrewd smile. 'No matter what happens to be right.'

Anne put them in a cab outside the restaurant and waved them off for an afternoon's shopping at Macy's. Then she turned and began walking the short distance back to the Fifty-Seventh Street store. It was a bright spring afternoon, unseasonably warm, the air fresh and the city gleaming in sunlight, full of vitality and fun. Walking was a pleasure. She had gained not one ounce of excess weight, and so presented a tall and pretty figure with a high-riding decorative bump; a fashion plate pregnancy. As she walked she was working out details of her new line of maternity clothes, One Plus One, sophisticated designs for the older working mother, a liberation from smocks and fusty collars. She had a new young designer, a pretty girl with frizzy hair who reminded her of Sarah O'Brien. She looked forward to the afternoon's work.

The baby kicked, once, twice, a good solid thud now. She made a note in her head to call that Nanny agency that Elizabeth had recommended and secure one of their polished, Edinburgh-trained girls. A special girl for a special baby, but she had no doubt that she would find one. No problem; things were great. Ahead she saw the awning in her maroon and cream colours bearing the letters 'Anne Conti' in graceful curling script. Thinking of Elizabeth brought back a quick remembrance of her first, hand-painted sign, above the Grassmarket shop. A good name. Twenty years and still going strong. A good name.

Names. She stood briefly at a corner, waiting for a light to change before crossing to her side. A small jam developed, blocking the crossing, and a herd of yellow cabs filled up the street, blaring horns with that unique New York sound that always made her blood run fast. Names. Catherine, after Nonna. Too staid. Louise. Perhaps. Jenny. Elizabeth. Marion. There were too many women in her life to whom she owed debts. All of them. Or none of them. Something new; a special name for a special child. Something from the Bible. Hannah, Mary, Sarah. *Grace*. She heard Simon's voice as he walked about the Christmas room, the dictionary in his hands. Grace. The undeserved salvation . . . Grace. Grace Conti. That would be lovely.

The traffic cleared. She picked her way across the road. A man in dungarees and a work shirt standing with a shovel by a hole in the road looked up as she passed and whistled. She glared at him, exasperated. *Asshole. I'm seven months*. But he smiled cheerily anyhow.

She turned her back, her small short coat swirling, and walked with quick swinging strides to her entrance. There was a man standing in front of it with that look of a waiting husband whose bank balance was being ravaged within. She smiled slightly seeing him, hunched over, staring gloomily into the window at some display of female garments that could not possibly interest him. He wore a beige trenchcoat and had a nice slim build, sandy hair, a small, almost unnoticeable balding patch. He turned quickly at the sound of approaching steps and she saw it was Bob.

At once she turned away. *Go on. Just go. Before we say anything that's going to hurt*. He did not, of course, go. Instead he came up to her where she stood in front of the shop entrance with her back to him. He did not touch her, only stood behind her so she, street sensitive, could feel his presence there.

'I feel like a teenager. I'm reduced to hanging around the street hoping I'll see you.'

'You know why.'

'I don't, Anne. I swear I don't.' She turned slowly. She looked at him carefully, deliberately suppressing any emotion, even familiarity. He was still very attractive.

She said, 'We've said all we're going to say. We've said it face to face, over the phone, and in writing. Saying it again, saying *anything* again, is just picking a scab.'

'How's my daughter?'

'My daughter's fine.' She tightened her coat about her, and suddenly brushed past him, and continued walking down the street as if she had never intended stopping at all.

'Hey, aren't you going to work?'

'I'm going for a walk.' She did, and of course he followed.

'Do you mind?'

'It's a free city.'

'Would you talk to Jenny at least? Jenny agrees with me completely.'

'Fine. Jenny and I never agree about anything.' He stopped walking. She did also.

'Anne, you're going to need my help.'

'I expect your help. Not only your help, I expect special consideration. I expect *house calls*.' She was smiling, in spite of herself.

'They're very expensive.' He was smiling slightly too.

'Money's no problem,' she said. 'No problem at all.' She stepped back so she could see him more clearly. 'And, if you're quite serious, I mean *really* serious, and God, Bob, there's enough to be serious about . . . then I'll have my first house call on Saturday morning. There's a stack of wood beside the porch that needs splitting.' She grinned and then turned her back and walked away from him, up Fifty-Seventh Street, a tall woman in black, contentedly, confidently, alone.